KILL CALL

JEFF WOOTEN

KILL CALL

CamCat
Books

CamCat Publishing, LLC
Fort Collins, CO 80524
camcatpublishing.com

Hardcover ISBN 9780744307597
Paperback ISBN 9780744307658
Large-Print Paperback ISBN 9780744307672
eBook ISBN 9780744307665
Audiobook ISBN 9780744307689

Library of Congress Control Number: 2023940752

Cover and interior design by Olivia Hammerman (Indigo: Editing, Design, and More)
Interior art courtesy of Pixabay.com

5   3   1   2   4

For Martha, who never wavered, even when I did.

Kill Call: In American football, a predetermined call the quarterback makes to "kill" the play at the line of scrimmage in order to run a previously determined call best suited for the defense being played.

"Success isn't measured by money or power or social rank.
Success is measured by your discipline and inner peace."
—Mike Ditka

CHAPTER 1

On August 12 at one thirty-two in the morning, Hanna Smith is going to die.

Nine days. That's all she has.

She stands less than a hundred yards from me, texting in front of Markle's, a designer jeans store. Two bags stuffed with clothes hang from the crook of her left arm, a huge purse on her right.

She's in workout clothes, and her long blond hair is pulled back in a ponytail. She's seventeen and goes to Miller's Chapel. I go to Bedford with the rest of the public school kids.

It's Thursday afternoon, and the mall is packed. People swarm around me as I sit on a bench in the middle of the promenade. Somewhere a baby is crying.

I feel ya, kid.

I don't want to be here. It feels way too stalkerish. That's not what I am. This whole thing feels wrong, but Dad says it's important, so here I am, trying to be cool.

I don't feel cool. I feel like I have a huge spotlight on my head and everyone is staring. Only no one is actually staring at me. I'm not antisocial, but crowds put me on edge. I've always been like this, but I've wondered in the last few months if it isn't also, partly, because of what I am. Since the Dream, I've been second-guessing my entire life.

I lean back, trying and failing to be nonchalant. I'm bad at this. Hanna's in her own world, hammering away at her phone with her thumbs.

In nine short days, Hanna Smith will be dead.

But only if I'm not there to save her. A life for a life. It's the only way.

My phone vibrates in my hand and I jump, almost dropping it. I check the text, trying to be chill. Nothing to see here, just a dude sitting in the mall on his phone.

Party Sat—B thurrrr!!!

It's a huge group text from Jacoby Cole. My phone buzzes with replies before I manage to mute it. How do people type so fast?

"Hey, Jude."

I flinch at the sound of my name and look up.

Molly Goldman smiles down at me, her hazel eyes bright and warm. "Did you get Jacoby's text?"

I feel like I've been caught stealing as I glance over at Hanna, but she's gone. She was standing there for ten minutes, and I look away for a second—

"Jude? You okay?"

I look up at Molly. She's still smiling at me. So far, I haven't completely blown my cover. I return her smile. It's not hard. I'm actually happy to see her. Any other moment in time would have been preferrable, but such has been my life lately. "Sorry. I was just— Yeah, Jacoby's text. Just got it. Guess you did too?"

"Yep. Bet you're dying to go, huh?"

I'm wound tight and the short bark of laughter that escapes me is a little much. "You bet, can't wait."

Molly raises her eyebrows and smiles. She knows me well enough to know I won't be attending Jacoby's little back-to-school get-together. I think she's about to say goodbye and move on, but she doesn't move. "Want some company for a minute?"

"Uh, *yeah*, absolutely." I make room for her on the bench, my mall experience suddenly much brighter, if not more complicated. "Have a seat."

She sits, pushing a lock of curly red hair out of her face. *"Soooo, are you waiting for someone?"*

"No, just chilling for a minute." I try not to, but I can't help but glance one more time to where Hanna was.

Still gone. I should go. Dad would certainly tell me to leave now that I've lost the Chosen. *But* Dad's not my favorite person right now, and besides, I really want to talk to Molly.

"Back-to-school shopping then?" Molly thumps my leg. "I have to know why Jude *I don't like people* Erickson is hanging out on a bench in his least favorite place."

"I've decided to embrace my social side," I say, gaining a grin from Molly.

"Unlikely story."

I shrug. "Need new practice cleats." It's not a lie exactly. I do need new cleats, but I'll probably order them online. Malls really aren't necessary.

"Okay," Molly says, nodding and smiling. "That is a believable story. You boys and your football." She shakes her head, but she's still smiling. She has a really nice smile. "You excited about the season?"

I sit up, on comfortable footing. I love football, always have. I'm good at it too. "Yep," I say. "Coach thinks we can win state. How about Lucas? He excited?"

Molly looks down. "Last I heard."

My Spidey-Senses tingle. All is not well in Munson-Molly land.

Lucas Munson is Molly's boyfriend, my teammate, and a Grade A dick. Next year he'll be playing college football somewhere big. I don't even know if college is a possibility for me.

I lean back against the seat and watch the people. "Are things cool with you and Lucas?" I ask as casually as I can muster, hoping very much that things are not cool with her and Munson.

She places her hands on either side of her and pushes up slightly. Her voice is low and tinged with something close to regret. "No. No, they aren't Jude. We aren't seeing each other anymore. It happened yesterday, actually."

I try not to smile. The mall is starting to grow on me. "Huh," I say. "So, what happened?"

"Stuff, you know," she says wistfully. "He wants to move away for college. I don't. Honestly, we've been headed this way for a while. But enough about that. What have you been up to this summer? You've been kind of off the grid."

Molly's words are true. This summer has been a nightmare, literally.

"Eh. Football, mostly. Roofing some with Dad . . ." I tap my foot. *Planning my first kill,* I add to myself. I need to chill. I make my stupid leg stop bouncing and shrug. "You know, the usual." I make an involuntary noise halfway between a grunt and a laugh.

Molly elbows me. "What's so funny?"

"It's nothing," I say.

"It's something. And now you have to tell me."

For a fleeting few moments, I consider throwing it all away. Letting it all out, telling her everything. The Dreams, what they mean, what Dad is, what I am. It's ridiculous. Molly would think I was crazy. Sometimes, I think I might be.

All this goes through my head in seconds. I shake my head and shrug, trying and failing to think of what to say.

"Awkward silences are fun," Molly says, "but I want you to use your words, Jude."

"Well, awkward silences are kind of my thing, and I hear you're single now." I hesitate, not sure where that came from. "Uh, sorry."

Molly's laugh lets me know she's not offended. "Honestly, I appreciate you not giving me a pep talk about Lucas."

"Not a chance of that," I say, surprising myself again. Molly laughs harder this time. I'm on a roll and decide to take a leap. "Can I ask you something?"

"Oh, this sounds interesting. Asking permission. Go on."

This whole conversation feels like a release, like all the weirdness in my life recently isn't real. There is freedom in being pushed to the edges of sanity. Mundane stuff, like Molly's love life, suddenly seems trivial. And I have questions. "Why Lucas?" I ask. "I never understood that at all."

Molly grimaces, and I wonder if I crossed some unknowable social line. "You know your problem, Jude?"

"*My* problem? I thought we were talking about Lucas?"

"He asked, Jude."

He asked.

"Uh," I say. "That's it? He asked? It has to be more than that."

Her eyes measure me. "Sure, but it has to start somewhere."

I still have doubts, but I think newly single Molly Goldman might be flirting with me.

I swallow and force the next sentence out of my mouth. "You want to come . . . help me pick out some cleats? We can head over to the food court after. Mall pizza is, surprisingly, not horrible."

Molly's eyes narrow like she's appraising me. "You're such a bad liar, Jude. I've had the pizza. Spoiler alert: it's horrible."

"Not if you eat it fast."

Molly belly laughs. "That makes absolutely no sense."

"Sure it does. You'll see."

"How about I get a salad?"

"So, yes, then."

"Sure," Molly says and stands. She reaches for her bags.

"Let me get those for you." I stand up and grab the bags, turning, enjoying the mall for the first time since I was a kid . . . and Hanna *Freaking* Smith is right there.

An annoyed look crosses Hanna's face as she brushes past me. Her shoulder meets mine, the faintest of touches. It's instantaneous.

The light twists, time slows, and I'm not in the mall anymore. I'm in Hanna's house. Hanna's at my feet, blood pooling around her head. The hammer in my hand feels good, like truth and power. I feel . . . electric. Everything is right. I am at peace, finally. If only for a moment.

Then I'm back in the mall. No more than a second has passed, but my head reels, my stomach turns, and my feet falter as I watch Hanna walk away. Dad's words echo in my ear. *The first time will make you queasy.*

Molly stops, watching my gaze. "You okay?"

"Yeah. I just—"

"Was that Hanna Smith? Do you know her?"

"Uh, no," I manage. The world is still tilting, and I need a second. I ask the only question that comes to mind. "How do you know her?"

Molly shrugs. "I don't. She goes to Chapel, and I see her around." Her tone softens. "She always seems sad."

She walks on, and I fall in beside her. The euphoria and queasiness the vision brought are still warring in my body, but my feet are steady.

"Fall Happening auditions are next week," Molly says. "We're doing *The Crucible.*"

"That's the one where the woman has to wear the red A, right?"

"That's *The Scarlet Letter*, Jude." Molly looks at me as we walk. "Did you really not know that?"

I give an exaggerated frown. "Sorry, Molly, but no, I did not."

"Whatever," Molly says with a laugh. "You can't fool me. All these years you've been playing the part of the dumb jock while harboring a love for classical literature. I think you've been hiding the real you all these years."

I almost trip but have a second to recover as a gang of middle school girls, all on their phones, nearly run us over, not a one of them ever looking up.

Molly's joking, but that comment hit a little close to home. "You see right through me, Molly Goldman."

"I do," Molly agrees with a quick glance and a sharp grin. "So, never lie to me again."

Molly has no clue. My whole life has been a lie.

I have a sudden urge to share, to share something real with Molly. I let out a wistful breath. "When I was a kid," I say, "Mom would bring me here on the weekends. We'd go to a movie and eat in the food court. I loved that. It was, you know, good times."

"That's sweet. How is your mom?"

"Not sure. I haven't seen her in three years."

Molly slows her pace. She knew my folks were divorced, but she didn't know about Mom. Hardly anyone does. It's not something I talk about. "That's horrible, Jude."

"It is what it is," I say, trying to sound casual. I'm positive I fail.

Molly moves closer until her arm brushes against mine. People flow around us, but we are an island in the flood. "You're a different kind of guy. You know that, right?"

"Yeah," I say. "I know."

Molly elbows me playfully. "Don't sound sad. It's a compliment. Normal is boring."

She's not wrong. But it stings. Three months ago, before the Dream took over my life, I at least had the option of normality. I want that back.

I look over at Molly.

"What?" she asks.

Something warm simmers in my chest. Something normal. "You want, uh, you want to go to Jacoby's party with me?"

As soon as the words are out, I wish they were back in, but it's too late. Molly's expression is unreadable, and I want to crawl away.

"Are you asking me out? I think you're asking me out. Bold."

"Just hanging," I say. "No biggie."

Her expression turns serious. "Don't you hate parties?"

"I don't know. It is our senior year. Maybe I need to live a little. Break out of my shell. If you were with me . . . it might not be so bad."

"Might not be so bad, huh?" Molly asks.

I know she's going to say yes, even before she says yes, and I can hardly believe it. "Yeah, you know. Less than horrible anyway."

She laughs. "Well, when you put it that way, sure."

"Date then," I ask, a part of me needing confirmation.

"Date," Molly agrees.

We walk into the food court, the mix of a dozen different cuisines vying for dominance. I take it all in.

I think I've changed my mind about the mall.

I love it.

CHAPTER 2

Dad's still up when I get home. He's got his feet up, watching the ten o'clock news. "You're out late," he says, still watching the TV. "Thought we agreed you'd only follow her to the mall?"

"I did, but I saw Molly Goldman and . . ." My words trail off. The truth is, we spent hours talking. It wasn't *what* we talked about at all, but rather *how* we talked. Spending time with someone I really click with hasn't been something that's happened a lot in my life.

But it isn't just that. I really like Molly, always have, and for the first time she's shown more than a passing interest. It's a new kind of experience for me, and I want more of it.

"We were talking," I say, the simple explanation not even close to what really happened.

Dad looks at me for the first time, and I see way too much knowing in the expression. "Molly Goldman?"

I don't respond. It's a test. Everything lately has been a test.

"How well do you know her?"

I shrug. "We go to school together. I've known her, like, forever."

Dad stares at me, waiting.

People hate lulls in conversations. Guilty people especially. A part of me wants to fill the void with something, anything, but I know better. Never give up what you don't have to. Dad's always been like this. When I was a kid, he'd make it a game. Since I Dreamed, it's been way more intense.

After a few seconds, Dad gives me a small smile. "I remember her now. Redhead, right? She seems nice."

"Yeah, she's nice. We, uh, might be going to a party together Saturday."

"A date?" Dad never encouraged me to date. Considering what he and Mom went through, I can understand why.

I shift uncomfortably. "I don't know. Maybe. We're friends. It's a party. Back-to-school thing."

"Party, huh? Not at the Bluehole, I hope."

"The Bluehole?" I snort. *Once you go in, you never come out.* The singsong refrain runs through my mind. The Bluehole is an abandoned bauxite mine, from when Rush Springs was a booming community. That was even before Dad's time. When Dad was a kid, it was a place where they used to party. All that stopped when three kids took a dare to jump in. Their bodies were never found, and an urban legend was born.

Once you go in, you never come out.

"No, Dad, nobody does that anymore. That's—no."

Dad pushes up from his chair and joins me in the kitchen. I'm as tall as my father, but he's bigger. I see myself in him, so does everybody else. His black hair is salted with gray, and he carries some cushion around his gut, but he's about the last person anyone wants to mess with. Like me, he was all-state football back in his day. Someday I'll probably look just like him, and that's cool. "So how did it go?" I have no question what we're talking about now. "You kept your distance, right?"

I stare at my feet. According to Dad, physical proximity strengthens the bond. The closer you get, the tighter the connection. It makes the Dream more vivid. The more vivid the Dream, the better your chances of success. That's why I was there in the first place.

But Dad also told me under no circumstances was I to touch Hanna. The whole vision thing could have gone way worse.

Way, way worse.

Hanna could have shared the vision. But that didn't happen. No harm, no foul is how I see things. I doubt Dad will be as forgiving.

Dad senses my hesitation. "You got too close, didn't you?"

He's right, and that makes it worse. I snap my head up. "So that's the first conclusion you jump to?"

He says nothing, just waits. How does he know? It's hard keeping stuff from him. Impossible really.

I take his disapproving stare for a second or two, trying, and failing, to think of an explanation. Molly distracted me, but it wasn't her fault. I shrug and walk to the kitchen. I get the milk out of the fridge and pour a glass. Dad comes in and leans against the kitchen wall.

I pull out the ham and mayonnaise to make a sandwich. "I was with Molly. Hanna was going the other way, but she must have . . . I don't know. She came back and ran into us. She brushed by me. We touched."

Dad's fist slams into the wall, crunching through the sheetrock. "Physical contact? You made physical contact with the Chosen?"

I look up at him, my face a mask.

It's a test. He's done stuff like this lately. It's completely out of character. That's the point. If I get caught, if I find myself having to answer difficult questions, I'll have to keep my cool. He's doing all this to help me. Still, I'm so done with it. All of this, from my first Dream until today. Why me? I don't want this to be my life.

"Yes," I say with no emotion. No hint of surprise, despite my racing heart.

His hand's bleeding, but he pays it no mind. "Tell me what you saw."

I start back on my sandwich. I spread the mayonnaise on the bread, finish up, and take a bite. I chew the bite and take a sip of milk before I answer. "I had a vision, just me. She kept on walking like nothing happened."

His eyes study me coolly. "You're sure?"

"Positive," I say.

"Okay," he says. "That's possible. Likely, in fact. Go on."

I take another sip of milk. "I was in her house. Standing over her body, a hammer in my hand. Just like the Dream."

Dad glances at the cut on his hand and gets a towel from the drawer. He wraps it up, his eyes never leaving mine. "How did it . . . feel?"

"During the vision or after?"

He shakes his head, annoyed. "During?"

I hesitate. I think I'm tough. I know I'm tough, but the words don't want to form. "It felt real. Like, not dreamlike at all. Real." I hesitate. "It felt . . . It felt *right*. I was happy. No, not happy, thrilled. I felt like it wouldn't last, but I knew I'd never be sorry. I felt good. Powerful."

"And now?" I hear a hesitancy in my father's voice I've never heard before. He's scared. Scared of what I might be.

I take another bite of sandwich, but it might as well be cardboard for all the joy I get from it. "It makes me sick to think about it. To enjoy," I sigh, "doing that."

Dad nods. "Good. That's good."

"How'd you *think* I'd feel? Geez, Dad, sometimes you're worse than Mom."

The words sting him. It's plain on his face. It's rare I can upset him. A part of me wants to twist the knife.

"Your mother," he says slowly, "knows better than most what we are." He flexes his bandaged hand.

"Does she?" I ask. "Does Mom know I'm like you?"

"You screwed up," Dad says, not answering my question. "I told you not to get close. If the Chosen had shared the vision—" His face flashes with equal parts concern and anger. "In the mall? It would have been over. We'd have to pull back."

I shake my head. Sometimes Dad contradicts himself. "A life for a life. Isn't that what you taught me?"

"It is," Dad says, softening his tone. "But *you* are what's important." He comes and puts his uninjured hand behind my head and pulls his forehead to mine. "I love you, Son. I'm trying so hard to make this better, easier for you. There will be others. Sometimes you won't succeed. Sometimes . . . you have to let them go." Dad's hand falls from the back of my head and he turns his back to me.

Dad has told me about a few of his Dreams. Once the killer got away, and the Chosen was killed later, but this is different. He at least tried. "Let them go," I say incredulously. "Did you ever do that? Did you ever walk away and let someone die?"

Dad turns back to me, and his eyes hold a lifetime of regret. "I know what it's like. The call of the Dream. It feels like if you don't answer it, it will destroy you. But you have a choice. It won't be easy, but I'll help."

"You didn't answer my question," I say, my voice rising. "Did you *ever* walk away?"

Dad shifts on his feet. "What I did or didn't do doesn't matter." He holds up his hand as angry words form on my lips. "Listen, Jude. It's still on. You messed up, but nothing has changed." He steps toward me. "I need you to focus. Stay as far away from that girl as you can. If you touch again, the vision will be shared, and we abort. We go on vacation."

Vacation is the plan in the unlikely event we have to call it off. Dad even bringing it up makes me want to scream. "You'd do it, too, wouldn't you? You'd let her die."

"Of course I would. You are all that matters." He looks away. "This is dangerous business. You want to end up in prison for the rest of your life, or worse, dead?" He looks at me and his expression hardens. "You're my son. I won't let that happen. If things go wrong, there can be nothing that ties you to the Chosen."

Chosen. Not once has Dad said Hanna's name.

"Her name is Hanna," I say.

Dad grimaces. "I thought you were ready. Obviously not."

"If I'm not ready, it's your fault. You think I wanted this?"

"That's enough," Dad snaps, the hurt clear in his eyes. "Go get your workout clothes on. We have work to do."

"It's ten thirty. We're finishing the Howards' roof in the morning. Then I have football."

"And I'm your boss. Lenny can run the crew fine without us for an hour or two." He turns and stalks off to his room.

I take another bite of sandwich. Why does he have to be such a hard-ass all the time?

The half-eaten sandwich hits the bottom of the trash can, and I go get dressed and meet Dad in the garage. There are no cars, just a wrestling mat, a heavy bag in one corner, and a Wing Chun dummy in another.

We spend the next hour sparring. Dad pins me over and over. Once I manage to almost get him in an arm bar before he escapes it. It's grueling work, and when I take my shower and finally get into bed, it's close to midnight. I'm beat, but I can't help reliving parts of my day. I think of Molly and how my life would be different if I weren't what I am. Dad says daydreaming is a weakness. Things are how they are. Right now, I don't care what Dad thinks. Nothing wrong with a little fantasy now and then.

When the time comes, I'll do what's right. I'll make my first kill.

CHAPTER 3

Hanna's house is a smoky outline in the gathering fog and dense foliage. I pull out my phone and check the time. It's one-seventeen, Saturday, August 12. The time and date are the only thing not distorted on the screen. I can't even tell what kind of phone it is. Likewise, my hands are smears of black and gray. I might be wearing gloves, but I might not be. The hammer, the murder weapon, too, is hazy and distorted, giving away its basic shape only.

I am a passenger, being carried by another, unable to do anything but watch as the future, unhindered, unfolds.

The moon cuts through the clouds and fog, sending rivulets of silver shining down through the leaves. Drops of water fall from the canopy far above, but it's not raining.

I move forward through the pine and oak, stumbling occasionally through the dark woods. Twigs and brambles snap under my feet, and I have to look down a few times to disentangle myself from the clutching greenbriers, but it's a short walk. Adrenaline pumps through my veins as I stand on the edge of the woods, watching the house.

The light haloing Hanna's home is from the streetlamps out front. The back porch light is off. My breath moistens the already damp air as I let out a deep breath. The hammer bounces in my hand, almost on its own.

I walk to the back door and quickly kneel next to the potted plant. I tilt the pot up and then fumble around with a gloved hand under the planter. It takes longer than I want, but I finally have what I need. The metal house key glints silver in the moonlight. Something warm and satisfied pulses through me with each heartbeat.

I stand, peering through the door's glass into the house. My reflection catches my eye. My ski mask covers my face all the way down to my neck. It's as black as my clothes that cover my arms and the gloves that cover my hands, amorphous things with no hint of design other than color. My eyes, the only thing visible of the person behind the clothes, are shadows, gray-black holes reflecting nothing but night.

The whole image is distorted, not from the glass, not from any natural process. One side of my head is large and bulbous, the other slim and elongated. My body is hazy and pulsating. I slip inside, no hesitation in my steps.

Purpose and excitement course through me as I slip through a kitchen, into a den, and up the stairs. Blood throbs in my ears as I come to stand before her door. For a second, I hesitate, gripping the hammer tight, and then push the door open.

Hanna lies facing me in her bed, her eyes closed. I take a step forward, and a floorboard squeaks. Hanna stirs and pushes up on an elbow and looks at me with the blank stare of someone awakened from deep sleep. I can hear my own heart beating now. It sounds like the beating of drums, and I tremble. Is it fear? Joy?

Yes, and yes.

I leap forward and raise the hammer. I bring the hammer down, but Hanna rolls, and it misses her head by the barest of margins. She's screaming at me from the other side of her bed, but the words are incoherent, and they only make my heart beat harder, louder, until it's the only thing I *can* hear.

I jump up on the bed, and she darts around the end, headed for the door. I jump back down and swing the hammer. It catches her in the arm, and she spins, screaming, in pain and terror this time.

Still, she manages to lunge toward the door, but the room is not big enough for her to get away. I bring the hammer down on the back of her head. With a sickening crack, Hanna's body crumbles and is still.

My chest heaves with deep inhalations as I look around me. The bed is large, heaped with blankets and comforters. An open MacBook sits on a desk next to a walk-in closet, the open door revealing lines of clothes and shoes.

The shades on two large windows are down, glowing white with the reflection of the streetlight out front. On Hanna's nightstand, the digital clock reads one thirty-two in neon red.

I look down.

Hanna's at my feet, blood pooling around her head. The hammer in my hand feels just so . . . like judgment come to the wicked. I sway on my feet like I'm on drugs. I feel so good. Everything is right. Everything is as it should be. I look at the body at my feet and feel no regret, no shame, no remorse. I am awash in satisfaction. Hanna deserved to die.

My eyes snap open, and I sit up in bed sucking in a lungful of air like a drowning man breaking the lake's surface. I'm soaked. Sweat evaporates from my skin under the ceiling fan even as my bed sheets cling to my damp skin.

Fear and revulsion churn my stomach. An invisible taint skims the surface of my soul like curdled milk. Slow at first, my body trembles but with gaining force until my whole body shakes. I shut my eyes, trying to ride out the nausea threatening to empty my stomach.

I don't know how long I sit there, shaking, willing myself not to vomit, but when I open my eyes, I see Dad is at my desk, and I have no doubt he's been there for a long time.

He leans back. "Tell me," he says.

A second or two passes as I clear my mind. This is what we do. I am a Dreamer, like my father. I see murders before they happen, through the eyes of the killer, in and around the places close to where I sleep, to where I Dream.

This is our calling. It is my job to stop the killer, to save the Chosen.

As far as Dad knows, we are alone in the world, Dreaming of future evil, given a righteous mission to save an innocent life. I often wonder about that. Where did this gift or curse come from? Dad says he's never met anyone like himself. Now that I've had the Dream, I can see how it works. How Dad came up with the rules. Once he told them to me, I felt the rightness of them. Dad had to work it all out on his own. I am so thankful for him.

He was alone. I am not.

Three months ago, I had my first Dream, and I knew the girl who died, kind of. Hanna Smith isn't my friend, but I did recognize her.

Dad called it a *lucky* break.

The Dream gives you what you need. Sometimes it gives you more, sometimes less. The fact that I knew Hanna made finding the murder scene easy, but *lucky*? No. Nothing about this has been lucky.

Dad was right about one thing, though. Being close to Hanna made the bond between us tighter. The Dreams before were vaporous things, insubstantial. They were, well, dreams. Tonight was different. It was so *real*. I felt the killer's emotions like never before. The sicko enjoyed the murder, like a thrill kill. They wanted to do it so very bad, but it was also personal. One thing I am sure of now: the killer knows Hanna.

I take a slow, steadying breath, not sick anymore, but on edge. I force myself to relax. Aching muscles reluctantly slacken.

I nod once at Dad, and I tell him about the Dream. I tell him everything.

CHAPTER 4

My car isn't the nicest. It's an old Cadillac my grandmother left Dad and me. We fixed it up some, replaced the spark plugs, redid the suspension, changed out the brake pads, rotors, and brake lines. The engine was in good condition since Grandma only took it to church and the grocery store. There is a lot of sentimental value in the car, but that's about it.

It's two-tone blue with a V6. We call it the Beast because it's a sled of a ride. Some girls wouldn't be caught dead in such a thing. Not Molly, though. Thankfully.

As soon as she got in, we were talking. Much like that afternoon and evening at the mall, the conversation is effortless and fun. Spending as much time as I can with Molly is my goal. Once we get to the party, that won't be possible. So, I take the long way while driving ten miles below the speed limit.

"Want to hear some good news?" Molly asks brightly.

"Sure. I love good news."

"I got the part of Abigail Williams."

"Really," I say. "The Big Bad? Think you can pull it off?"

"Not a problem," she says with a confidence that I have always admired. Molly believes in herself. She's one of those people who sees what they want and isn't afraid to go for it. "Oh, and she is so deliciously evil," Molly goes on. "Has an affair with John Proctor and then tries to have his wife hung. I'm going to love playing her. Mr. Sampson wanted me to audition for Elizabeth Proctor, but I told him I'm all about some Abigail Williams."

Neighborhoods turn into trees and old clear cuts as we head deep into the county toward Jacoby's grandmother's house.

"I don't know," I say, feigning sincerity. "You don't have a bad bone in your body."

"Acting, Jude. That's why they call it *acting*. Besides, we all have our dark side, Jude. Even you."

I laugh, but it comes out quick and loud, more like I'm choking. "Well, I can't wait to see you in the play," I say. "I'm glad you got the part you wanted."

Molly smiles, pleased, and for the first time in our little trip, the conversation lulls. I search for something else to say. We're getting close to Jacoby's, and I want to get a better idea of how she feels about me. She did just break up with Lucas, but she also said the breakup had been coming for a long time. Is she ready for a new relationship? The last thing I want is to make her feel uncomfortable. Besides, do I need this? It's kind of a complicated time for me, having to kill someone on August 12 and all.

What would a normal person on a normal date say to the girl he likes? Nothing comes to mind. *Nothing.*

"I'm glad you asked me to come," Molly says, saving me from my internal struggle.

I keep both hands on the wheel, watching the road as the sun sets and the Beast's headlights illuminate the country road. The next words out of my mouth are maybe the truest things I've ever said. "Me too." I glance over at Molly. Despite the low light—maybe even more so—Molly is lovely, her dark-red hair framing her face, a mischievous grin on her full lips.

"There are going to be a lot of people here," she says.

"I know," I say with a small laugh. I'm not even sure when I told Molly about my aversion to crowds. Ninth grade maybe. I do remember she thought it was funny. Even then, I was one of the most athletic kids at school. Normally that means one of the more popular kids, too, but in my case, that wasn't true. It still isn't.

All day, the thought of so many kids together in one place has made me slightly ill. Molly is, literally, the only reason I'm here. "It's cool," I say, trying, and failing, to sound nonchalant.

Molly reaches over and pats my leg. "A lot of people, Jude. These parties are huge."

I glance over at her.

"So many people, Jude."

I take the turn to Jacoby's house, slowing down and looking at Molly. Her smile seems a little more predatory than before.

"You're enjoying yourself, aren't you?"

Her smile twists, turning sly. "You should see your face right now. I'm sorry Jude, but wow! You're like this football-playing tough guy, but more than three people get together and you're trying to find an escape route. You've got a lot going for you."

"Not really," I scoff, but I want to hear more.

Molly sighs dramatically. "Jude, Jude, Jude. My poor naive Jude. Let me tell you how it is."

I shake my head with a little laugh. "Okay. Tell me."

"Well, you're smart, athletic, not too bad on the eyes," Molly says with laughter in her voice, "and soooo polite. You're like a parent's dream. My mom barely knows you, but I bet she asks about you at least once a month."

"Yeah?" I ask.

"Yes," Molly says matter-of-factly.

I don't know a ton about Molly's parents. I know they own a business, construction slash remodeling. They work a lot in Little Rock on office buildings, but they also do local stuff. I've only been around Mrs. Goldman a time or two. "Really," I say. "She asks about me."

"Absolutely. She thought you'd be a good influence on her little tomboy. She wanted a little princess. Someone different from me.

And you, you've always been, like, this nice kid with your *yes ma'ams* and *no ma'ams* and asking her how she's doing. *Thoughtful, charming,* I think are a couple adjectives she's used."

Her words carry a hint of something. Sadness? Resentment? I'm not sure, but I understand. I'd like to tell Molly just how very much I understand. How my mother feels like she got the short end of the stick, kidwise. Molly and I have a lot in common. But I'm not talking about that tonight. My anxiety is a low buzz now. Molly's mom is Team Jude. That certainly can't hurt.

I make the last turn to Jacoby's. His place is back in the woods, down a dirt and gravel road. The Beast's wheels bump over the uneven drive as I avoid some of the larger potholes.

"Almost there. How you feeling, big guy?" Molly asks.

"I'm great. Never better. How many people can be here, anyway?"

My headlights light the field in front of Jacoby's house, and there are *so* many cars. Something small dies inside me as I groan.

Molly giggles, enjoying my discomfort way too much. "Relax, Jude. You probably know everyone here. Most everyone. Probably only a few hundred you don't," she says, still enjoying her game.

"I'm good," I say, swallowing. "As long as I'm here with you." I cringe at the cheesiness of the line and change the subject. "Where should I park?"

Molly points. "Over there by the tree." She whistles. "This is crazy. Half the school must be here."

"Uh-huh," I say, spiders crawling up my spine. I park the Beast and shut off the engine. The lack of its comforting hum is like an amputation.

Molly reaches over and squeezes my hand. I glance down at our interlocked hands and up into Molly's smiling face. My heart pounds. The spiders disappear, replaced by warmth. For once, the spreading heat in my cheeks is nice.

"Let's have fun tonight, okay?" Molly says.

"Yeah. Sure. It's a party, right?"

Molly's smile widens, and it amazes me how such a simple thing can make me so happy.

"It's definitely a party." Molly's eyes twinkle. "Now let's work on your social skills." She lets my hand go and gets out of the car.

"Molly!" someone yells as soon as I step out of the Beast.

A small group of girls waves us over.

I take two steps, and someone yells my name. "Erickson. Oh, yeah." I turn. Rob Thomas, our starting fullback, comes over.

"I'll be over here," Molly says. "Have fun."

She walks to her group of friends as Rob approaches. His walk is kind of off and as he gets closer, I understand why. He's got a red Solo cup of beer in each hand. "Woooh! Jude Erickson at the par-tay. I salute you, captain of the football team!" He takes a drink from the beer in his left hand.

Rob is built like a tank, short and thick with a chest as big as a bull's. We've played football together since third grade. He's a friend, a good guy, hardworking, but, if I'm being honest, not the brightest bulb on the tree.

He cuts his eyes at Molly as she walks away. "You guys here, like, together, man?"

"Yep," I say.

Rob hesitates. Takes a drink from the cup in his right hand. "That's"—a smile splits his face—"awesome." He offers me the left-handed beer. "Drink up, man."

I don't drink. The idea of being out of control, not in charge of my emotions and reactions, has never appealed to me.

"I'm good," I say.

"Suit yourself."

People stand in groups talking, some drinking, some not. Laughter and conversation fills the field, Jacoby's house up the hill awash in lights, the low thump of bass rolling. A few football guys stand in a knot near the porch. There are plenty of people here I don't know. Andre Anderson, our starting tight end, comes over. We clasp hands and he pulls me in to slap my back. "My man, never seen you at one of these things."

I nod. Big Andre's cool. Kind of a straight-laced type of guy. Tall, broad, and genuine. His father's the pastor at the Methodist church, preaches fire and brimstone from the pulpit but one of the nicest guys ever. "Your pops know you're here?"

Andre gives me a broad smile. "The Lord detests lying lips. Proverbs 12:22."

"So, you didn't tell him?"

Andre nods. "Avoided him all day. But you? This is something. Never thought I'd see you here."

"What?" I ask. "Just trying to get my party on."

"Party on, huh? Okay." He laughs. "If you say so. Wish I wasn't here to be honest. Jess wanted to come." He nods at one of the girls chatting up Molly. She's petite, with dark hair and eyes. Jessica Brashear and Andre have been dating since . . . well, as long as I can remember.

Rob takes a sloppy drink of his right-handed beer and wipes his mouth with the back of his sleeve. "Both you guys here with dates, and me all alone. Makes me feel like the smart one! Have you guys seen how many ladies are up in here? Chapel girls too."

"You came with someone?" Andre asks me, but I ignore him.

"Chapel girls?" I ask. "Really?"

Rob nods. "Maybe, who knows? Lots of folks I don't know, for real. Jacoby sent up the Bat-Signal. Good thing he lives in the middle of nowhere or the po-po would already be here!" He screams the last part to prove his point. A few people outside cut glances his way, but most ignore him.

I search the faces. I recognize most from school, but there are people I either don't know or can't make out. If Hanna's here, I have to go. But she's not here. No way.

"So, who are you here with?" Andre asks again.

"Molly-freaking-Goldman," Rob answers for me.

"Really?" Andre sounds surprised. The music coming from Jacoby's house changes. The bass deepens, and the music takes on a slower, rhythmic quality. I can't make out what it is, but if the bass gets any deeper, the house windows might explode.

Rob belches. It's long and loud, like a cartoon. "I saw it with my own eyes. Molly and our boy getting out of Jude's ride."

Andre shifts his body weight. "Molly, huh? Like a friend thing?"

"Here come the ladies," Rob interrupts, saving me from answering. In truth, that's all Molly and I are. For now. I follow Rob's gaze and indeed Molly and her friends are coming our way. "You think Jess could set me up with Payton?" Rob asks Andre.

"Uh. I'm not sure. Maybe," Andre says with a hint of *no way* in his tone.

"Sweet," Rob says, oblivious. He takes another swallow of beer. "She's so smart, man, uses words I gotta Google. I think we'd be cool together. You know, like opposites attract."

"Uh-huh," Andre says.

Rob takes another drink of his left-handed beer as Molly, Jess, and Payton join us.

"What's up, Payton?" Rob says. "You got Mrs. Alverez for English second block? 'Cause I might need help in that class."

The conversations diverge. I'm not included in any of them, and that's okay. Molly's not participating either. She's frowning, glancing up at Jacoby's house, and I wonder what's happened in the last few minutes. She's different somehow. Different in some fundamental way from who she was a few minutes ago. She takes the beer from Rob's right hand.

"Hey," Rob says. "I was drinking that."

Molly takes a sip of beer. A little bigger sip than maybe is necessary.

"Oh yeah," Rob hoots, "now it's a party."

Molly looks down at the cup like it materialized from thin air, and she takes another, longer, drink. When her head comes up, her eyes almost seem to sparkle in the low light, but not in a good way.

Of all the possibilities of tonight, Molly chugging beer wasn't something I'd considered.

"Thanks, Rob," Molly says. "Why don't you go get me another?"

Rob nods like she's just shared the most righteous tidbit, like how God makes rainbows. "Oh yeah. *Oh, yeah!*" he says. "Coming up." He runs off toward the house.

"You okay?" I ask Molly. "Didn't know you drank. Your mom might rethink her position on me if I bring you home tipsy."

Molly never looks at me, doesn't even acknowledge the joke. "It's a party, Jude. Live a little." She takes a slow breath. "I think I'm ready to go inside."

CHAPTER 5

Jacoby Cole's grandmother's house smells like old people, and that's not a bad thing. It smells lived in. Years of cooking permeate the air, like a house well lived in and well loved. It's familiar, friendly, like a home.

The living room is crowded with people, some sitting around the dining room table playing cards, but most talk in close groups; a few people dance and laugh. Music bumps on a neon-flashing Wi-Fi speaker turned up way too loud. I walk a few steps into the living room and take it all in. There's a hallway to the right and an open kitchen to the left. In the kitchen, five or six people stand around a keg, Solo cups on the counter, towers of red plastic reaching up.

One of the people in the kitchen is Lucas Munson. Two years ago, he was at Chapel.

But something happened, something with his dad. I don't know the details, but it involved alcohol and redneck behavior. Something un-Chapel-like. Now Munson's back at Bedford. He's six-five, two hundred and twenty-five pounds, strong and fast, with over twenty scholarship offers to play division one football.

He's also Molly's ex-boyfriend.

I lean in close to Molly. "Do you want to leave?"

She doesn't even acknowledge my question. Her glare is focused on the kitchen, on Lucas.

Rob materializes in front of us. His smile broadens as he holds up a beer. "Got that drink, Molly."

"Thanks Rob," she says, taking the cup from him, her eyes never leaving Lucas.

I lean in so only she can hear. "If you want to go, that's cool."

She looks at me, and her expression that's been hardening over the last few minutes softens a bit. "I'm sorry, Jude. Lucas was supposed to be visiting A&M this weekend. I didn't know he was going to be here. And—" She stops midsentence as her eyes cut to Lucas. "I need a minute, okay? I-I-I'm going to the bathroom." She turns and leaves me alone with Rob.

Someone yells Rob's name. He yells back, pats me on the shoulder, and leaves without saying another word.

I reluctantly take a seat on an empty couch as Jess and Payton come in from outside. They seem like they're on a mission. Payton is especially acting odd, glancing at me as she walks through the living room and into the kitchen.

It's obvious Molly is upset with Lucas being here. It hurts, but I get it. They dated for a while, but I'm still trying to understand what all the *other* people are so concerned about. I know Molly's friends care about her, but they're way overreacting. Eventually, Molly was going to be in a room with Munson. They attend the same school. I'm smart enough to know that I'm missing something, but I'm not smart enough to see what it is.

Jacoby comes from the kitchen, with Jess and Payton behind him. He's a tall, lanky kid, his skin dark and smooth. Looks like he got a haircut for the party, too. His fade is way too tight to be over a day old.

He sees me across the room and smiles weakly with his hands stuffed in his pockets. He strolls over, leaving the girls behind, and plops down beside me, slapping my thigh in greeting. "Jude, finally you decide to show. Make one of my epic parties."

I scan the room of mostly drunk or soon-to-be drunk teenagers and nod at its epicness.

"Glad you came, really," Jacoby says.

His words do not match his demeanor. I feel a *but* at the end of his statement that he's hesitant to drop.

Dad has taught me how to choke someone out, how to break limbs, how to strip down any number of firearms and reassemble them. He's never taught me . . . *this*. "I need to ask you something Jacoby, and I need you to be honest."

"Okay. I can do that."

More people have come in from outside. Jacoby's small house is way over capacity. Many are kids I go to school with, but people I hardly know. Not because this is the party crowd. The group I have the least in common with. It's deeper than that. I don't belong here. In fact, I don't belong anywhere. I've felt like this my whole life. Dad's revelations about what I am only made that feeling worse. I don't care why Jacoby came over now. I have a question that I want him to answer. "Jacoby, why do you invite me to your parties?"

Jacoby leans forward, his elbows on his knees. "It's a party. I invite a lot of people."

"Yeah," I say. "That's it?"

"Pretty much, yeah. You're cool."

"How am I cool?" My words come out a little more accusatory than I mean.

Jacoby lowers his head and taps his foot. "Look, I'll be honest. I sometimes wonder why I invite a guy who never shows, but, well, I'm like that, magnanimous and stuff. Taking you off the group text isn't really worth it. And I see you at school, hanging out with football dudes, but I don't know. I never see you out."

"So, you're worried about my social life?"

He laughs at that, but the laugh is off. He keeps glancing toward the kitchen. "Nah, man. I don't really have a reason. It's like I said, I invited almost everybody I knew. You're cool. Be a lot cooler if you hung out more." He grimaces like this next part is going to hurt. "But tonight is not your night. You've got to go. For your own good."

"For my own good," I say out loud, as if speaking the words will make them make sense, but they don't. "Why? Why do I have to go?"

Jacoby looks at me like he's not sure if I'm joking. "You really don't know, do you? Do you even know Munson?"

Molly appears from the hall. Her posture is rigid. She stands taller, straightening wrinkles in her jeans that don't exist, and walks to the kitchen.

Jacoby groans and stands. "Don't do it, girl. It's not worth it." He looks down at me. "See what you did? Come on. You need to fix this." He takes off through the throng of people.

I hesitate for just a moment and follow him.

CHAPTER 6

Jacoby doesn't make it in time. I stand behind him as Munson spots Molly. An entire range of emotions washes over Munson's face, settling into Hand Caught in the Cookie Jar.

"Hello, Lucas," Molly says. Her words aren't angry. They're maybe a bit too pleasant. More still, her words carry across the room. It might be my imagination, but I think someone turned down the music. More than a few people seem interested in what's cooking in the kitchen.

My heart sinks as I see why. Part of the reason people have been acting strange finally makes sense.

A girl is standing next to Munson. Molly's gaze turns to her, and I freeze. It's Hanna Smith. The dead girl. I take an involuntary step back but bump into someone. This isn't happening.

Hanna, for her part, looks about as comfortable as I feel. She leans back against the countertop as if trying to fade away. Relatable. I'd melt into the floor right now if I could. I need to get Molly and leave, but stepping any closer to Hanna Smith seems like a bad idea. The bond between us is as strong as it's ever been. If we touch again, it will be so much worse than that day in the mall. Hanna would share the vision this time. That would be a complete disaster.

"Hi," Molly says to Hanna. "It's so awesome you're here."

I'm the social equivalent of a garden slug—no denying that—but even I know the sincerity in Molly's voice is fake.

Lucas Munson swallows and lowers his voice. "This isn't what it looks like."

Molly smiles up at Lucas. "It's fine, really. I thought you would be in Texas. And now you're here." She shrugs. "It's fine. I just wanted to come say hi before any awkwardness happened." She glances around the room, and for the first time notices her audience. Someone definitely turned down the music.

Munson sets his beer down on the counter behind him. "Can we talk?"

Molly's next words are soft. "Not right now. I . . . anyway, okay. Bye." Molly shakes her head and turns away. Her eyes lift and meet mine. She smiles apologetically, and I am so relieved. "Let's go, Jude," she says.

"Jude Erickson," Munson says. "You came with him? *Jude.*" He says my name like I'm a little kid.

I give a quick bark of laughter at that.

Munson gives me the briefest of glares before speaking to Molly again, his voice softer. "You're right," he says. "This is . . . awkward. I didn't think you'd be here either. Please." He steps closer to Molly and lowers his voice, but everyone in the room hears, because someone turned the music off. Who needs music when you have this kind of drama? "Can we . . . can we just talk?"

"Later, okay," Molly says. She walks past me, and I let her by, but Munson is on her heels. I don't stand in his way, but the room is packed, and Lucas is a huge human being.

He puts a finger on my chest. "Get out of my way, Jude."

I wasn't in his way, not really, but now I am. "You need to chill," I tell him.

He grunts and grabs my shirt. No one has ever tried to bully me before. Not like this, not with physical violence. I don't even think about it. It's reflex, muscle memory, like I saw a mosquito and had to swat it. I grab Munson's wrist with both hands, turning his palm up while moving my feet to his side, bending his wrist in ways it wasn't supposed to move. Munson is strong, but he's never experienced a wrist lock. He instantly releases my shirt, his knees bending toward the ground to get away from the pain.

I stop. What am I doing? This is so stupid.

Maybe someone spilled beer on the floor, maybe the linoleum in Jacoby's grandmother's house is extra slick, or maybe Munson's a little too drunk, but Munson's foot slips, and he slides down, pulling me with him. I let go of the huge kid, but he pushes out even as he's falling, and he is strong. People move, beer flies as I slide back, spinning to catch myself on the kitchen counter. Only one problem—Hanna is in my way.

I slide to a stop less than a foot away from her. She hops up on the counter to get away from me. Hanna's eyes meet mine, and she frowns. I stare back, knowing the vision is about to take me. My heart thumps . . . and nothing happens. Of course nothing happens. We didn't touch.

I spin around to get the heck on up out of Dodge, but Munson is on his feet, glaring at me with eyes so cold they could break glass. He lunges at me, all six-five, two hundred and twenty-five pounds of him.

It's hard to explain exactly what happens next. My heart rate slows, my muscles relax, and I'm at peace. The anxiety is gone. The exact opposite of what I would have thought. The crowd disappears into white noise, and I no longer feel eyes upon me. I've never been in a real fight before, but Dad told me it would be like this. This is part of what makes us what we are. I never knew if I believed him or not.

I move back half a step, stop, and shoot forward to meet Munson, striking out as I sidestep his awkward attempt to grab me. My hand slides up past his clumsy, groping hands to deliver a quick strike to the throat. Lucas's eyes bulge as he stumbles, his red face turning scarlet.

"Stop, you idiots," Molly says, appearing between us like a referee at a boxing match.

The calm that surrounded me is gone in an instant, and the weight of all the eyes in the room bears down on me. Lucas is ten paces away, his hands at his throat, and he's panting like a fish out of water.

I tapped him in the trachea. Hit someone hard enough and you can kill them. Dad says that's only for the movies, but I'd almost let that strike really fly. The realization scares me. I'd almost tried to kill Lucas Munson.

"Munson," I say slowly, my hands lowering. "We need to think about this."

In answer, Lucas shakes his head. He stands straight, all his breath back, his eyes focused on me. The room is silent. Everyone is still. Not because I'm in some kind of killer trance. The whole party is waiting for what's coming next.

Molly's friends drag her out of the way. She doesn't leave quietly, telling Lucas and me how stupid we are. She's not wrong, but I'm trapped. Munson won't let me leave. And I suddenly know the other reason why some kids have been acting odd tonight. Jacoby all but told me on the couch. *Do you even know Munson?* They are scared for me. Scared Lucas would take offense to me being here with Molly.

Dad has trained me to fight since I was old enough to walk. Alone in the garage, we've trained: Brazilian jiu-jitsu, boxing, Krav Maga, Muay Thai. Any type of fighting skill Dad could learn, he has, and he's taught them all to me. I know how to shoot, how to fight with a knife, but mostly it's the hand-to-hand stuff Dad pushes. *Any dumbass can pull a trigger*, Dad says. *Not everyone can throw a right cross.*

I'm not scared of Munson, but I should be, if I were normal.

Lucas Munson jumps forward and takes a swing at me. It's bad—bad form, bad angle, bad technique. I step back, and his motion pulls him forward. Without thought, I strike him hard in the ribs, bringing a grunt from him, but more importantly bringing his arms down as I step past him.

Dad teaches me to attack the groin in this situation, but I'd rather not do that. I'm holding back. I don't want to really hurt Munson. I want him to stop. My hesitation is my undoing.

Lucas turns, crazy fast. Faster than someone as big as he should be able to. The reason why every college in the country wants him to play football for them.

He jabs at me, not a wild swing like before, and I'm caught off-balance. I duck at the last second, but it's too late. Lucas's huge fist grazes the top of my head. I fly back. The punch landed, and it hurts, but worse, it causes me to lose balance. I turn to stop my fall. Hanna is there, still sitting on the countertop, and I can't stop my momentum this time.

I fall into her lap.

I'm not in the kitchen anymore. I'm not in Jacoby's house anymore. I'm climbing the stairs at Hanna's house. She's there on the bed. She wakes, sees me, and moves. My hammer misses. I swing again as she rounds the bed, clipping her shoulder. She falls, and I attack her. I stand over her body as the blood pools. The images assault my brain in rapid-fire succession, making me want to puke, and cry, and laugh all at once.

The vision bursts like a bubble, and I'm back in Jacoby's grandmother's kitchen. Hanna stares at me in disbelief. She's scared. Horrified. A tear leaks from the corner of her eye to roll down her cheek. *Oh. No . . .*

I disentangle myself from Hanna, turning in time to see Lucas's meaty fist coming straight for my head. If the punch lands square, it might break my face. I don't have time to think. I react, tucking my chin in and lowering my head. Lucas's hand connects, not with my nose, but at my hairline, the hardest part of my skull.

Lucas's hand cracks against my head, and he screams in pain. My already weak legs buckle, and I'm seeing stars of black. I fall to my knees, the blow reverberating down my spine.

Lucas is hopping back, holding his hand. "Ahhh!" he screams again. "Ahhh! My hand!"

Something both triumphant and nauseating bubbles up inside me. The dark stars get larger, converging on one another. I tip forward, falling. The floor tiles rush up at me.

Mercifully, I'm too stunned to feel the full impact of my face hitting the kitchen floor.

CHAPTER 7

Coach Davis stares at us from across his desk, his dark eyes going from me and back to Lucas. With his lean, hard face and blond hair cut drill sergeant-like, Coach D is an intimidating man on his best day.

Today is not his best day.

The party was on Saturday. Dad doesn't know anything, other than I went to the party and had a super-awesome time. He can never know anything different.

Coach, on the other hand, heard about it as he always hears about things. The fact it took until the end of practice Monday is nothing short of miraculous. All the players are gone. All the coaches too. Coach D made us wait. Now, our wait is over.

"You two are the best players on the team. We have five captains, and two of them"—he points to me and then to Munson—"are punching each other at weekend parties." He shakes his head like that's the most ridiculous thing he's ever heard. "You're both senior leaders. Both of you." He spits the last words, literally. Spittle's been flying from his mouth in random intervals for the past ten minutes. "Were either of you drinking?"

Lucas answers first. "No sir." He glances a warning my way. "*I* wasn't."

My forehead is sore. I'm not positive what whiplash is, but I think I have it. Despite all that, I don't have a mark on me. "I don't drink," I say in a level tone. "Ever."

Lucas rolls his eyes and sinks lower into the seat he's already slouching in. His right hand is in a soft cast. He can practice and play, but he has to wrap the injured hand up and won't be able to grab anyone for four weeks. Coach D isn't happy.

"We have a real shot at winning the conference this year. You guys know that, right?" Coach doesn't wait for an answer. "But I've seen more talented teams take a nosedive when the chemistry wasn't there. And you two are the heart and soul of this team."

Coach gestures at Lucas's cast. "You're a D lineman. You need your hands."

"I'll be fine, Coach. Doc says I was lucky, only fractured the one bone . . ." Munson trails off as Coach D glares at him.

"You broke your hand," Coach says slowly, emphasizing each word, "because you *punched* your *teammate* in the head?"

Lucas grunts an acknowledgment but keeps his mouth shut this time.

"And you?" Coach says to me. "I hear you instigated the whole thing."

Lucas sits up at this, unable to keep a grin off his lips.

Coach eyes me expectantly. Most of Coach's questions are rhetorical, but he wants an actual answer this time. "No?" I say, more like a question than an answer. Truth is, I'm not sure. Everything happened so fast. But I'm smart enough not to try and explain myself. This really isn't a conversation.

Coach shakes his head in disgust. He lets out a long sigh. "Women aren't property to be fought over. Y'all understand that, right?"

"It wasn't like that, Coach," Munson says, and I cringe. Munson obviously doesn't understand how this type of interaction works. He should. He's been in enough trouble.

Coach leans forward on his desk, storm clouds in his eyes. "All right then. Let me tell you what it *is* like," he says. "You embarrassed yourselves, you embarrassed your teammates, and you embarrassed me."

Coach's words sting more than he can know. I am embarrassed. I haven't tried to contact Molly, and I haven't heard from her either. Things were going so good too.

I never lost consciousness that night. My vision went wonky, and I was disoriented for a minute or two, but when my head cleared, Molly was gone. Andre and Jess took her home. Andre texted me to let me know.

The last two days have been full of uncertainty. I'm constantly wondering what she's thinking, but too afraid to text her. Calling her is out of the question. I know I messed up. I'm not sure I could handle hearing the disappointment in her voice.

Coach leans back in his chair. "Is there an *I* in team, Erickson?" The abrupt change in topics is jarring.

"Uh, no," I say.

Coach shakes his head. "*That's right.* No *I* in team. Either you are all-in and ready to ride, or you're out. Which is it, Erickson?"

I hesitate a moment, mulling over Coach's words of wisdom. I nod like expected. "I'm in, Coach."

He looks at Lucas. "Munson? How about you?"

Lucas nods as if he's ashamed by the whole thing. It's fake. I know Lucas. He's never been contrite about anything, ever. "You bet, Coach. Just a misunderstanding." He looks over at me. "We're cool."

I'm positive Lucas Munson and I are not *cool.* "That's right," I say. "We're good, Coach."

Coach Davis leans back farther in his chair and levels his gaze. "Women are to be respected. What you two did," he shakes his head, "in another time, in another place, *maybe* it would have been acceptable, but it would have been bullsquat all the same."

I swallow and nod. Coach doesn't cuss. When he almost cusses, you know you've messed up. He's right too. That only makes it worse.

"Both of you will have extra running after practice this week, so you remember how *cool* and *good* you both are. And if I hear a peep, if a little birdie whispers even a hint of you two acting like fools again, things will only get worse. Is that clear?"

Lucas sits up, nodding. I do the same.

"Good," Coach D says. "That's all."

It's our cue to leave, and we don't have to be told twice. I almost trip standing.

"Erickson," Coach says. "Stay a minute."

Lucas smirks at me where Coach can't see and goes out the door. Reluctantly, I turn and sit back down.

Coach taps a finger on the desk. Outside we both hear the field house door open and close. Munson has left the building.

Coach sighs. "Munson's a real jackass."

My jaw drops a fraction. I shut it as quick as it opened. I don't say anything. Coach goes on. "But not everyone is as fortunate as you, Jude. You know Quinn Munson, Lucas's pop?"

"Not really," I say.

Coach seems to consider his next words. "I'm going to level with you. Munson's home life isn't the best. This community of ours, we don't have much. We have a lot of broken families, poverty, and drugs." Coach grimaces, the last one hitting too close to home. Tommy Davis, Coach Davis's son, has a very public drug problem. He is two years older than me and was the starting quarterback my sophomore year. In a small town like ours, a former high school football star dropping out of college and going to rehab is big news.

"I know your parents are split up," Coach Davis continues, "but you're one of the lucky ones. Your pop takes care of you, teaches you right from wrong. A lot of people don't have what you do. You need to keep that in mind." Coach Davis studies my face. "Is it true you hit Munson first?"

A lump forms in my throat. Technically, I put Munson in a wrist lock, thought better of it, and released him. Munson then tried and failed to hit me. But I don't explain any of that. I nod.

"Violence begets violence, Jude." Coach gives a small laugh. "Might sound funny coming from an old football coach, but truth is truth."

Violence begets violence. The words resonate deep within my soul.

He hesitates, and I know he's about to drop some knowledge on me. "You have talent. I know your dad would welcome a full ride to college. Football can do that. Being smart helps, but any academic money you get won't pay all the bills. An athletic scholarship will pay for room, board, and give you a stipend to live on. But you get into fights, at parties, with teammates, and you can bet word will get around."

I keep my mouth shut. Coach Davis taps his fingers on the desktop. "Keep your nose clean. You understand?"

Time for me to speak. "Yes, sir."

Coach nods. "All right then. Go on, I've got work to do."

I get out of my seat and walk to the door. Two pictures on the wall I've never noticed before catch my eye. I stop a second to check them out.

The top picture is of Coach D and his wife on their wedding day. Coach D's tuxedo is at least two decades out of date. Mrs. D, on the other hand, looks great in her white wedding dress. The other picture is of Coach D, his wife, and Tommy. They stand in front of several rows of red fish with white bellies. The smallest is over a foot long. A sign above them reads "Sailor's Delight, Destin, Florida." In the photo, Tommy can't be more than twelve. He's grinning wide, holding up one of the huge fish.

"Thought you were leaving," Coach says, but his voice holds no irritation. He pushes up from his squeaky office chair and walks over.

"Your tuxedo is pretty sweet," I say with a grin.

"Ha," he laughs. "Well, that was the style twenty-five years ago."

I tap the glass of the fishing picture. "What kind of fish are those?"

"Snapper," Coach says. "Red snapper." He grunts. "That was a great day. I'll remember it the rest of my life."

His voice has a hint of sadness, and I wonder if it's because of Tommy. From what I've heard, Tommy is back from rehab and doing great. I'm rooting for Tommy. Everyone is.

"You fish a lot?" I ask.

"When I can. Me and the missus are planning a quick overnighter the weekend after homecoming." He pauses. "How about you? You a fisherman?"

"No," I say. "I've never been fishing."

"Never? That's hard to believe."

I shrug. "I don't even have a pole."

"Now that's a shame," Coach says. "I have a ton of old tackle up in the attic. If you want it, it's yours." Coach takes a deep breath. "Stay clear of Munson outside of football, okay?" He shakes his head. "Of all the people to get into a scrap with, *Lucas Munson*? Know your limits, Erickson."

"Right, Coach," I say. "My limits."

CHAPTER 8

I leave Coach D's office and head out. The air is thick with humidity, and gray-black clouds cover the sky. *Odd.* It was sunny and dry when I went into the field house an hour ago.

My eyes drift down from the clouds and fall on Munson. He's still here, lingering in the parking lot, and his dad is with him.

The elder Munson eyes me while Lucas looks at his feet. Munson's father is as big as his boy. He's about my own father's age. The few times I've found myself near him, he's reeked of stale beer.

I walk toward my car, trying hard not to look in their direction.

"Hey, you," Mr. Munson yells at me in a tone way south of polite. I stop and stare down the hill at the pair. "Come here, boy."

I consider ignoring him. What's he going to do? But it's Lucas who makes me change my mind. He's still staring at the ground. It's odd seeing Lucas like that, and for a second, I feel sorry for him. That second passes and a slow-boil anger creeps back in. Mr. Munson wants to intimidate me? He picked the wrong guy.

I walk toward the pair. Lucas looks up as I approach, and something hard crosses his face. All the sheepishness is gone, and he stands tall. He glances at his dad and then glares at me, like this whole situation is somehow my fault.

"You broke my kid's hand," Mr. Munson says.

"*He* broke his hand," I snap.

Mr. Munson gawks at me, the twist of emotions playing across his face more entertaining than a ticket to the fair. He steps close. "My boy's got scholarships riding on this season. And *you* break his hand?" Alcohol and tobacco are thick on his breath, and the challenge in his voice is almost more than I can take. For an instant, I understand why Lucas is such a jerk.

Another snide comment forms on my lips, but out of the corner of my eye I catch Munson shuffling his feet. He gives me the slightest of head shakes. He's pleading with me to stop. Not threatening. Pleading. All at once, the air goes out of me.

"You hear me, boy?" Mr. Munson says.

I step away from him, unable to look at him or his son. "Yes, sir," I say, my eyes downcast. "It was a misunderstanding. It-it won't happen again."

The elder Munson grunts. "*This* boy broke your hand? All hype, just like his old man."

The comment burns, and I stare up at him.

"Yeah, I know your daddy," Mr. Munson says. "You tell him Quinn Munson says hi. You tell him that if his kid don't walk the straight-and-straight, I might come pay him a visit. A visit he won't like."

It's comical, this drunk, threatening Dad. The laugh that escapes me is completely involuntary. Mr. Munson's eyes turn cold, and his lips curl into an ugly grin. He opens his mouth, but up on the hill, the field house door opens.

Mr. Munson turns, the fake smile already cracking his face. He raises his hand to Coach D. The transformation is astounding. "Hey, Coach. Thought I'd come by and make sure my boy's doing right. Makin' sure we stay tight as a team."

Coach D frowns as he comes down the hill to join us. He stands beside me and takes in the situation. "Quinn, to be honest, this is a team matter. You can discipline Lucas as you see fit, but I'd appreciate if you let me handle the other kids on the team."

Quinn Munson gives Coach a weak, mocking salute. "This is your ship, Captain. All right then, we'll be going. Can't wait for the season to start. My boy here's gonna put on a show." He swats Munson on the arm, glancing over at me. "Hope everybody carries their weight."

Coach Davis doesn't respond, just crosses his arms and waits.

Mr. Munson's fake smile dissolves, and he turns. "Come on, Lucas," the elder Munson says, walking toward an old, battered pickup in the parking lot below.

Coach and I watch as they get in the junker four-wheel drive and take off. "You all right, Erickson? Old Quinn didn't threaten you, did he?"

"A little," I admit.

Coach grunts. "Figures. Once a bully, always a bully. Stay clear of him. If he gives you any more trouble, let me know."

"I will."

"Good." Coach D makes to leave, but his eyes linger on the dark horizon over the practice field. "Didn't know it was going to rain today. Best get home before that hits."

We part ways. My phone vibrates in my pocket as I stalk downhill to the Beast. I take it out but don't recognize the number. It's local, so I answer it. "Hello."

Someone is on the other line. I can hear them, but they don't speak.

"Ah, hello."

Nothing.

"I'm hanging up in one, two, thr—"

"Jude? Jude Erickson?" It's a girl, but I don't recognize the voice.

"Yeah."

"Hey." The girl's voice is steady enough, but I also hear a slight hesitation. "This is Hanna, Hanna Smith."

My phone nearly falls from my hand. This isn't good. I probably should have prepared for this, but I didn't.

Be cool, I tell myself. Be . . . cool.

"Do you know who I am?" Hanna asks, her voice all trepidation.

"I . . . uhhh. I . . . Hanna Smith?" I stammer, unable to get a sentence out.

"Yeah," Hanna says. "I was at the party. I was there when you got into a fight."

I notice she doesn't say who she was there with.

"Anyway. Can we, I don't know. Get together and talk? Like, face-to-face? I know this is . . . weird, but, well—" She seems to get irritated, at herself or at me, I'm not sure. "It's not that big a deal," she says, and the irritation is definitely pointed at me now. "I just want to talk."

I'm speechless. Literally. My brain won't work.

"Jude? You still there?"

"Uh, yeah. I'm here."

"I can be at Regional Park in like ten minutes," Hanna says. "Can you meet me by the old train?"

"Now?" I ask. "I . . . ahhh . . . can't you ask me over the phone?"

"No, I can't," Hanna says, her voice clipped and demanding.

"I don't know—"

"Look," Hanna says more forcefully than before. "Come talk to me. Five minutes. Or I can come to your house."

I imagine Hanna knocking on my door and Dad answering it. "My house? No. I can meet you at the park."

"Great, and maybe don't tell anyone. This isn't, you know— I just want to talk. At the party something . . . just, yeah. I'll see ya. Ten minutes, and don't make this any weirder than it has to be."

The line goes dead, and I stand there for a second, my phone still to my ear.

What. Just. Happened?

Above, thunder echoes in the clouds, and a light rain begins to fall.

CHAPTER 9

I take the side road to the park. Water sprays up around the Beast as I hit a deep pothole full of rain and red clay. My wipers screech against the added strain of mud on the windshield. It's raining hard. The weather matches my mood.

Hanna wants to see me. Hanna wants to talk. With each passing second, the dread grows. What will she say? What exactly does she want?

The vision freaked her out. Understandable, and I hate it for Hanna. I know she's probably confused and angry. Scared, too, but it will all be over soon. Then she will *see*. Dad has told me how it works.

The Chosen must *see* means that we share one last vision that will erase any doubts she has of what I am and what I did for her. After it's over, I take her hand or touch her shoulder, whatever. Physical contact and we share . . . something. Dad tells me to trust him on this one. Despite knowing he's keeping stuff back, I do. On this, at least.

I speed up, pressing the gas pedal down. My phone is on the passenger seat beside me. I drove toward my house, turned it off, and backtracked toward the park. My phone can't be tracked now.

Nothing will go wrong on August 12, but if it does, I can explain away one phone call. Dad can't find out though. Never. He'd freak.

We'd go on *vacation*.

We'd leave Friday after football and drive a hundred miles to Northwest Arkansas. We'd stop a lot, our cell phones on, and make ourselves memorable to gas station attendants, waitresses, and anyone else we met along the way. We'd make sure we were on camera everywhere, which isn't hard. Everyone has cameras. In every hotel, every restaurant, every gas station, someone is watching. We'd check into a nice hotel and make sure we're seen by as many people as possible, at the pool, in the lobby, everywhere.

In short, we make an alibi so tight nobody could question it.

That's not going to happen though.

I put all that aside. I need to prepare myself for Hanna.

The one thing I keep telling myself is that the visions are done for now. I could walk up to her and give her a high five, and nothing would happen. We shared the Dream. Dad says once that happens, once physical contact is made and the Dream shared, it's done . . . until the very end. "Rule four: The Chosen must *see*," I mutter.

I pull up into the parking lot in front of the old steam engine. It sits under a huge awning, on tracks bolted into the concrete. A red Jeep I don't recognize is the only other car in the parking lot. Huge oaks surround the train and awning, their thick limbs bending and twisting in the storm.

Under the awning, right next to the train, a lone figure stands. Hanna is wearing a clear rain poncho over shorts and a T-shirt. The poncho twists in the wind as I peer at her through the windshield. "You could have stayed in your car," I say to myself. I flash my lights at her, but she stays where she is, her arms crossed, hugging herself. She's not moving.

I tap my finger on the steering wheel. Am I doing the right thing? Dad would flip if he knew, but I can fix this, and after August 12 at one thirty-two a.m., it won't matter.

I turn the Beast off, take a deep breath, and open the door. The wind-driven rain hits me like a slap to the face. The train is about forty yards away across a short grassy field. I run, splashing through the wet grass. Hanna waits, watching me. I slip under the awning, soaked as if I'd hopped in the shower fully clothed. The awning above and huge antique steam engine blocks most of the wind and rain. I lean against the train, flicking rainwater from my hands.

Hanna hasn't moved. I glance up at her, afraid to stare too hard. I don't want to spook her.

The corners of Hanna's lips turn down, but she doesn't speak. Her eyes are blue. Really blue. They pierce me, trying to see through me. I feign nonchalance. "I'm here," I say. "What's up?" My heart pounds harder against my ribs.

She steps toward me. I take an involuntary step back, mentally shake myself, and stand my ground. Until Hanna's murderer is dead, the visions are over.

If Dad is right. The thought gives me pause, but I remain still, outwardly calm. I attempt to make my heart stop racing. I take a slow breath.

Hanna's frown deepens. "Are you afraid of something?"

"No," I say. What is there to be afraid of? My stupid voice cracks for some dumb reason, probably the wind and rain.

She blinks, and her expression changes. Her shoulders sag, and her eyes refocus. "I-I— Something weird happened last time we were in the same room."

I hear the uncertainty in her voice. This is good. The vision for her couldn't have been as strong as it was for me. Hopefully, she'd had a drink or two as well. Hooray for bad decisions.

"I saw something," Hanna says. "Something disturbing."

"The fight," I say. "Yeah. Sorry about that. Lucas and I are cool now."

Hanna shakes her head. "That's not what—" she starts, but stops herself as her eyes harden. "Why did you knock him down?"

"*Knock him down?*" I repeat her question as if she asked why is rain wet. "He grabbed my shirt and—"

Hanna doesn't give me a chance to continue. "The whole thing was stupid. You could have defused the situation."

"Defuse the situation?" I laugh. "While Lucas Munson tries to kill me? And what were you doing there? What's Munson to you?"

"Is that any of your business?"

She's right. It isn't any of my business, and it's not why I'm here. She's totally doubting herself. This is good. I did the right thing coming. She won't tell anyone what she saw. She doesn't even want to tell me. After this is over, she'll understand, and we can both continue on with our lives. But right now, I need to make a speedy exit.

"Honestly," I say, "I thought you wanted to apologize for Lucas."

She opens her mouth to speak, but I don't give her the chance. "No worries. It's cool. No hard feelings at all, but it's raining, and I've got to get home. This was fun. Bye." I turn away from her and leave a frowning, very unsatisfied Hanna Smith on the hill.

The ground is slick and wet as I splash through puddles growing larger by the second. My sneakers are covered in dead grass and mud. I'm going to have to vacuum out the Beast when I get home.

The wind pushes at me as a hand clamps down on my shoulder, pulling me around. My left foot slips, and I nearly fall. "We're not done!" Hanna all but screams at me. She grabs my wrist, pulling me with surprising strength close to her, staring intently into my eyes and . . . nothing.

I pull my arm free. "Let go."

The intensity in her eyes tells me all I need to know. She was trying to get sucked back into the vision. Well, joke's on her. It's perfect. Now she has to accept what she already wants to believe.

"You know what I'm talking about," she says, her voice rising. Her poncho hood is down and she's getting soaked, but I don't think she cares. "You saw something. I know you did. I saw how you looked at me." She shakes her head, looking away, trying to make it make sense. "I was in someone's head. Someone who killed me." Her eyes come back to me full of fierce determination. "It wasn't you. I know that.

How do I know that? I'm not crazy. I know what I saw. I know what I felt. Tell me I'm not crazy!"

I lick my lips. I may have miscalculated Hanna Smith's stubbornness.

The rain beats down. I can't tell her. The future must unfold as it is in the Dream. Otherwise, things get unpredictable, and I lose all advantages. I don't want to lie to her, but it's for her own good.

I raise my hands in a placating gesture. "I'm sorry you're going through . . . some things," I say. "But it's going to be all right." I leave so much unsaid. But after she is safe, after I have done what I must, she'll *see*. One last vision to set this all straight.

I turn without another word and walk away. Hanna's eyes burn into my back. I open the Beast's door. Hanna's still standing in the rain, like it's a clear Sunday afternoon and not a torrential downpour.

The Beast's interior is getting wet. Thunder rumbles above and something aches in my chest. It didn't go perfectly, but it's over. She'll drop it. Probably. Maybe.

I raise my voice to make sure Hanna hears me. "I'm sorry, but you're going to be okay."

She doesn't move, doesn't react to my words. Her stare is one part ice, one part fire. I get in my car, start it up. As I back out, Hanna still hasn't moved.

I put it in drive and get out of there as fast as I can.

CHAPTER 10

O nce I get back on the road, I have to drive under the speed limit to see in the storm. I pass other cars doing the same thing. One poor guy was changing a flat. On any other day, I would have stopped and helped, but not today.

Eventually, I can turn my phone back on. As soon as it lights up I have a notification.

I know what I saw. Call me!

Hanna. Now there is a text. Great. I pitch my phone on the passenger seat, mumbling to myself as the rain beats at my windshield. It doesn't matter if Hanna texts me a million times. I'll save her and everything will work out.

Lightning cracks nearby, making me swerve. My radio pops on, blaring white noise. The Beast's electrical system is a mess. It's always doing something odd. Annoyed, I switch off the radio.

Lightning again cracks, even closer this time. I blink against the flash of light as the radio pops on again and white noise once more fills the interior of the Beast. I want to punch the thing. Can't anything go right today? I take a deep breath and reach for the radio. Deep within the cracks and pops, for an instant, I swear something laughs.

My hand stops inches from the radio. I listen. Nothing, just static.

Juuuuuddddde something in the white noise rasps. I pull my hand back from the radio. Lightning crashes a third time right above me, hitting one of the power lines next to the street. Sparks jump and spit from the transformer, falling in the road like molten rain. I have no time to react as the transformer breaks free, swiveling down toward me, swinging on the power lines it's still connected to. I slam on the brakes, but I know I'm too late.

The transformer misses my front bumper by inches, falling into the road, pulling down the power lines. The road pulses with blue electricity as the transformer spews electric fire. The Beast vibrates with the surrounding energy. I hit the gas, shooting forward, swerving around the pole that's halfway in the street now.

The Beast's tires bump over spitting power lines, like great black snakes twisting in the road. In seconds I'm clear, but my heart doesn't seem to know it. My hands shake even as my knuckles turn white from gripping the steering wheel. I almost died.

Almost. Died.

Almost died in the most bizarre way imaginable and someone—something—

I stare down at the radio. Nothing but static comes from the speakers now. I turn it off.

It was my imagination, the voice. I take a deep breath. Of course it was my imagination. Near-death experiences will do that . . . maybe. But as I replay the events, I know the voice came *before* the swinging transformer of death. Had it been real?

"No, nope," I say. "You've been under a lot of stress, that's all."

In the rearview mirror, the rain is already swallowing up what's behind me, but I can still see sparks dancing in the road. A fraction of time and mere inches saved my life. Never have I wanted to be home so bad. I glance down at the radio, hesitate, and quickly smash the power button. Music plays, a mariachi band singing in Spanish. I listen to the music for a minute, my nerves calming slightly. I turn off the radio and concentrate on driving.

The rain comes down in blinding sheets as I drive on, passing by the high school and football field. I drive slowly, allowing my windshield wipers to keep up. Somewhere along the way, the noise of the storm changes. The telltale beating of hail pounds at the Beast's roof and windshield.

It seems like forever until I'm in the garage, the door closing behind me. Dad is training in the other bay, shirtless and panting like he's been working out for some time. He's got more than a few scars. The worst is on his left shoulder. I'm almost certain it's from a gunshot, but he won't tell me how he got it.

"Be cool," I tell myself as I grab my phone and get out of the car.

Dad watches me, still panting from his workout. "You're wet," he says.

I'm not just wet, I'm soaked. "Yeah, got caught in the rain."

"Go get changed," Dad says. "We need to work on your side control. Maybe do a few escapes, too."

I nod dumbly and head to the door. "Yeah, okay, let me, you know—"

Dad's firm grip squeezes my arm as I pass, and I meet his gaze for the first time. His eyes narrow. "You all right?"

In all my life, I can't remember a single time I lied to Dad. Not like this, not about anything that mattered. "Yeah. I'm good." I look away, and I know I messed up. I'm acting guilty. I am guilty. I force myself to meet his gaze. "I . . . it's nothing. Really."

Dad's eyes narrow a fraction farther. My heart skips a beat. This man can smell lies. "Okay," he says. His face softens. He reaches out and pulls me in a bear hug. He's sweaty, and I'm soaking wet. But what's that between us? "I love you. You want to talk later about anything, let me know. I push you hard, too hard. I know that. But there is no other way for us. You know that, right?"

"Sure, Dad."

The garage door rattles, buffeted by more wind and rain. Dad releases me. "Wasn't even supposed to rain today." His voice carries

54

a bit more concern than the statement deserves, but he gives me a slight grin. "Go get cleaned up. And hurry." He rubs my wet hair as my phone vibrates in my hand. I try to clear the screen, but instead I unlock it. The phone slips out of my still damp hand.

To my horror, Dad bends, reflexes stupid quick, and catches the phone inches from the concrete. The phone is screen up and a text from Hanna is there for us both to read.

You saw it too. Don't lie to me!!

"Who—" The phone vibrates in his hand, a call this time. It's Hanna's number. Dad answers the call before the first ring dies.

"Dad!" I say, taking a step forward, but he holds up a hand.

He says nothing as Hanna begins to rant. I can hear her voice. She's angry. I can't make out any words, but I don't have to. Dad's face says it all.

He lowers the phone slowly as Hanna continues to talk. He ends the call, but his gaze doesn't waver from me. We stand there for a long minute, an intensity in my father that I don't recognize. He seems poised on the edge of a cliff, deciding whether to jump or not. Slowly, everything drains from him, and he seems smaller, diminished somehow. He looks tired.

"It's done," he says. "It's off. We aren't—you aren't doing it."

"Dad? We can't—"

"You lied to me, Jude," he says, the words sharp and clipped. He breathes in and out deeply through his nostrils. When he next speaks, his words are much softer. "You don't know the pain it caused me when you Dreamed. To find out you were like me. I would take this all from you if I could." He shakes his head. "But I can't. There are dangers—" He hesitates and can't find the words.

"I know the dangers, Dad," I say.

"You don't know anything," he snaps, and I see the instant regret in his eyes. He moves closer, handing me my phone. Never in my life have I seen him so miserable. He pauses as if collecting his thoughts. "It's off, Son. We let her go. No argument, no question. Friday, after football, we go on vacation." He leaves me, walking up the three steps into the house, and shuts the door behind him.

CHAPTER 11

Overhead, the sun bears down on all of us.

The french fries under the heat lamp at McDonald's can't be as hot as I am right now. *August in Arkansas, ain't it grand?* Coach blows the whistle, and we all line up. Only shorts and helmets on Fridays, so no contact drills, but running? Oh yeah, lots of running.

Football is pretty much year-round, but right now it's crunch time. School starts Monday. Our first game is against Chapel, Friday. We haven't beaten them in four years.

But this is our year. We can all feel it.

Coach blows the whistle again, and we take off. I'm in the tight end and linebacker group. We have twenty seconds to run the hundred yards. We have to do it five times in the next fifteen minutes. If we fail our conditioning runs, we'll have extra running after practice. Since I've had extra running all week because Lucas Munson is a dick, I don't want that. Not that there is any real danger of me missing my time. I lead the pack. The next closest to me is big Andre, and he's a good three strides behind as we reach the fifty.

It's one of the reasons I'm a good player. Speed kills.

I reach the opposite goal line, cross the line, and stand tall, placing my hands behind my head. It's the best position to get air after a sprint, not slumping over like a few sophomores are doing as they finish their test. Andre's upright like me, sucking wind. "You're fast. You know that?"

I wink at him. I don't want to ruin the compliment by trying to talk and passing out. Truth is, I haven't slept much since Monday. Hanna calling, the storm, and Dad. The Dream, too, seems to know I won't be answering its call. It's taken on a new life, a new intensity the last four nights. The calling is with me all the time now, the undeniable urge to go to Hanna's. It's been growing every day, almost like some force knows what Dad has planned and will not have it.

Lucas Munson crosses the goal line, first in his group of big boys. Linemen, tenth through twelfth graders, some the size of small cars, cross behind him. Their time is twenty-five seconds, but Lucas might have given me a run for my money in my group. Speed kills. Speed plus size destroys. For a brief instant, our eyes meet. Something sharper than a smile cuts his face and disappears. I really don't like that kid. Not at all.

Coach blows the whistle, and it starts again. I take my place on the line. Behind me, someone laughs. I turn.

Munson is with a small group of his cronies, mostly senior linemen. Several in the group have been giving me side-eyes and sly grins all practice. One of the guys staggers like he's been shot with a tranquilizer dart and leans his head forward, smacking his hands together in an approximation of someone falling on their face, much like I must have looked after Munson clocked me. The whole group laughs, most of them anyway. A few of the juniors and sophomores try to join in too, but as their gazes meet mine, they cut off.

The whistle blows again, and I take off, not as fast as I can, but still leading the pack. The hundred yards go by quick. Andre and I finish nose to nose.

"Slipping, Erickson," Coach Rubacker, the D coordinator, says from his spot on the goal line, stopwatch in hand. He blows his whistle, indicating time's up. Everyone in my group made the cut. "Anderson might have nosed you out that time."

Andre gives me a shrug, breathing deep with his hands behind his head. "Don't let those guys get to you." His hands come down as he gets closer. "'Be strong and courageous. Do not fear or be in dread of them, for it is the Lord your God who goes with you.' Deuteronomy 31:6."

"You got a Bible verse for everything," I say, still eyeing Munson and his group.

Andre grunts. "PK, man. Preacher's kid, yeah. If you got a problem, I got some knowledge."

Munson's group finishes. A few younger boys, sophomores mostly, almost don't make their time, and Munson gives them an earful, to the delight of a few of his squad.

Munson. Of all the people in the world he could have brought to Jacoby's, he brought *Hanna freaking Smith.*

My stomach knots up as I remember my reflection in the backdoor glass of Hanna's house. The black mask covers my face, and my clothes are nondescript. In the Dream, reality is distorted. It's hard to judge distance and size. The masked face I catch a glimpse of in the reflection is hazy and undulating, like a moth trying to break free of its cocoon.

My body, too, is distorted and disjointed; my fingers on the doorknob, a giant's or a kid's, roll like snakes. I could be five-foot-three, or I could be six-five, like Munson. It could be Munson. The thought makes me sick. Sure, he's a huge jerk and a narcistic bully, but I know him. And why would Munson want to kill Hanna? But he's in her life, somehow. Close to her. And after the Dream became sharper, I am now positive the killer knows Hanna.

Could I kill Munson? I don't know, but I'll have to kill someone . . . someday.

Tonight would have been the night. *Is* the night. But Dad's called it off. I begged until my throat hurt, but it's no use. He won't listen. We are leaving town after practice. Going on vacation, and definitely being recorded on security cameras in gas stations, being seen in restaurants, using our phones to ping off cell towers all the way to Northwest Arkansas.

We'll have as airtight an alibi as anyone can have. Because Hanna Smith is going to die tonight. It's almost more than I can bear.

The whistle blows again. Time to run, not think.

The rest of practice goes by in a flash. After the conditioning test, we split up into groups and do drills. I don't have to be around Munson much, but the same thought in the back of my head won't go away. The killer *could* be Munson.

Coach blows the whistle to end practice, and all eighty-five members of the Bedford High School football team form a circle around him. "The season starts Monday. Game week," he says, his voice loud so all can hear. "The first step on a journey." His steady gaze is met with utter silence. "In the last ten years I've been a coach, I've never had a more talented group." Munson nods and grins. "But talent alone won't do it." He raises his voice. "Who here thinks Whitehall, or Dollarway, or Conway are going to lie down come game time?"

I'm shaking my head without even realizing it. We all are.

"Monday will be the start, but this season is going to be a marathon, not a sprint. Fellas, look at your seniors. Look at 'em."

Across the circle, eyes find me and lock on. Surprisingly, Munson's looking at me too. He nods, almost imperceptibly, a slight movement of the head. It feels as if lightning is trapped in my chest. I want to be a normal kid with normal dreams. I want to win state.

I want to go to Hanna's.

"These are the men who are going to lead you," Coach says. He pauses as we all stare at each other. Despite the heat, despite all my problems, I'm drawn in by the speech. I'd run through a brick wall for Coach, for my team.

Coach barks, "Munson, Erickson, get in here." The spell Coach Davis had woven so carefully breaks. I blink. Me and Munson? What is this?

Someone gives me a gentle push from behind, and I shuffle forward toward Coach, toward the center of the ring. Conversations rise and fall, quick words between teammates. Everyone knows what happened at Jacoby's. Most of these guys were there. The mumbling dies as

Coach speaks again. He grabs me around the neck. At the same time, he pulls Munson in for a hug, too. "These two *captains*," he stresses the words, "got into a scrap the other night."

Nothing but silence meets this statement of fact. "Look around, fellas. Look at the man next to you. Being on a team—a football team—is like being part of a family. When you're all old and gray, you'll remember this year, this season. You'll remember the wins and losses, sure, but more than anything you'll remember the men standing next to you, around you. These are your teammates. Brothers born in sweat, blood, and tears."

Coach has a way with words. He's good. And he says the words with true emotion in his voice. *He* believes, so we believe.

"All of you, everyone, are brothers now. White, Black, Brown, senior, junior, sophomore. All that stuff doesn't matter now." He shakes me and Munson playfully. "And like brothers, sometimes we're gonna fight." He pauses as the silence turns a bit uncomfortable, for me, at least. Every face I can see is grinning.

"We can have something special this year. All that other stuff. All your problems. Leave those things behind while you're out here on this hundred yards of grass. You have a whole lifetime to figure all that other stuff out, but here and now? Here and now, boys, you have this one year, this one perfect year with your team. With your brothers. Do you hear me?"

No one says a word. "If you hear me," Coach says, his voice rising, "the correct response is: 'Yes, Coach.' Do you hear me?"

I scream with the crowd. "Yes, Coach!"

"Good," Coach says. "Hard work on Munson. Bring it in!"

Bodies rush forward as Munson raises his hands high as we crowd in around him. The press of bodies moves us close. We begin to bounce. I match him, as do all around us. Lucas howls like a dog. We howl with him.

Munson screams the next words, "Hard work on three. One, two, three!"

Along with my teammates, my brothers, I scream, "Hard work!"

There is a lot of backslapping and chest bumps around me. Then the crowd sloughs off until it's just me, Coach, and Munson.

"All right, men," Coach says. "Time to pay the piper."

We don't need any more instruction. We put our helmets back on and jog to the goal line. The sun bears down even harder, cooking my brains. Coach blows the whistle, and Munson and I start running, the afternoon sun and Coach the only witness to our penitence.

Thirty minutes later, Coach blows the whistle a final time, and I fall to my knees a second later, then to my stomach, all thought of proper breathing posture gone from my mind. I force myself to roll over as Lucas collapses beside me, breathing as hard as me. I lie there, every muscle screaming, staring up into the blue sky. Even my face hurts.

Coach's shadow looms over me. "Respect," he says. "Neither of you puked all week." He pulls his cap from his head, mopping at the sweat inundating his buzz cut of blond hair. "I've got church, so you two hit the showers and be gone in thirty." He hesitates. "I meant what I said earlier. You guys can have a great year. It's up to you." He turns and leaves us.

For a while, I do nothing but breathe. Asking my body to do anything more would be cruel. A jet moves across the sky. Billowy clouds of white trail behind, cutting a line through the blue. Munson follows the plane with a finger. A cool wind blows, and I don't want it to ever stop. Munson's hand falls to the ground as the plane moves on to parts unknown.

"I bet there's a rich guy up there in first class with his feet up eating a steak," Munson says.

"Maybe," I say. "Who knows?"

Munson grunts. "There is. If not on that plane on some plane somewhere. You never look up and wonder about where all those people are going?"

Munson's getting weird on me, but it is an interesting question. I answer honestly. "No, not really."

Lucas pushes up on an elbow. "You ever been on a plane?"

I sit up, warily. "No, never. You?"

"Nah." He takes a big breath and looks back up into the sky. "I'm going on a recruiting visit in a few weeks. I've never left the state. Going to Florida, flying."

After Munson got in trouble at Chapel, a lot of the colleges recruiting him backed off. It occurs to me that the fight we got in could hurt his recruitment even more if word got out. It's unfortunate, but he chose to do what he did. No one made him punch my head.

"I've never seen the ocean in real life," he goes on. "All that water. I want to put my feet in and just feel the waves. I've never seen a mountain, either. Two weeks after Florida, I'm going to Colorado. The colleges are paying for it. Good thing too. Pop always said we had everything we needed at home. I've never been anywhere."

I wait, certain Munson has a point, but not sure what it is.

"My aunt died a few years ago," he says. "The funeral was in Oklahoma. I never met her, even though she was Pop's only sister. I was excited 'cause I knew we'd drive over to Oklahoma. *Oklahoma*," he shakes his head. "I was excited about going to Oklahoma."

I snort. "I've never been outside the state either." I hesitate; sharing a moment with Munson is a new experience. "So how was Oklahoma?"

Munson stands and offers me his unbroken hand. I take it, and he pulls me in close. "I don't know. We didn't go. Here's the deal. I'm getting out of this place. Leaving this town, this state, wiping the dust from my shoes and never looking back. I matter. *Me*. You don't matter. Not even a little bit." He squeezes my hand hard, and it's all I can do not to cry out. Lucas is seriously strong. "You broke my hand, Jude. *My hand*. If I wouldn't have been able to play this year, you and I would have finished what we started at Jacoby's. Watch yourself. Stay out of my way." He leans in and lowers his voice. "And stay away from Molly Goldman."

He lets my hand go, not waiting for an answer, backing up, his eyes still on mine. "Listen to me, Jude. Listen." He turns and walks off, his six-five frame moving like some kind of machine.

I bite my lower lip, surprisingly calm. The world makes perfect sense. For a minute, I thought Lucas Munson was going to do the right thing. Mercury colliding with Mars. But no, the planets still orbit the sun, all is right in the universe, and Munson's still a dick.

I've never disobeyed my father in anything that mattered, but if I don't go to Hanna's tonight, I won't be able to live with myself. The second my mind is made up is like a huge weight being lifted from me. A part of me has always known what I'd do.

I'm going. For the first time in my life, I don't care what my father wants, what he might think or say. One way or another, I'm going. Something deep in my chest tightens like a tug or a pull, not unpleasant, but a shifting of something vital, something long out of place locking home. My decision is made.

I'm saving Hanna Smith tonight.

CHAPTER 12

Dad isn't here when I make it back home, and I'm disappointed. I had the speech prepared. I was going to tell him I was a man, capable of making my own decisions. I was going to Hanna's, and he'd have to knock me out or lock me up. I'd make him understand. I'm not going on *vacation*. I'm not running away.

But my house is silent. Dad's not here. Since he caught me in the lie, he's been coming home early. He should be home. It's almost like he knows what I'm planning.

I call him on his cell phone, but his voice mail box hasn't been set up, so I call it again. I'm annoyed more than anything when the robot lady tells me, again, that Dad hasn't set up his voice mail. Is he ignoring me? It's possible.

I find Lenny's number, Dad's foreman on most jobs, my thumb hovering over the call button. After half a minute of indecision, I click off my phone and set it down.

I *am* going. I'll forever be haunted if I don't. I'll go without telling him if I have to, but I want to tell him. I want to look him in the eyes and make him understand. He can't stop me. Probably not. Not without hurting me, anyway, and I know he wouldn't do that.

I make a sandwich and get a Gatorade from the fridge and a bag of chips from the pantry. I walk into the living room, find the remote, and sit on the couch. I click on *SportsCenter*, trying to distract myself. The Cardinals beat the Cubs in ten innings while Coach Davis was trying to run me to death, and despite all that is wrong, I take a minute to watch the highlights.

The ceiling fan whirls comfortably as I finish off the chips and snuggle deeper into the couch. MLB highlights are replaced by golf. I don't play golf. Golf is for country club people. Miller's Chapel people, not me. Dad has to be back soon. We planned on leaving as soon as I got home. I bet he knows I'm going to fight him on this. The call to go is so strong. He knows what it's like. He's waiting until the last minute. He'll come in all in a hurry, thinking to get me in his truck, on the road, and out of town before I can blink.

It won't work.

Nothing will.

I'm going, and that's it.

I close my eyes for a second, for a heartbeat.

I'm in a field of knee-high golden grass. This is not a dream, but I'm not awake. Above, the clouds swirl, blue-black, purple, and vanilla. The air is thick with humidity. The storm swirling the clouds above holds back, waiting for something. I turn my head up to the heavens. The land is flat, flatter than any place I've ever been.

The wind stirs, and like golden waves, the ocean of grass rolls and bends. I am at peace. I am alive like I have never been alive because I am the wind. I am the grass. I am the gentle rain that starts to fall lightly on my face.

I am the storm that comes.

Off in the distance, I feel something drawing near. My eyes scan the horizon, and a tiny black dot appears. I watch as it grows larger, rushing toward me on leathery wings. My breath quickens as predatory eyes find me, measure me, and find me wanting. In that instance, I know what the gazelle knows when it spots the lion hiding in the tall grass.

In my mind, something screeches. *Juuuuuuuuude!*

I sit up, panting, bleary-eyed, not sure where I am. I can still hear something bestial screaming my name.

The living room comes into focus, the swirling ceiling fan above the TV, Dad's recliner. I steady myself. What was that? I wasn't asleep, I'm sure of that. It was a trance more than a vision. Was it stress-induced? Can stress cause hallucinations? I don't think so. So much of what has happened to me since the Dream seems unreal. Dad has prepared me since I was little, told me what I was these last months, but he never said anything about this.

My phone rings, and I know it's not the first time. I pull it out just as the call ends. I've missed three calls from Dad. Relief and annoyance replace my unease. My phone rings and vibrates in my hand. It's Dad again. I answer the call, careful to keep my voice calm and collected. "Hey."

"Jude Erickson?"

It's not Dad.

"Who's this?"

"Jude," the man says again, his voice self-assured and smug. This time it's not a question. "We have your father."

I hesitate as the man's words sink in. Despite what I feel, I keep my voice neutral like I was taught. "You have him? What's that supposed to mean? Who—"

The man cuts me off. "Tad Erickson is with us. He will remain here until your task is complete."

Again, I manage to keep my voice calm, but just barely. "Look, I'm calling the police if you don't—"

The man grunts, amused. "You won't call the police. You're different, Jude. You've known it all your life. You feel the truth of what your dad *taught* you." The word *taught* comes out smarmy and mocking.

I swallow as a deep sense of unease creeps up my spine. I'm on the verge of slipping down a hole of panic and fear, but I regain control. "Who is this?"

"Your father failed you, failed us. He kept you from us, thinking he could hide you."

"Who are you?" I say again, more forcefully this time, a great portion of my emotions turning into anger. "Who is *us*?"

The man sighs. "If you must, call us the Society."

"*The Society?*" I say with scorn. "Seriously? Okay, whatever. Look, tell me where my father is."

"Ticktock, Mr. Erickson," the man says. "Every second we speak is one less second in Hanna Smith's life. She will die if you do not fulfill your sacred duty. I should add that, unlike yesterday, it won't just be Hanna Smith's life you're saving. There are repercussions to your father's lack of discernment."

My blood turns cold. "Is that a threat?"

"No. It's a promise. Let me speak bluntly. There is always a price for failure, but know that if you are a coward, and you choose not to go tonight, your father's life is the price."

I don't say anything. I don't move. It isn't until a few seconds later that I realize I'm gripping my phone so tight it hurts.

"I'll take your silence as understanding," the man says and takes a deep breath, as if all of this is an inconvenience for him. "If you are caught, keep your mouth shut. Your father has told you this at least, correct?"

I swallow. "He has."

"And the rest? Has he told you the rules?"

I hesitate. Dad has always trained me, even before I knew why. But it wasn't until the night of my first Dream that he sat me down and told me the four unbreakable rules. I asked him how he knew them, and he told me that I'd understand soon enough. He was right. Each time I Dreamed, the rules solidified in my mind, like they had been there my whole life. It's hard to explain. Perhaps it's a lost human instinct. I know the rules are true, as if they were etched in my bones. They are part of me.

Rule one: You go alone.

Rule two: Bring no weapon but yourself.

Rule three: A life for a life.

Rule four: The Chosen must *see.*

"I know them," I say.

"Tell me now so that we are clear," the man says.

I tell him.

"Good," he says when I am done. "You feel the truth of the words coursing through your veins. The same as you feel the undeniable pull to save the Chosen. This is what we are. What makes us. Prove yourself worthy and all is well for now. Or don't, and we will clean up your father's mistakes. In the end, it matters little."

I hear shuffling on the line and another voice speaks, "Jude?"

"Dad! Where are you? Who was that guy? Are you okay?"

Dad's voice is calm but strained. "I'm fine. Don't worry about me. This is— I'm sorry, Jude. I didn't want it to go down like this."

"What's happening, Dad? Is this— Are you testing me? That guy is lying, right?"

"This isn't a test, Son, and he's not lying. He's a prick, but he's not lying."

I hear a sharp whack, and Dad grunts.

"Are they hurting you?" I say, my voice rising.

"A little," Dad admits, "but that doesn't matter. Listen to me now. You don't have much time. I . . . I wanted to make you better. I wanted . . . I wanted to protect you, shield you. Because I didn't want you to end up like me."

I open my mouth to speak but have no words. What is he talking about? All I've ever wanted was to be just like him.

"You've got to go, Son. We don't have a choice now. Do it like we planned. In and out. Be quick. Be merciless. Don't give the killer a chance. You hear me?"

My mouth is dry.

"Do you hear me, Jude?" Dad asks, louder this time.

"Yeah, yes, Dad. Like we planned."

"Good." His voice cracks, and the impossible happens. I hear tears in my dad's voice. "I love you, Son." He pauses as if collecting himself. "Don't trust these pricks. They're liars. They want us dead or in jail, but they want us to do it to ourselves. They're everywhere, run everything— Stop, no!"

The line goes dead.

"Dad!" I scream. "Dad!" But no one is listening. I call his number three times in a row; each time, it goes directly to the voice mail that's not set up.

I stare at the phone. Questions tumble in my head, making me dizzy, as tears well up in my eyes. I knew Dad was keeping things from me, but the magnitude of his lie is staggering. I thought it was me and Dad against the world. The two of us fighting against evil. Now *this*. There are others?

So many angles. The possibilities are infinite, but my choice is finite. There is only one.

I check the time on my phone. It's just past midnight. Hanna Smith has less than two hours to live.

I can do this.

This is who I am.

This is who my father made me.

CHAPTER 13

The fog has gathered as I wait. From my vantage point in the woods, Hanna's house is a smoky outline in the soft white light filtered through the fog hugging the ground. My breath disturbs the thick moisture with each exhalation. As vivid as the Dream has been, it did not, could not, completely prepare me for this, being here in the flesh.

In the Dream, my hands never shook.

Knowing I am truly alone makes this so much worse. I take a deep breath and try to stop my shaking hands. It doesn't work.

I check the time. It's five past one. Time to go. I move forward through the pine and oak, gliding through the foliage. The greenbriers slide off my boots, and each step is as soundless as the last.

This is what I've trained for; this is what I am. Do this and Dad will be safe. Do this and Hanna lives. Do this and I become what I am meant to be.

Across Hanna's backyard, a shadowy figure emerges from the line of woods. The fog is so thick, I can barely make heads or tails of the figure. It could be anyone, even Munson, all six-five of him.

At seeing the dark silhouette of the murderer, my heart beats so hard and loud, for a second, I'm afraid I might be heard. In the moonlight I can see the glint of the hammer in the murderer's hand as they stride forward, toward the back door.

It's time to do what I was born for.

In the Dream, I'm in the killer's mind, a hitchhiker, vaguely experiencing their emotions but never able to read thoughts. But I am here in the flesh now, and the hunter is the hunted.

I'm a killer.

I kill the killers.

The fog is dense, my heart loud in my ears, and whoever they are, they are at the back door now, bending over to get the key. I move forward a fraction, and my foot finds the only dry twig in the forest. The *crack* of the limb is a shotgun blast in the still wet night. The figure hesitates, and although I can't tell where they are looking, I can feel them searching for me. I don't move.

Dad warned me of this. In the Dream, I was not here. In the Dream, it is only the killer and his victim. We alter the future. We save those who would die at the hands of evil people. If I alter reality and the killer is spooked off, the Chosen is as good as dead. Time and human degradation play out. The killer strikes again, but there will be no Dream alerting me to the time and place of the murder. It might be the next day or five years later. A person's fate is not set, but time has a path, and the future resists change jealously.

Dad messed up once, and the killer got away. The man's life he was supposed to save that night was lost six months later. The killer never identified. I won't let that happen.

The masked man opens the back door and slips inside. I move quick. Dad and I rehearsed this every day for months, and I'm at the door in a matter of seconds. I feel a tug at the core of my being. I've never felt it before, but I was expecting it. The Dream and reality are merging, and Dad told me there are repercussions of that. This sensation isn't unpleasant, but it is insistent. It's a guide, Dad says. Timing is important. I kill Hanna's murderer at the point of no return. Even now, the killer has a choice, I suppose. They have free will. They could leave, walk away, and go home, leaving this evil behind.

Even knowing this, I know as sure as I have known anything that the killer won't leave, and there is only one way this ends. *A life for a life.*

I wait a few seconds, then a few more, until the pull on my soul can't be ignored. It is time.

I follow the killer in.

The house is large and quiet. I shut the door carefully behind me. My heart races as I move through a house I've never been in physically. *Be quick. Be merciless.* Dad's words come back to me, fueling me. In seconds, I'm taking the stairs two at a time, bounding up on muscles honed for years for this moment. This is what I am. I am going to save Hanna's life tonight by killing her murderer.

The dead girl will live.

I grunt with exertion as Hanna shouts from her room. It's just like the Dream. I am on time. An overwhelming sense of purpose and duty fills me, driving me upward. I have a sudden and distinct feeling of being watched. Dad never said anything about this. But it is undeniable. I know. Somehow, I know.

Whatever power that brought me to this moment . . . is watching.

I'm at the top of the stairs. Hanna's door is cracked. Through the thin sliver, I see movement. But that's not right. In the Dream, it is closed. The little tug at my soul does a flip. It's unpleasant, like the floor dropping out from under me.

The door swings wide and someone bursts through, dressed all in black. I have less than a second to comprehend that something is very, very wrong. The ski-masked person does not hesitate. They dive at me. It is so unexpected, so unlike the Dream, so stupid, that I am caught off guard. I have one foot on the landing and one on the last stair.

I grab the killer as we slam together. I'm off balance, my momentum all wrong. My back foot slides off the stairs and we are falling. I try to move this insane murderer to the bottom, so I don't take the brunt of the stairs, but before I can, the back of my head cracks against a wooden stair. I see stars.

I'm sliding down the stairs, the killer on top. My head hits another stair. More bright stars bloom in my vision.

My head slams into another step, and my limbs turn to jelly. One last hard and unyielding surface slams into the back of my skull. The tile at the bottom of the staircase.

The pain is sudden and intense. The killer is off me, scrambling away. I roll feebly, trying to grab an ankle, but I am a useless pile of concussed bones. The stars and dark grow and coalesce as the killer disappears, headed for the back door, still clutching the hammer.

My eyes flutter. I try to stand but slip and crack my forehead against the floor. One last thought goes through my neurons before I black out completely.

Hanna.

I failed.

Hanna is dead.

The darkness consumes me.

CHAPTER 14

Light.

A thin crack of dull fire stings my eyes, and a sharp bolt of pain cuts through my already throbbing head. A half-moon of brightness is all I see. After several bleary seconds that seem like forever, it dawns on me my eyes are half closed.

"Wake up, Jude," a familiar voice tells me. I should know it. I try to rub my pounding temples, to coax my foggy memory back, but my hands won't move. It's almost like I'm tied up.

I open my eyes all the way and find Hanna standing over me, a softball bat clutched in her hands. My memories come crashing back. "You're alive!" I shout. It hurts. I groan as the second part of the equation sinks in. "They got away."

Hanna kicks me in the shin. It hurts but doesn't compare to my head. "Who got away? And why did you try to kill me?"

I blink. My eyes focus. My mind's still foggy, but she knows better. "You know it wasn't me. I-I . . ." How much can I tell her now? How much does she already know or suspect? "I was here to save you," I mumble.

Hanna sniffs. "You think I can't protect myself?"

I look down at my chest. My hands are behind me, thick bands of some sort of tape crisscross my chest. The stuff is all over me, looping around me like a mummy. Worst of all, it's not your garden-variety duct tape. It's covered in hearts and . . . ponies.

"What is this?"

Hanna rolls her eyes, and— Is she blushing? "It was a present, from a long time ago. Does it matter? Tell me why you tried to kill me."

The pounding in my skull is rhythmic, in time with my heart. I've played football all my life and never had a concussion, but I'm sure I have one now. I shut my eyes against the agony. This can't be happening. The murderer got away, and the *Chosen* caught me and wrapped me up like a three-year-old's present.

"You know I didn't try to kill you."

Hanna taps her foot. She's wearing workout clothes, not the night clothes she was wearing in the Dream. "I know," she says, annoyed. "How exactly do I know that?"

Maybe it's the concussion. Maybe it's the hopelessness of my situation. I have to make her *see*. But will that work now? Did Dad and I even discuss this possible scenario? No. No, we never discussed an outcome where I got knocked out, taped up, and interrogated.

I need time for my head to clear. To think rationally.

I was sure she'd died. That the killer got her before I could stop it. My head pounds. I need to start there. "How?" I ask. "How did you not die?"

"I'm asking the questions," Hanna says, looming over me with the bat. "Not you."

For half a heartbeat I think she's going to smack me. But then her expression softens. "The . . . thing that happened when we touched. Those things I saw. You think I could sleep after that?" Her eyes drift off. "Mom and Stan left for a night in Little Rock. They'll be back in the morning. I asked them not to leave, but they wouldn't listen. Mom would have stayed, but Stan threw a fit." Her eyes come back to me. "I wouldn't beg. I don't think I totally believed . . . whatever just happened was going to happen. How do I know things? How is any of this possible?"

She has a lot of questions, but I'm not sure what to tell her. Once I make her *see*, none of this matters. If it will even work now. Which I'm not certain it will. First, I need to get free. I need to have options. Right now, I'm at Hanna's mercy. I flex my hands behind my back, trying to make some room in the tape. My feet and legs are free. That was a mistake. I could stand if I wanted, but then Hanna would use my head as a piñata. So . . . I'll just keep her talking.

"Tell me what happened and maybe I can explain." My thumb is free. I twist my wrist back and forth, the adhesive on the tape warming and softening. I can get loose, I'm positive of that, but how long will it take?

Hanna's gaze turns hard. "I hit the creep with my bat as soon as he came in. I didn't get him good, though. The door got in the way. He tried to fight, but he brought a hammer to a bat fight. He couldn't win, so he took off and ran into you, right? I saw the end of it. You hitting the tile and the other one running away." She pauses. "I almost called the cops then. You have no idea how close I was to that."

I tap my head gently on the cold tile beneath me and use the motion to distract Hanna from my shoulder, moving up in a sharp tug. My right hand is free. I feel for an edge of tape on my left hand and start working it with a fingernail at first.

"Why didn't you? Why not call them now?" I'm taking a chance, a big chance, but Hanna knows I'm not the bad guy. I hope.

"Maybe I will," Hanna says.

"I came here tonight to help you," I say as calmly and matter-of-factly as I can. "I failed, and I'm sorry."

"You might have failed," Hanna says placing the barrel of the bat in her hand and tapping it menacingly. "But I didn't."

I don't react to her implied threat. If she was going to hit me, she already would have, and she needs to hear the truth. No matter what happened, I did fail her. Telling her the truth is the least I can do now. I shake my head gently. "The person who tried to kill you tonight won't stop. Ever. They got away, and we don't know who they are. Do you understand what that means?"

She doesn't respond, mulling it over. I think I've got her. It's time to end this while I still have an ounce of dignity. "Now please, put down the bat, let me up, and let's talk." I take a deep breath, willing every ounce of confidence I possess into my next words. I look Hanna straight in the eyes. "You know I'm on your side."

The corner of Hanna's lip turns up, and she laughs like I just told the best joke. She pokes me with the bat. "Do I? I don't think so. Sure, there are things I can't explain, but I'm like ninety-nine percent sure I'm calling the cops. Why I haven't yet is the only real mystery. You're in my house and someone just tried to kill me."

Well, that didn't work. I guess it's time for plan B. I pull hard on the tape. It lets go easy but makes a horrible racket. Hanna's eyes widen. "You . . ." She raises the bat.

I'm on my feet in a second, my left wrist pulling free of the hearts and ponies. Both hands are free now, but the tape still has me wrapped up around the elbows, giving me T-rex arms. No time to think. I duck under the bat as it whistles past my skull. "Stop," I yell, somehow keeping my balance. "We were just talking."

She's not having it. She's attacking. The bat comes at me again, this time a waist-high slice. I jump back in time, wrenching at the tape still holding me. "Stop! What are you doing?"

She swings at me again. "Defending myself from a home invasion."

It's ridiculous. She knows better. I know she knows better, too, but she's angry. She won't listen. I do the only thing I can. I turn tail and run.

"Hey!" Hanna screams. "We're not done!"

I sprint, my head still throbbing, and my balance is off. I bump into the wall several times but manage to keep my feet. The house is dark, but I know where I'm going. I hear Hanna behind me, giving chase. I can almost feel the bat connecting with the back of my skull.

She's completely out of control.

The back door is to the left. I sprint through the kitchen, but the door is closed, and I know when I stop to open it, I'm done, but I'm not leaving, not yet. I have one more thing to do.

I push out with both arms with all I'm worth. The tape pops and tears, my arms come free, and I spin. Hanna's right on top of me, and she can't stop or get the bat up in time. I close the distance between us, wrapping her up, pinning her arms.

I'm not in Hanna's house anymore. I'm nowhere. I'm everywhere. And I'm not alone.

Sights and sounds, joy, fear, and pain. Love, envy, and love. All these things I experience, but I am not me. I am not Jude Erickson. I am so much more.

Hanna.

As I take in all that is Hanna Smith, I, too, give all that is me. Everything that is me flows out as everything that is Hanna flows in. There is no secret we can hide. I see her truth. I see her. She is not perfect. There is darkness and pain, wrongs both received and given.

She is not a perfect person, but she is beautiful.

I see Hanna Smith.

And she sees me.

Then it is gone. The sense of loss is almost as overwhelming as whatever that had been. No wonder Dad had trouble speaking about it. And I know. What just happened could never be verbalized.

Hanna is on top of me, panting. How we got here, I don't have a clue. She doesn't move, and I never want her to. Our faces are inches apart. Her breath has a hint of cinnamon, and it occurs to me she brushed her teeth minutes before her murderer came for her, and that makes perfect sense. That's just what Hanna would do.

Because I know her, almost like I know myself.

Even as I make this realization, the sense of her is fading like light from a sunset. My headache is gone. My heart is full.

Hanna swallows. Her eyes hold an intensity I feel reflected deep within my marrow.

Her lips part. Her voice is a whisper. "What the actual hell?"

CHAPTER 15

The magic fades. The sense of oneness, of knowing another person on such an intimate level, dissolves like mist in sunlight.

The spark in Hanna's eyes fades too, and she clears her throat, pushing herself off me. The bat is a few feet to my left, but she doesn't even look at it. She stands, turning away from me.

"Hanna," I say.

She holds up a hand. "Give me a second, okay?"

I prop up on my elbows, afraid to move. The situation could still go south, and I don't want to startle her.

After a long minute, Hanna turns. She rolls her eyes at seeing me still on the floor. "Get up."

"So you're not calling the cops?"

She takes longer than I'd like to answer. Her voice is soft. "I don't know. Maybe. Convince me not to."

"I think I just did."

She looks up to the heavens for support and lets out an exasperated huff. "What was that?"

I slowly stand. Hanna is not short, but I tower over her. She's not afraid, though. I don't think she ever was. She met me at the park alone. She's known from the start I'm not the bad guy, but I still worry she might call the cops out of frustration more than anything.

"I'm not sure," I say. "Dad told me, but I— That was . . . a lot."

"You think?" Hanna says sharply. "So, your dad's in on this too? Where is he?"

"That's a long story."

Hanna raises her eyebrows. "Can we cut to the end where you tell me what's happening? It's been a long night with the attempted murder and the total mind"—she makes a vague gesture to the floor we just occupied—"whatever."

"I'm . . ." I start but trail off. "I-I don't know if I can."

"You don't have a choice."

I consider the statement. "Not sure where to start," I say. Should I tell her she's doomed first or save it for the grand finale? It makes me sick, but the killer is in the wind. There will be no dream the next time the killer comes. And he will come. I failed, and now Hanna Smith will die. "Can we sit?" I ask. "I'm a little dizzy."

She sighs wearily and walks off without a word. I follow her to a large room with a fireplace and lots of dark wood cabinets and brown leather furniture. A huge bookcase holds tons of immaculate books that look like they've never been touched. Hanna takes an oversized chair. I take the couch.

We stare at each other for a long moment. How much do I tell her? Dad never went over this. *Dad.* The thought of him makes my chest hurt. What will happen now? I failed. Hanna's doomed, and I can't help her anymore, but Dad . . .

Hanna watches as I take a deep breath, calming myself.

"This is all going to sound crazy."

"Uh-huh," Hanna says. "We're way past crazy."

She's not wrong. This girl saw into my soul. She already knows so much. What will it matter if I tell her the details?

I put my head in my hands. This is sooo messed up. Dad's Chosen never even knew his name. He was this avenging angel that came and saved them. Hanna knows my name and where I go to school. The way she planned and blew up tonight, she probably has my Social Security number.

Truth is, I want to tell Hanna. I need to tell her—someone—what I've been through. Hanna's the only person who won't think I'm insane. At least that's my hope.

I sit up straight, and after several attempts, I find the right words. "About three months ago, I had a Dream about you."

It's hard, and I have to start and stop, but I tell her my story. I tell her what I am, what Dad is. Hanna squirms a bit when I tell her how Dad's trained me since I was a kid to be a weapon, to fight with my hands and feet, with knives and guns.

I tell her the rules, how I had to come to her alone. How I couldn't bring a gun. I had to give the killer every second of free will until there was no turning back. How killing is the only option. A life for a life. And finally, how the last vision, the total mind mixing that happened only moments ago, is necessary. I understand the importance of the last rule now. So does Hanna.

I tell her Dad is missing, but not about the Society. Not yet. Not sure what they'd do if I did.

She looks at me with intelligent blue eyes, her face a mask, as I tell her she is doomed. I clear my throat. "The killer escaped. The Dream is done. I can't see what the future holds. Maybe a week, maybe a year, the killer will come for you again."

"I can move," Hanna says, her voice low and soft. "I can get out of here."

"Can you?"

She frowns. "I only have a year left of high school."

"Are you going to stay awake every night with a bat?"

"Maybe," she says.

"It can happen anytime, anywhere, and one thing Dad's made clear is that it *will* happen."

She groans. "Will you stop saying that? There are no rules to the universe. It just is."

I laugh at that, the sound bitter. "I wish." The frustration and anger of the whole situation wells up inside me. "Tell me how the Dream is possible, then? Aren't you paying attention?" I cringe at the frustration in my voice.

Hanna doesn't seem to notice. "Well," she says. "You sure don't know much about"—she waves her hands around, as if encompassing the universe—"any of this. Why is that?"

She is so infuriating. "Because Dad lied to me," I say more forcefully than I had intended. I want the admission back as soon as it is out, but it's too late.

Hanna flinches. "All right, calm down."

The wind goes out of me. "I didn't want this to happen. Someone *took* my dad, okay."

"Who?" Hanna asks.

"I can't say. No," I say as Hanna frowns. "I don't know for sure, but they . . . well, they made threats, and it's not safe. I can't tell you. Powerful people." I close my eyes, miserable as I speak. "A week ago, I had a plan. I had Dad. Now . . . the killer got away, and I got caught by the freaking Chosen." I look up at her and can't keep the disgust out of my voice. "I don't know what these people are going to do now."

Hanna twists her mouth into a grimace. "Will they . . . hurt him?"

The compassion in her voice catches me off guard. "I don't know," I say honestly.

I hang my head. The tears that squeeze through my eyelids burn like fire. I hate myself for failing Dad, for failing Hanna.

Hanna stands, walks over to the couch. She sits down cross-legged, facing me. "I'm not going to die," Hanna says. "I don't accept that's the only possible outcome."

I nod, but I don't encourage her. She's doomed.

Hanna punches me in the arm. Hard. "Hey," I say.

"I'm not dying. Neither is your dad."

I look at her. "How can you know that?"

"Because I'm not dead. You haven't failed . . . yet. Help me find whoever was here tonight." She frowns at me, waiting.

I swallow, trying not to let the indecision show on my face. I was ready to kill the killer. That is what I was trained my whole life for, but I'm no detective. Without the Dream—

Hanna's frown deepens as I think. "I could still turn you in," she says, but I don't believe her.

"You turn me in, and you still die," I whisper.

"Stop saying that," she says. "You're the one who broke into my house. Help me or go to jail. And don't say I won't do it. I'm desperate. Desperate people do desperate things."

It's a loser's deal. The cops can't help her. I can't help her. Hanna Smith is going to die, and there is nothing anyone can do about it.

Hanna's gaze doesn't waver. "Help me find whoever tried to kill me. That can only help your dad, right?" Her voice is full of emotion as she holds out her hand, her nails manicured and perfect.

"They might have already killed him," I say. "Or let him go. He might be home when I get back."

"Do you believe that?" Hanna asks. "Do you believe they let him go?"

"No," I whisper.

Hanna's hand is still outstretched. "Then help me."

I want to believe I can help her. I want to believe she can somehow help me. There is a deep ache in my chest as I think of Dad.

I look at her hand and then into her eyes and take her hand gently, a man catching a butterfly. Hanna squeezes my hand as hard as she can.

CHAPTER 16

The water is hot on the back of my neck. But there will never be enough water, never enough heat, never enough scrubbing to wash away my sin. I failed.

I make the water hotter, turning the shower knob as far to the left as it will go. Part of me expected Dad to be here, waiting for me, the Society an elaborate trick to test me in some new way. But Dad isn't here, and the house feels emptier than I can ever remember it.

The heat from the water is painful now, but I don't care. I think of how many ways I'm messed up. Death by hot shower would be an appropriate ending for me. The heat intensifies. Too much. I shut the water off to the sounds of my own gasping, my skin on fire. I step out and grab a towel.

As I'm drying off, my phone dings in the kitchen. *Dad.* I wrap the towel around my waist as I run to my phone, almost busting it on the kitchen tile. It's a text, but it's not from Dad.

It's from Molly.

Awake?

I read the text again, then glance at the clock on the stove. It's two forty-five in the morning.

My phone dings again.

???

I haven't talked to Molly since the party. I'm not sure I want to right now. I take a deep breath and text back.

I'm up.

Almost immediately, my phone dings again.

I'm outside. Can I come in?

I read her text two more times. I can't help but glance toward the front door. Which is stupid because it's hidden behind at least two walls. I text back.

You're here? My house?

The next text takes longer, the little bubble telling me she's typing.

Yes. Didn't want to wake your dad.
Please, can we talk?

I stare at the screen, the mention of Dad like a dagger to the heart. I stand there for a moment more, my grief making me immobile.

I don't want to do this right now, but this is stupid, texting Molly when she's twenty feet away. I jog to the door and swing it open. Molly looks up, her face illuminated by the phone in her hand.

Molly gives me an apologetic smile, then her gaze travels the length of my body. "Jude. You're in a towel." It's a statement of fact. A fact I just remembered.

I grab the towel secured around my waist and hold it tight, determined to remain dignified. "And you're at my house in the middle of the night."

She frowns. "Fair enough. Are we going to wake your dad?"

"He's, ah, away, on, ah, on business."

"Okay," Molly says. "Can I come in, and maybe you could, I don't know, put on some clothes?"

I swallow, looking away, my face warming. "Ah, yeah. Come in." I step aside as she walks by. I shut the door with one hand, still holding the towel firmly with the other. "Have a seat or something. I'll be right back."

Before Molly can respond, I run to my bedroom, flipping the den light on for her as I exit. I put on shorts and a T-shirt in my room. I also put on a hoodie. Layers seem appropriate.

When I return, Molly is on the couch. "Why are you here?" I say, not unkindly. "It's, like, three in the morning."

The social lives of most people are a mystery to me. I've heard about kids staying out all night and doing stuff, but I don't have those types of friends. I don't have real friends at all.

Molly shrugs. "I couldn't sleep, so I got in the car and went for a drive. It helps me clear my mind sometimes, you know, the cool night air, the empty roads." She shrugs. "I ended up driving by here. I saw lights on. I don't know. I thought I'd see if you were up too. I've been thinking about the other night at Jacoby's and, well, I wanted to see you."

I shift on my feet, suddenly very self-aware. Molly wanted to see me.

I sit at the end of the couch. "I'm glad you—" My words freeze as Molly slides her leg up and turns toward me. Her right eye is bruised. "Uh, Molly, what's wrong with your eye?"

Molly winces, her hand going to her cheek. Her fingers probe the dark, swollen skin around her left eye. She has a shiner. A black eye. It's not horrible. I've seen worse, but against her pale, smooth skin, it stands out. She frowns. "It's nothing." The frown dissolves as she returns my gaze. "I'm a klutz is all." Her smile is slight, the corner of her lip curling up. Molly is pretty, even with the bruise, but I can't help the sinking feeling in my gut.

Molly has a motive to hurt Hanna, kind of. I stare at her eye.

Falling down a flight of stairs or getting hit with a bat could certainly cause that kind of injury. I try to shake the thought away, but the stupid thought won't leave me.

It would be a bizarre, cruel world if Molly tried to kill Hanna over Lucas Munson.

"So, where were you tonight? At home?" The question is out of my mouth before I can think.

Molly's eyes narrow, and I see a small glint of hurt. She wanted to see me, but the moment is gone. I've squashed it.

"No," she says. "I wasn't home. I was at Jess's spending the night, but I couldn't sleep. Why?"

I take a deep breath. It wasn't Molly. It couldn't have been. Molly couldn't knock me down a flight of stairs on her best day.

Yet, there had been that tug on my soul. I've been thinking about that. It must have been the instant Hanna altered the Dream. The Dream got out of whack, causing me to falter. At that moment, Molly could have knocked me down those stairs. A ten-year-old could have.

I'm being ridiculous. All I have to do is ask. "Why do you have a black eye?" My tone is more accusatory than I intended.

Molly pats her thigh, not meeting my eyes, a self-deprecating smile on her lips. Thankfully, she misses my tone. "It's embarrassing, okay?"

"It looks like it hurt," I say, trying to sound more casual.

"It did. Not so much anymore," Molly says dismissively. "We started rehearsal on *The Crucible*, and Marcus didn't fasten the coffin lock—"

"Coffin lock?" I interrupt.

"Yeah. It holds backdrop scenery in place. It's nothing. Two panels came loose. It fell and hit me. Marcus almost cried. But it was my fault, really. I should have been paying attention. I had my head down reading lines and I look up and *bam*."

Now that I'm closer, I think the black eye has to be at least a day old. Also, her story sounds legit, *and*, more importantly, easily verifiable.

I seriously need to chill. I can't go around suspecting everyone I know is a murderer.

My shoulders relax. It wasn't Molly. Of course it wasn't Molly.

"Look, Jude," Molly says, leaning forward, oblivious to the stupid going on in my head. "I've been thinking . . . thinking about a lot of things."

"So have I," I say. And it feels like we're having two different conversations. I shake my head. "I'm sorry, Molly," I blurt out. "About the other night. Munson and all. It was wrong, what I did." I want to make excuses, but that would be defeating the purpose of apologizing, so I let the statement stand.

Molly takes a steadying breath, and a tiny tear forms in the corner of her eye. "Thank you. Thank you for the apology. I . . . I wasn't happy with you *or* with Lucas, but I'm at least partially to blame. I should have walked away."

"You don't need to apologize," I say. "I messed up, not you."

"No, Jude," Molly says, forcefully. "I did mess up. And I'm big enough to admit when I do something wrong. It was unfair to you, Jude. I came to the party with you, saw Lucas, and got jealous." She absently touches her bruise. "I should have left when you asked me if I wanted to go. We were having so much fun in the car. That's what I like about you. We can just hang and talk. I like you, Jude. I'm not sure what that means, but I do like you."

Molly slides closer to me so that her knee is touching my leg. If I wanted, I could take her in my arms. I could kiss her. I very much want to kiss her. The moisture in her right eye breaks free and rolls down her face. I wipe the tear away. Her skin is warm under my touch, so warm. "I like you too, Molly. I think I always have."

Molly places a hand on my chest. Through layers of clothes, it burns. Her hand stays there, and I know she can feel my heart beating. We are so close. The house is quiet.

No. I lean back. It's not right. She's vulnerable, not in a good place. And the thing with Hanna tonight—the mind mixer or whatever it was—still lingers. The memory of Hanna is fading, being burned away with every second, but it's not gone, and I don't like how the two situations play in my head.

"You, ahh, want something to drink?" I say.

Molly bites her lip unconsciously. There is no mistaking the disappointment on her face. She clears her throat, not meeting my eyes. "Sure. A drink."

"Water okay?" I ask, wondering if I blew the opportunity of a lifetime. But I know it was the right thing to do.

"You wouldn't have Perrier, would you?"

I laugh. "I don't even know what that is."

Molly returns my laugh and, just like that, the tension is broken. "It's French mineral water. It's what we sophisticated types drink."

"Right," I say. "Let me get you one and maybe some fresh caviar, too?"

"Only if it's beluga."

"Uhm. Yeah. Now I'm totally lost."

"Water will be fine," Molly says.

I go to the kitchen and get her a glass of water with some ice, the everyday act making me think of Dad. My heart quickens, but I can't do anything right now. Maybe at all.

I take the water to the den. Molly sits on the end of the couch, and I take Dad's recliner. The conversation is hesitant at first, but before I know it, I'm back on the couch beside her, and we're talking, even laughing. I didn't stop the killer. Dad is still gone, but this small bit of normality feels good. There are moments when I can pretend everything is okay.

"So why are you up so late?" Molly asks. "I thought you liked to go to bed early so you could get up and build roofs and work out."

I have a strong impulse to tell Molly about Dad, about Hanna, and what happened tonight. Molly senses my discomfort. She sits up. "What? You don't look so great right now, Jude. Are you okay?"

I shake my head. "Not really."

"You want to talk about it?"

"I had a bad night." I shrug as if it's not that big of a deal, even though it is. "Lots of stuff that's out of my control is happening. None of it's good." I rub my tired eyes. "You ever feel like you're on this ride you can't get off? Like all this stuff is happening, but you can't do anything about it?"

"Is this about your dad?"

I blink, caught off guard.

"Do roofers leave town on business a lot?" Molly asks with a raised eyebrow. "Staying overnight?" She makes a face like she's trying to puzzle it out. "Conventions for new shingles? Vendors paying for trips? Really, Jude? I've known you forever. I could tell something was wrong the second I asked about your dad."

I close my eyes and tilt my head to the ceiling. "Yeah. There's something wrong, and it's got something to do with Dad. But . . . can we not talk about it?"

She touches my cheek, pulling my head down. Her fingers are soft on my skin. She leans in and gives me a kiss right where her fingers were. Her hazel eyes are full of sleep. "You can talk to me about anything. Okay? I'm a good listener."

"Yeah, okay."

Molly yawns. "Sorry. It's so late." She rests her head on my shoulder. I put my arm around her, and she snuggles against me. As Molly's breathing becomes slower and deeper, I shut my eyes, too. Never have I been this tired. A part of me realizes tonight there will be no Dream.

That thought and Molly's rhythmic breathing pull me down into sleep.

CHAPTER 17

wake up in the field of golden grass once more. This time I instantly recognize it for what it is—not a dream, but something more. The fresh wind blows, a light rain falls, and the grass sways, an ocean of gold.

I feel the storm within me.

On the horizon, something is coming.

It starts as a dot but moves fast, impossibly fast. The same monster as before. A huge bat. A dragon. No. It's a cross between a dragon and an insect. It flies toward me, covering miles in seconds.

The storm above turns angry. Lightning flashes. The thing is massive, a twisted sacrilege to life. The head large and insectoid, the neck long and serpentine, on leathery wings the size of football fields, it comes. Its maw widens, ancient and terrible.

Juuuuuuude. Juuuuuuude. Juuuuuuude.

I awake in a sweat, alone on the couch. For a second, I'm still caught in the nightmare, my breath ragged and deep. I press my hands to my ears, still hearing the thing call my name.

I'm lost in panic and fear, but like an avalanche of emotion, the past day's events crash into me. I lie back into the couch as my breathing becomes normal and steady. What's up with that? It wasn't just a dream, but what was it? Maybe something related to what I've been through.

What I've been through.

The thought hits me like a ton of bricks. I failed. Dad is gone, and the killer got away. Hanna . . . Molly. *Molly?*

I stand up, in T-shirt and shorts. Sometime in the night, I must have yanked off the hoodie. I put it back on and head into the kitchen.

Molly's gone. I have no doubt about it. I feel her absence almost as sharply as I feel Dad's.

I grab my phone off the charger as I shake off the last clinging residue of the nightmare.

Molly texted me about an hour ago.

Sorry had to run B4 Jess's parents got up. TTYL

I read another text below it.

You talk in your sleep

The text is followed by a smiley face emoji and a winky face emoji.

I read that once again, wondering what I said. Hoping I didn't incriminate myself in any way.

My whole body hurts. I roll my head from one side to the other, and pain shoots up into my head. I wince and rub the back of my neck, the muscles sore under my fingers. No surprise. Sliding down a staircase and smacking your head on tile will do that. I should probably see a doctor, but I have more important things to do.

My phone vibrates in my hand. It's Hanna. I groan and consider not answering it. I swipe to take the call. "Hello?"

"Is your dad home?" Hanna asks before "hello" is fully out.

"No," I say, a little more petulantly than I intended.

"I'm sorry," Hanna says, and, despite myself, I believe her. She moves on. "I made a list of everyone who might—*might*—want me dead. It's a surprisingly long list." Her voice, so full of energy and drive, is annoying.

"Add one more," I mumble.

"What was that? Are you joking? You sound like you were asleep."

"I was—it's—the sun just came up."

"You fell asleep after last night?"

"Molly came over and—" The words are out of my mouth before I even know they left. Stupid concussion.

"Molly Goldman came over to your house last night?"

"Yes, but—"

"She's on my list, Jude."

"Molly? No way."

"How well do you know Molly? You don't know her as well as you think. Lucas has told me stuff."

"Lucas Munson needs to keep his mouth shut," I say. "He's on *my* list."

"If you think Lucas tried to kill me, you're clueless, and I need to find a better assistant. And you don't have a list."

"Assistant? What do you think this is?"

"It wasn't Lucas, but it could have been Molly," Hanna says, but her voice wavers with doubt. "What did she say, anyway?"

"I—that's between me and Molly. It was nothing about murdering you, though."

"Huh," Hanna says. "So, no confession. Did she have any signs of being hit with a bat or falling down stairs?"

"No . . . I, well—"

"What?" Hanna asks.

"It was nothing."

"Tell me, Jude."

I want to cry. I take a deep breath. "She had a—small—bruise under her eye."

"She had a black eye?" Hanna asks.

"It wasn't black, just bruised."

"That's the same thing, Jude," Hanna says in a tone I don't appreciate.

"Whatever," I say. "She had an excuse that I can easily check out. And if she was the killer, wouldn't she stay as far away from people as she could, until her eye heals? Her coming over here proves she didn't do it. You don't seriously believe Molly Goldman tried to kill you."

I listen to the long pause on the other end. If Hanna says yes, I'm hanging up.

"Listen, Jude. Just come over, okay? We can talk about this face-to-face. I need to go over some things and . . . I need your help." The last bit sounded like it physically hurt her to say.

I'm irritated and consider telling her to forget it . . . but Dad. The thought of him sends new spikes of pain through me. No word from the Society yet. I failed. What will they do?

"Fine," I say. "I have some things I have to get done, and then I'll be over."

"Good. That's awesome," Hanna says, but I'm not sure I believe her. It must really gall her to have to ask for my help. "I'd give you directions," she says, "but you already know where I live." She hangs up without another word.

CHAPTER 18

I pay bills before I leave for Hanna's, doing as Dad taught me, transferring all of our savings into the business account.

We have two full crews. More than a few of the men Dad's hired had drug issues in their past. Dad's always collected strays, taking chances on people others wouldn't. It's paid off.

Of the current roofers, the two that have been with us the shortest time have been here three years. I've worked beside them all. They treat me like a kid brother, teasing and joking.

For the most part, they stay out of trouble, but they need their checks. Until Dad comes back, Lenny can run the crews, but I've got to make sure the money is there.

We have an emergency fund in the gun safe, some cash, and a few old hunting rifles I can pawn if it comes to it, but I hope it doesn't.

They can't keep Dad forever. Eventually, something will have to give.

I text Lenny next.

> Dad's out of town. Will be for a while.

Lenny texts back in less than a minute.

> Yeah, I heard. Sorry about your aunt. No worries. I got you. Prayers.

I stare at the text. *Aunt?* I don't have an aunt, but Lenny talked to Dad. I know instantly what it means. I shudder. The Society let Dad contact the outside. Let Dad set up a plausible reason to be gone.

Understanding dawns on me. The Society is watching me, giving me room to fix my mistake, but they are keeping Dad. His life is still in danger, but he's safe . . . for now. I break down and cry, alone, at the kitchen table. When I'm done, I take a shower and get dressed. As I walk into the living room, I stop a minute and look at Dad's recliner. I sit down and put my feet up, feeling his presence more keenly. Dad's counting on me. I'm going to fix this.

I leave the house and drive to Hanna's, my resolution to fix things morphing into irritation at the rich girl who has me on such a short leash. It's unfair to her. There is a lot of blame to assign, but none of this is Hanna's fault. Despite knowing this, I'm still irritated.

Small homes, trailer parks, and duplexes turn into middle-class neighborhoods that finally morph into golf courses and mansions. Miller's Chapel doesn't have a school district, being a private school, but there is no doubt where the imaginary lines are drawn between the haves and have-nots.

I turn into Hanna's driveway. It's a big house of stone and brick. A water fountain of three carved stone women is in the middle. The women hold upturned pitchers. Water flows from the pitchers to a basin at their feet.

Rich people. Sheesh.

I pull up behind a red four-by-four Jeep parked next to the fountain and cut my engine. It's the Jeep from the park. It's nice, new, and, by the looks of it, recently detailed. The Cheer Academy decal in the lower back glass removes any doubts who it belongs to. I bet she paid someone to wash it for her.

It's the first time I've seen the front of the house in the daytime. The landscaping is immaculate, the grass thick and green, and the hedges in the flowerbeds manicured to precise angles and smooth curves. I get out of my car and realize how out of place the Beast is—how out of place I am—in this neighborhood.

I knock on the front door and a middle-aged man answers. He's about an inch taller than me and slim like a runner. I've never met Hanna's dad, but this has to be him. His eyes are the same piercing blue as Hanna's, and he's dressed in khakis and a polo. He looks me up and down, frowning. "Can I help you?"

"I—"

He rides right over me. "If you're selling something, you should know we require a permit in Sterling Oaks. If it were up to me, we wouldn't let you people in the neighborhood at all. If I wanted a magazine subscription or a new security system, I'd buy it."

I'm a deer caught in headlights, not scared, just trying to understand what's happening.

"So, what is it?" he asks.

I blink at him. "I . . . ahh. I—"

"Stan!" Hanna barks, as she pushes past him and grabs me by the arm, pulling me inside. "This is my friend Jude. I told you he was coming over."

Hanna says all this without looking at the man who may or might not be her dad. She hurries me across the den and up the staircase to her room.

"Friend?" her dad calls, still standing at the open door. "Another one? Are you going to your room? Keep the door open."

Hanna snorts. "Whatever, Stan."

"I'm your *father*," Stan yells up at us. "Stop calling me Stan."

Hanna pulls me along, and I let her guide me up to her bedroom.

"The door open!" Stan screams right as Hanna slams the door shut.

She turns, catching her breath. "Sorry about that. Now, like I said, I made a list." She goes to her MacBook on her desk.

Hanna's room looks different with the lights on, but it's still the room I watched her die in. Suddenly, I don't feel so good.

"So, this list isn't—" Hanna stops. "Jude?" she asks. "Hello, earth to Jude!"

I snap out of the daydream. "Sorry. It's, well, I've been here before. A lot of times and . . . I've never actually *been* here."

Hanna flops down on her bed. "This is where I died."

"Yeah," I say, feeling the full weight of that statement. "This is where he killed you."

"He *or* she," Hanna shoots back.

I grunt noncommittally. "You said you had a list?"

Hanna looks at the space beside her on the bed. "Come on," she says.

I sit by her. On her screen, she has a document pulled up with six names. "I put at least one pro and one con on most of them," Hanna says.

I lean in and read the first name out loud. "'Molly Goldman. Pro: Is jealous of me for hanging with Lucas. Manipulative. Con: Maybe not as big as the person in my room. Motive is weak. They were breaking up anyway.' Manipulative? Really?"

Hanna shrugs. "Live with it."

"Hold on, no. You're telling me Molly is *first* on your list?"

Hanna gives an exasperated sigh. "The order isn't important. Stop arguing and read."

I shake my head and return to Hanna's list. "Jerry Thomas," I say, recognizing the name. "Y'all's quarterback?"

Hanna nods. "Jerk-faced weasel, but also starting quarterback."

I read the sentences beside his name out loud. "'Pro: Kept asking me out over and over. Wouldn't take no for an answer. Big ego. Thinks everyone should do what he wants, especially girls. Con: Did not take rejection well but hasn't bothered me in a while.' Sounds pleasant," I say, and keep reading. "'Kristi or Tabby Wallace. Pro: Beat Kristi out for cheerleader. Left Chapel because of losing her spot on cheer team to me. Mom's a nut job who wants to be her daughter. Both super competitive. Con: Tiny person and maybe way too Lifetime movie to be true.' Kristi Wallace?" I ask, the name ringing a bell. "Is she that Chapel girl coming to Bedford this year? Molly told me about her."

I stop as Hanna frowns at me. Her eyebrows go up expectantly. "Live with it," I say.

Hanna shakes it off with a grimace. "Yep, that's her."

"Huh? And she wants you dead because of cheerleading?"

Hanna shrugs. "It's a long story. Basically, I went out for cheerleader last year for the first time. I cheered competitively in town before, and I made the team and Kristi didn't. That's why she's going to Bedford this year. She made the squad there."

"Yeah," I say. "That's what Mo— That's what I heard. You think she'd want you dead over that?"

Hanna shakes her head. "Probably not," she admits, "but her mom's another story."

"I don't know," I say. "Cheerleading?"

"You'd be surprised," Hanna says.

The next name is one I don't recognize at all. "'Josh Stroup,'" I read. "'Pro: May know I found out. Con: Almost impossible he knows.'" I sigh. "Is this code?"

Hanna taps her foot. "Kind of, yeah."

"Mind explaining?"

Hanna rubs the back of her arm, her laptop still bouncing with her tapping foot. She does not like sharing. "Stan is an accountant. Josh is the son of Stan's biggest client. Josh is possibly redirecting some money. Stan, possibly, is helping. Josh may know I know and not be happy about it."

"Redirecting money? They're stealing?"

Hanna pushes a loose strand of hair behind her ear. "Almost one hundred percent yes. Stan is stressed over the situation and talks to Mom. I've been able to put most of it together."

"Love or money," I say, nodding more to myself than to Hanna.

"What?" Hanna asks.

"It's something Dad says. Most killers are motivated by some twisted version of love or money."

Hanna scratches her forehead. "I never thought of it like that, but it makes sense."

"So," I say, getting back on track. "This Josh guy may or may not be stealing from his own father, and Stan may or may not be helping, and Josh may or may not know that you maybe kind of know about the whole situation and might have tried to kill you last night because of it?" I blurt out in one long breath.

Hanna looks at me like I'm a slow middle schooler. "You summed it up perfectly." Her tone is less than flattering.

"Fine," I say. "Money it is. Moving on."

I read the next name, but it's not a name, it has no pros and cons, it's just a description. Again, I read it out loud. "'Creepy guy at the mall who follows me.' Someone followed you at the mall?" I ask, thinking about the day I followed her. She can't be talking about me, right?

"Twice now," Hanna says.

"That sounds like a possibility."

"They're all possibilities," Hanna says. "That's why I made a list." She focuses back on her MacBook, and she makes a hurry-up motion for me to keep reading.

I hesitate to let her know she's not in charge before going back to the list. Only one name is left, and it's not even a full name, just initials. "'T.D.,'" I read. "Who's that?" I look back at the screen to make sure I didn't miss something. I didn't. It's just initials and no explanation behind it.

Hanna frowns. "I don't think it's him, but it could be."

"Okay," I say. "Who?"

For a moment, I think Hanna will balk, but she seems to get past whatever is going on in her head. "Tommy Davis."

"Tommy Davis?" I ask, the question full of scorn. "Coach Davis's son. My friend Tommy?"

Hanna nods. "Didn't know you were friends, but yes."

"We played football together," I say. "Of course we're friends."

"Is that how that works? Okay, fine. He's your friend."

"How do you even know Tommy? And why is he on the list?"

"You don't get to know everything, Jude. For now, just know he might be a suspect. If—and I do mean if—we need to talk about it more, we will."

"How am I supposed to help if you won't tell me everything?"

"We're not negotiating," Hanna says. "Isn't it bad enough you knew someone was going to murder me and didn't tell me?"

"That's not how it works," I say.

"Because your dad said so?"

"Yes."

I stand all in a rush and pace her room. "We have to be straight with each other. This whole thing is messed up. If we're going to do this, we have to be honest, completely honest with each other. You need to tell me everything. Even if it's hard."

"Like you're telling me everything?" Hanna asks with scorn. "I know you're not."

"No, I'm not telling you everything, but if I do, will you do the same?"

She shrugs, not backing down. "I don't know, depends."

I look right in her eyes. This is it. The moment of no return. I mull it over one last time and come to a decision. I think of how Dad described the Society in the last seconds before we were cut off. *Don't trust these pricks . . . They're everywhere, run everything—*

"All right," I say. "My father was kidnapped by a secret society that may be running the world."

Hanna's eyes narrow. That got her attention. "Okay," she says after a moment. "What kind of people?"

"People like me," I say. "People who Dream."

Hanna ponders that for a moment. "Go on. I'm listening."

I tell her about the Society and about Dad keeping things from me because he thought the Society wanted us dead. I tell her about the phone call.

Hanna listens quietly. When I'm done, I can tell I've convinced her. "Why is Tommy on the list?" I ask.

"It's embarrassing, okay?"

"I think we should be past that by now."

Hanna's lips form a thin line as she looks at her computer. The words come rushing out all at once. "He's my brother."

It takes a few seconds for that to register. "Brother?"

She still won't look at me. "Tommy's mom and Stan . . . whatever. Tommy found out about it somehow and wanted to talk to Stan, but Stan wasn't having it. Mom knew," Hanna's voice cracks. "She was angry Tommy found out, not for what Stan did. They fought that night. Loud. Mom cried, broke stuff, and Stan . . . he talked her down, eventually. That's what he does. Makes sense out of the senseless. Truth out of lies." Hanna takes a quavering breath. "I've seen Tommy around town a few times. He . . . he's never said a word to me, never threatened me, but the way he looks at me." Hanna's words trail off. Her bottom lip, a thin line, begins to tremble.

I start pacing again. "Tommy wouldn't do that. He wouldn't hurt you."

"Then who?" Hanna says, slapping the bed with her palm. "Who *would* want to hurt me?"

I stop pacing as a thought strikes me. "Why isn't Munson on the list?"

"Stop, Jude. Just stop, okay?"

"Seriously, why isn't he on the list? Most all murderers, by average, are male and people you know. Husbands. Boyfriends."

She shakes her head and tosses her MacBook on the bed. "Because he didn't do it. He wouldn't hurt me. We're going to start with the kid at the mall. He seems the most likely."

I rub my sore neck. If Tommy's on the list, Munson needs to be on it too. Munson *could* be the killer, maybe. The attack on the stairs happened so fast. But looking into Hanna's eyes, I know I might as well argue with a kitchen table.

"Why the kid?"

"Because he's *following* me. Isn't that reason enough? And he'll be the easiest to check off the list."

"And why is that? Unless that's a secret, too."

Hanna rolls her eyes. "I tried to confront him once, but he walked the other way. He would have run, I bet, if I'd chased him. I'm not even positive what I would have done if I'd caught him."

"And now?" I ask.

Hanna looks up, her lips moving slightly, as if praying for relief. She takes a deep breath and looks at me. "Now I have you."

"What makes you think I can make him talk?"

"How hard did you hit your head last night?"

I blink at her. She stands and walks over, shaking her head. She takes my upper arm in her hand and squeezes it appraisingly, like a rancher might inspect a prize bull. My cheeks turn red hot as she looks up at me and smiles. Her eyes are so blue, it's stupid. I take a step back, pulling my arm free. Hanna releases me.

"The fight with Lucas was stupid," Hanna says. "You're both complete idiots."

"Are you trying to persuade me to help? Because it's not working."

Hanna ignores me. "You're kinda intimidating when you want to be, Jude. The fight *was* stupid. The thing is, any sane person would have run from Lucas. But I saw it. It was Lucas who should have run. There is something about you, Jude. You're . . . dangerous."

I grimace. I've never thought of myself like that. I don't like it. Wild animals are dangerous. Criminals are dangerous. I'm a good person.

She's right though. I can help her. Of every person Hanna Smith knows, I doubt she knows anybody more uniquely qualified to help her than me.

Hanna's blue eyes try to read my thoughts. She needs me. She can't do this alone.

I clear my throat. "You think the creep's at the mall right now?"

CHAPTER 19

Hanna gets into the Beast without hesitation or comment. Her father, on the other hand, comes out to watch us from the front porch like he just ate a whole bag of lemons.

"I get the impression he doesn't like me," I say as I back the Beast out of the driveway.

"Oh, don't take it personal. He just thinks you're white trash."

"Seriously?"

"In his mind, if your family hasn't been a member of Rush Springs Country Club for three generations, you're white trash."

"And unworthy of hanging with his daughter?"

"Unworthy of more important things than that," she says, not looking at me. "So, do you have a plan or what?"

I put the Beast in drive, leaving a still glaring Mr. Smith behind. I tell her my plan as I navigate her neighborhood and make it out to the expressway. She listens and grunts here and there but is silent when I'm done.

"That's it?" she finally asks. "That's the plan?"

"Yeah. It's elegant in its simplicity."

Hanna blows a raspberry. "We're in trouble, aren't we?"

I shake my head and turn on the radio. We ride in silence the rest of the way. Thankfully, it only takes a few minutes to get to the mall. The parking lot is crowded, and it takes some time to find a spot. I park and offer Hanna my keys. "If I get him, you'll need to drive."

She frowns at my keys, and I think she's going to argue, but she takes them and gets out of the Beast without protest.

I sit, giving her plenty of time to get inside the mall and into position. My leg starts bouncing with nervous energy. Hanna's right, my plan isn't great, but at this point, nothing I do will be great. Great is way, way behind me in the rearview mirror. The only thing I can do is plow forward. A bad plan is better than no plan, maybe. I'm not sure, but what I do know is doing something is way better than doing nothing. The inside of the Beast gets toasty as I ponder my stupid life. It's time to go.

I step out into the summer day. The parking lot is full, and the smell of exhaust, hot asphalt, and Cinnabon permeates the air. It's Sunday, school starts tomorrow, and it would appear some last-minute shopping is going on. If hell was a place on earth, this would be it.

I cross the parking lot and manage not to get run over at the crosswalk. Once inside, I navigate the ebb and flow of shoppers and make my way to the fountain. As much as I loathe this place, the fountain is pretty cool. Arcs of water shoot out from the edges, almost, but not quite, meeting in the middle. Three separate bursts of water shoot up from the center in regular intervals, forming a complicated dance.

Within a few minutes, Hanna passes by, headed toward the food court. She glances at me and frowns, straightening out the pockets of her jeans that don't need straightening. She's not very good at this.

I get on my phone, trying not to look at her, and pull up a game I haven't played in over a year, halfheartedly playing as I scan for anyone following her. No such luck. In about fifteen minutes, Hanna comes back by, a soda in her hand. This time, she manages not to look at me, but I can tell she wants to. Seconds pass, then minutes. Are we wasting our time? Then I spot him.

A kid in black pants and a white shirt. He's younger than me, skinny, with dark hair, pale skin, and ruddy cheeks. Odd that he wears the same clothes every day, but he matches Hanna's description to a T.

As he fades into the people milling about, I stand and follow. It only takes a few minutes to confirm the kid's stalking Hanna.

Like we planned, Hanna is in Markle's, visible through the storefront glass. The kid is watching her, trying to act casual and failing. He seems to be having a conversation with himself, all while staring at Hanna. He takes two confident steps toward her, and then takes two back, slapping his forehead. He does this several times, and I'm becoming more and more certain he's the guy. This is the killer, a deranged secret admirer. My blood pumps hot. *Finally.*

Killers are what I'm here for. Killers, I can handle.

I glance at Hanna, and she's staring right at me. *Don't,* I think at her, but it's too late. She throws her hands up in exasperation and points at the kid. My eyes dart back to Skinny, and he, too, is staring at me. His face goes still, and he swallows, looking left and then right.

Don't run, I think. *Don't—*

Like a rabbit catching scent of the hound, he bolts. I curse and, like the dog that I am, give chase. If he gets away, we'll never get this chance again. For a skinny kid, he's fast, running past startled shoppers as I close the distance. Someone shouts behind me, and I turn to see a mall cop waving at me to stop. The guy is middle-aged with a substantial gut. No way he's running me down, but he does have a walkie-talkie. He pulls it from his belt and holds it up to his mouth.

I run faster and watch the skinny kid dart into the arcade. He's mine now. Only one way out of that place. I rush to the entrance, glancing back to make sure mall cop is out of sight.

I duck into the arcade. The place is filled with people, kids mostly, but a fair number of adults as well. The lights are low. Some are black lights, making the carpet and people's clothes glow. Lights flash, games roar, and people scream in delight or frustration. I haven't been in here in a long time. I don't remember it being this big.

I scan the place, trying to find Skinny. If I leave the entrance, he could double back. If I stay here, he could hide until the security guard finds us. Only one choice. I move through the crowd, doubling back several times, hoping to catch him as he makes a dash for the exit. He doesn't fall for it, which means he's hiding. I let my eyes wander, looking for likely hiding spots. The bathrooms against the back wall are a possibility, but I'll search them last. The car games are another spot.

I wait and watch. It doesn't take long for me to see something odd. A boy, no more than seven, goes into the photo booth. Someone pushes him right back out. He begins to point and cry.

In seconds, I'm there. The curtain is drawn, but there are no feet showing below the curtain. I yank the curtain back, and Skinny's sitting inside, his knees to his chest. He moves quick and tries to run past me, but I slide in front of him and wrap him up in a bear hug. I move fast, grasping his wrist and twisting it behind his back like Dad taught me.

A man, likely the crying boy's father, steps in front of me when I turn around. "What's going on?" he asks, his eyes narrow.

"My brother was hogging the photo booth," I tell the man. "Sorry about that. We're leaving."

"He's not my broth—" Skinny starts, but I twist and bend and his words cut off in a yelp. "Mom's going to be real mad at you," I tell him. "Let's go."

I push past Angry Dad and move Skinny out the front. As we break free of the noise and black lights, someone yells. "Hey you! Stop!"

I look over to see the same overweight mall cop. He's at the far end of the food court, headed our way, and he has a friend. This guy is younger and probably faster.

"Let's go," I growl, twisting Skinny's arm again. He yelps as I push him to the front door. He tries to slow me down, pushing back against me. I put a little more pressure on the hold and he moves forward like a shot, trying to outrun the pain, all while the security guards yell at us to stop.

We make it out the front door and, blessedly, like the last lifeboat on a sinking ship, Hanna is waiting for us by the front door behind the wheel of the Beast. The sound of the Beast's rough idle has never sounded so sweet. I push Skinny into the back seat. Hanna takes off, laying down rubber like we stole something.

CHAPTER 20

"What is wrong with you people?" Skinny yells at me.

I push him into the corner of the back seat with one hand. "Stay quiet."

Hanna glares at me in the rearview. "What happened in there?"

"We got him. That's what happened."

"*Okay*," Hanna says with an admirable amount of scorn. "Now what?"

It's a good question. "The Bluehole," I say without thinking.

Skinny bucks in his seat. "Wait, the Bluehole. Why the Bluehole?"

Once you go in, you never come out. The words sing inside my skull. I turn on him, my voice ice. "Be quiet."

The drive goes by faster than I want. When we reach the dirt road leading to the Bluehole, Hanna takes it without even looking back at me. An old steel swing gate meant to keep out curious teens lies broken on its side. Rare anyone comes out here anymore, not in at least twenty years, anyway.

It's a hot dry day, and the Beast's tires bounce off baked mud. Trees fold in over us, thicker as we drive deeper into the woods, blocking out much of the sun. In under a minute, we reach the other side and break through the trees into sunlight.

Flat rocky ground stretches fifty yards to the cliff's edge. The Bluehole itself, an almost perfect circle, is at least a football field across. This part of Arkansas is dotted with abandoned bauxite mines. The Bluehole is ours. Even from here I can see the cobalt blue water, so far down. It's beautiful and eerie all at once.

Kids used to party here in Dad's day until three teenagers took a dare and jumped from the cliffs. Their bodies were never found.

Once you go in, you never come out.

Hanna parks the car halfway between the woods and the cliff's edge. She spins around and glares at Skinny. "Why were you following me?"

"Sheesh," the kid says, regaining some of his swagger. "Can't a guy walk in the mall without being chased like a criminal and"—he looks over at me—"roughed up like muscle boy's prom date?"

I slap the back of his head, not hard, but enough to get his attention. "You were stalking her."

The kid glares at me, and I swear if he were as big as me, I'd be scared. His face smooths out, defiant. Despite myself, I admire his grit. He should be spilling his guts, but he's tougher than he looks. His glare softens as he looks at me and back to Hanna. I can almost see understanding wash over him. He smiles and starts nodding. "I'm on *video*." He says *video* like it's a word he created. "Of course I'm on video. This is some kind of internet challenge, right? What is it? The Kidnap Challenge? The Imma Go to Jail Challenge? Y'all got hashtags? Sure you do. Don't tell me. Let me guess #StealaKid, #FelonyFreakShow, #18AndLife? Where's the cameras?" He pulls at the seats, checking the upholstery.

Hanna wrinkles her nose. "Internet challenge. You think this is a joke?"

"Come on," Skinny says. "You got me. You don't have to keep lying." He lowers his voice comically and tilts his head from side to side with each word. "I. Don't. Believe. You."

Hanna sputters. "I'm— This is serious."

"Seriously *lame*," Skinny says. "Now where's the cameras?"

I smack him again, harder this time. "You're trying to distract us, and it won't work. You're going to tell us what you were doing."

He rubs the back of his head. "Can't a guy—"

I hit him a tad bit harder, and he yelps. "Hey dude, ever hear of a concussion? Oh, wait. You play football, so . . ." He shrugs. "Explains a lot. Like why you geniuses kidnapped me in broad daylight with like a thousand witnesses."

"How do you know Jude plays football?" Hanna asks, before I can smack the little jerk again.

"Yeah," I say, wishing I'd asked first.

"Duh," the kid says, sharp and angry. "We go to school together."

I stare at him. "Who are you?"

He laughs. "Perfect. You really don't know. I knew it. You are so in over your head. Kidnapping is a serious offense. Take me back now and maybe I keep my mouth shut."

Hanna leans back and groans. "You know him? Really?"

I'm about to tell Hanna I definitely don't know the kid, but I stop and study his face. "You . . . you were in my algebra class last year."

The kid's eyes narrow. "Duh, of course. You cheated off me the whole semester."

His words unlock a flood of memories. "You're the smart kid that skipped a grade. Ken, Kyle—"

"Coop," Skinny says. "My name is Coop. Sheesh, are you really going to act like you don't remember me? We were in class *all year*."

The truth is, I didn't remember him until this very minute. He's changed since I saw him last. "You grew a lot since last year."

Coop sits a little straighter. "Protein shakes. It—"

"If you guys are through making friends, can we get back on subject," Hanna cuts in. "Why are you creeping on me?"

"I wasn't," Coop says.

Hanna reaches into the back seat and slaps him in the back of the head.

"Come on!" Coop complains. "Stop doing that."

Hanna moves to strike him again, but he holds up a hand. "Okay, okay. I'll tell you, but first—"

He moves quick, tugging the door latch, pushing the door open, and springing from the car like a shot. I lunge but miss him as Hanna curses. "Get him, Jude."

I take off. The little guy's headed for the woods. I sprint toward him, and unlike the mall, filled with people and clutter, this space is wide open. Like a football field. Coop doesn't get far before I have him by the scruff of the neck. "Really," I say. "You think you can outrun me?"

Coop shrugs in my grasp. "Protein shakes, man. I mean, I've been drinking a lot of those things." He takes a swing at me. I dodge it, still holding him. He kicks me in the shin, but I don't even grunt.

Hanna catches up to us, breathless, and I shake Coop like the little weasel he is. I look around. At the edge of the woods, a huge oak has fallen recently. I march him to it, with Hanna following. I sit Coop down on the trunk. "Don't move."

"I didn't do anything," he whines. "Why are you guys harassing me?"

"You've been following me at the mall. Don't lie," Hanna says.

Coop, for once, seems lost for words. "Okay, fine. But I'm not a freak, okay? I have information. I found something."

"Found what?" Hanna asks.

"It wasn't me. Okay? I didn't make the thing. You'll think I'm a weirdo and call the cops, and I'll end up in jail or juvenile hall or . . . look at me." He scratches nervously behind his ear. "I won't last ten minutes in the big house."

"What did you find, Coop?" Hanna asks, her voice hard.

"Like, I don't know, a book . . . or something. It has, it has stuff in it. Stuff about you." He looks at Hanna. "Bad stuff, and pictures, too."

"Pictures?" Hanna's face drains of color. "What type of pictures?"

Coop grimaces. "You jogging in the park. Cheerleading practice. Pictures of your car, your license plate. I don't know. Like you have a serious stalker."

I'm not sure I believe him, not yet, but if he's lying, he's a good liar. "Where did you get the book?"

"I told you. I found it."

"Where?"

Coop takes a deep breath. "Someone left it at the food court."

"The food court? At the mall?" I ask incredulously. It seems my whole life always comes back to that cursed place. "Who left it? And how did you end up with it?"

"And why are you always at the mall?" Hanna asks. "It's like you're waiting on me."

"Seriously, guys," Coop says. He pulls at his white shirt. I glance at Hanna to see if she understands. She shrugs.

"Are you both that unobservant? Or does someone like me not merit your notice? The food court," he says. "I work at the food court. Hunan Buffet City? The HBC?" He blinks at my blank stare, glancing at Hanna. "I've served both of you food before. Like, more than once."

For the first time, I notice the small, stylized red dragon on his shirt. It's so faded it's almost pink, but I recognize it as Hunan Buffet City's logo.

"So, you found this thing?" Hanna asks skeptically. "And it's not yours. You're not a creep, but you follow me around the mall?"

"I was trying to tell you, okay? But how do you do that? 'Hi, I'm Coop. I'm supercool, and I found this book with pictures of you, and maybe you want to have a look, and no, I'm not a huge weirdo that totally made this book for attention.' Don't you see? I was afraid you wouldn't believe me."

Hanna shakes her head. "Why not give it to the police then?"

Coop snorts. "Aren't you listening? I give it to them and who do you think is suspect *numero uno*? I mean, I looked through it. It has my fingerprints and, like, DNA all over it."

"He has a point," I say.

Hanna turns her rising frustration on me. "A point?" she asks acidly.

I hold up my hands in surrender.

Her upper lip twitches before she turns her attention back to the little guy. "Fine, *Coop*. Tell us—exactly—how you found the book."

Coop rubs at his head. "It's not like a cool story or anything. I was cleaning tables and found a shopping bag. It happens all the time. People leave stuff and come back for it later. So I put it behind the counter. I closed that night and was cleaning up when I noticed no one had come for the bag. My manager had already clocked out, and they were closing the food court, so I took a peek inside to see if there were any names in there. There was only one thing in the bag. The book. After I looked inside, I knew no one was coming back for it. It's straight serial killer, right?"

Hanna groans in frustration. "How long have you had it?"

Coop won't look at her. "I'm not sure. A little over a week. Ten days tops."

"*Ten days?*" Hanna says dangerously. "Someone tried to kill me, and you had this for ten days?"

Coop's head pops up. "Someone tried to kill you?"

"That's right. Someone tried to kill me."

Tears form in Coop's eyes.

"I could have died," Hanna says.

Coop swallows hard, and the tears start to leak. He licks his lips. "Do you know how hard it is to be me? Unnoticed. By myself. I mean, you two should recognize me. You should know who I am, but no. I'm a loser. I'm nobody. I may as well not even exist. I tried to talk to you, but how do you start up that conversation? Do you know how hard it is to talk to someone like you?" Coop bites off the last word. He looks like he wants to crawl under a rock.

Hanna's going to plow into him now, I think, but when I glance over, her face is still. Coop's head bows. "I'm sorry, okay? I should have showed it to you. It was stupid."

Hanna comes over and sits by him on the oak trunk. She puts her arm around him. Of all the things I thought she might do, this isn't one of them. "It's all right," she says, patting him on the shoulder.

He looks up at her, his eyes red. "I messed up, I know it. Can you forgive me?"

Hanna takes a deep breath. "I forgive you."

"Thank you," Coop says, grasping Hanna in a bear hug. "Thank you." For an instant I think Hanna will push him away.

Instead, Hanna pats his back. She looks up at me, frowning, Coop still clinging to her. Finally, she gives me a small shrug.

CHAPTER 21

We take Coop back to work after he agrees to bring the book to Hanna's house. "Security will believe whatever I tell them," Coop assures us. "This little event doesn't even register on the strange meter at the mall, trust me. That place is like a different universe or something."

After dropping Coop off, we head to Hanna's house. She seems to be mulling things over, and I'm happy to ride in silence.

I glance over at her. The kindness she showed Coop surprised me, even though it probably shouldn't have. I had a sneak peek in her soul, after all, but still, I didn't see it coming. I had expectations of who she would be, what I imagined most Chapel girls would be like, and I realize, that's on me. She's not the stuck-up rich girl of my expectations. She almost catches me as I glance again. I turn on the radio to cover myself.

"Jude?" she says.

I don't dare look at her. "Yeah?"

"Thanks for helping today. For the first time, I feel like we're going to find whoever was in my house last night."

"Sure. No problem." I change the station on the radio, but not before I catch a slight smile on Hanna's glossy lips.

"I'm starving," Hanna says out of nowhere. "Are you hungry? I think we have some leftover pizza."

At the mention of pizza, my stomach growls. "Is your dad home?" The question comes out a little hard.

"Probably."

"Your dad thinks I'm white trash, remember?"

Hanna's tone becomes serious. "My dad's not a good person. I know that. It sucks, but it's true. If I lived my life according to what he wanted or expected, I'd be like him. I won't let that happen."

I put both hands on the wheel as I drive. I get what Hanna's saying. If my father did what Stan had done, I'd be less than a fan. It's still hard for me to believe that Tommy isn't Coach D's biological son.

I swallow as a horrible thought strikes me. If Coach D found out Tommy wasn't his son, would he want to hurt Hanna? Like some type of revenge thing. He wasn't on Hanna's list. Should he be?

I shift in my seat, needing very badly to stop thinking. "What kind of pizza we talking about?"

Hanna laughs. "Does it matter?"

"Not at all," I say with a smile.

It doesn't take long, and we are turning into Hanna's neighborhood. When we get to Hanna's house, a deep-purple GMC truck is blocking the driveway. It looks new, like it just rolled off the lot. I whistle. "That's a sweet ride."

Hanna frowns, her eyes on the GMC. "Not this guy," she mumbles to herself. "That's Josh Stroup's truck. He's on the list, Jude."

"Huh? The guy who may know that you know that he's stealing?"

"Yeah," Hanna says flatly. "Exactly. Come on."

I hesitate for a second and follow Hanna. I have to jog across the perfectly manicured lawn to catch up.

The front door flies open and a guy, a year or two older than me, stalks out. He's tan with blond hair, short on the sides, long on top. He's thin, not that tall, but wiry like a lightweight boxer. He's wearing a long-sleeve white shirt and tie. My first impression is a slick preacher boy, but when our eyes meet, I know he belongs in a prison yard, not a church. He looks familiar, but I can't place him.

He grins, exposing white, straight teeth as he alters course to stand right in front of Hanna. Hanna freezes, and I almost run into her. In a second, I size him up. He could have a gun, either in the small of his back or an ankle holster . . . but this guy looks like a knife guy. I bet he's got a blade in his pocket, something expensive, tactical, and worthless in a real fight.

Hanna takes a step back and to the side until she's even with me.

The guy gives me a quick dismissive glance as he bars our way to the house, pushing fingers through his hair. His grin broadens. "Hanna," he says. "How nice to see you." His tone implies the opposite. "You stayin' out of trouble?"

"Most days," Hanna says. Her voice is calm, measured. The guy holds Hanna's gaze, but Hanna doesn't even blink.

I've met a few people over the years whom I instantly disliked. The dislike I have for this guy is tenfold. It's something almost visceral.

I hold out my hand. "Jude Erickson," I say.

Amusement washes over his face as he ignores my hand and turns back to the house. Stan is at the door, half in, half out, a lamb about to bolt from a wolf. "I'll be back tomorrow for that paperwork," the guy shouts. "Get it right this time." It's a totally unnecessary display. Yep, I have no doubt now. This is Josh Stroup, and he likes making people uncomfortable. Well, Hanna did ask me to help. Time to poke the bear.

"Josh, right?" I say.

Slick Preacher Boy narrows his eyes at me. "Yeah."

"Nice truck. Two years out of high school and you buy that all by yourself?"

Hanna snorts. It's awesome.

Josh glances at her with malevolence before his attention laser focuses on me. "That *your* ride?" He points at the Beast. "Looks like something an old woman would drive."

"Well, it *was* my granny's," I say, with no shame in my game.

Josh's nostrils flare. "Who are you?"

"I already told you," I say, all amusement gone from my voice. "You're not listening, Josh."

"You got a problem, kid?" Josh says, stepping to me. He's in my face, trying to intimidate me.

This is it. If I'm wrong and Josh is just some rich kid with daddy issues, I'll feel bad, but I have a hunch that Josh Stroup is a powder keg, always looking for a match.

I sniff. "I think you're a punk who wouldn't be able to keep a job flipping burgers if it wasn't for *Daddy*." I push him with both hands. Not hard, but enough to make him take two steps back.

His lips twitch, and I think he might be in shock. It's clear he's not used to being treated like this, and I see the wheels spinning in his head. What will he do now?

I see the instant the decision is made. He moves fast, reaching behind him. I was trying to provoke him, but I'm stunned by this reaction. Despite my shock, I have no doubt what's happening, and I absently wonder if it's a knife or a gun he's reaching for. I close the distance on instinct, ready to end the fight before he can pull his weapon.

A dog barks, loud, shrill, and incessant. It's a little yapper. An old couple dressed for a tennis match stand staring from the sidewalk, walking their ancient lapdog. Josh and I freeze.

Stan yells from the door. "Hey, Mark, Patty, nice day." His voice is two octaves too high, and his words are fast and clipped.

The spell is broken. Josh straightens, his hand falling away from whatever he was about to pull. I would bet a thousand dollars it's a knife. He glares at me. "You messed up, boy. Got lucky." He brushes past me, intentionally ramming his shoulder into mine.

I let the blow turn me but don't react to his violence. Josh thinks I'm nothing, certainly not a threat. Good. Let him keep thinking that.

The little dog is going crazy, trying to get off its leash to destroy someone's ankles. Mark and Patty give us disapproving frowns, like we don't know the difference between our salad and dinner forks.

"Nice dog," I say to them, waving, as Josh gets in his truck.

Josh doesn't leave right away. He sits in the driver's seat and glares at me through the window. I have my answer and then some: Josh Stroup is comfortable with violence.

Hanna comes to stand beside me, her arms folded. "You see why he's on the list?"

"Totally," I say without looking at her.

"You know," she says, "you could have just taken my word for it." She grabs my arm and pulls me away from the still-glaring Josh, the little yapper still going nuts.

I follow Hanna to the house as Josh starts up his GMC, revving his engine like a redneck. He burns rubber in Mr. Smith's nice white driveway.

Hanna lets me go when we reach the stairs and walk to the door, Stan barring the way. "It's time your friend went home," Stan says through clenched teeth, still holding the smile for Mark and Patty, the yapper still yapping.

"Sure thing, Stan." Hanna moves past him, forcing him to move. "Come on, Jude."

I hesitate and follow her in. "Sorry, sir."

We visit the kitchen first and eat cold pizza. It's got pineapple on it, but I don't care. We keep the shop talk to a minimum though because Stan keeps walking by, stopping in the door to frown at me. Hanna ignores him like a pro.

After pizza, we make it upstairs, and Hanna flops down on the bed, finally free to talk. "I told you."

"No doubt," I say. "Who is Josh, exactly?"

"You really don't know, do you?"

"No. That's why I asked."

"That's Big Hank's son, Jude." The name tickles something in my subconscious but doesn't register.

"Big Hank's Homes," Hanna says, exasperated. "Hank Stroup is, like, the richest man in town. His billboards are everywhere."

It clicks. That's why Josh looked familiar. Father and son look a lot alike. Big Hank is older obviously, white hair and leathery skin. He wears a white cowboy hat on all the billboards, but the resemblance is there.

"He was reaching for a weapon at the end," I say. "I didn't expect that."

Hanna bites her lip.

"What?" I ask.

"Nothing," she says, a little too emphatically.

I get the distinct feeling Hanna Smith is being less than honest. "Are you sure?"

Hanna sighs. "The Stroups aren't great people, and my family is all wrapped up with them. Stan used to be this person I looked up to. When I was a kid, I thought he was the greatest. We went places, did things, had this whole life, but he isn't that person."

I search for the right words to comfort Hanna, but I know all too well, nothing I say will ease the pain. My own mother abandoned me. I let out a breath. "It sucks, no doubt."

Hanna shrugs. "It is what it is."

I grimace. Her words are the exact words I used in the mall to tell Molly about my mom situation. Hanna notices my discomfort, and I think she's about to ask more questions, but I'm saved from any further awkwardness by an ear-piercing scream from downstairs.

CHAPTER 22

Hanna bolts out her door and to the railing overlooking the foyer. I join her, taking in the scene below.

Stan Smith grasps and swipes at Coop, who twists and bobs like an eel, darting side to side, backing up. Stan flounders and stumbles. Coop has a book grasped protectively against his chest, but his feet are moving as Stan tries to corner him.

I laugh. Hanna elbows me. "It's not funny," she says, but her words are betrayed by the warm smile.

Coop looks up at us as he dodges another one of Stan's clumsy attempts. "Hanna, will you tell this guy I'm your friend?"

Mr. Smith makes one last lunge at Coop. Coop slides to the side as Stan falls and hits the hardwood. His way open, Coop skips past him. He hits the stairs at a run.

"I asked him over, Stan," Hanna shouts down at her father.

Stan rolls to his back, panting. He looks up as Coop joins us. Mr. Smith points at Coop. "How many of these little urchins can I expect?"

Coop snorts. "Urchin? Who am I, Oliver Twist?"

Mr. Smith glares at him. Coop shrugs as best he can, clutching the book like some ancient and valuable treasure. "Right. I'll—" He looks around. "This your room, Hanna?" He nods to Hanna's open bedroom door.

Hanna's too busy with the stare-off between her and Stan.

"Right," Coop says, backing up into Hanna's room. "I'll wait in here."

"Me too," I add, quickly following Coop.

"Who was that guy?" Coop asks, as I make my way into the room.

"Hanna's dad," I say.

Coop grunts, sitting on Hanna's bed. "Dude's got issues."

Hanna comes in, closing the door behind her. "Is that it?" she asks, nodding at the book Coop's still clutching.

"Nah, I left the real one back home."

Hanna blinks.

"Come on, of course this is it."

"Well, let's see it."

Coop hesitates. "Remember, before you look at it . . . just remember I didn't make it, okay? I wouldn't . . . I couldn't—"

Hanna sits by him on the bed. "I believe you," Hanna says gently. "Now can I see it?"

Coop taps his foot, probably not even realizing he's doing it. He hands the book to Hanna. She places the book on top of her knees, and I sit on the bed next to her as she opens it.

The first page is a large picture of Hanna. "It's my Insta profile pic," she says.

Hanna runs a finger down the page, then starts flipping. The book is thick, full of printed pictures of Hanna pasted to each page, a lot of selfies and pics of her and friends, several pictures of her Jeep. There are a couple of her and Lucas.

"They're from social media. All of them," Hanna says as she flips. She stops on a page with a lone picture less staged than the others: Hanna jogging. "This one isn't though." On the next page is a picture of the back of her house taken from the woods. "Neither is this one." Hanna turns the page. It's the same picture of the back of her house, only zoomed in. In red pen, someone has circled a plant on her back porch. The swirling red encircles the plant over and over.

"The key under the planter," I say.

Hanna's hand trembles as she turns the next page. It's a picture of her sunbathing in a swimsuit. It appears the picture was taken from the same vantage point from the woods, but it's hard to tell for sure, because red pen marks cover the page.

Red circles swirl like vortexes, X marks and dashes cover the picture. The page is ripped in more than a few places from the pressure of the pen on paper, the picture a mess except for Hanna.

Like the eye of a storm, Hanna is unmarred, untouched by the red.

Hanna shudders. My hand is on her shoulder. I must have unconsciously placed it there. I freeze, not sure what to do. Hanna reaches up and places her hand on top of mine.

I squeeze her shoulder reassuringly. "This is the killer," I tell her. "Whoever was in your room that night made this. It's a smoking gun. This is someone who has something personal against you."

"Yeah," Hanna says in a small voice. "You're right. This feels personal . . . very, *very* personal."

"So now what?" Coop asks. "The police?"

"No," I say. "We can't."

"Why not?"

"It's the first rule. No help."

Coop's face screws up in confusion. "First rule? What are you talking about?"

My hand slides from Hanna's shoulder. "I . . . It's," I stammer, realizing my mistake. Coop doesn't know about the Dream, and I'd like to keep it that way.

"Jude's right," Hanna says. "We can't call the police because the police might be involved."

I do a double take at Hanna. She threatened to call the cops nine thousand times last night. Now she's saying we can't call the police?

Coop frowns. "Why would the police be involved?"

"Yeah, Hanna," I say. "Why *would* the police be involved?"

Hanna has to hear the irritation in my voice, but she chooses to ignore it. She closes the book in her lap. "One of the people who we think may have tried to kill me has a lot of money, power, and connections," she says. "He has major—and I mean major—sway over Rush Spring's PD. Chief Jamison, in particular."

"This is new," I say, my voice a little too pleasant. "Now, which suspect is this?"

"Well, you just met him, Jude," Hanna says with equal sugariness. "Josh Stroup."

Coop sits up a little straighter. "Big Hank's son?"

"That's right," Hanna says. "Big Hank is the one who really has the power, but it's all the same. Whatever Josh wants, Big Hank gives him."

Coop grunts like he's putting stuff together. "Does this have anything to do with the Stroups being huge drug dealers?"

I laugh. "Drugs, no. They sell mobile homes." I look at Hanna for backup. She is frowning hard at Coop and, pointedly, won't look at me.

"Uh, Hanna," I say.

Hanna turns to me, and her expression is defiant. "What?"

I facepalm. "Seriously, they sell drugs?"

Hanna stands up, slinging the murder book onto her bed. She stares down at Coop. "How do you know the Stroups sell drugs?"

"Uh, doesn't everyone?"

I groan. "*Definitely* not everyone," I say.

Hanna has the audacity to side-eye me. "Spill," she demands of Coop.

"Uh, well," Coop starts, shifting on the bed. "I'm kind of drug adjacent. Got some relatives who have had issues. Big Hank and meth are kind of common knowledge in certain circles. But that doesn't explain why Big Hank's son would try to kill you over money."

Hanna rubs her forehead like a headache is coming on.

"Telling me Joshy-Boy was a drug dealer would have been helpful," I say. "You know, before he tried to *murder me* on your front lawn."

Hanna huffs. "You did fine. And I never told you to push his buttons like that."

"*Told me*," I say, my voice rising. "You are not in charge." I grind my teeth. "You know everything about me." I glance at Coop. "*Everything*," I hiss.

Hanna shrugs. "Live with it."

Hanna spends the next several minutes pacing and explaining how Big Hank is the biggest meth distributor in the South. How he supplies drugs not just to Arkansas but to Oklahoma, Missouri, Mississippi, and parts of Tennessee.

She explains how her father launders money for Big Hank, how Josh is making Stan divert funds, and how Josh may know Hanna found out and want her dead because of it. Several times Hanna slips and mentions something about my part. During the story of the night someone tried to kill her, Coop keeps glancing at me despite Hanna never mentioning me being there at all.

"Okay," Coop says. "I think I have more questions now than when we started." He taps his foot, and I can see the wheels spinning in his head. Coop is a smart guy. I don't like where this is going. "I think I can help, maybe. There are cameras in the food court. I don't know if they work, or if they were even on when whoever dropped the bag came and ate, but I might be able to get the video."

I jump from the bed. All my problems seem to evaporate. "That's freaking awesome," I say. "If we can get video evidence, we're going to catch the killer red-handed."

"Yeah," Coop says. "But there's a price."

My excitement goes to anger. "A price?" I ask coolly.

Coop doesn't flinch. "You guys aren't telling me something. Something big. And it has to do with you." He nods at me. "How do you fit into this? Why are you even here?" He looks at Hanna. "The story about the night someone tried to kill you makes zero sense. What aren't y'all telling me?"

I open my mouth to speak, but the little guy rolls right over me. "If you lie to me, I'm done. I'm not kidding. This is big, dangerous stuff, and you're asking me to help. Fine, I want to help, but I won't help people who lie to me. Period. End of conversation. Full stop."

I huff. And then stand there in silence. I can't tell this kid the truth. I hardly know him. But what do I do? We need his help. We need the video. If there is someone on the video, Hanna is saved. I can do my job. Dad can come home.

Hanna's hand rests on my shoulder. I flinch but don't pull away. "It's the only way," she says. "We don't have a choice. He knows too much already."

"Ah," Coop says. "You guys aren't going to murder me, are you? 'Cause I thought we were past that?"

I look at him. "Murdering you might be easier. More fun too."

"Murder me or not. You want my help? Don't lie to me."

"You won't believe the truth," I say.

"Bet," Coop says.

I grunt. Because that is exactly what this is. I'm betting this kid I hardly know won't blab about my family's dark secret. But I don't see any other way.

For the second time in less than twenty-four hours, I tell another living being who and what I am.

CHAPTER 23

It's Friday. School started Monday, and it's been almost a week since someone tried to kill Hanna. Dad is still gone. There are no messages, no phone calls. I must assume the Society is watching, wanting me to fail, to get arrested or killed, like Dad believes, but who knows. It would seem the Society has a distorted sense of honor that I don't understand.

Right now, I can only control what I can control.

The possibly homicidal cheerleader, Kristi Wallace, is my responsibility. All five feet, three inches of her.

"This is ridiculous," I tell Coop, scanning the hallway to make sure no one's in earshot. People are hanging out, waiting for first bell. "She's not big enough. The person at Hanna's was bigger."

"You sure? Hanna says it was all dark, and it happened kinda fast, and Tiny Cheerleader Girl would absolutely fit the bill of making the crazy book. She's got crazy eyes, man."

"None of this would be necessary if you'd get the video," I say a little too harshly.

Coop doesn't seem to mind. "Patience, grasshopper. I can't just ask for the video. Chuck will ask too many questions. I'll get the code, trust me."

I grunt. We've been over this too many times. The video, if it exists, is stored on computers inside the security room in the mall. The security room has a passcode lock and is off limits to everybody but mall security. Coop is working on Chuck, the mall cop, trying to get the code so we can sneak in and watch the video from the day Coop found the book.

While Coop works on getting the video, all three of us are going through Hanna's list. Time is important, and the video of the killer might not even exist. So, the more people we can clear, the better.

Coop and I are supposed to befriend Kristi, maybe even get invited over to her house to get intel on her momma, but making friends isn't exactly something I'm good at. It irks me that my job is *this*. I'd much rather punch someone.

"Hanna isn't running things," I tell Coop.

"Right," Coop says. "I guess you could tell Hanna you decided, again, that the time wasn't right."

I groan.

"Right?" Coop says with a mock shudder. "Even the thought of it makes me want to pee."

This is the third attempt to approach Kristi. I've bailed the other two times, and Hanna isn't happy.

"The time is now," Coop says. "The perp is right there."

"Perp? Really?"

"Lingo of the trade," Coop says. "We doing this or what?"

"Fine. But you're coming with me."

"Uh, that's the plan."

I ignore him and take the first reluctant step toward Kristi. Petite with short black hair, Kristi stands in the hallway, talking to Natalie Su, a sophomore cheerleader.

"You got this," Coop says. I drove him to school all week, and it might be my imagination, but I think he's taller. He's definitely chattier.

We brush by kids at their lockers, standing in groups, talking. If first bell would ring a few minutes early, I'd be totally cool with it. "I don't like this," I hiss at Coop. "What should I say?"

"I don't know. Maybe tell her your name. In fact, try not to say too much, just smile and, I don't know, flex. I'll do the friend making."

"Flex?"

Coop gives me a little shove from behind, and I let him move me, unwilling to make a scene. I stumble, my cheeks warming.

Coop sighs. "Or you could tell Hanna you're in charge now, or that you're afraid of girls."

"She's not in charge. And I'm not afraid of girls," I say, as a kid half my size pushes me toward a tiny cheerleader of a girl.

Natalie looks up as I approach. Kristi follows her gaze. It's game day, and both girls are in their cheerleading warm-ups. Kristi's dark eyes appraise me as I get close.

"Kristi?" I ask, my voice cracking. I clear my throat. "Kristi, right?" I already sound like a moron.

Kristi nods, her eyebrows rising. "And you're Jude Erickson."

I nod at her and look over at Nat. "Nat," I say in greeting.

"Jude," Nat says back. "Are we going to win tonight?"

"They better," Kristi cuts in. "I mean, we better. I've got to get used to saying that. I'd still be at Chapel, but the honors department is better here. So, here I am."

"Honors?" I ask, surprised. "I thought it was about chee—" I stop as Nat gives me a slight shake of the head. Kristi watches me. "Ch . . . urch?" I finish with an awkward laugh.

"Church?" Kristi asks. "Why would I change schools because of church?"

"Yeah." I throw my hands up. "Crazy, right?"

Kristi's eyes narrow.

"Ladies," Coop slides up beside me. "How bad is this guy going to stomp Chapel tonight?" He holds out a hand to Kristi. "Coop Harris," he says. "Welcome to Bedford, m'lady."

Kristi laughs. At least, I think it's a laugh. It's a nasally snort that goes on way past being normal. She takes Coop's hand and shakes it.

"Did you ask her yet?" Coop asks me.

I stare at him. The heat in my face is a slow burn, the pit sweat cold as ice.

"Ask me what?" Kristi says, eyeing me suspiciously, but she's unable to keep a smile from her lips.

"Oh," Coop says. "I thought he—" He looks from me to Kristi and back again. His face scrunches up like he smelled something sour. It's a caricature of confusion. It's *bad*, real bad, but it has the desired effect. Nat snickers at Coop's absurdity. Kristi absolutely loves it, her odd laugh drawing the surrounding students' glances.

What is happening?

"Jude?" Coop prompts. Both girls look at me. "You came over here," Coop continues, as if speaking to a child, a slow child, "to ask Kristi if you could buy her a coffee sometime."

I can't speak. This was not the plan. I don't want a date. *A date? Molly.* What would she think? *No, no, no, what is Coop doing?* All this goes through my head, but I can't speak, so I just smile. Kristi looks at me questioningly. The smile from before has been replaced by something less inviting. I manage a nod.

Kristi considers me for what seems like a very long time. Coop is still as a statue. Nat looks like she's about to head to the lobby for popcorn. I swallow.

To my total bewilderment, Kristi's lips part and the smile is back. "You know," she says, stepping closer, "I've noticed you noticing me. This was cute. *Cute.* Having your friend help."

She takes a pen from her backpack, grabs my hand, and writes her number on my palm. She finishes and smiles up at me just as first bell rings. "Text me," she says, walking off.

Nat stares up at me, her dark eyes laughing. "Smooth." She giggles and heads off too, her ponytail swishing as she almost skips away.

"Are you having a stroke?" Coop asks.

"No," I say sharply. "I— What about Molly?"

Coop narrows his eyes. "Molly Goldman?"

"Of course Molly Goldman," I say, irritated.

"Y'all don't really have anything going, do you?"

I hesitate. *Do we?* She came over that night, and we've talked and texted. School started Monday. Molly's been rehearsing for her play. I've had football. We've hung out at school, but that's about all I've had time for. There's also my preoccupation with making sure Hanna doesn't get murdered.

In all honesty, I thought there would be more going on with me and Molly, but things have moved slow. I didn't think that was a problem until now.

"She . . . I don't know. Go to class."

Coop shakes his head. "You, man. I swear. Did you even say two words to Kristi? And still she gave you her number. Superpowers, man. Superpowers wasted."

"Just go to class." I walk off to English, leaving a grinning Coop behind.

The rest of the day goes slowly. At lunch, Kristi sits with other cheerleaders. Their eyes all seem to follow me as I make my way across the room to where a handful of football guys sit. Rob Thomas hoots when he sees me. "Jude. The Man. Erickson."

I sit down between Rob and Big Andre. "The Man, huh? Did I get a promotion?"

"Word on the street is," Rob says, "you asked Kristi Wallace out."

"What? It's been like four hours."

"So, it's true? Molly first, and now Kristi," Rob nearly shouts. "Dang, dude."

"Does Molly know?" Andre asks.

"I don't know," I say miserably.

Andre slaps my back. "Jess said you and Molly were still talking."

"We are," I say. "Kristi is . . . it's a misunderstanding."

Andre glances over at Kristi and her crew. I take a chance and look, too. Kristi catches me and gives a little wave. "Yeah," Andre says. "I'd say Kristi misunderstands for sure."

I don't return Kristi's wave, poking at my mashed potatoes. "So, everybody knows?"

"Rob knows," Andre says. "So yeah, everybody knows."

I drop my fork and rub my forehead, my appetite gone. Andre is cool enough to change the subject, and we pass the next twenty minutes talking about the game tonight. Kristi and her friends leave, finally, and Andre and Rob soon follow. There are only a handful of kids left in the cafeteria when the bell rings.

As I'm putting up my tray, I run into Tommy Davis. He has a custodian's uniform and a mop in hand. He smiles warmly when he sees me. "What's up, Jude?" He holds out a hand, and I clasp it. Even though Tommy is also on Hanna's list, I can't help but return Tommy's grin.

The fact that he and Coach Davis aren't really related is hard to reconcile. They are a lot alike. Nature versus nurture, I guess. Thank goodness he seems to have taken on Coach D's personality and not Stan's.

"Tommy. When did you start working here?"

"Today, actually," he says, popping his collar. "One day, you too can have the job your father gets you."

I chuckle with him. "It's not what you know but who you know."

"Truth," Tommy agrees. "Honestly, this is the perfect job for me. Staying clean is hard some days. This job helps. Dad's just down the hall."

The confession doesn't surprise me. Tommy has always been an open book. It's why people like him. When his drug use went to the harder stuff, people said that Tommy went away. I didn't hang around him any by then. He was older, at college most of the time an hour away, and running with a totally different crowd. It wasn't my fault, but standing in front of him, I wonder if I could have done anything. Called him or something.

"I'm proud of you, man," I say. "Seriously."

Most guys would blow that compliment off, but not Tommy. "Thanks, Jude. I appreciate that." He looks down at his feet and shifts the mop from one hand to the other. "Not everyone is so understanding. Once a junkie, always a junkie. I get it." Despite his best attempt, Tommy can't hide all the scorn of that comment. The anger is a little un-Tommy-like. At least the Tommy I used to know. He looks up at me, and his expression is somber. "I did some stuff. Stole from friends, family." He sniffs. "That crowd that's still using, some call me, want to hang even though they know I'm trying to kick, others want . . ." he hesitates, and I see a brief yet powerful glint of rage, "more than they should."

Tommy smiles at me awkwardly. Tommy, the open book, almost said too much. And I wonder what "more than they should" means. I hate myself for it, but I wonder if it's possible Tommy did try to kill Hanna, but for something other than being Hanna's half brother. Could it be because of his entanglements with the drug world?

"So, we gonna beat Chapel tonight?" Tommy asks, changing the subject and interrupting my mental gymnastics.

"That's the plan," I say. It's hard for me to imagine Tommy Davis trying to kill *anyone*, much less Hanna. But that glimpse of rage . . . I shake the thought away.

"You coming tonight?" I ask.

Tommy grins and he's the old Tommy again. The one incapable of murder. "Come on. You know I won't miss it. What else is a twenty-year-old single guy living with his parents going to do on Friday night?" It's a joke, and I laugh appropriately, but I can see the disappointment in Tommy's eyes.

"Well, these floors aren't going to clean themselves."

"You know a girl from Chapel named Hanna Smith?" I blurt out before he can leave.

His head snaps up and I see suspicion and something else—guilt, maybe—wash over his face, but he smooths it out fast. Before he speaks his next words, I know I'm about to be lied to. "Chapel girl? You kidding? You think I'm high society now? Nah, man, never heard of her." He frowns. "Why? You trying to date above your station?" The frown is replaced by a sly smile. "Don't go chasin' waterfalls."

I laugh. In Bedford, "Chasing Waterfalls" is not only an awesome '90s song, it's also when one of us tries to hang with the Chapel kids. "No way," I say. "Just somebody I met at a party."

Second bell rings.

"Stay away from those Chapel kids," Tommy says. "Most of them have more money than sense."

I nod at his words but don't move. Tommy stands his ground as well, like a man with more wisdom to impart, or, perhaps, something to confess. An awkward moment passes, then another. Tommy rubs at his five-o'clock shadow. "You're going to be late for class," he says. "Good luck tonight." He proffers his mop. "Clean up on aisle nine."

I watch him walk away. I don't want to believe Tommy could be the killer, but he did lie to me, and the anger he has bubbling below the surface wasn't there two years ago. How much has my friend changed in the two years since he was a senior? There was also something left unsaid at the end. It was almost like he wanted to get something off his chest.

Anger, plus suspicious behavior, plus more suspicious behavior. I let out a breath. I'm going to keep believing it wasn't Tommy, or, for that matter, Coach D. The alternative is way too hard to contemplate.

The rest of the afternoon drags on. Class after class comes and goes. During my day I have three opportunities to see Molly: in the hall between early lunch and late lunch, between fourth and fifth periods, and at the end of the day, cutting across the soccer fields to the field house for football.

Most days we stop for a chat. Today, I didn't see her my first two opportunities. She usually waits for me in the hall so we can talk for a second or two, but after a no-go my first two chances, I have a very bad feeling about what Molly may or may not have heard.

The soccer field is my last chance. After that I'll have to call, or text, or maybe stop by her house. I have to let her know . . . what? That I asked Kristi on a date? I shake it off as I hustle to get to the soccer field. I'll figure it out. Maybe she hasn't even heard.

To my relief, Molly is with her friends on the soccer field. It's not until I'm halfway to her that she notices me. She spots me and looks away almost as quick.

Not good.

She keeps talking to her friends as I come close.

"Hey guys," I say to everyone.

I get a few icy nods, but not much else.

Not good at all.

Of everyone in the group, I know Marcus best. He's also the one who inadvertently gave Molly the black eye. I checked with Andre, and Molly did spend the night at Jess's the night she came over. Further exonerating Molly, the accident did happen. Coop talked with multiple theater kids. Molly got wacked pretty good by scenery. The dangers of theater, who would have thought?

After that, I'd decided Andre and Coop's intel was enough, and I had better things to do than chase down dead-end leads, but . . . here he is.

"Hey, Marcus, Molly ever forgive you for the black eye?" I say it kindly, trying very hard to keep my comment light.

Marcus gives me a tight smile. "Sure, she forgave me." For a long minute he scrutinizes me like one might inspect week-old leftovers. He sniffs and leaves the group without another word. The three girls still with Molly join Marcus, leaving me and Molly alone.

Yep, I'm toast.

Any final, last-second hopes I have of Molly being unaware of the Kristi situation evaporate as she won't meet my eyes.

"I've got to go, Jude," she says, still not looking at me. Her posture is hurt, wounded, embarrassed, and I want to explain, to tell her it's stupid. To tell her whatever I need to.

The seriousness of the situation didn't really hit home until this very second. I hurt Molly. It seems ridiculous that anything I could do would have this type of effect on her. I was pretty sure she liked me, but I'm not worth this, am I? It would appear so, and it's almost more than I can bear.

"Molly, can I please talk to you?"

For an instant, I think she'll refuse. She still hasn't made eye contact, but then she looks up at me and tilts her head without speaking. The hurt is replaced in a second by something much sharper.

Oh boy.

"Uhhh," I stutter. Her change in demeanor completely knocks me out of my game. "How was your day?"

She raises her eyebrows. A smile too sweet to be true forms on her red lips. "It was great. How was yours? Anything noteworthy happen?"

"No. Not really."

Her smile turns thin. "I hear Kristi Wallace is having a good day. She's letting everyone know she and a certain football player are together."

"Together? Like . . . *together*?" I ask, unable to keep the confusion from my voice. "What does that even mean?"

"I don't know, Jude. Maybe you should ask Kristi."

"It's not like that. It's this stupid thing Coop did."

"You don't owe me an explanation," Molly says, with a startling lack of emotion.

"Coop asked—" I stop. Blaming Coop is wrong. I could have blown it all up, but I didn't. Truth is, finding the killer and saving Dad are the only things I should care about. I take a deep breath. "I asked Kristi to get coffee, but I don't want anything more than to be friends with her."

Molly shrugs. "No explanation needed."

"But I want to," I say. "I want you to understand."

Molly crosses her arms. "Great. Explain it."

I open and close my mouth several times as Molly's expression becomes more brittle.

"I need to talk to Kristi about some things," I finally say. "That's it."

"I understand completely now," Molly says in a way that makes it clear the opposite is true. She starts walking, following her friends, who are standing by the entrance to the auditorium on the far side of the soccer field.

I keep pace with her. "It's really stupid, and I will explain it better later, but I don't want to, you know, be less than, uh, clear."

Molly pulls up short, and I have to check myself before tripping. "Will you make things *clear* before or after you make it *clear* why you've been hanging with Hanna Smith?"

The bottom of the world drops out from under me. "What?" My voice wavers even as it goes higher. If I had a sign around my neck saying "Guilty" in neon paint, it wouldn't be any more obvious.

"Wow," Molly says. "It's true."

Molly walks. I keep pace, trying to understand. A thousand lies run through my head, but nope, I'm going to try to keep the deceit to a minimum. I have too many secrets as is. I cough, my throat tight. "Hanna's a friend of mine. That's it. A friend."

"Really? Because at the mall the other day, you acted like you didn't know her. And you sure are making a lot of friends, Jude."

"That's fair," I say. "There is nothing going on with Hanna Smith, though. Trust me. To be honest, she's kind of annoying." A question pops into my head, and I can't stop it from coming out. "How do you even know about me hanging with Hanna?"

Molly stops again. I'm ready this time and don't almost fall.

"Is that what you care about? How I know?"

I sigh. "No, that's the last thing I care about, but it might be important for me to know how you know." I groan at the total stupidity of that statement because it would only make sense if Molly knew someone wanted to kill Hanna.

"Your car, Jude. The Beast. Some Chapel girl put it on Insta. She was making fun of it parked in front of that mansion. Hanna's house. They're making fun of you. Is that the people you want to be around? To be friends with?"

I run my fingers through my hair and try to explain. "Hanna's annoying, but she's not a snob." Molly's face darkens at my words, and I wish I'd learn to shut up.

"Is that right?" Molly asks dangerously. "Well, last I checked, Hanna was also spending time with Lucas."

Molly wants a reply, but I am speechless.

Molly shakes her head, and I see a little of the hurt and embarrassment from earlier. "Look, Jude. I'm not into love triangles, or squares, or whatever this is. I thought you were different."

"I *am* different. You are the only person I'm interested in. Kristi and Hanna are literally just friends."

"*Friends*," she says, the word so flat it sounds like a curse. "I can't, Jude. With what happened with Lucas, I just can't." She steps close. "We've been having fun together. I felt like things were going somewhere. Then this? Put yourself in my place. Kristi Wallace and Hanna Smith?"

I put as much sincerity in my voice as I can. "I know what it looks like, but I'm telling you I am only interested in *you*."

She shakes her head. "Actions and words, Jude." She pokes me in the chest and there is no denying the simmering anger in her hazel eyes. "I have to go." She backs up. "Good luck tonight." Her tone turns impossibly sweet. "I'll be *cheering* for you."

CHAPTER 24

The air is crisp, charged, full of electricity, not only in the excitement of the game but in the black clouds that have moved in over the last hour. Despite the brewing storm, the stadium lights above are bright, lighting the field like noon on Sunday. The band plays "Crazy Train" as the cheerleaders and steppers dance. It's fall in Arkansas.

It's time to play football.

As messed up as my life is, I can't help but be pulled in by the thrill of a game I was born to play. For a little while, for four quarters, I'm going to allow myself to have fun. I know that's what Dad would want.

The whistle blows and the band stops playing. All I can hear is my heart thumping in my chest as Cade, our kicker, moves forward. I move too, breaking the line at a sprint as the ball flies off Cade's foot. Then I'm running, all thoughts of dreams and the evil that men do leaving me as I focus on the kid who caught the ball.

The ball carrier, number six, runs five yards as I close in. A blocker tries to cut me off, but I shrug him off and keep moving. Number six sees me and jukes, but it's too late. I drive through him, wrap him up, and drive him to the turf. The ball flies free, and I scream through my mouthpiece, "Ball!"

I disentangle myself from number six to get the fumble, but Munson beats me to it, scooping the ball up with one meaty hand while running full speed. He flattens a Chapel player trying to tackle him and saunters into the end zone.

The entire kickoff team runs to Munson and celebrates. I slap Munson on the back as others jump around him. "Good stick, Erickson," Munson says as we jog off the field together. The animosity between us is still there, but it's game time, and we're teammates. We'll have time enough to hate each other later.

We trot back onto the field. And I am drawn to the thick boiling mass of clouds that fill the sky. They look ominous, oppressive in their weight. As strange as it sounds, I almost feel a connection with them. The stress of the last few weeks knots up my muscles like coiling snakes, threatening to break free at any moment.

We kick off again. This time Chapel manages not to cough the ball up, and our defense takes the field. I get the call from the sideline and bark out the coverage and formation. Chapel's offense comes up to the ball, and I get my first clear view of Jerry Thomas. He's a tall kid, but thin. Not frail, but long. Long arms, long legs, and a light in his eye I recognize. The kid's a baller.

Jerry wears the number two jersey. I have a quick laugh at that. He was number two on Hanna's list. He's also a pushy, narcissistic rich boy who doesn't take no for an answer. Does that mean he's a killer?

Love or money.

Hanna rejected him hard, and Hanna, being Hanna, she let everyone know what a creep he was.

It's not quite love. It's twisted, but it tracks with what Dad taught me.

It's up to me. Hanna's got nothing, hasn't been able to provoke him or get anything out of their mutual friends.

Coop, Hanna, and I all have jobs. Coop's job is to watch Kristi and her mother. See if they do anything suspicious. Hanna has been snooping around Stan's office and probing Stan with questions. She thinks it's unlikely Josh knows about her, but she's not certain yet.

Tonight, cheering for Chapel, Hanna will be on the lookout for anyone acting odd, possibly stalking her. I've given her tips on what to look for. Loners, people who don't belong at the game, or anyone giving her the stink eye or staring too much. It's not likely to happen, but I suppose anything's possible.

Right now, my job is Jerry Thomas.

Jerry scans our defense, making his reads on the line. "Kill, kill, kill!" he screams. It's a kill call. In the huddle, he called two plays. After reading our D, Jerry killed the first play, checking into the second.

I step up to the line. "Shift, shift, shift!" I call. Munson and the rest of the D line shift to the right, our weakside linebacker walking up. This is a chess match Jerry and I will be playing all night.

Jerry's back in the shotgun. He hikes his leg, setting his slot into motion. I watch his eyes. Some QBs have tells. Their eyes, lingering on the receiver or back they are going to prior to the play. Part of being a good middle linebacker is being able to pick up on these tells and anticipate what's going to happen. Jerry doesn't give anything away.

He claps his hands, and the ball is snapped. The offensive linemen pass block. Jerry holds the ball high, his eyes lifting to the receivers, but I'm already moving. As soon as I saw it was a pass, I was moving. Coach D thinks we can rattle Jerry. Coach D says I'm the special weapon. Jerry is a good runner, but he might be an even better passer. I'm his spy.

Wherever Jerry goes, so do I. If he drops back to pass, I blitz. My job is to hound Jerry Thomas, and that's what I'm going to do, in more ways than one.

Jerry sees me coming, but too late. I hit him, and he grunts as we land on the turf with me on top, our face masks pressing against each other. "Why'd you do it?" I ask over my mouthpiece.

Jerry looks at me, his eyes narrow, and he pushes me up, giving nothing away. I stand and offer a hand to help him up, but he ignores it. Linemen I blew past to sack their quarterback surround me, giving me stone-cold glares. I push past them and trot back to my huddle, getting high fives and slaps on the back.

The game goes on. It's not a blowout like most of our meetings with Chapel. We're hanging with them this year, matching them play for play. Every opportunity I get, I ask Jerry a question. *Why'd you do it? Did falling down the stairs hurt you as bad as me? Do you still have the hammer?* Jerry is getting frustrated, but he's giving nothing away. With each question, Jerry's irritation and obvious confusion grow. It doesn't help that I'm up in his grill all night.

At the end of two quarters, the game is tied fourteen to fourteen, and both teams trot off the field for halftime.

In the field house, we get hydrated as we sit in small groups with our position coaches. After ten minutes, Coach D calls us all in. "Two more quarters, gentlemen," he says, every eye on him. "Four years. That's how long it's been since we beat these guys. You seniors were in the eighth grade. We know these kids," Coach Davis says, pointing his finger through the walls to where Chapel is probably getting a similar halftime speech. "We go to church with them, shop at the same store with them. Some of your parents work with their parents." He pauses dramatically, the intensity of his eyes flickering as a smile plays on his lips. "Well. Most of your parents *work* for some of their parents."

Rough laughter echoes throughout the room.

"Tonight though," Coach says, the smile growing, "money and position and whose house is bigger, whose car is nicer . . . none of that matters. Pop these rich kids in the mouth, make them bleed, and watch them quit. Be relentless. Don't let them up for air. Let's take the fight to them. You hear me?"

A roar goes up that I add my voice to.

"You hear me?" Coach almost screams.

We stand and roar that we hear him. I love Coach D. There is nothing I wouldn't do for him.

Coach eyes us. "Good. We're receiving, so I want return team ready to go. Everyone in on Munson."

We crowd in and Munson screams, "Bulldogs on three. One, two, three."

"Bulldogs," we scream as one, and exit the locker room for the second half.

The next two quarters are a blur. Black clouds swirl above, and the wind on the field is strong enough to affect play, the storm threatening to break at any moment. We score, they score. We make a big play. They make a bigger play. I am on Jerry Thomas like white on rice. He can't get away from me, and every chance I get, I ask him another question. *How long did you plan it? Why her? Was it a jealousy thing or was it revenge?* In the first half, he ignored me. Now Jerry gives short, often obscene answers to most of my questions. Most of his suggestions are imaginative but, anatomically speaking, impossible.

By the end of the game, I still don't know if Jerry tried to kill Hanna.

I'm out of time. Chapel is in the huddle. It's fourth and goal from the seven-yard line. We're up by four, thirty-eight to thirty-four. Three seconds remain on the clock. This is it. One play. They score, they win. We hold, we win. This is the closest game I've ever played against Chapel. They usually have the game won by the third quarter. Not tonight. Grim determination paints Chapel's faces as they come to the line in a packed formation. It's killing them that they aren't dominating us like usual. I love it.

There's not an empty seat in the house, and hardly any fans are sitting down on either side. Even the bands, usually the best of sports, are playing over each other as Jerry scans our defense.

I have daydreamed about this moment for the past three years.

Joy and anguish, victory or defeat, are separated by seven green yards.

The bands stop playing, Chapel's side goes quiet, and our fans scream like wild banshees. I point at Jerry across the line from me, and scream, spittle flying from my mouthpiece, "I'm bringing the *hammer,* Jerry!"

His eyes narrow for an instant, but he dismisses me just as quickly. Confusion or guilt. I don't know.

One play is all that's left.

I get the call from the sideline. "Fifty-three fire mike weak," I call the play as Jerry moves his tailback to the other side of him. We've made adjustments and I haven't blitzed in over a quarter, but if they spread it out, I have the all clear. I'll make a beeline to Jerry. My mouth waters as Jerry calls the audible. "Kill, kill, kill. Blue, blue, blue. Omaha. Omaha," he yells, telling his guys what play they are going to run. The packed formation spreads out. The back moves out wide too.

Empty set, five wide. I shiver with anticipation.

Jerry's alone back in the backfield. The call is perfect. Munson will stunt too, slant right into B gap, and I will ride his coattails through A gap. If the play goes right, I might have a shot at another sack. If that happens, the game is over, and we win.

Munson yells something incoherent, and the kid across from him blinks. Despite myself, I admire Munson at this moment. I am a good football player. Munson is on a different level. Munson has hit Jerry even more times than I have. Mr. Thomas is gonna be sore in the morning.

Jerry barks out the cadence, and the ball is snapped. The world becomes high definition.

There are times in your life when you are free. When you truly are ten feet tall and bulletproof. Times when you are an unstoppable force, a thing of power and glory. This is one of those times. Munson crashes down. Chapel's center, big number sixty-eight, is confused by the stunt and moves with Munson. A hole in the offensive line opens like the gates of heaven.

I lose myself. The crowd is gone. Every worry I've ever known is nothing, not now, not in this place, in this moment.

After an eternity, after one lone heartbeat, Jerry Thomas sees me coming. His eyes go wide. He tucks the ball and tries to scramble, but the outcome is inevitable. The football gods have spoken.

Above, the black clouds that have gathered erupt with thunder and lightning. Harsh streaks break the sky, pitchforking out, doubling and tripling their number as if some unseen dam has finally burst. Jerry's eyes widen at the spectacle and drift up, even as he tries to spin away. I am not overcome with any such emotion. The storm is within me, and it is good. It is mine.

I hit Jerry Thomas at a full sprint, driving him into the turf. He grunts as the air rushes from him, just as rain splatters the back of my neck. The world comes back in a flash of sound and fury. The whistle blows and the horn sounds, ending the game.

I'm face-to-face with Jerry, the ball pinned between us. He groans. Hanna didn't want me to use her name. I was to rattle him and judge his response. But Hanna Smith isn't the boss of me. And this is my last chance. "We found your book, Jerry. Why'd you do it? Why'd you try to kill Hanna?"

His eyes focus, and he pushes me off him. I get up, offering him my hand once more. He eyes my hand and stands up on his own. The rain begins to fall in earnest as both teams jog out onto the field to shake hands. Coach D and Chapel's coach are at the fifty. They share a few words and the briefest of handshakes as most people head to the locker room.

The stands are emptying out, all except the band. Every kid up there has donned raincoats and is playing us out. The tubas start by laying down the baseline. DA-DADA-DA-DA-DA-DU-DUDU. It sounds just like heaven. I love those guys.

Jerry pulls his helmet from his head, letting the rain flatten his sweaty brown hair. "You are the weirdest—" The deluge of words that follow are classic Jerry. I let him ramble as I take in the hurt he is experiencing at the loss. True loss, true emotion. And confusion. True, true confusion. Jerry Thomas really thinks I'm a weirdo.

He pushes the football he still holds deep into my chest. "Enjoy the win. Just know, tomorrow, when you wake up, you'll still be white trash."

I clamp down on the football and smile. "Scoreboard, rich boy. Scoreboard. Now get off my field."

His mouth works, but he can't seem to find the appropriate response. "Prick," he finally settles on. It's pretty tame for some of the other things he's called me tonight. I take off my helmet. I don't smile.

We stay that way for a few seconds, then he mumbles something about loser, turns, and walks away. He joins the last few stragglers of his team leaving the field. I turn my head up to the rain, letting it wash over me as the band plays on.

One thing I'm now certain of: Jerry Thomas isn't the killer. I saw it in his eyes. I heard it in his voice. I know all I need to know. Jerry is a good athlete, and he's a jerk.

But he's not like me. He's not a killer.

CHAPTER 25

I run from the field, water splashing up around me as lightning strikes and thunder rolls. A whole group of kids are huddled under the stands waiting for a break in the downpour. Over the wind, someone calls my name. I turn, and Coop motions me over. I jog over and slip under the bleachers.

He's wearing one of the cheap see-through rain ponchos they sell in the concession stand. "Good game, dude. You're, like, really good at football."

"Thanks."

He motions me away from the crowd, and I follow him, but there's not a ton of room under the bleachers. He pulls his rain poncho away from his face so he can speak quietly. "So, uh, I need to start with some bad news. Get it out of the way."

"All right. What's up?"

"Chuck was at the game, and I took a few minutes to interrogate him. Outside his normal surroundings, he was a little more loose-lipped. I think he might have been a little drunk, too. He and his boys were whooping it up pretty good."

"Mall Cop Chuck?"

"You know any other Chucks?"

"I don't even know *that* Chuck."

"Right, anyway. The cameras in the food court are on the fritz. They haven't worked in years, apparently. Something about the management company of the mall being on the brink of bankruptcy. The front door cameras are out too. The only cameras that work are in the parking lot. There is no video, dude. None that would help us."

It's a gut punch. I was counting on video evidence. I close my eyes. "That . . . really sucks."

"I know," Coop says, and I hear real disappointment in his voice. I consider the little guy. "It's not your fault. We move on. What else you got?"

Coop adjusts the poncho again. "Kristi's mom spent all her time taking selfies and posting stuff. I caught most of it."

"Did you learn anything?"

"Loads. She really, really likes taking pictures of herself and posting them on the internet."

"Anything *useful*."

Coop shrugs. "Besides writing out a confession on Twitter, only to delete it and start over seven or eight times?"

"Really?" I ask.

"No, dude. Of course not."

I take a deep breath. "Then what did she do?"

"I'll tell you what she didn't do," Coop says. "She didn't watch one snap. She didn't even watch Kristi cheer. She was on her phone the whole time. Posting and whatever. I mean, she has like an electronics problem or something." He leans in closer. "Wacky for sure, but maybe not homicidal. More like garden-variety nutty. I don't think she's the one, but I can't be positive. What about Jerry?"

I shake my head. "I don't think so."

I catch Molly in the crowd as I speak. Our eyes meet, and she looks away. She's with friends, talking under the far side of the bleachers.

Molly glances back, and she holds my gaze this time. A small, reluctant smile even parts her lips.

"Jude!" someone yells, and before I can even comprehend what is happening, a one hundred-pound cheerleader grabs me. Kristi Wallace comes up to my breastbone, but she squeezes me like a bear. "That was awesome," she says. "You were awesome."

"I'm soaked," I say, trying to find a way to dislodge her.

"So am I, silly," she says. "I was out there too."

I look over at Molly, and she's already leaving. I want to call out to her, but Kristi chooses that moment to break the hug, and she pushes me. She's not big, but she's surprisingly strong, and I take a step back. "Get out of here," she says. "We beat those Chapel snobs," she says with relish, conveniently forgetting she was one of those snobs a few months ago.

"We did," I say. Molly runs out into the parking lot with her group of friends. Most I recognize as theater kids. They angle toward us, laughing and splashing through the puddles and rain. Molly never even looks my way.

"Are you going to the Banjo?" Kristi asks.

Molly disappears in the downpour. Something breaks inside me.

"Jude?"

I look at a smiling Kristi. "What?" I say.

She pushes me again. "Stop it!" she squeals.

"I—"

A woman whom I imagine Kristi will look like in twenty years, only taller, interrupts me. "Is this him?"

Kristi nods. "Yep."

"He *is* cute," the woman says.

"*Mom*," Kristi complains, but she's smiling.

"Let me get a pic," Kristi's mom says. Kristi obligingly slides into me.

"Bend down," Kristi complains. "You're too tall."

What's happening? I went from the one place where the world makes sense, the football field, to this? Kristi pulls me down so that our cheeks are touching as her mother snaps off at least twenty pictures in quick-fire succession. Then her fingers work as she starts posting.

"Tag me in those," Kristi says, but her mom is only half listening.

"So," Kristi says. "Are we going to the Banjo or not?"

I'm dizzy. Things are spinning out of control. "I . . ."

"Yes," Coop says from beside me. I didn't even notice him. "Yes, we are going to the Banjo."

"You're coming, too?" Kristi asks.

Coop shrugs. "If that's not a problem. Jude promised me he'd take me. I've never been."

"That is adorable," Kristi says, patting Coop's cheek like he's a kid. It's a comical scene. Coop doesn't seem to mind at all. Kristi looks up at me. "Pick me up in thirty?"

I'm speechless. Moments ago, I got the most satisfying win of my life. Now I'm . . . going to the Banjo with Kristi Wallace?

"Kristi, come on, we have to get you home and dried out," Kristi's mom says. The crowd under the bleachers has dwindled, and the rain is finally slacking off.

"This is going to be fun," Kristi says, grabbing the collar of my shoulder pads and pulling me down to plant a soft peck on my cheek. "Don't be late." She hurries off to catch up with her mother, who's still on her phone.

I look over at Coop. "What did you do?"

Coop cuts his eyes at me, annoyed. "My job. We have to interrogate the suspect."

"Interrogate the suspect? You watch too much TV."

"I used to, then I met you. More entertainment than a boy needs. Why don't you hit the showers? You smell like a wet bull."

"You think Molly will be at the Banjo?" I ask.

Coop lets out a long breath. "Of course she will. She's a cool kid. All the cool kids will be there. Do you know where Kristi lives?"

A bitter laugh escapes me. "No."

"Better text her then." He looks over at me. "And cheer up, man. I mean, Kristi might be a psycho hammer murderer, but she seems fun at least."

"Yeah," I say, not meaning it at all. "Fun."

CHAPTER 26

I suppress a groan as we roll up into the Banjo parking lot. It's packed. For someone who hates crowds, I seem to be seeking them out a lot lately. Kristi sits in the passenger seat. Her mom took at least seventy-five pictures before we could leave. She's applying something to her lips in the visor mirror. Coop is in the back seat. Coop and Kristi chatted the entire drive, but I can't bring myself to make small talk. No one seems to mind.

By tomorrow, there will be a year's worth of pictures on the internet of me and Kristi, and I imagine Molly scrolling through them all. Will she be able to see how miserable I am? I look over at Kristi. The sooner I can clear her and her mom, the better. "You know Hanna Smith?" I ask.

Coop makes a noise between a groan and a sigh as Kristi whips her eyes over at me.

"Sure. I know her. Why?" Her words are sharp and clipped.

It's the first real thing I've said all night, and I get a little thrill from Kristi's reaction.

Coop clears his throat awkwardly. "We . . . She's, like, the worst?" Coop's words sound like a question.

Kristi frowns, but I'm not sure it's genuine. "That's a horrible thing to say, Coop. Poor thing. You can't blame her. It's no wonder she is the way she is."

"The way she is?" I ask.

"I don't gossip, Jude Erickson." She waits, and when it's obvious no one's going to respond, she continues. "Fine. Everybody knows, anyway. Her parents hate each other."

"Okay," I say. "That's not too uncommon."

"No, Jude. I mean, they *hate* each other. They fight. In public," Kristi says, scandalized. "It's all that money."

"What money?" Coop asks.

"I thought you knew her," Kristi says, enjoying this a little too much. "Hanna's dad is a big-time lawyer and—"

"Wait," I say. "I thought he was an accountant."

Kristi is annoyed at my interruption. "Lawyer, *accountant*, whatever. He made all his money in real estate and has, like, an ironclad prenup. If Hanna's mom leaves, she gets nothing. So, she won't leave because she likes all her nice things, and he's, like, Mr. Toxic Masculinity and won't let her leave anyway.

"Hanna can't stand either one of them. Do you know what she calls her own father?" Kristi doesn't wait for a response. "Stan. She calls him *Stan*." She flips her short dark hair. "Poor, poor thing. I feel sorry for her," she says, with a little too much sympathy in her voice. "Anyhoo, can we stop talking about Hanna Smith? We came here to have fun, so let's have some fun." She bounces in her seat and leans over and punches me, not too lightly, in the arm. "Come on! It's happy fun-time." She gets out of the Beast and shuts the door behind her.

Coop doesn't move. "She's a high-energy type of girl, huh?"

"High-energy is one way to describe her."

"She's not that bad," Coop says.

I turn in my seat and lower my voice. "Seriously?"

Coop glances at an oblivious Kristi outside the passenger window. "You really have a skewed view of people. No one is all good or all bad. Most people are a little of both. Kristi is obviously jealous of Hanna. People twist their pain in strange ways sometimes. Besides, she let me come, dude. She's nice. She could have made me feel unwelcome. People do that, you know."

"Who?"

"Lots of people. You don't notice because you're, well, you. You're kind of operating outside normal social structures, being really good at stuff involving running and sweating. Lucky you. But I notice. Trust me. I don't think she did it."

Kristi's waving at us to come on. I try to smile at her, but I don't think I pull it off. "Uh-huh," I say noncommittally.

We get out, joining Kristi. The rain has moved on, leaving the night colder than normal. "Ohh, there are so many people here," Kristi says, eyeing a group of cheerleaders. "Why don't y'all order a pizza. I'll be there in a sec. Cheese," Kristi says. "Gluten-free. Get me a water too." She skips off to talk to her friends.

"This is your fault," I tell Coop.

We leave Kristi to her friends and enter the Banjo. The crowd outside was light compared to the throng of humanity inside. People are everywhere: in booths, at tables, or just standing. There're hundreds of conversations going on and lots of laughing. A rap song, popular when my dad was a kid, plays. The bass thumps in my chest as the hook asks if you want to take a ride.

I get the usual greetings. I also catch a few awkward glances thrown Coop's way. I think about our conversation and how he has to navigate a world of social acceptance I was oblivious to. He's all smiles though, lit up with a grin that covers his face. "This is how the other half lives, huh?"

"Yep," I say. "It's all downhill from here."

It takes a while, but we find a table and order right away. Kristi comes to join us a few minutes later. "This is so much fun," she says, and squeals for emphasis. And I realize this is her first time at the Banjo, too.

"What does Chapel do after a game?"

"Nothing really," she says, looking out over the crowd. "This is like something out of a different time. It's so, I don't know. It's like we went in a time machine. You guys are so cute. So quaint."

I share a glance with Coop. He just smiles.

We sit and hang out for a while. Kristi rattles on about one thing after another, never waiting for, wanting, or expecting a response. I try to nod or grunt at the appropriate times, but I don't think Kristi cares. Our pizza comes pretty quick, and I dive in.

Coop nudges me and juts his chin toward the front door. Munson is in the house. Hanna is with him. I let out a long-suffering sigh. There's a killer on the loose, and Hanna is putting herself in dangerous situations. The killer hid their identity the first time, but who's to say they will again? If the killer doesn't care if they're caught, they could have shot her in the parking lot or run her over with a car.

She says she won't live her life scared, but she should try a little harder than this. She could have at least told me she was coming.

"Speaking of the devil herself," Kristi says, sipping her water and eyeing Hanna. "She's a Chapel cheerleader. You'd think she'd know better than to come here."

Munson's crew of D linemen and hangers-on swarm over their boy. A few girls chat with Hanna. Kristi eyes the whole procession, sipping water.

Coop leans in so only I can hear. "If looks could kill."

He's right. Kristi is bad at hiding her emotions. I would call her present expression unadulterated malice.

Kristi stands up. "I'm going to mingle. Don't eat all the pizza." She pats me on the shoulder and leaves.

Coop tears into his fourth piece of pizza like he's never seen food before. "Whatcha think, my dude? Is our cheerleader the bad guy?"

I lean back in the chair. "I don't think so, but this is hard."

"Yeah," Coop says. "A confession would save us a lot of time."

I watch Kristi make the rounds. She's only been at Bedford a week, but she's more popular than I've ever been.

"I'm almost certain the killer was bigger," I say, "but Dad says memory in stressful situations is unreliable."

"The whack to the head probably didn't help either," Coop says.

I take a bite of pizza and talk with my mouth full. "Hanna says the killer might have been wearing puffy clothes like a skiing jacket. I don't remember that at all." I swallow my food and take a big gulp of water. Kristi moves on from the dude she was talking to and heads right for Hanna.

"Oh boy," Coop says, sitting up. "You seeing this?"

I groan. It's doubtful Kristi will strangle Hanna with all these witnesses, but I'd rather not have an awkward scene, either.

"Dinner and a show," Coop says, feeling the opposite of me, apparently. He frowns. "Wait. What's the chances Kristi has a hammer hidden up her sleeve?"

Hanna smiles as Kristi approaches. It appears genuine, but Hanna is good at hiding emotions . . . and huge secrets, too, like her family's involvement in drug empires.

The girls hug, Hanna bending down for the smaller girl. Coop and I eat pizza and watch the interaction. If anything, it appears to be warm and genuine. Kristi even waves over some of her fellow cheerleaders and appears to introduce them to Hanna. Soon they're all talking and laughing. Even Munson and his guys join in.

Hanna catches my eye from across the room and gives the slightest of shrugs.

Coop grunts over a mouthful of pizza. He takes a long drink of soda to wash it down. "Well, Kristi just moved way down the list, wouldn't you say?"

"Looks like it," I agree.

"You know, Jude, something's been bothering me."

"What's that?"

"I understand how this works, kind of," Coop says. "You kill the killer blah, blah, blah, but—it's one thing to kill someone when they are actively trying to murder someone else, but to kill someone in, well, cold blood. Kristi or even her mom? Could you do that? Would you?"

It's a good question. One I've been asking myself ever since that night. For an instant, I think of Dad. I have to do this for him. A pang of guilt shoots through me, and I'm not sure if it's guilt over what I might have to do, or what I won't do. "It's what I was trained for," I say, avoiding the question.

"So, could you?" Coop asks again.

I sigh. "I don't know." But that's not true. I shift, suddenly uncomfortable in my chair. "It depends, I suppose. If it's Josh Stroup, for sure." I bite my lip. "If it's Tommy or Kristi or someone like that . . . I don't know."

A weight seems to be lifted from Coop, relief evident in his face. "That's what I thought." He sits up straighter, looking past my shoulder. "Holy smokes. Those dudes aren't in high school."

I follow Coop's eyes, and my heart starts to thump in my chest. Josh Stroup just walked in like he owns the place. Two massive humans are with him, and I know them both: Brian Barnes and Billy Blake. Both are two years older than me.

In junior high, everyone called them the BBs because you rarely saw one without the other. They always got into trouble at school too, so much so that they dropped out in tenth grade.

All three are wearing long sleeves and their haircuts are similar. Shaved on the side and long on top.

"Do you know them?" Coop asks. "Looks like three dudebros looking for a frat party."

"The smallest one is Josh Stroup," I say. "The other two are Billy Blake and Brian Barnes. The BBs."

"Daaaaaaaaang," Coop says, drawing out the word. "Maybe all the suspects will come eat pizza tonight and we can solve this caper."

I glance at him. "Caper?"

"That's what these are called," Coop says. The sauce formerly in the corner of his mouth has migrated to his chin as he continues to eat. He's having way too much fun.

The sea of teenagers spreads before Josh and the BBs as they walk over to a table occupied by a group of sophomores. Words are exchanged. Words I can't hear, but the message is clear: the sophomores clear out, eyes downcast.

Staring at Josh from across the room, it's like the day I met him on Hanna's lawn and he almost pulled a weapon on me. This guy evokes something primeval inside me, something less evolved, something angry. The caveman inside me roars.

"Dude," Coop says. "Are you growling?"

The trance is broken in an instant. "No," I say a little too quickly.

A waitress comes to take Josh's order. She shakes her head a few times, uncomfortable. She scurries off, and in a minute, the manager is at the table taking their order instead. She also shakes her head. Josh is all smarmy smiles as he produces his ID. The BBs do the same. The manager frowns at the IDs, shuffling them in her hand as she studies each one. Her frown deepens as she gives them back and exchanges words with Josh. She hesitates a second or two more and hurries off, returning after a time with a pitcher of beer and three mugs.

Kristi comes back and sits down. "What'd I miss?"

"Nothing much," Coop says. "Just some old dudes crashing the party."

It doesn't take Kristi long to find Josh and his crew. "Eww, Josh Stroup."

I glance at her. "You know him very well?"

Kristi prepares her utensils like she's at cotillion. "He went to Chapel, sold weed, pills, that kind of thing. Coop! How many slices did you eat?"

"Dunno," Coop says, his mouth crammed. "I . . . hungry."

Kristi cracks up at a grinning, cheek-bulging Coop.

"Saw you talking to Hanna," I say as casually as I can.

"Why wouldn't I? We used to go to school together."

"Yeah," I say, "but back in the car I got the impression y'all weren't close."

Kristi takes a piece of pizza off the dish and puts it on her plate. If she uses her fork to eat it, I might have to leave. "In all honesty," Kristi says, "we didn't really care for each other at Chapel. She was always a little jealous of me. But I decided to let it go. Life is too short. I went and made peace."

Coop, for a second or two at least, has stopped eating. "So you went and buried the hammer?"

"Hammer?" Kristi laughs. It's the odd nasally variety, a high-pitched hooting like a cracked-up baby owl. "It's *hatchet*, Coop, not hammer. But yes. Yes, I did. And I feel good about it."

Coop gives me a raised eyebrow as Kristi rearranges her plate with the lone slice on it.

"I love pizza," Kristi says, picking up her slice. "I don't get it near enough. My mother doesn't eat pizza. Can you believe that?" She takes a bite.

"That's just wrong," Coop says. "Why not?"

Kristi holds up a hand as she chews and swallows. "She doesn't eat or use any animal products. She's vegan."

"Vegan? I've heard of them," Coop says. "Kind of like I've heard of aliens, but I never met one. So, your mom never eats meat."

"Never. She thinks meat is murder."

Coop cuts his eyes at me and back to Kristi. "Huh, and what does she think about murder?"

Kristi laughs. It's the real thing, no hesitation, no awkward silence. "She's against that too. She even marched last year against the death penalty. Taking a life is always wrong, no matter why."

"Well, that's nice to know." Coop looks over at me nonchalantly, as he chews his pizza.

"I mean, I'm a vegetarian," Kristi says, unaware of the silent conversation going on between Coop and me. "But cheese is too good, and ice cream." Kristi rubs her belly. "Yum. Oh, and I eat fish too."

Coop hee-haws, almost falling out of his chair.

"What?" Kristi asks, all smiles, swatting at him playfully.

"I'm no expert, but you're not a vegetarian."

Kristi shrugs. "Fine, but I don't eat the *cute* animals."

They both laugh, having a legit good time with each other, and I can't help but think of Molly. I should be here with her. I look around the Banjo, but I don't see her.

Coop and Kristi laugh at another of Coop's jokes.

My fake date and a kid I didn't know a few weeks ago, having a great time. It's suddenly clear that I'm not needed. I'm useless in more than one way.

Why I had to go on a date with Kristi and hurt Molly to get to this point is beyond me, but at least now the pretense can end. I stand and Coop and Kristi look up at me.

"Where are you going?" Kristi asks.

"To the bathroom."

"I need to go too," Coop says.

I want to tell him to stay, to enjoy himself some more with his date, but that would be petty. That would be weak.

As Coop stands, Josh Stroup spots me. I don't like the grin that spreads across his face, but honestly, I'm too tired to care. I head to the bathroom with Coop on my heels.

CHAPTER 27

Coop looks up as we wash our hands. "Kristi's nice, huh?"

I grab a paper towel. "Yeah, she's a real *hoot*."

Coop misses my sarcasm, or ignores it, fixing his hair in the mirror. "Yep. She is."

The door opens, and Brian and Billy come in. They let the door shut behind them but don't move away from it.

I close my eyes and lower my head. I should have seen this coming, but I thought the Banjo would be safe. There are so many people here.

Josh Stroup, despite a relatively weak motive, has won the honor of the top spot on my list.

I take in the situation. Besides getting into trouble, the second thing the BBs enjoy is working out. Both are rock solid with muscle. One of them, Billy, I think—I can never remember which is which—whistles. "Jude Erickson. I hear you like to mad-dog people. How 'bout you try that on *us*?"

Until one of them spoke, it was all just conjecture. Now it's real. To my surprise, Coop laughs. "That's—no, man. That's really bad."

The BBs share a confused glance, but Coop isn't done. "Your intimidation game, dude. It needs serious work. Like maybe," he deepens his voice. "Jude Erickson. I'm here to claim your throne. No, no, no, that's weird given we're in the bathroom. Toilets, thrones, you know. Maybe something short and sweet." He clears his throat and does the deep voice thing again. "Jude Erickson. Time to diiiiie." He draws out *die* way too long, his voice going down an octave. Coop holds his hands out, palms up, expectantly. "Better, right?

"Shut it," Billy says.

"Honestly," Coop says. "I think you're a lost cause. Maybe just loom. Speaking kind of ruins the whole *I crush you* vibe."

I glance at Coop. "*What are you doing?*" I try to whisper, but the bathroom isn't that big.

"When I get nervous, I start talking," Coop whispers back. "It's kind of my thing. You should know this by now."

Billy shakes his head. "Not here for you, little boy. Stay quiet and maybe we only slap you around a little. We're here for the football wannabe."

Coop makes a face. "*Football wannabe.* Yeah," he says. "It's official. You're bad at this."

Billy ignores Coop. His gaze fixes on me. "You disrespected a friend of ours. That can't stand."

Brian—I think that one is Brian—has been trying to bore holes in my skull with his eyes this whole time. Now he grins at Billy's pronouncement. They came for violence. I have no doubt about it now.

Years ago, so far back it seems like it was in another life, Dad taught me the first rule of any fight. Avoid it.

"I don't want this to happen," I say. And I mean it.

"I'm sure you don't." Billy laughs. In my mind's eye, the next few minutes play out. I'm going to have to play dirty—groin shots, eye rakes, whatever it takes. My muscles tense, ready to move. I can't win, two big brutes against me, the tight space, but I'm backed in a corner, and I need to give Coop a chance to get out of here unhurt.

With that decision made, an overwhelming sense of calm washes over me. This is what I am. This is what I do. The world goes still . . . and the bathroom door opens.

"What's going on in here?" A cop stands in the door, coming in and letting it shut behind him. Billy and Brian are forced farther in the bathroom. The cop is middle-aged, with a thick middle and thick black eyebrows over an unremarkable face. His gaze flicks to me, Coop, and the BBs.

"Not now, Uncle Fred," Brian says. I think it's Brian, anyway. Okay, that one is Brian from now on. Someone really should give them nametags.

The officer's face goes red. His name badge reads Jamison. It clicks. This is Chief Fred Jamison. The bought and paid for police chief of Rush Springs.

"Is there any reason I got a call about some underage kids trying to pass off fake IDs? Milly called my cell phone. My *cell phone.*"

"Not now, Uncle Fred," Brian says. "We're in the middle of something."

Jamison looks me over but addresses the BBs. "Seems to me if I was supposed to be looking out for a certain person, help keep that person out of trouble and such, I'd be with him and not in the john."

"*John,*" Coop says like he's discussing a fine wine. "Did y'all know bathrooms are sometimes called johns because of Sir John Harrington? He was a godson of Queen Elizabeth I. He invented the flush toilet. He was kind of a freak, though, liked to write dirty poetry."

All eyes go to Coop. Chief Jamison looks especially confused. "Who is this kid?"

"Nobody," Billy says.

"Uh-huh," Chief Jamison says. "Welp. Billy, Brian. Pizza time is over. You guys are leaving. Now. You don't pass go. You leave, and you head to your car. I'm right behind you, and if you so much as shuffle your feet, you'll regret it. We're leaving. Together. Fake IDs? What the hell?"

"What about Josh?" Brian snaps, anger in his voice.

Jamison huffs. "The Big Guy says Josh can find his own ride home."

"Big Guy?" I ask. "Who would that be?"

Jamison's face goes even redder. He slipped up, and he knows it. "I'm just here to keep the peace, young man. Good game tonight, by the way."

I don't say anything. Coop, thankfully, doesn't start spouting nonsense either.

Jamison nods at the door. "Get," he says to the BBs. They give me and Coop one last menacing stare and leave like dogs with their tails between their legs.

Jamison waits several seconds after the BBs leave before turning a disingenuous smile on me and Coop. "Sorry about those fellas. My nephews ain't got much manners." His fake smile broadens. "Y'all boys have a good night." He follows his nephews out the bathroom door.

Coop whistles after he's gone. "Well, that was . . . intense. Thought I might have to open a can of whoop-ass on those boys for a minute."

This night is getting on my last nerve. I take a deep breath and let it out, the adrenaline of the past few minutes draining from me. "Can you give me a minute, Coop?"

"Uh, sure, yeah, no problem." He walks to me and stops. His mouth twists, but he finally decides on a nod and leaves without another word.

I go to the sink and turn on the faucet, staring at myself in the mirror. Why is my life like this? My reflection has no answers, and I have the sudden and unexplained desire to break the glass.

Some kid comes in, and the spell is broken. I wash my hands again and leave the bathroom.

The noise of the Banjo washes over me as I make my way through the crowd. Jamison and the BBs are nowhere to be seen. Coop is right outside the door, talking with a group of kids I don't recognize. Their eyes are wide as Coop talks, gesturing with his arms. That kid needs to talk less, a lot less.

I move on, and Rob Thomas stops me to chat me up. Something about Andre finally getting Jess to hook him up with Payton. I half listen, grunting and nodding, but my heart's not in it. After a while, I find an opening to leave and hurry on through the crowd. The Banjo is rocking tonight. As I turn to the table I left Kristi at, my heart sinks.

Josh Stroup is sitting in my chair, talking with my date.

CHAPTER 28

Kristi doesn't look comfortable.

She's leaning back in her chair, and the smile on her lips is as tight as her shoulders. She catches sight of me. Her eyes tell me to hurry up. When Josh sees me, his eyes widen for the briefest of moments. He reaches in his pocket and pulls out his phone, reading something as I come to stand over him.

"You're in my seat," I say.

Josh takes his time with his phone, not even glancing up at me. A half-finished mug of beer sits on the table in front of him. I can't see what he's reading, but I'd bet one of the BBs just texted him from the parking lot.

Kristi tilts her head at me as if to ask what I'm going to do. "This is Josh, Jude. Do you know Josh? You know, Big Hank's son."

Josh looks up from his phone, then up at me. A slick smile cuts his face. He turns back to Kristi. "Now, what were we talking about, sweetheart?"

Something in me twists. *This guy.* My blood boils and turns to steam. Insult after insult has ruined me. I'm a failure at what I was born for. My father's gone. Molly doesn't want to know me. And the jerk who sent two dudes to hurt me—most likely a murderer—is sitting in my chair. *My chair.* With *my* date. Fake date, sure, but *my* date.

"You're in my chair," I say again.

Josh's fake smile is gone. He picks up his beer, then slides the chair to face me. He leans back, the front two legs of *my* chair coming off the floor, his eyes never leaving mine. It's posturing. He's showing me, showing the world, he's not afraid. Dark eyes fix on me, and he takes a slow sip, taunting me. "You still here?"

The world sucks. My life sucks. I cross one person off the list and add two. The BBs. It could have been either of them, sent by Josh.

Bullies, drug dealers, murderers, crooked cops, and pushy rich girls. I close my hands into fists.

All I wanted was to have a fun, *normal* senior year.

The moment I lose control doesn't feel like losing control at all. It feels good. It feels right.

I move fast, darting my right leg out and catching the front right leg of the chair below Josh's leg. I pull back, my foot slides, catching the cross bar. Josh's eyes go wide as his weight is all wrong, and the front of the chair comes up.

Josh Stroup, drug dealer, leader of muscled-up high school dropouts, and all-around slimeball, falls unceremoniously onto the floor, a half-full mug of beer splashing his preppy white shirt and smug, smug smile.

The room goes from a hundred voices talking at once to dead silence in the instant Josh, *my* chair, and his beer hit the floor. Every eye in the Banjo presses down on me.

Kristi pushes away from the spilled beer. Josh's eyes are wide. He's frozen with rage. Then he's on his feet in a second, his hand moving to his pocket, and pure murder in his eyes.

It's all wrong. *What was I thinking?* I wanted a fight. I wanted to show him he wasn't better than me. I wanted to show him *I* was the better man. Worse still, I hesitated, and that is my undoing.

Josh's hand emerges from his pocket, and the knife in his hand isn't a mere tool, it's a weapon. I was right. Josh Stroup is a knife guy.

He flicks his wrist and the blade, thin and sharp, springs out.

The world slows.

Josh cuts the air in front of me as I step back to give myself room. He slices the air again, his eyes gleaming with malice and joy. Again, the knife moves. Wide, broad strokes. It's comical. Dad would laugh.

Josh must think what he's doing looks cool or intimidating. It's not. Josh Stroup, potential killer and all-around tough guy, is an amateur with a blade.

The Banjo is alive with movement and sound, a storm of shouts and confusion. A wide circle forms around us. Chaos swirls around me, but I am calm. I am still. I am the eye of the storm.

Josh commits, lunging like a fool. Instinct brings me inside Josh's guard. Even as he tries to stick me in the gut, one of my arms knocks his hand wide, and I grab his wrist. All I have to do is twist, bend, and shove the pointy end into his left breast. The knife will slide off rib, cut through muscle, and enter the heart. Josh will be dead in a sec. But if he's not the killer, what then? That doesn't matter. Josh is trying to kill me. I need to kill him. It's perfect, justified even. More public than I wanted, but— My right foot slips on spilled beer.

Josh takes advantage of my slip and my stupid internal struggle and pulls free of my wrist hold. He swipes the blade awkwardly at my face, and I'm too close, my right foot way far in front, my base of support off, and too caught up in my feelings.

The blade cuts a line across my right cheek. There is no pain, but warmth rolls from the cut, blood instantly spilling onto my chest.

He cut me.

It's hard to comprehend. Josh is like a kid with a toy and . . . He. Cut. Me. I take a step back, then another, disengaging.

Josh's eyes gleam as he mistakes my tactical retreat as fear. He charges and makes another pitiful swipe at me. I catch his wrist, twisting hard this time, using his own momentum against him. He cries out as I wrench the bones of his forearm, pushing them far beyond their normal range of motion. Josh's hand goes limp as I slam him down on his knees before me. He cries out in agony as the knife clatters to the floor.

Bang! Bang! Bang! Gunshots ring out.

Kids crouch and run, some hitting the deck, some finding cover, but most hauling tail. At the entrance, the BBs watch me with dead eyes. Billy has a gun pointed up in the air. He puts another round in the ceiling. *Bang!* He points his weapon at me, striding across the now silent room with the gun.

Blood runs down my mangled cheek. I raise my hands in surrender as Billy Blake comes close and presses his gun to my forehead. I don't move. I don't blink, my hands up, palms facing Billy. Josh gets up, his injured arm cradled against his chest. Never have I seen such hate, such malice in anyone's eyes as I do Josh's.

The room is silent. Josh Stroup licks his lips, his eyes hooded and mean. He nods to Billy. "Do it."

Even as Billy's eyes come back to me, I'm moving. He got too close. Billy wanted to scare me, wanted to press the cold barrel to my skull. It was a mistake.

I grab Billy's wrist with one hand and the barrel of the gun with the other. My feet move without me even having to think about it as I rotate the barrel up and Billy's hand down. The gun comes free in my hands.

Billy and Josh look at me, stunned, as I point Billy's gun at his chest.

The room is quiet. Many of the kids I go to school with stare at me from the floor or behind tables. One kid, lying flat on the floor, has his phone out, recording. Billy's expression darkens, and I think the idiot might charge me.

Josh glares, his breath coming in deep gulps. If before I thought his gaze held malice, now the hate in Josh's eyes is like a living, breathing thing. Never in my life has anyone looked at me like Josh is now. I move the gun so that it points at Josh's chest.

His nostrils flare as he looks to the gun and back to me.

Josh's motive is strong enough.

He found out Hanna knew about him stealing money from his father. He wanted to silence Hanna and at the same time punish Stan for being careless with his business.

It makes perfect sense.

Josh is the killer.

The trigger beneath my finger is light as a feather, the slightest pressure and it could all end.

"Jude?"

Molly is here. Her eyes are wide. They contain a sort of strange mix of awe and tenderness. She's scared too, terrified in fact, but there is something else in her demeanor, in her expression, something I can't quite decipher. Something promising help, comfort, and relief from my pain. "Don't," she says, ever so gently.

Josh licks his lips. He's breathing hard, but his eyes have lost some of the recklessness. He bolts, running from the room, stumbling as he goes. After a heartbeat, Billy follows, joining Brian at the door, and they leave.

I pull the pistol to my chest. I'm not sure what make it is, but my thumb finds the mag release, and I drop the magazine. It clatters on the floor. I pull back the slide to eject the round in the chamber. My hands work, knowing what to do on instinct. The takedown lever is below the slide, and I work it, pulling the slide free from the frame. The gun comes apart in my hands, and I drop the useless pieces to join the magazine on the floor.

It's not until I'm done, I realize what I just did—in a room full of people, a few of them with phones out, recording. I find Coop and Kristi standing together, Hanna and Lucas watching me intently. So many people, so many faces.

In the distance, sirens wail. I hang my head, not able to meet any of the eyes on me. Molly wraps her arms around me and squeezes.

I shudder. All this time I thought I was so hard, but I'm not. I never was. I never will be. "It's okay," Molly says, letting me go. Her eyes are so calm, so penetrating. Her hand moves up to my face and her fingertips come away red. Her eyes linger on the blood, my blood. After a long second, her hazel eyes find me. They see me, really see me.

Tears leak down my cheeks. Molly reaches up and gently pulls my head down to her. The tears flow. I'm losing it, but I don't care. Neither does Molly.

"It's okay," she whispers in my ear. "It's okay."

"I'm-I'm getting blood on you," I say through ragged breaths.

"That doesn't matter," Molly says.

I shudder again, harder this time.

What is wrong with me? I am so weak, so very weak. Dad would be ashamed.

Dad. I could have ended it all tonight.

Molly holds me tighter, and I wrap her up, clinging to her. And I'm so thankful to have her holding me. Without her, I might fall.

Kristi takes that moment to walk over, her face pale. "Jude?" she says.

Molly breaks the embrace, taking a step back. My blood is red and dark against her alabaster cheek.

I swallow, trying to control my emotions. "Yes."

Kristi points to me and back at herself, her face apologetic. "I don't think this is going to work out."

CHAPTER 29

The interrogation room at Bedford PD isn't like in the movies; no one-way glass, no small table with two chairs facing each other. In fact, I'm not even positive this *is* an interrogation room. Maybe it's storage. Piles of rickety cardboard boxes are stacked on one side of the wall, and I'm sitting at a desk, just a normal desk.

Jamison cuffed and stuffed me, even as the paramedics were patching me up, even after tons of kids came forward to say Josh Stroup had been the one with the knife. The cuffs are gone, but I can still feel them. My fingers probe the bandage over my face. The paramedic said I was lucky it missed my eye, said the cut wasn't deep and might not leave a scar.

The only door in the room swings open, and Jamison and another man come into the small room. The other man is short and thin with snakeskin boots and a white cowboy hat. I recognize him at once. It's Big Hank. He sits down behind the desk and smiles a wide and toothy grin as Jamison stands by the door.

"You're Tad Erickson's son, ain't ya?"

I nod. "And you're Josh Stroup's dad."

Big Hank returns my nod. "So, we know each other now."

"Your son tried to kill me tonight," I tell him.

Jamison takes a step forward. "Watch the tone, boy."

Big Hank raises a placating hand. "It's all right, Fred. We're just two men getting to know each other." His eyes move to me. "Did he?" Big Hank asks. "Did my boy try and kill you?"

I tap the bandage over my cheek as proof. "Yeah, pretty sure he did. I'm also sure there is video evidence. Lots of video evidence."

Hank leans forward, props his elbows on the desk, and winks at me. "I once saw a video of Bigfoot. Don't make that hairy sucker real." He leans back. "Josh is in a tight spot, no doubt, but what you say, what you do, will have a profound effect on future events."

We stare at each other for a long while. Big Hank sighs. "Look, son, people get out of line on occasion. They act out of character. They make mistakes, but one man's mistake can be another's opportunity." Hank gives a quick laugh. "The way you're looking at me. I swear. You and my boy have a lot more in common than you might want to admit."

"We're nothing alike," I all but spit at him.

"Oh, but you are." Out in the hallway someone yells, at least two people arguing. Big Hank ignores it. He takes off his cowboy hat and throws it on the desk. His hair is white and thick. "You want a job, Jude?"

For half a heartbeat, I'm sure I misunderstood. "What?"

"A job. I want to offer you a job."

I stare, not comprehending what he's getting at. Is this some strange opening to a threat? Of all the things I expected Big Hank to say, that wasn't it. And it dawns on me. He's trying to buy my cooperation. People like Big Hank think money solves all their problems. Most times, he's right. Not this time.

"I already have a job."

"You mean roofing? You work with that group of degenerates your dad hires out."

"They're not degenerates," I say, my words sharp and clipped.

Big Hank raises his hands. "Just a concerned citizen, but I'd bet some of them boys did time." He glances over at Jamison. "How many of Tad's crew been on the inside? Any on parole?"

"More than a few did some time," Jamison responds sourly. "Lenny Allen went upstate for a stint back in the day. Probably should go by the worksite, make sure they got all their permits, make sure they don't have any contraband, not falling back on old habits."

I lean forward, placing my hands flat on the table. "Leave them alone."

Big Hank raises a single eyebrow. "Rest assured, my intentions are pure. Benevolent, in fact. Question is: What's your intention?" He doesn't wait for a response. "I'm offering you gainful employment, Mr. Football Stud. I'm not talking about a summer job, working for your old man. I'm talking a full-time job. Twenty an hour. Forty hours a week."

The numbers take me off guard, and I do the math in my head. Eight hundred dollars a week. He's offering me eight hundred dollars a week. The number is staggering. For a moment, I imagine taking the money. And I hate myself. Big Hank has brought so much misery onto so many people.

Hank sees my wheels turning and is encouraged. He sits up as he tries to seal the deal. "You wouldn't have to do much. Heck, you don't even have to show up. Collect a check. I'll have my people direct deposit it right into your bank account. You could even keep working for your dad. Double-dipping's what we call that."

Before he's even finished, I'm shaking my head. "There were too many witnesses, and Billy shot up the place."

"Billy ain't Josh," Hank says, his cool demeanor slipping. Out of the corner of my eye, Uncle Fred Jamison winces.

The arguing outside is getting louder, the voices moving toward us. Big Hank rubs at his perfectly shaven chin, reining in his anger. "All I need is for you to make a statement. You and Josh were horse playing, messing around, having fun."

"Fun? He cut me." The noise becomes clearer. Someone is yelling now, but the voices are muffled.

"Well, make up anything you like," Big Hank says, "as long as Josh and you weren't trying to kill each other. Maybe refuse to give a statement at all. Hard to proceed with a case if the injured party refuses to cooperate. I have people who could help you find the right words to say." Big Hank smiles and this time, it's not pleasant. "Or we could do this . . . another way."

There it is. The threat I expected. I want him to say it, though. I want to hear it from his lips. "What *other* ways are we talking about, Hank?"

Jamison's eyes widen. "Watch your mouth."

"Fred," Hank snaps, raising a hand. "Me and the boy are having a conversation."

Jamison is duly chastised and even takes a step back.

"Son," Big Hank says, "if there is one thing I've learned, it's that anything is possible with the right motivation. Question is: What motivates you? I already offered you money and you ain't bit yet. That limits my options. Limited options are bad for you and for your family."

The noise outside reaches a crescendo and the door busts open. "Ma'am, now, ma'am, you can't be back here," an officer I don't recognize says.

"Get out of my way," says a voice I would know anywhere. Lia Renee Erickson steps past the officer and into the room, her head high, her eyes taking in the scene in an instant.

It's as if time stops.

The fight with Josh, being here in the police station, even Hanna's impending doom, loses all its importance.

Three years. No phone calls. No birthday cards. Nothing. My mother left me and never looked back.

Time catches up. Jamison moves in front of her. "Whoa, whoa. What do you think you're doing?"

Mom ignores him, eyeing Big Hank.

Hank's smile shifts from me to Mom and it's the nice one again. "Lia. So nice to see you." He doesn't offer any explanation.

Mom pushes past Jamison and comes to stand behind me, looking down at Hank. She places a hand on my shoulder. I can smell the cigarettes on her. Another smell mixes with the odor of stale tobacco, something familiar, awakening emotions of times gone and buried. I haven't seen my mother in three years, despite the fact she lives only a fifteen-minute drive away. Tears want to leak from me, but the well is dry.

"What's this?" Mom asks. "You a deputy now, Hank?"

"Just a concerned citizen. Came down to make sure the boy wasn't hurt in the little misunderstanding tonight."

"Misunderstanding?" She cuts her eyes to Jamison. "Is Jude charged with a crime? Because from what I hear, he's a hero. Josh Stroup pulls a knife and starts—" She hesitates, turning my cheek up to her. When she came in, she couldn't see the bandage. Mom sucks in a sharp breath. "Has my son received medical care?"

Big Hank leans back in his chair. "You see the bandage, don't you?"

"Jude is a minor," Mom says, her words ice. "Why wasn't I notified he was in custody? We want a lawyer."

Big Hank regards my mother with cold cruel eyes. "No need for all of that."

"Can we leave, then?" Mom asks.

"This is a police matter," Jamison says. "And you—"

Mom cuts Jamison off with a quick, mocking laugh. "I wasn't talking to you, Fred. I was talking to the man in charge."

"Your boy," Chief Jamison sputters, but Big Hank holds up a hand, quieting Jamison with the slightest of gestures. If there was any doubt who ran Rush Springs, there is none now.

Big Hank picks up his cowboy hat and turns it over in his hands. "This whole situation seems so much bigger right now than it will in the morning. Lia, Jude. You can both leave, with my blessing." He tosses the cowboy hat back down. "But one thing first."

Mom says nothing, waiting for the demand.

"It would be in everyone's best interest if Jude not talk with law enforcement outside of Chief Jamison here. Not for the foreseeable future, that is."

No one moves or says a word for several seconds. Mom clears her throat. "Come on, Jude." She pulls me up from my chair, and hurries me to the door, getting between me and Jamison. It's comical. Mom, my shield.

"Jude," Big Hank says. It's a command. Mom stops, her breathing slow and deliberate.

I turn and look at Hank.

"Think about my offer. It's a wonderful opportunity for you . . . and for your family."

Mom's hand tightens on my shoulder, and I let her guide me out of the room.

CHAPTER 30

Mom's car isn't the same vehicle she had three years ago. Three years. It's hard to believe it's been that long. The car isn't the only change. At forty-five, Mom's face is harder and the lines and creases in her face are deeper. Her long, dark hair is streaked with some gray too. Something vital is missing from her eyes, a hollowness that was only hinted at the last time we were together.

Before she starts the car, she lights a cigarette and rolls down the window to blow the smoke outside like she did when I was a kid.

"You need to quit that. It's really bad for you."

She takes another drag and gives me a little sad smile. "Buckle up, Jude. I'm taking you to my place." She puts the car in reverse, the cigarette grasped expertly in her first two fingers as she uses her palm to move the shifter.

"Just take me back to Dad's. He'll be worried."

Mom backs the car up, puts it in drive, and drives slowly to the exit. "Your daddy's not home."

I turn my head sharply to stare at her, studying her face. It doesn't take long for me to see the truth. "How much do you know?" I ask.

She takes another drag on her cigarette as she turns right and accelerates down the road, glancing in the rearview like she's afraid someone's following. "You're not a good liar, Jude. Not yet."

We slow down and take a right onto the service road. Fifteen minutes, and we'll be at her house. Fifteen minutes . . . that's all that's separated us.

Fifteen minutes.

Up ahead, on the right, is a billboard for Big Hank's Mobile Homes. Big Hank smiles down on us. Funny, after not paying any attention to the billboards for years, now I can't unsee them.

"I know you had your Dream," Mom says. "I know it didn't go well, and I know your father is gone."

The admission is shocking, and I have no idea how she knows any of this, but instead of denials, I take a moment to feel the relief her knowledge brings me.

Mom knows. Can she help? A familiar low buzz of hurt and anger instantly replaces my relief.

I've wished for this moment for three years—Mom coming back, making things right. But I'm not a little kid. I know how the world works.

I compose myself before speaking, pushing my emotions down like Dad taught me. "How?" I ask, my words flat.

Mom glances at me. "You're like him now. Hard on the inside, my baby boy—" Her words trail off, but her face is still cold. This is my mother, the emotional range of stone.

"How do you know, Mom?"

"You used to call me Momma. I love you, Jude. I hope you know that."

Part of me wants to believe her, but it's been three years. "Do you know where he is?"

She shifts in her seat, and I feel some type of explanation coming on. "No. I don't know much more than you do, I suppose." She takes a drag of her cigarette. "He thought he was protecting us. He lied to us."

I want to yell at her, tell her that *she's* the liar, but I don't have the strength to argue, and she's right. So, I sit quiet and wait.

Mom takes another, slower drag of her cigarette and flicks her eyes to it like it's disappointed her in some way. She expels the smoke from her lungs and tosses the cigarette out the window. "Tad thought he could make it better for you. He made up a fairytale where you were the hero."

To my utter amazement, she begins to cry. Not a racking sob that shakes her body, more like an ice sculpture melting.

Mom takes the on-ramp to the interstate, accelerating as she does. Traffic is light, just a few eighteen-wheelers hauling freight. Mom's voice is the slightest bit hoarse as she speaks. "Lewisboro, New York; Oak Ridge, Tennessee; Waterloo, Illinois; Vadnais Heights, Minnesota." The words flow from her like a litany of some kind, like a prayer.

"What are those? Towns?"

Wetness glistens on her cheeks. "Have you ever wondered why we live in Rush Springs?"

"I . . . it's where we've always lived."

Mom nods. "Those towns I named have the lowest crime rates in the country. Year in and year out. No one's been murdered in Oak Ridge, Tennessee in twenty-five years." Mom grimaces. "You ever wonder why we live here?" She throws an arm out, indicating the expressway and all around us.

"It's not that bad," I say, but at the same time, I know she's right. We could have moved to a lower crime area. Dreamers only have the Dreams of murders that occur close by. I may never have had a Dream if I'd lived in one of the towns on Mom's list.

Dad's forty-five and has had six Dreams in his lifetime, his first one at eighteen. Rush Springs isn't the worst place in the world, but murder, premeditated murder, does happen. The kind of violent crime a Dreamer would Dream about. Suddenly, I have a deeper understanding of Mom's pain, but that only fuels more questions. "So why didn't you take me, take me somewhere safe?"

"I think you know," Mom says.

It clicks. "The Society," I say, tasting bile on my tongue.

Mom grips the steering wheel and scrunches up her face. "Never trust them, Jude. Ever." Her words hang in the space between us, and we ride in silence.

Another mile down the road, Mom takes the off-ramp toward her place. Out here in the country, it's dark, so dark that the stars above shine down with more clarity than in the city. The thick pines on the side of the road gather close to one another like giants huddling in the cold.

Mom's working up her courage to tell me more. I sense it. I see it in her posture. Her fixation on the road, her unwillingness to look at me. I give her time.

Another mile passes, and she speaks. "Your father came home one night with a bullet hole through his shoulder, and he wouldn't let me take him to the emergency room. He was raving about being set up. He made a call, and a stranger came over and stitched him up, put in a chest tube because your daddy's lung collapsed. The whole time your father held a gun to the man. Even when the chest tube went in. Tad told the man he knew what 'they' tried to do." She shifts in her seat. "The man denied it all, but he was lying. Even I could tell."

"His scar," I say. "It is a gunshot wound."

Mom nods.

I run a hand through my hair. "But why'd they try and kill Dad?"

Mom blinks at the road. "Tad had a Dream once, and the killer got away. The killer eventually killed the Chosen."

"Yeah," I say. "Dad told me."

"Well," Mom continues. "The Society's attitude toward him changed after that. They took his failure . . . personally. Said he wasn't worthy. Cut off communication, stopped helping. The very next Dream, your father was almost killed. Tad said the killer knew he was coming. He only survived because he sensed something was off with the Dream." She shrugs. "I don't know how that works."

"I do," I say softly, remembering how Hanna altered the Dream, and it felt like the floor falling out from under me. "That's why Dad tried to hide me," I say, putting it together. "That's why he lied to me, why he was going to stop me from going to Hanna's. He was protecting me from them. Only he didn't know the Society was already watching."

Mom's body shakes a little, but her eyes remain dry. "That's right, Jude. He did it for you."

We're getting close to her house. I've driven by a few times, telling myself I was going to stop and knock on her door, but I never managed to find the courage.

"So much your father would never share," Mom says. "You can't understand what that was like. He lied to me. He married me, we had you, and I never knew what he was until the night he came home shot."

The pain in her words stirs something in me. Tears well in my eyes. No other person in the world could elicit such a range of warring emotions inside me. This woman, my mother. "And I'm like him," I say. "I'm a monster. Who'd want to be a monster's mother?"

"You're not a monster, Jude," Mom says, slamming her palm into the steering wheel. "Don't ever say that. You're my baby. *My baby.*" She shifts in her seat. "You hunt the monsters, Jude, but it's so hard to live like that. Watching you grow, wondering if you'd be like him. Tad training you but keeping it all a secret." She pauses and takes a deep breath. "But I didn't leave you."

I look at her, the old resentment rising in my chest. "Yes, you did, Mom. Three years. You and Dad split, fine, but you stopped calling and coming to see me. Dad said you needed space. But three years?"

She shakes her head. "You know the story of the day you were born?"

"Um, yes," I say, confused. I'd heard it a million times. A tornado warning was in effect when Mom went into labor. She delivered me just as the tornado was coming for the hospital. They carried me into the hall. Mom held me as I screamed while Dad stood over us. The tornado wrecked the parking lot outside and flattened the surrounding neighborhood. They said it was a miracle no one died.

"What does any of this have to do with you having nothing to do with me?"

"My storm child," Mom says. "That's you. There's nothing I wouldn't do for you. Fight a tornado." She pushes her hair behind her ear to look at me better. "Even make you believe I abandoned you. The Society, Jude. I was going to take you. They told me if I did, they'd kill us all."

My whole body tingles. This isn't—This isn't real. I can't speak.

Mom's bottom lip quivers. With visible effort, she pushes down her emotions. When she speaks next, her voice is softer. "They knew you were a Dreamer, Jude. I don't know how, but they knew. They said you had to stay, and I had to go. They wouldn't let me tell your father anything, just that I was leaving. They said if I told Tad about their threats, about their involvement, none of us would last a week. I believed them, Jude." Her next words are a choked whisper. "I still do."

We pull into Mom's driveway, and she puts the car in park. With the engine still running, she looks at me. "The Society told me no contact, but I was there, Jude. I've seen every home game you've played since freshman year." She takes a deep breath. "You're like your father. Born to play football."

Tears run down my cheeks. "I-I never saw you."

"The hill overlooking the field. I parked there. I never came into the stadium. I didn't dare."

"You . . . were there?" My voice is soft, like I'm seven again.

Mom licks her lips. "Every snap, every play."

I swallow, fighting back the pain, and the love, bubbling up inside me.

"They called tonight," Mom says, "and told me to get you. But this is it. Tomorrow you have to go back. They were clear."

"No," I say. "They . . ." I shudder. "Momma—" I lean for her, and she embraces me. I hug her tight, and she returns the hug.

Momma holds me tighter. "You can stay here tonight. In the morning, I'll tell you all I know about your father, then you got to leave, baby. I'm sorry, I am. I'm so sorry."

I bury my head in her shoulder. "Okay, Momma. Okay."

We cling to each other, and I can feel the love, the pure emotion, coursing through her. *My Momma.* She didn't leave me.

And I know in that moment of both hope and awful surety that nothing in my life has ever hurt so much.

CHAPTER 31

The next morning, in a robe and slippers, Mom makes me breakfast. The eggs are too runny, and the bacon and toast are extra crispy, but that's Mom. She never was the domestic type, and that's okay. I wolf the food down, feeling lighter than I have since Dad went missing.

Mom smiles as she watches me eat, her hair hanging loose around her face. I note a hesitancy to her that wasn't there three years ago. She bares the emotional scars life has given her, but there is a glow to her, too. A presence that I remember from long ago, when I didn't even know what a Dreamer was.

For a time, as the morning sun shines in through the kitchen window, Mom and I talk.

We talk about school and about life. We talk about my plans for the future. How two state colleges have sent out feelers to Coach D about the possibility of me playing football for them, and how I don't know what I want to do yet. I tell her a little about Molly. Mom smiles but doesn't ask any questions.

We laugh and talk until a soft and comfortable silence falls. Then she takes a deep breath as if she knows the fun has reached its end. "You're a lot like your father, Jude. Like he was when we first started dating. So full of ideas and hope." She takes a sip of coffee. "But what he does, what you do, it changes you. How could it not?" She looks at me with her sad brown eyes. "Taking a life changes you, Jude. It makes you into something even you won't recognize in ten years. Each time Tad Dreamed, each time he trained for it, each time he went out . . . when he came back, he was different, like a piece of him was missing.

I didn't know what was going on until later, when he almost died, but looking back, I saw the changes in him." She turns away from me and stares through the bay windows to her backyard and the woods beyond. "You deserve better, Jude, better than what I gave you, better than what the Society has done to us."

I grind my teeth. It always comes back to the Society. I need to understand. "Is there anything else you can tell me about them?"

Mom sets down her coffee mug and stares into the black liquid for a moment. "They have money and power, and guard both jealously. But the way Tad described them, the money and power are nice, but secondary. Most are true believers."

"Believers in what?"

Mom laughs, an unpleasant sound. "Themselves mostly. They believe every innocent they save, every evil person they kill, tips the balance in favor of the good. They believe they're fighting a war."

"A war against whom?"

Mom shrugs. "Tad said it depended on the individual. The Society has believers of all faiths and believers in none. They believe they were given a gift by God or by the Universe or by whatever or however the person wants to rationalize it, but in the end, all that matters is that the innocent is saved, and the killer is killed." She pauses. "Even your dad believed that. I always wanted to know why the killer had to be killed. I wanted Tad to call the police."

"That doesn't work," I say.

Mom's eyes snap to me, a challenge on her lips, but her face softens. "That's what your father says. Did Tad tell you the story of the first time he Dreamed?"

I shrug. "Kind of."

"I knew your dad then, of course. He was eighteen. We weren't dating, that came later, but we were friends. He told me he was confused when he had the first Dream but knew what he had to do. He found the man he was supposed to save and, well, he saved the man, but the police got involved."

"*What?*" I ask incredulously.

"That's right," Mom says. "Your father didn't even know the Society existed. He told the police the truth about the Dream. In less than two hours, the Society came in with lawyers. Tad wasn't ever even charged."

Mom taps her nail against her coffee cup. "Tad said the Society were surprised to find him, called him a weed. Something that sprouts up unwanted and useless. But they did save him from charges. In the beginning, they helped him. Until he failed."

I rub my forehead. "Why didn't he tell me? Why didn't he tell me about any of this? He could have trusted me."

"Do you even know your dad?" Mom asks in a voice harder than at any other time this morning. "What army would he not fight through to protect you? I couldn't stay with him, but you have to know how strongly he loves." Her tone softens. "Maybe he was misguided, but he did it for the right reasons."

I can't argue with her, so I don't.

Mom looks down and takes another sip of coffee. "I wish I could tell you more. I wish I knew more, but I don't. Your father tried to protect us both." She looks out the window, her eyes going distant. "Isn't it funny, Jude? It's the things we try to protect most that we end up doing the most damage to."

She shakes her head as if coming out of a trance and reaches for my hand on the table. "I love you, baby, but that's all I've got."

Her words feel like an ending. It's time for me to go. "Give me a ride back to Dad's?"

Mom smiles at me, a knowing smile full of regret. "Sure. Just let me finish my coffee."

After her coffee, Mom takes me home. We don't speak much in the car, driving with the windows down while Mom chain smokes.

She pulls into Dad's driveway and parks but leaves the engine running. She reaches over and gently pulls my head to her lips, planting a soft kiss on my forehead. "Be safe, Jude," she whispers. "As safe as you can be. Don't let them change you. Fight them if you can." She looks me in the eyes. "Mercy and grace are the strongest powers in the universe . . . remember that."

I don't trust myself to speak, so I nod as I pull away from her, open the door, and get out. I watch Mom back out and pull away. I stand under the morning sun long after Mom's car is gone, thinking about all she told me.

How would my life be different if Dad had trusted Mom with the truth from the beginning? Would I even be here? Would Mom and Dad still be together?

After a moment, I pull out my phone. I find the number and tap the screen.

"Jude?" Molly's voice is more than I can take.

"Hey," my voice cracks with emotion. "I need to see you. I need . . . I need to talk."

CHAPTER 32

It is a credit to Molly, the person she is, that she doesn't call me crazy. She doesn't run. She doesn't even interrupt. We sit in her car in the Walmart parking lot, and she listens. I tell her everything, the words flowing from me.

Despite knowing every word is gospel, I fear what Molly will say when I'm done. With every word, the fear grows, and I become certain I'm making the biggest mistake of my life. Molly will tell someone, maybe a counselor at school, and I'll find myself in a padded room on the top floor of some mental hospital for the rest of my life.

Stupid, stupid, stupid.

I am stupid for believing I was special. I am stupid for letting the killer escape. I am stupid for telling Molly the truth.

Since this summer, I thought I was the hero of the story. I kill the killers. I save the Chosen. I follow the rules my father set before me, never really asking why, and I make the world better. But I'm not the hero. I'm not even the villain. I'm the henchman doing the dirty work. But it's even worse than that. When it comes down to it, I don't *know* what I am.

I glance at Molly occasionally while I speak. She listens, sipping a bottled water, but mostly I look out the window, or at my feet. I can't look at her. If I see doubt or alarm in her hazel eyes, I won't be able to finish, and I have to finish.

I tell her about Mom picking me up from the police station, and what the Society did to my family. It's the last piece, the final chapter in my story. But I'm not done.

I still can't look at her, but she gives me time while I find the courage to say the rest. "That's the reason I called you," I say. "I know we aren't really a thing. But I think . . . I think we can be." I close my eyes tight.

After several heartbeats, I look at her. It's clear Molly isn't scared, and her eyes don't tell me I'm crazy. There is a compassion and warmth in her bright eyes that I have rarely seen.

"I believe you," she whispers.

Her words sink in, but I don't dare move or speak. I can tell that there is more she wants to say.

She shifts in her seat to face me better. "I believe you aren't lying, but that's not the same as me believing everything you say is true."

I don't argue. What would I say?

She goes on. "I believe you, because the only other alternative is this is an elaborate lie or you're delusional. I don't believe either of those two things are true."

She reaches out and touches the bandages over my cheek. Her fingertip slip down to my chin, her touch warm and gentle. She looks into my eyes. "If you were delusional, I could see that, but I knew the night I came over something was wrong. Something real. I believe someone kidnapped your dad."

Her fingers fall from my chin, find my hand, and squeeze. She lets out a sigh. "It's the little things too. So much adds up now. You asked Kristi Wallace out." The hurt in her voice is tinged with anger. "I've known you since we were kids, and you doing that right when things were starting to happen with us made absolutely no sense. It wasn't like you at all. And making friends with that geek Coop?" She rolls her eyes, but her smile dulls the slight.

"Hey, Coop's cool," I laugh, feeling a wave of relief at Molly's joke.

"I love Coop," Molly says, "but you guys might as well be from different planets."

She bites her lip, and her expression becomes dangerously serious. "Whatever happens from now on, you've got me to help you through it."

Her words wreck me. Molly has no idea how much this means. She looks out the front windshield and her voice becomes softer. "I've always believed there are things in this world we don't understand. Just because we don't understand something doesn't mean it doesn't exist. People want to put everything in a box and label it." She turns her gaze back on me. "People try to put *me* in a box, but I don't fit. You don't either. I've always known that about you." Her tone is defiant, and I have never felt closer to Molly.

She squeezes my hand again. "I want to be absolutely clear on something. You're not crazy, and I believe you aren't lying, but I haven't completely ruled out some type of mental breakdown. I plan on staying close to you from here on out, Jude. I want to see more proof. Is there any way we could contact this Society?"

"No," I say a little too hard, a little too fast. "No," I say softer. "That would be a very bad idea."

Molly frowns but doesn't argue. "Then I want to talk to Hanna and Coop, and I want to help."

I hesitate.

"What?" she asks.

"Uhhh . . . Well. Hanna may think, may consider you to be, well . . . you're a suspect."

"A suspect?" Molly says, her voice dropping into the danger zone. "Hanna thinks I tried to kill her?"

I nod like a man trying not to startle a bear. "Yeah, kind of. I don't know, maybe. I think you're on the list mainly because it annoys me. Hanna's . . . a lot."

Molly looks like steam might come from her ears. "There's a list?"

"Yeah."

"And I'm on it?"

I shrug in answer.

"And what do you think? Did I try to kill Hanna?"

It's an easy answer. "No way. The black eye threw me for a loop, but Marcus backed up your story."

"You checked my alibi?" The danger is back in Molly's voice.

She wants me to be real. Well, I'm going to be so real it hurts. "You had a black eye, Molly. The night I fell down the stairs with a killer. Then there was you and Munson and Hanna. This whole love triangle thing."

Molly surprises me by laughing. "Now that's a good one. Hanna thinks I would kill her over a boy. Over Lucas? That's . . . I don't even know. Outrageous isn't even close. I think you were right, Jude. Hanna *was* trying to annoy you."

She shakes her head. "Call Hanna and call Coop and tell them to meet us at your house." She leans back in her seat. "This is kind of exciting. Even if it's all some weird misunderstanding, I really want to see what happens."

"Are you sure you want to get involved? Once I make the call, there's no turning back."

Molly looks over at me and her eyes are wide, full of questions and excitement. "Yes, of course." Her reaction is so much better than I'd expected. Better than I could have even hoped for.

"What?" she asks, and I realize I've been staring.

I lean toward her, and I see her swallow in anticipation. I lean in a fraction more, and Molly moves forward fast to meet my lips. We kiss. It's the most intense moment of my life. And that's saying a lot, considering I've tried to kill someone.

Then she pulls away. Her cheeks are scarlet, and her next words are breathless. "What took you so long?"

I shake my head. "I want to do that again."

She giggles and leans back in for another kiss.

CHAPTER 33

We swing by to get Coop because he doesn't have a car. His mother waits with him by the front door of their double-wide. She's a large woman in a floral print nightgown. Three dogs under the porch lie on top of one another. Only one bothers to raise its head at our approach.

When Coop sees us, he hops off the porch and jogs to meet us on the gravel drive. Molly stops and I get out, pushing the seat forward so Coop can climb in.

"Y'all don't get my boy in any trouble," Coop's mom yells at us.

"Mom," Coop whines, "we talked about this."

"I know what pot smells like," his mother warns him. "I got high back in the day. Until I was washed in the blood of the lamb."

"Mom," Coop pleads, but she pays her son no mind.

"It's a wonder Coopy came out so smart. Don't need to go makin' my mistakes."

"Yes, ma'am," Coop says. "No getting high, stoned, baked, or blazed."

"You mocking me, Coopy?"

Coop's face goes red. "No, ma'am."

"Good. Don't do the things I've done. I love you, Coopy."

Coop glances at me. "Love you too," he mumbles and gets in the car.

I follow him, ducking in quickly. Molly backs up as slow as possible, as if trying not to disturb the gravel. "Coopy?" she asks.

Coop groans. "Don't repeat that."

"Sure thing, Coopy."

"So, you call Hanna yet?" Coop asks me, changing the subject.

It's my turn to groan.

"No," Molly answers for me. "He's scared."

Coop laughs. "I would be too. You know you're on the list, right?"

"I've heard," Molly says, her playfulness gone. "Jude, please call Hanna now."

My phone, resting on the console, is like a snake about to strike. "You sure?" I ask one more time.

"Call," she says.

I take a deep breath, pick my phone up, find Hanna's number, and make the call. Hanna picks up on the first ring. "Hey."

I open my mouth to speak, but she rolls right over me. "Yeah. I have company, so I can't."

"All right," I say, annoyed. "This is important. Get rid of them. Wait, is it Munson?"

"You're so smart," Hanna says. "Let me call you—"

"Molly knows," I blurt out before she ends the call. "Molly knows because I told her. She's going to help, and we're going to my house with Coop to talk about it. Make a plan."

The other end of the line is silent, silent like the tomb. The need to fill the void is real, but I don't. "Is that right?" Hanna asks after a moment, her voice all sugary sweet. "A plan, huh? That's nice. Great news," she says, but I don't believe her.

"We'll be at my house," I say. "If you leave in the next couple of minutes, you might beat us there. Coop lives out in the sticks. Just ditch Munson and come on."

"I'll think about it," Hanna says. Her voice is losing its soft curves, getting sharper with each word. "Just give me a few. Okay. Bye." Hanna ends the call before I can respond.

"That went well," Coop says.

"Lucas was over there," I say and immediately regret it. "Sorry, Molly."

"It's a little uncomfortable," Molly admits, "but Lucas deserves to be happy. So does Hanna."

When we pull into the drive, Hanna's not waiting for us.

"She's not coming," Coop says.

"She'll be here."

We go inside, and I ask if anyone wants something to drink, like a good host.

"Whatcha got?" Coop asks.

"Water," I say. "Money's tight."

"Water's good."

"Molly?" I ask.

"No thanks," she says.

I step into the kitchen. A pile of laundry I haven't folded yet is visible just inside the laundry room. I shut the door—out of sight, out of mind—and grab a cup from the cupboard and am getting some ice when the doorbell rings.

"I got it," Coop yells at me.

I pour some water into the glass from the sink, glad Hanna decided to show.

I hear the door open and Coop make some type of exclamation, but I can't catch it. I take the water and head back into the living room. Molly's on the couch, staring at the front door, frowning.

As I round the corner, I see why.

Hanna brought a friend. Hanna brought Munson.

"What's he doing here?" I say, my words clipped and sharp.

Lucas says nothing, standing beside and slightly behind Hanna. His uncharacteristic sheepish expression changes at my words though, and he glares at me. "Trust me, Jude. It wasn't my idea."

"You told your friend, and I told mine." Hanna says. "If Molly's in, so is Lucas."

"Awkward," Coop whispers, way too loudly.

I shove his water at his chest. "Come on," Coop says as I glare at him. "This is crazy." He takes a long drink, looking between Molly and Hanna.

"Has Hanna told you what's going on, Lucas?" Molly asks.

Lucas nods. "Most of it. Not sure I believe"—he looks at me—"all of it."

"Yeah." I ask, "What part don't you believe?"

"He thinks you might be a homicidal stalker who has me confused," Hanna says. "But I already *told* him. I know that's not true. So, here's the deal. This is *my* life. *My* life we're talking about. So, all of you are going to sit down, and I'm going to tell you what's up. When I'm done, we're going to come up with a plan. That's it. We aren't going to argue or fight. We're going to do this, and that's all there is to it. Any questions?"

No one argues.

Coop and I join Molly on the couch. Lucas takes Dad's La-Z-Boy and Hanna sits on the loveseat.

"I'm starting from the beginning," Hanna says, "and I'm telling everything."

I sigh, loudly.

"Everything," she repeats. "And then we are coming up with a plan."

She looks each person in the eyes one by one, then she tells the story of the last few weeks, leaving absolutely nothing out.

CHAPTER 34

Molly is the first to speak when Hanna is done. "Motive," she says.

"Was that a question?" Hanna asks with more than a little snark.

"It's a statement," Molly says, her voice firm. "This Josh guy is definitely unhinged. I saw what he did at the Banjo. But his motive is weak."

I open my mouth to speak, but Molly holds up a hand. "I know Jude, trust me. I still see that lunatic trying to stab you when I close my eyes, but killing Hanna to punish Stan or keep her quiet is weak as far as motives go. I don't buy it." She looks right at Hanna. "Why kill you? It doesn't help him in any way other than possibly turning your dad against him. I could see him killing the both of you, but why just you?"

Hanna smirks. "You could see it, huh?"

"I could," Molly says and readjusts her seat, moving a little closer to me.

"I know I was on your list," Molly says. "Can we address that real quick and get on with trying to save your life?"

Hanna's lips press into thin lines. "Sure."

Molly turns to Munson. "What are the chances, Lucas, that I tried to kill Hanna over you?"

Munson sits up. "Uh."

"Don't hold back," Molly says. "Say what's on your mind."

Munson squirms uncomfortably in Dad's La-Z-Boy and makes the weakest shrug I've ever seen. "Like, less than zero." He looks to Hanna for support. "But you didn't put Molly on a list, right?"

Hanna taps her foot. "Maybe."

Munson scratches his nose, completely lost. "Huh. That's . . . huh."

"Hanna," Molly says, her voice soft. "I know I may not be your favorite person, but I can help. I'm really good at making connections and solving puzzles."

"Solving *puzzles*?" Hanna asks, and I recognize the tone. It's not the good one. "It's a little more than a puzzle to *me*."

Molly purses her lips. "You're right. I'm sorry." She shakes her head. "Honestly, I've been trying not to think about it, someone coming into your house while you're asleep, trying to beat you to death with a hammer. It's almost too horrible to believe. And I think," Molly's voice wavers the slightest bit. "I think if I dwell on that too much, I won't be able to sleep ever again." Her next words are spoken with care. "You don't deserve this. Any of this. I want to help."

Hanna watches Molly, her cold demeanor thawing a fraction. After a very long pause, the air seems to come out of Hanna. "Fine," she says. "I *may* have been a little hard on you. Tell us what you're thinking."

Molly straightens, collecting her thoughts. "All right. Good. So, I agree with you. This is personal. *Very* personal. If the killer just wanted you dead, there would be a thousand easier ways to do it, but breaking into your house with a *hammer*? That's messed up." She slowly folds her hands together, thinking. "And there's one person not on the list. An individual with a very personal reason to want you dead."

"Okay," Hanna says slowly, her eyes narrowing. "Who?"

"Coach Davis," Molly says.

"No way," I say. "Coach D wouldn't do that."

Molly shakes her head. "He has motive, Jude. Strong motive. Revenge. If he knows about Tommy not being his son, maybe he decided to, I don't know, deprive Stan of his daughter."

"*Damn*," Munson says. "That's cold."

No one speaks for a long moment.

Hanna stands and presses a hand to her head, turning her back to the group. "That's really good, actually. I never considered that."

I keep quiet. Admitting I'd thought of this possibility earlier doesn't seem like a necessary admission. It wasn't Coach D though. No way.

"What else do you have?" Hanna asks.

"Well," Molly says. "It's all about motive. Find who has the most to gain, who has the biggest grudge. Tommy and his dad both fit. Josh Stroup does too. He's a psycho. Killing someone with a hammer would be right up his alley, but, again, his motive is weak. Is there any other reason Josh may want you dead? Have you ever told anyone else what is going on with Josh and Stan?"

Hanna still has her back to us, but she tenses slightly. A few seconds pass, then a few more.

"Hanna?" I ask, already knowing what's happening. Hanna has a bad tendency to hold things back. "Who else did you tell?"

Hanna turns and the pained, angry grimace is all the confirmation I need.

"Unbelievable," I say, standing. "Who?"

"Besides the people in this room?" Hanna snaps. "No one. That's who." She taps her foot, defiant, and I can already hear the *but* coming. "But," she says as I groan, "I may have driven to the FBI office in Little Rock."

"Whozza," Coop quips. "Bombshell."

I throw up my hands. "And you thought that wasn't pertinent information to share?"

Her nostrils flare. "I wasn't going to tell them just about Josh. I was going to burn it *all* down."

"That doesn't matter at all," I say.

Hanna crosses her arms. "I didn't go in. I sat in the parking lot, trying to have the courage to do the right thing and turn Stan in, but I didn't because I'm a coward."

"That st-still doesn't—" I stammer.

"Calm down, Jude," Molly says with gentle reproof.

"Yeah, Jude," Munson says from the recliner. "Sit your ass down and listen. Hanna's talking."

I glare at the big guy and hesitate several heartbeats. Only then do I sit back down.

"This is important," Molly says to Hanna. "Did anyone see you?'

"No," Hanna says. "I mean, yes. One lady, but it wasn't a big deal."

"Who saw you?" Molly asks.

"I don't know, a woman. It was nobody. I was crying in my car, having a meltdown. Some woman knocked on my window and asked if I was all right. She offered me a tissue. I took the tissue and told her I was fine."

Molly listens intently. "And you didn't know this lady?"

"No," Hanna says. "Never seen her before. I drove home after that."

"This is dumb," Lucas says, suddenly all belligerent. He leans forward, his elbows on his knees. "I'm supposed to believe Jude's some type of hero? Is that it? But he can't figure out who the"—he makes air quotes—"*real* killer is? My money says Jude and his dad are both nut jobs. His dad was probably the one who tried to kill Hanna and accidently knocked dumbass here down the stairs."

I stand, seeing red. Literally. The whole room is tinged with red. "Watch what you say," I warn him.

Munson stands, all six-five of him. "It's, like, Aaron's Razor," he says. "The easiest explanation is what really happened."

"Uh," Coop says. "You mean *Occam's razor*?"

"Yeah, that," Munson says. "And Jude and his dad being the killers makes the most sense. All this magic and dreams and whatever. It's all lies. It's impossible, and Jude's got Hanna and Molly brainwashed."

I take a step toward him.

"Stop!" Hanna screams. "How long have you known me, Lucas?"

Munson's eyes stay locked on me.

"How long?" Hanna says.

Munson finally looks at her. "You know how long."

"That's right," Hanna says. "In all that time, you ever see me acting weak or easily manipulated?"

"No," Munson says, albeit with reluctance.

"Do you think I'm lying to you about the vision and what I've seen with my own eyes?"

Munson looks to Hanna, to me, and back to Hanna. He sits down in Dad's recliner as aggressively as I've ever seen anyone sit.

"Good," Hanna says. "And you," she turns on me.

"What?" I say.

"Just, I don't know, stop provoking Lucas."

I huff and shake my head, but I can't think of a reply that would fit the ridiculousness of Hanna's statement. I sit back down on the couch next to Molly.

"Let's get back to the matter at hand," Molly says. "Coop, there is no video, right?"

Hanna covered that bit of bad news earlier when she told the story. Coop shakes his head miserably. "That's right. *No bueno.*"

"The parking lot cameras, though," Molly says. "Maybe they caught Josh or someone else on it."

"Doubtful. The cameras only cover a portion of the parking lot and . . ." he trails off. His head drops into his hands. "Uhhh," Coop moans. "The parking lot. That stupid camera." He drags his head up, his face twisted in anguish. "Hanna's the take-no-guff hot one," he says. "Jude's the bumbling hero, but I'm the brains. I'm the brains!"

"What are you talking about?" I ask.

Coop shakes his head. "It's like in the movies." He points at me. "There's the dude with muscles who's lovable but not too bright." He points at Hanna. "There's the girl, hot and strong and a little cold." He falls back on the couch, grimacing. "But I'm the smart one.

"The parking lot cameras. One is turned facing the glass wall of the food court." He rubs his chin, thinking, and sits up. "It was cloudy that day. The sun wouldn't have reflected off the glass. The table I found the bag at is right next to that huge wall of glass."

He looks at us in turn, expectantly. "Don't you see? I bet that one camera in the parking lot recorded whoever dropped off the bag through the glass window. It was right there the whole time. I must have looked right at that stupid camera a thousand times. It's in the parking lot, but it's facing the building. It's up high, and at an odd angle, but it's, like, laser-focused right where the killer sat. I'm so sorry, Hanna. I should have—"

"It's okay, Coop," Hanna says. She's excited. We all are. "It doesn't matter now. Tell us how we get the video."

Coop nods and brightens a bit, but he still looks miserable. He takes an overly dramatic breath and lays out his plan.

Unfortunately, the plan hasn't improved since he first came up with it. Coop gets the code to the security room somehow, someway. Then, he and I break in and watch the video from the day he found the murder book.

Coop is going to get me arrested. But if this works, if that one parking lot camera caught video of the person who left the book, it's game over. No more being a detective. All I have to do is what I am meant for.

All I have to do is kill whoever is on the video.

CHAPTER 35

The HBC, Hunan's Buffet City, is not good. In fact, bad would be a step up. The egg foo yong is a mushy shrimp pancake, and the sweet and sour chicken is like eating a plate full of last year's Halloween candy.

I've only eaten here a handful of times before. This time I thought I was playing it safe with the chicken fried rice. Stupid me. The rice sticks together on my plate in big doughy balls and the chicken somehow manages to be spongy and dry at the same time. I'm no connoisseur of fine dining, my idea of a gourmet meal being panfried potatoes and onions served with an ample supply of ketchup, but I cannot understand how the HBC is still in business.

I glance up at Coop across the food court. He's behind the sneeze guard working the wok, "Hunan Buffet City" in neon red above him. He's going at it, cooking and mixing, smiling like he knows what he's doing. He sees me and gives me a bright smile and a thumbs-up. His eyebrows rise, asking how the food is. I give him the best fake smile I can muster and return his thumbs-up. Coop's grin broadens as he flips whatever unfortunate ingredients he's cooking, catching only about half on the descent.

Coop finally got the keycode for the video room last night. It took him four days with everyone hounding him, but he came through. It feels like the last stage in this ordeal.

I can only hope.

If the video exists and the killer is on camera, I can do what needs doing. Dad comes home, and my life returns to—not normal, but as close to normal as I'll ever have.

I stifle a yawn. I left football practice only an hour ago. I even stayed late, watching film with Coach Rubacker. We play Jacksonville tomorrow. After we beat Chapel, we got ranked first in conference. Jacksonville is ranked second. It's a huge deal for both schools. Even more so for Bedford because it's also our homecoming game.

More and more, I've realized how much I need football. I have a lot going on, but keeping some normalcy in my life might be the only thing keeping me sane.

I look back at my plate and put my fork down. Soon, Coop and I are going to break into the security room and find the video footage from July 27 between three thirty and five thirty. My stomach turns at the thought, and I'm not sure if it's the breaking and entering or—I look down at my lumpy half-eaten fried rice—something more gastrointestinal.

Josh Stroup is going to be on the tape. He's going to be the one who forgot the bag. I've convinced myself of that.

I check my phone. It's eight forty-five. The mall closes in fifteen and already people are beginning to file out the doors. I get more than a few side-eyes from the cleaning crew telling me it's time to leave.

Coop finishes up with his last customer, boxing up his latest culinary delight in a Styrofoam box and wiping his hands on his black apron like a real pro. He motions me over as a girl I don't know checks out the last customer. I throw away my food, half of it untouched, and walk to the counter. Coop nods his head to the employees' entrance at the side.

"Hey Charlotte," he says to the checkout girl. "My buddy and I are going to clean up. Thought you might want to take off early."

Charlotte looks at Coop with dark eyes and a frown. "Whatever," she says in a Valley girl sort of way. "Just clock me out when you're done. And do it right this time, like, last time, you totally did it wrong. I got docked, like, fifteen minutes." Charlotte grabs her bag and leaves without saying bye.

The food court is empty now except for the cleaning crew. Coop grins at me. "You going to stand there all day or help me clean?"

"Charlotte could have helped."

Coop shrugs. "We needed her gone. She usually leaves anyway."

"She ditches you? You shouldn't let people do you like that."

Coop laughs. "Walk a mile in a man's shoes, you know? Come on. We really do have to clean. My manager's a lot like you. Anger issues."

There's a commotion by the front doors as the last of the shoppers leave. Coop and I both turn to see what the shouting is about. Lucas Munson is ignoring the cleaning crew that are telling him the mall is closing. Chuck, the mall cop, comes from Andrew's, the only dine-in restaurant in the place.

He saunters over to Munson on an intercept course. He meets Munson halfway to us. Chuck rolls his shoulders as the two talk. After a brief interaction, Lucas makes a waving motion toward me and Coop.

"Oh boy," Coop says. "What is he doing?"

I bite the inside of my mouth. "Screwing us over," I say.

The plan was for Munson to stay with Hanna and Molly outside and pick us up after we watched the video. Apparently, Munson had other ideas.

Chuck and Munson make their way over as Coop and I watch.

Chuck stops at the counter with Munson looming behind him. Munson wears a dower expression as he stares me down. I know why he's here. He's only told me about a thousand times.

Chuck sucks his teeth. "Mr. Lucas Munson says he's here to help you clean up, Coop." Chuck's eyes flick to me and recognition dawns. "You're the Erickson kid, the one who played that practical joke on Coop this summer."

I just nod, afraid to speak. Chuck can blow this up in a heartbeat. "You helping Coop too?"

I nod again, a little more vigorously.

Coop, normally Mr. Chatty Kathy, only manages a shrug and a weak smile.

Chuck sucks his teeth again. "All right, then. Well, better get to it." He takes a few steps, stops, and spins back to us, giving us six-shooter hands. "What chance we got against Jacksonville tomorrow?"

I stammer, "I, uh, well—"

Munson clears his throat. "We're going to stomp a mudhole in their ass, sir."

Chuck's belly shakes when he laughs. "That's what I wanted to hear. Go Bulldogs." He thumps his chest. "Class of '92, *represent*." He does something with his hands, like a magician's flourish after pulling a rabbit from a hat. He turns and leaves us without another word, his steel-tipped cowboy boots clicking on the floor as he heads deeper into the mall.

"Dude. Why are you here?" Coop asks Munson.

For the thousand-and-first time, Munson tells us, "I don't trust Jude."

"Right," Coop says. "Stupid me."

"Well, come on. These pots won't wash themselves."

"Wait," Munson says with a grimace. "We're actually washing dishes?"

"Yes," Coop says. "Yes, we are."

Munson glares at me like it's my fault.

We spend the next thirty minutes cleaning and stowing the assortment of pots and pans, throwing out whatever foodstuff couldn't be reheated for the next day. It was a lot less than I'd hoped. Munson does not give a hundred percent.

When we're done, Coop clocks himself and Charlotte out and turns to me. Coop's eyes narrow. In a deep, overly dramatic voice, he says, "And now we wait."

"You enjoying this?" I ask.

"Kind of." He slides a five-gallon bucket my way. Then another for Lucas. He grabs one too, flips it up, and sits on it. I do like he does. Munson reluctantly joins us, and we wait.

The plan is stupid simple. Chuck hangs out in the security room for most of the night, probably napping, but at ten, he does rounds. Rounds entail him going straight to the arcade and playing video games. So, the plan is to wait until Chuck comes by on his way to the arcade, then make a mad dash for the security room.

Last night, Coop finally got the code, standing by Chuck as he punched it in. That's it. He stood beside him. Chuck didn't notice or didn't care. After our last encounter earlier, I'm leaning toward the latter.

We sit in awkward silence as Munson keeps shifting his huge frame on the bucket, making too much noise, trying to get comfortable. At a quarter past ten, Chuck comes by whistling. We wait until the whistling fades out before sprinting to the security room. In under a minute, we're at the keypad. Coop punches in the code. The door clicks open. Munson pushes past me to be first in, like I might plant evidence.

The room is larger than I expected, with four rolling desk chairs at four large workstations. A row of filing cabinets lines the wall next to the door. Of the four workstations, only two appear to be in use, one neat and clean, and the other with an array of empty fast-food cups and pictures of kids and a woman. A younger, slimmer Chuck is in most of the pictures.

"This place is a dump," Munson complains.

The far wall is covered in monitors. Ninety-five percent of the cameras aren't working. Some are blank, some are staticky, but a few, a small few, are on.

I point at the monitor in the lower left corner. "There's Chuck."

The picture is clear. Chuck is in the arcade playing *Galaga*.

"He's got like the top ten high scores," Coop says. "What is it with old dudes and that game? Help me keep an eye on him. If he moves, we run." He goes to Chuck's desk, pushing Munson out of the way like he owns the place, and plops down in Chuck's chair. He moves the mouse. The monitor pops on, and the computer is password locked.

"Tell me you know Chuck's password," I say.

"Duh," Coop says, as he punches in a word. "*Password* is his password," Coop says, laughing. "He told me that forever ago. He thought it was funny."

The computer lets him in. "Now we're cooking."

Thirty minutes later, Coop still hasn't found the file. He sits at the workstation, scrolling through folders. "It's got to be here somewhere."

"So you've said," I say, sitting in an office chair, my eyes on Chuck. Munson's been pacing, cursing under his breath most of the time.

Chuck's still playing *Galaga*. Ten minutes ago, he gave himself a high five. It wasn't as awkward as I would have thought. "You need to hurry, Coop."

"Yeah, Lucas may have mentioned that thirty seconds ago," Coop says, his fingers moving over the keyboards. "I just have to find the right directory... bingo."

I pop up and come to stand behind Coop. He's got the cursor hovering over a file dated July 30. "Is that this year?"

"Yeah, sure. I think." Munson shoulders his way right beside me as Coop double-clicks on the file and hundreds of individual video archives blossom on the screen. "Well," Coop mumbles, the curser moving. It stops on a file titled *3:00 p.m. – 6:00 p.m. CT Parking Lot East 1*. Coop clicks on it.

The video player pops to life and loads. "Geez," Coop hisses. "Upgrade your software, Chuck."

The video plays. It's from outside and the windowed wall is a bright blank wall of nothing.

I groan. "This was a waste of time."

"That's what I've been saying," Munson adds unhelpfully.

"You guys are like an old married couple," Coop says. "Just hold on. It was sunny that morning, but the afternoon..." He fast-forwards the video and sure enough, like a curtain falling, the camera picks up the inside of the food court. He lets the video play.

The video quality is surprisingly good, as I can almost make out faces even through a pane of glass.

"We got him now," Coop says. He taps the screen. "There's the table. So, let me just..." He fast-forwards the video again, and the people walking and sitting inside the food court start doing the time-lapse hop, moving in and out of the frame, eating and carrying on with their lives at breakneck speed. Most of the people are blurs, but the people closest to the glass are relatively clear. For the first time today, I let myself hope we have the killer.

Twice Coop stops the tape and backs it up as someone either sits at the table in question or walks by it. Neither time is it our guy.

I watch as the time speeds by: 4:00, 4:05, 4:10, 4:15, 4:20, 4:25, 4:30. Someone does fast-forward dance, sits at the table and eats a sub sandwich. He's up and gone, doing the fast-forward shuffle again, leaving behind something at the base of the table.

"Stop!" I say. "That's him."

Coop jumps, hitting the fast-forward by mistake, and the people on the screen go into warp drive. Coop swears, "Dude, you scared me." He stops the screen as the video version of Coop finds the bag. He lets it play. "That's me," he says happily. The on-screen Coop kicks the bag by accident, picks it up, looking around the court.

The present-day Coop hits rewind and the time-lapse dance goes backward. Video Coop is gone in an eye blink, and the man comes into the screen again and sits, eating in reverse, the sub growing longer. In seconds, the sandwich is whole again and wrapped back up. The person stands and walks out of the video.

"There," I say. "Stop."

This time, Coop gets it right and plays the tape. I watch as the killer's face comes into focus and my breath catches in my throat. I recognize the killer... and it's not Josh Stroup.

I feel sick.

"No way," Munson says, and I am certain that despite video evidence, Munson does not believe what he sees. I don't want to believe it either, but I can. It was the anger in his eyes that day in the cafeteria that gave him away.

On-screen, Tommy Davis strolls to the table with a sub sandwich cradled like a football in the bend of his arm, a drink in one hand and a bag in the other. He sets the drink and sandwich down and slides the bag under the table. He sits, unwraps the sub, and eats, wolfing down the sub, a typical jock eating alone. It takes less than ten minutes. When he leaves, he takes his trash to the trash can but leaves a bag behind.

"That's messed up," Coop says.

Munson turns away in disgust.

It hurts so bad. It's a betrayal. Sure, he has his issues, but Tommy is still one of us. He was my teammate, my friend. "Back it up," I say. "I want to watch it again."

"Dude," Coop says. "It's him. It's Tommy. I'm sorry, but it's Tommy."

"Back it up," I snap.

Coop sighs and does as I say. We watch it again. There is no doubt. It's Tommy.

"Hey," Munson says sharply.

"What?" I say with all the anger and frustration churning in my gut.

"Look," Munson says, pointing at the arcade feed. "He's gone."

My already sick stomach lurches as I see. Chuck is no longer in the arcade.

"There," Coop says, pointing at a screen in the middle of the monitors. It's one of the few cameras working inside the mall. "He's almost here." Coop closes the video, sleeps the computer, and hops up, but I know we're already too late. Chuck—overweight mall cop—is here, punching in the code right outside.

I grab Coop by the shoulder and haul him away from the door. Munson follows. We all three crouch behind the filing cabinets as the door swings open. Munson's too big. If Chuck looks over...

An office chair squeaks as Chuck sits down. Munson doesn't wait for us, he slides to the door, silent for a kid the size of a small tree. I pull Coop with me as Munson exits. I expect a shout. I expect the door to shut before we get there. I expect to have to run for it, but as I pull Coop through the narrowing opening of the still closing door, no cry of stop or halt or I'll shoot follows us. As soon as we're clear, the door shuts behind us.

Munson, surprisingly, waited on us. He points to the front of the mall, but Coop shakes his head. "No, this way is faster," he whispers.

We follow Coop, and in less than a minute we are outside in the back parking lot of the mall.

"What if he saw us?" Munson asks.

"Nah," Coop says. "He'd be here already. He's not bad at his job."

"I'd say tonight disproves that theory," I say.

"Point well made," Coop says. "Good news is, if he's not here in the next thirty seconds, then it's for sure he didn't see us."

We wait, watching the bank of mall doors. Thirty seconds, a minute passes, and Chuck doesn't show.

"Clean getaway," Coop says. "And, wow. Tommy Davis?"

"Bro," Munson says, almost as if in warning.

Coop's eyes widen. "You saw the video, dude. What do you want from me?"

The full weight of what I saw hits me again. Tommy Davis is the killer. The sickness I felt before returns in a wave of nausea and anger. I pull my phone from my pocket and find Hanna's number as Coop, Munson, and I walk out of the mall parking lot.

Hanna picks up on the first ring. "Where are you?"

"You know the Texaco behind the mall?"

"Yeah."

"We'll be there in a minute."

We get to the Texaco and Hanna's Jeep comes flying into the parking lot. Her Jeep has the hardtop off. Molly is in the passenger seat, her unbound hair whipping in the wind as Hanna screeches to a stop.

Molly gives the front seat to Munson, and Coop and I join her in the back seat. Hanna wastes no time in exiting the gas station. "Did you get in?" she asks.

Munson won't look at her. I can't speak.

"We got in," Coop says.

"And?"

I swallow, not wanting to say Tommy's name. Coop must decide it's my job to tell her because he's looking at me. Molly grabs my hand and squeezes it.

I sniff. "Tommy Davis." I say quickly.

"No," Munson says emphatically. He turns in his seat to glare at me. "It's not possible." His lips twitch. "Coach D let me back on the team even after I left Bedford for Chapel."

I raise my hands. "What does that have to do with Tommy?"

"It *was* Tommy," Coop says. "We all saw it."

"It's a mistake," Munson says, as if his words alone will make it true. I can't even work up the strength to be mad at Munson.

Munson has no such issues. "*Tommy Davis* tried to kill Hanna?" Lucas almost spits. "Say it out loud, Jude."

I look into his eyes, but I don't say anything. I'm done arguing.

"Calm down," Molly says. "Just calm down."

Hanna keeps glancing back at me in the rearview mirror. Tears fill her eyes. "I didn't want it to be him, Jude."

"I know," I say.

No one speaks. Munson faces forward and slumps in his seat. The only sound is Hanna accelerating down the road and the wind whipping past us. She needs to slow down. She speeds up more.

"Can you slow down, please?" Munson asks miserably.

Hanna complies, her fingers gripping the wheel.

No one says a word. The wind whips by as we cruise down the road. Slowly, more gently than I'd expect, Munson places a hand on Hanna's shoulder.

Like a dam bursting, Hanna begins to cry.

CHAPTER 36

Somewhere up on the hill, Mom's watching.

I've felt her presence the entire game, and I've played my heart out for her, not letting up for one second, not for one play. Grass stains my jersey, my white pants, and a bit of turf is still stuck in my face mask from the last play. I ignore it. Right now, I focus on the problem in front of me, number twenty-one.

DeShawn Ballard is a beast. A man among boys.

Jacksonville is up 45–41. They have the ball with one minute and thirteen seconds left. It's first and ten on Jacksonville's forty. Everyone on the field, everyone in the stands, and everyone home streaming the game knows who's getting the ball.

I chew on my mouthpiece as Jacksonville takes their time lining up. The stands are full. It's homecoming. After the game we have a dance. Coop is my date . . . not date exactly, but we're going together, because neither of us has a real date. I wanted to skip the whole thing, but Coop's never been to a dance, and he was persistent.

Molly's going with theater friends, and that's for the best. After seeing Tommy on the tape, I've been doubting everything, even my relationship with Molly.

She knows what I am. She understands what's coming. But I won't do to her what Dad did to Mom. If we are going to be together, it's got to be her choice. I won't pressure her.

In a few days, maybe less, this whole ordeal will be done. How will Molly see me then, with blood on my hands?

I shake the thoughts away as I get the call from Coach Rubacker. I don't want to think about anything but football, anything but this game.

I don't want to think about how I have to kill Tommy Davis.

I call out the play, a run blitz, as I glance to the sideline, finding Tommy without trying. He's biting his nails, nervous for us, nervous for a team he's not on anymore. Is that the action of a murderer?

Jacksonville's QB slides under center, cool, calm. Why wouldn't he be? DeShawn Ballard is standing behind him.

"Blue thirty-two, blue thirty-two," he calls out the cadence. "Set. Hike." The center snaps the ball. DeShawn moves with a suddenness and a ferocity that even after four quarters of play is still hard to comprehend. He gets the ball, but I'm already moving, stunting, filling my gap perfectly. It's an inside trap. Jacksonville has been running away from Munson all night, running right at me.

It hasn't been my best game, DeShawn Ballard being the type of elite athlete that tends to make linebackers look bad, but I've held my own for the most part, and Coach Rubacker's call is perfect.

I meet DeShawn in the gap. My teeth rattle with the impact. DeShawn knocks me back two yards, falling forward on top of me. He pops up and offers me a hand. "Good stick, thirty-three. It's a shame we're gonna have to ruin that perfect record of yours."

I take his hand, and he pulls me up. The clock ticks away: 1:09, 1:08, 1:07. "We got time," I tell him. In the distance, thunder rumbles.

DeShawn jogs back to the huddle. The thunder rumbles again, closer, and I swear I can feel it, feel it deep inside me. I shake it off as tiny raindrops begin to fall.

The clock winds down as Jacksonville takes the line. They're milking the clock, in no hurry to snap the ball. We have only two timeouts left, and after this play, Coach Davis will start to use them. All Jacksonville has to do to win is make one first down. All we have to do to win is stop them, get the ball back, and somehow manage to score a touchdown with only seconds left on the clock.

The wind picks up, swirling around us. Thunder rolls again, the deep bass a counterpoint to my heartbeats. I glance at the sideline, finding Tommy.

A life for a life.

Tommy's life for Hanna's.

Dad comes home.

In front of me, Munson gets down in his three-point stance. He hasn't spoken to me all game. He won't even look at me. Munson will turn me in after I do what I have to. He's all but told me.

I kill Tommy. Munson turns me in, and I go to jail for life. It's probably what the Society is hoping for. I've thought about that a lot since last night. Why did they give me all this time? Will their twisted sense of honor be satisfied if I eliminate myself? Would they let Dad go if I wound up dead or in jail?

The phone call from the Society seems so long ago now, but the man told me . . . *it won't just be Hanna Smith's life you're saving.*

No matter what I do, I know one thing for sure: time is running out. One way or another, I have to end this, no matter what Munson does after.

Coach Davis walks in front of his son, pacing, watching the clock as time ticks away. Jacksonville comes back to the line and the QB, once again, barks out the cadence as the game clock winds down: 38, 37, 36.

"Make a play!" Coach D yells at me. "Someone, make a play!"

I swallow as the thunder above rumbles, echoing deep within my bones.

The center snaps the ball. DeShawn gets the toss on a sweep. I flow with the play as a lineman reaches the second level and tries to get his meaty paws on me, but I'm too quick for him and slip by.

DeShawn is faster than me, and my angle is all wrong. He's going to beat me. He's going to outrun me to the sideline, cut it upfield, and maybe score. DeShawn knows it too.

Something burns within me. Disappointment, anger, frustration, pain all mix together. So much is falling apart, so much I can't control. The sensation within me shifts, grows. Wind pushes at my back, urging me forward. I'm lighter, stronger, faster, and I move like I've never moved before, popping DeShawn with the smack of pads on pads, forcing a grunt from him. For the first time this night, I win the collision, knocking DeShawn onto his back. The clock rolls on. I hop up this time and offer DeShawn a hand. He takes it, and I pull him up. He pats me on the head. "Not bad," he tells me. "I like your game, thirty-three."

Coach Davis burns a time out, and the clock stops with nineteen seconds left to play. I jog to the sideline, and the defense huddles around Coach Rubacker and Coach D.

Coach Rubacker gives us direction, tells us what we're running for the next play. After that, his face gets serious. "All right, we need a turnover or a stop. If they get a first down, the game's over."

The whistle blows and the ref comes over to break up our huddle. "We know what's coming, right?" Coach D says. "More of Mr. Ballard. You know what to do."

"Grip and rip! Get the ball back!" Munson roars. For an instant, our eyes meet. He looks away just as fast.

Coach D nods at Munson's words. "That's right. Now do it!"

Tommy stands beside his father, wearing a Bedford ball cap turned backward. His eyes are fierce, like he's a player and not a spectator. "Come on. You guys got this."

I nod, hopping and backpedaling onto the field, unable to pull my eyes off Tommy. The pressure in my chest continues to build, not the normal adrenaline of a game, something . . . more. Thunder rumbles, and the rain picks up.

Jacksonville lines up, and like the black night clouds hovering above the stadium lights, I'm on the verge of combustion.

It's like all my problems are representative of the game unfolding right now. If I can stop Jacksonville, I can do anything. The rain intensifies, and a clap of thunder booms so loud that everyone turns skyward. The ref blows the whistle as Jacksonville comes to the line. I bounce on the balls of my feet, needing to move. The storm courses through me. The power, the strength.

The ball is snapped, and the QB, once again, hands the ball off to DeShawn. I meet him in a gap with the power of the storm within me. The wet ball slips free, firing straight up, high into the air. I stumble past DeShawn. I almost fall, sliding on the wet turf, my eyes on the ball.

One step, two steps. I reach out as the ball descends, thunder coursing through my veins, and my fingertips make contact. The ball is slick with rain, but somehow, I manage to grasp it, cradling it like the precious thing it is. My feet find purchase, and I run.

Ahead of me is nothing but open grass. The scoreboard in the end zone clicks off the time—seven seconds. Someone dives at my legs, and I lose my balance, stumbling again.

Five seconds. Four. Three.

Again, my cleat bites into the grass as my free hand keeps me off the turf, and I move. The end zone is so close. Never have I wanted something more.

Two. One.

The buzzer sounds, and I'm five yards from glory—
Something smacks into the back of my legs, and I trip, stumble, and fall... one yard from the end zone. A collective groan rolls through the stadium. DeShawn Ballard untangles himself from me and stands.

"Almost, man," he says. "Almost." Four or five of his teammates swarm him, knocking him away from my sight.

The game is over. We lose, and the rain intensifies. I lie there for a minute, my face to the dark sky, all the fight gone from me. Munson looms over me, hallowed in the field's lights, a vengeful demon sent to punish. My arm tightens protectively over the football still cradled under my arm.

Munson holds out his hand. I take it, and he pulls me to my feet. He holds my gaze and, after a few seconds, he takes the football from me. "Just so you know, me and Hanna were never together. Never will be. She's a really good person, better than you or me. But she's like a sister. A very close sister."

"All right," I say, not sure why Munson picked this exact moment to have this conversation with me. "Good to know."

Munson sees my confusion. He's like me, bad at conversation. He licks his lips and doubles down. "She's like my spiritual advisor. You get it? She's helped me through some . . . stuff, for no other reason than she wanted to. Now you understand?"

"No," I say. "I don't."

He grunts at that and looks up at the rain. "I've decided where I'm going to play football," he says.

"Really?" I'm still confused by this whole encounter but can't help but be curious. "Where?"

He gives a half grin. "Oklahoma."

"Ha! Really?"

Munson shares my laugh. "Yeah. I finally went. Oklahoma is actually pretty cool."

He rotates his upper body and launches the football into the air. "Hanna showed me the book, Jude. The one Tommy left. We can't," he swallows, "you can't let anything happen to Hanna."

A coldness creeps up my spine. "What are you trying to say?"

He looks at his feet, intentionally avoiding my gaze. His voice is low. "Dreams and murderers." He shakes his head, still not looking at me. "I'd be lying if I said I believed it." He tilts his head up to me, still looking down because he's a huge person. "But I believe Hanna. And that book." He lets out a long breath. "Make sure she's safe, Jude. Do *whatever* you have to, to keep her safe."

The rain picks up a notch and I understand what this awkward conversation is really about. "I will," I say, and nothing more because I can't say what's left unspoken. Neither of us can.

Because Lucas Munson just told me to kill Tommy Davis.

He leaves me standing alone, a foot from the end zone.

CHAPTER 37

The atmosphere after the game is somber. I feel it too. Even with all that's going on, losing the first football game of the year stings.

Most guys take showers, get dressed, and leave to pick up their dates for the homecoming dance. I'm in no hurry to go to an auditorium with the entire school stuffed inside. So, I take my time cleaning up.

Part of me would rather head home. Munson giving me the green light is both a blessing and a curse. My chances of ending up in jail have decreased, but now my path is set. I have a plan, and I want it done in the next twenty-four hours. But then there is Coop.

I promised I'd go to homecoming with him. The little guy has been growing on me. I've never had a close friend. Molly, Coop, and even, to some extent, Hanna are all close to me now.

It's odd what a little murder and mayhem will do for one's social life.

I get dressed, adjusting my tie in the shower room mirror and putting on a black suit coat I found in Dad's closet. It fits me, mostly, but I think it might be a couple of decades old. I put on the cleanest pair of white sneakers I own, a homecoming tradition going back to even before Dad's day.

Once I'm presentable, I leave the locker room. Coop is waiting for me, suited up too, his phone in his hand. He looks up and half smiles. Kristi Wallace is with him, wearing a black dress a couple of inches short of dress code and a long black coat with fur at the collar.

I stop, staring. Why is Kristi here? It doesn't make sense. Since that night at the Banjo, she's been nice in the halls but distant.

And that was fine. That was perfect. What has Coop done?

I steel myself and walk to them.

"Hey, man," Coop says as I get close, putting his phone down.

"What's up?"

"You know," Coop says. "Chillin' like Matt Dillon."

"Is that right?" I say.

Coop is obviously nervous, but I don't know why. He can't be trying to set me up with Kristi again. He knows better.

Kristi moves closer to Coop, and a piece of the puzzle falls into place. Kristi is *with* Coop. Of course, she is. That actually makes a lot of sense.

I grin at Coop, but he's back on his phone. He's acting squirrelly for sure. Does he think I'm mad he's ditching me?

"Tough loss," Kristi says.

I nod. "Yeah." We stand in awkward silence for a second or two. "So," I say. "You two?"

Kristi nods, embarrassed. "I asked Coop to the dance yesterday. Hope it isn't awkward for you."

"No," I say. "It's all good."

Coop glances at his phone again and scans the parking lot. A car pulls in from the highway and winds its way toward the field house. Coop watches it, sighing in satisfaction as the car parks.

Molly gets out of her car, and my breath catches. Under the streetlights, the long black dress she's wearing shimmers as she moves. Her hair is up in a way I've never seen it before. She's lovely.

Coop moves close. "You can thank me later."

I stare down the hill at Molly and back to Coop.

Coop's grinning ear to ear.

Molly comes up the hill, her dress silky and dark, and I see her gown isn't black at all but a deep purple. It's not something I'd normally notice, but Molly makes me notice. She joins our little group. "Hi," she says. "I'm looking for a homecoming date. You know anybody?"

I'm speechless, so I give her a hug while I think of something coherent to say. A minute ago, I was happy Coop had a date and I could head home. Now, seeing Molly . . . I don't know. "Didn't you have plans already?"

"I did," she admits, "but I was kind of hoping you would break them for me."

I should say no. After I do this, she'll feel different. How could she not? What's coming is so bad. I'm not sure she's thought it all out. I have this deep desire to protect her. Even if I'm protecting her from myself.

Still, her eyes hold me. "You sure?" I ask quietly so Coop and Kristi can't hear. "Are you absolutely positive you want to . . . to be part of my life?" I want to say more, but I can't. I can't.

Molly's expression turns solemn. She lets out a breath and then bites her lip. "I'm sure," she whispers as she nods.

I give her another hug and we hold each other for a long moment. When we break the hug, Molly is smiling. "Let's have fun tonight. Let's forget about everything for a few hours and just have fun. Okay?"

I nod, moisture in my eyes. I swear, if I start crying again. "Okay," I say. "Deal."

"Kristi," Molly says, glancing past me. "Wow, that dress. I love it. Wish I'd thought to bring a coat."

Kristi perks up as Molly lets me go and walks over to her. "Thank you," Kristi says. "Mom helped pick out the dress, but she doesn't know about the coat. It's imitation fur. Mom would totally have a cow anyway."

Coop comes over. "You're not mad, right? I mean Kristi asked and how could I say no. But I didn't want to leave you hanging."

"I'm not mad, Coop," I say. "Far from it."

No one is left on the hill; everyone is at the dance. Molly and Kristi's conversation ends. Coop and Kristi head to the auditorium, but Molly and I hang back. "Hi there, Mr. Homecoming date." Molly holds my gaze like we're the only two people in the world.

"Hello," I say. "You look ... great."

"Thanks. For a jock, you clean up well yourself." Molly shivers, goosebumps coming up on her shoulder.

"Here," I say, taking off Dad's coat and wrapping it around her. For a moment, our faces are close. I pause.

Molly's eyes twinkle, and she gives me a quick peck on the lips. "Sorry about the game."

"Yeah, thanks."

Molly pulls the jacket tight around her shoulders. "Come on." She takes my hand, and we follow Coop and Kristi to the gym.

Despite everything, the rest of the night goes great. I take Molly's suggestion to heart and forget my troubles. Molly makes it easy. I talk and mingle like someone other than Jude Erickson, hardly noticing the crowd at all. It's fun. I don't think much. I live in the moment.

The only odd thing I notice at all is Munson's absence. It's not like him to miss anything social, and all his friends are here. Catching myself worrying about Munson is a new experience. I push it away.

Munson's maybe not the person I thought he was. He's deeper, more complicated than I gave him credit for, but he's still Lucas Munson. He'll be fine.

Molly pulls me onto the dance floor, making me forget about everything but her. We dance, the music loud and fast. For the first time in my life, I don't notice the crowd. I don't mind the people.

The night wears on, and I don't want it to end. It's like I'm in an island of noise and motion, and when it stops, I have to go back to being me, to being Jude Erickson. I don't want that. I don't want to be me anymore.

The pumping music ends, and a slow song plays. Our principal, Mr. Ryerson, taps the mic. "Last song of the night, guys. Be safe driving home. See everyone Monday morning."

Molly pulls me close, and we laugh. The song plays, and we move within the crowd, alone. "This was nice," Molly says.

"The best," I say. She does something, her lips moving, and I swallow. I have zero game, but I read the signs.

I feel the moment like gravity, and I move my head toward hers. Our eyes meet and she smiles and—someone grabs my arm and pulls. Coop has his phone out, thrusting it at me. "Did she call you too?" A very confused Kristi stands behind him.

"What?"

"Check your phone," Coop says.

I hesitate.

"It's Hanna. Check your phone."

I pull my phone from my pocket.

"What is it?" Molly asks.

"Hanna called me three times. I have a voice mail."

"Play it," Coop says.

I play it, putting my phone to my ear as the last song ends and the lights flicker on. Voices come through the phone, several all at once. I hear Hanna screaming. "No, stop. Don't hurt him!"

Someone roars. It sounds familiar. Someone else curses, threatens, but I can't make out words. I hear a thump. Hanna screams again.

Then a male voice, muffled but clear. "Get her." It's Josh Stroup. I hear a clattering, static, and more unintelligible voices.

A man screams, "Don't touch my daughter!"

I hear more noises, like the phone is underwater. Followed by scraping sounds and a different male voice. I'm positive it's a BB. The voice mail ends.

"What's happening?" Molly asks.

"I have to go."

I move to leave, but Molly grabs my arm. "Tell me what's happening, Jude."

"It's Hanna," I say. "Josh—" I look over at Kristi, her face twisted in concern.

"I'm coming," Molly says.

We don't have time to waste, so I don't argue. I head to the door, but Kristi yells at us. "Where is everybody going? Coop, are you going to leave me? Alone?"

Coop runs back to her. Holds her tight, hesitates, and asks Kristi something. Kristi's eyes widen, and she nods. Then she leans in and kisses Coop. A real kiss. A few hoots ring out, and some kids even clap. Kristi lets Coop go, and he stumbles away, turning and running to us. "Let's bounce," Coop says, his cheeks flushed.

We head out the door, pushing through the crowd. Once outside, Molly slips her shoes off and we jog to where I parked the Beast. We get in and I pull out, beating most of the crowd.

I peel out onto the highway. Outside, the night seems to darken, making my headlight beams shrink into pinpoints. Overhead, lightning cracks and thunder booms. The storm from earlier, coming back from the dead. I tell Molly what I heard.

"It was Josh and the BBs? You're sure?"

"Without a doubt. I heard them. I heard Hanna screaming, and I heard Stan, and there was... fighting. I don't know. It's bad."

Rain begins to fall, light at first but picking up. *Tink, tink, tink,* the sound of the rain sharpens, becomes more solid. Hail, the size of nickels, begins to pelt the Beast.

"Uh," Coop says, his voice wavering. "Was there hail in the forecast? Maybe an Armageddon warning I missed?"

Visibility goes to near zero in half a minute. Hail pelts the car and road ahead, bouncing off the blacktop, some the size of golf balls.

"It's going to be all right," I say. But it's not. Nothing has been all right in a long time. I push the gas pedal to the floor as the hail beats down and the storm, once again, builds within me.

CHAPTER 38

By the time we get to Hanna's, the hail has stopped, but it's still raining.

Lightning flashes, but it's a regular storm now, a distant rumbling in the back of my mind. If things were different, I'd probably spend hours, days, weeks analyzing what is happening. Things aren't different, though. My life is too complicated as is.

I loosen my tie and take it off. Molly squirms beside me in her dress.

I make the last turn. Hanna's house is on the left up ahead and there doesn't seem to be anything wrong. The brick home stands tall in the night, outside lights on, illuminating the dark. I don't know what I was expecting: fire, ambulances, a gunfight, but the lack of any sign of trouble is worse somehow.

I stop the car in the driveway and hop out. Coop's already running to the house before I even put the Beast in park. Coop bangs on the door as Molly and I join him. The deadbolt thunks, and the large wooden door opens. Most of the interior lights are off, but the streetlight reveals Stan Smith's face. His eyes are distant, and his nose is swelling, caked with dried blood. Coop doesn't hesitate, pushing past him and running into the house. "Hanna!" he screams. "Hanna!"

There is a haunted cast to Stan's face. One I recognize. Stan Smith has given up.

I move past him, and he won't meet my eyes. Molly follows me into the foyer. Upstairs, Coop is screaming for Hanna.

Molly pulls on my arm and nods to the living room. Even from here I can see signs of a struggle. A lamp is lying on the ground, its bulb flickering. An older version of Hanna comes into view, bends over, and puts it back in its place on a coffee table. I've never met Hanna's mother, but I've seen pictures in the portraits hanging in the foyer. The woman in the living room only bears a fleeting resemblance to the portraits, though. She's tired, beaten down, scared. She adjusts the lamp shade, evening it out unnecessarily, her eyes blank.

"Where is she?" Coop yells down from the banister and immediately heads back to the stairs.

Stan joins Molly and me. He blinks as if coming out of a deep sleep, and the arrogant narcissist I've come to know is back. "Why are you here? Why are any of you here?"

"Because Hanna called us," Coop says as he hops down the last step.

My stomach is knotted and shaky. Molly takes me by the hand and leads me into the living room. The whole room is a mix of brown leather and dark wood. Paintings, vibrant with color, hang on the wall. One of Stan, sitting behind a desk, hangs above the fireplace. Whoever painted it was talented. It's a very lifelike rendition. I dislike the arrogant snob in the painting almost as much as I dislike the real Stan.

Mrs. Smith sits down in a large leather chair as we enter, not even acknowledging our presence. Her eyes are swollen and puffy from crying. Coop and Stan enter behind us.

"Can someone tell me where Hanna is?" Coop says.

Hanna's parents share a look, a ton going on in that brief moment. Stan looks away from his wife, muttering something. He goes to the wet bar and makes himself a drink.

"Where's Hanna?" Coop asks again, slow this time.

"The Stroups have her," Mrs. Smith says. "They took her friend, too. Lucas Munson."

"Lucas?" I ask. "Lucas was here?"

Stan bangs a glass hard on the wet bar, brown liquid sloshing. "Why are you telling these children our business, Jen?"

The look Jen Smith gives her husband could melt ice. "Why not?" Her gaze softens as it moves back to me. "Lucas stopped by. He's a good kid, a good friend. He was just here a minute. He was leaving when they came in."

"It's that idiot's fault," Stan says. "If he wouldn't have fought them, no one would have been hurt."

"Is Lucas okay?" Molly asks.

"They beat him pretty bad. He . . . he fought them so hard, but there were three of them . . ." Mrs. Smith's words trail off.

"Why?" Coop asks. "Why'd they take them?"

Stan drains the liquor in his glass and grabs the bottle again, pouring another, larger, drink. "They're trying to scare us, is all."

"*Scare us?*" Mrs. Smith says, her words mocking. "That's *all* they want? To *scare* us?" She grinds her teeth, anger erupting from her. "You stole from Hank. *Hank Stroup!*"

"I didn't have a choice!" Stan says, spittle flying from his lips. "Don't be a child!"

"Child?" Mrs. Smith stands. "You're the child. A child! You should have told Hank the minute Josh made you start stealing. Now Josh is blaming you. Who do you think Hank's going to believe?"

Stan's eyes widen. "Stop talking! Aren't things bad enough? These—Kids. Get out." Stan moves out from behind the bar. "Get out of my house!" He lurches forward, trying to grab Coop, but Coop easily darts away. "You," he spits at me. "This all started the day she brought you home." He takes a step toward me, then another. "Lie down with dogs and get fleas."

He closes the distance between us and raises a fist. At first, I don't react, the attempt at violence so pathetic. He swings at my face. I catch his arm and redirect his movement, spinning him around. I pull his arm up behind him, getting a satisfying yelp from him.

He stumbles. His socked feet slide on the immaculately polished hardwood floor, and he falls on his hands and knees. He cries out in pain. For several heartbeats he stays there. He takes a deep breath and flops over onto his rear end, looking up at me with loathing. He doesn't try to stand.

My lip twitches with pent-up rage. "Where's Hanna? Tell me now."

Stan's face goes slack. "Call the police, Jen."

She laughs. It's not a happy sound. "You want me to call the police? Fred Jamison. You want me to call him?"

Stan shakes his head. "The FBI, call the FBI."

"You're drunk!" Mrs. Smith screams, the anguish on her face heartbreaking. "You write the checks, Stan! Josh brags about who all is on the take. You know! They'll kill her! You know they will!"

Stan's breaths come in ragged shudders as he appears to come to some realization. "What else can we do?" He looks around, hoping an answer will materialize out of thin air. When it doesn't, he curls up into a ball on the floor.

Mrs. Smith stands. I move out of her way as she walks to her husband. She sits down next to him and rubs his shoulders. The act of kindness breaks something in him. He climbs up her like a drowning man coming to shore and clings to her like a child to his mother, his body shaking.

Mrs. Smith looks up at me as she pats her husband's back. She rocks him like a child. "How much do you know?" she asks me.

"Lady, I know everything."

Hanna's mom tilts her head to the side as if she'll argue, but then the small remaining light in her eyes fades. She gives a small, unamused laugh. Her voice is oddly serene. "Hank says we have until noon tomorrow to come up with the missing money. Two-point-five million. But we don't have that much. Even if we tell him his own son's the one who stole, Hank won't care. He'll kill us all and forgive that demented son of his."

I take a few steps closer. "I can help Hanna," I tell Mrs. Smith. "But I need to know where she is."

Stan shudders. He's a complete mess. Gone is any semblance of the arrogant man in the painting above the fireplace. "They could be anywhere," he says into his wife's shoulder.

I think of all the places they could have taken her, but the possibilities are endless without some starting point. Hanna had her phone when Josh and the BBs took her. What are the chances she still has it? Small, but it's all I've got. "Give me your phone, Stan."

Stan pulls away from Mrs. Smith and looks up at me. "My phone? Why?"

I'm done explaining myself to this miserable man who endangered his family with his greed. "Give it to me. Now."

He sits up, disentangling himself from Mrs. Smith, and visibly tries to pull himself together. He awkwardly gets to his feet. He rubs at his eyes with the back of his hand and stands a fraction taller. He pulls out his phone and hands it to me.

Without a word, I hold it up to his face to unlock the screen. I find his apps and locate the one I'm looking for. "Are you and Hanna on the same phone plan?"

"Yes," Mrs. Smith says from the floor, a small hint of hope creeping into her voice.

"She didn't have her phone," Stan says.

"Yeah she did," Coop says. "She called us."

"B-but," Stan stutters. "They wouldn't . . . let her keep it."

"Have you met the BBs?" Coop says. "They ain't too bright."

"I don't know," Mrs. Smith says, the hope increasing. She pushes up from the floor. "It happened so fast, Stan. Maybe they didn't notice."

Coop comes to stand beside me as the app to find your lost phone loads. Stan pushes in close too. Molly walks over, staying back but giving me a hopeful nod.

I find the device I'm looking for. I tap the device listed as Hanna's Phone. The screen goes to a map, a small circle swirling as it looks for Hanna's cell phone. Seconds tick by. Finally, a little bubble pops up with Hanna's name and picture on it. Hanna's icon is unmoving, somewhere out on County Road 8. The Wi-Fi signal with a cross through floats above it.

Coop studies it a second or two and groans.

"It's no good," Stan says, a sob escaping him as he looks at his screen. "There's nothing there. Her phone lost signal twenty minutes ago."

He's right. Still. "You work for this guy," I say. "You do his books. Does he own any property out here?" I tap Hanna's icon.

He started shaking his head even before I finished. "It's not—Wait. The old barrel plant." He clears his throat. "H&H Distributors. It's here." He points at the map on his phone several miles from Hanna's last reported location. "It's the only thing out there."

"I know where it is," I say.

"That's where she'll be . . . maybe. But you're a kid," Stan says. He looks to his wife. "He's a kid. This is insane."

Mrs. Smith stands from the floor. "We don't have any options."

"I'll go," Stan says, wiping fresh tears from his face.

"No," I say. "You won't."

Mr. Smith lets out a sound halfway between a sigh and a whine and covers his face with both hands, sobbing.

I drop his phone at his feet. "Let's go," I say to Molly and Coop, but Mrs. Smith stops me.

"Wait," she says, going to an end table. She reaches under it, Velcro cracks, and she pulls a gun out. For an instant, my heart skips a beat, thinking she's about to open up on us, but she walks over instead, offering me the gun, grip first.

Mr. Smith groans but doesn't speak.

"I don't want that," I say.

Jen Smith frowns. "Take it."

I hesitate for a heartbeat and take the gun. Stan Smith groans again.

The pistol is a Beretta. I pull back the slide a fraction and see the brass of the chambered round—9 millimeter. I release the slide and, with practiced movements, drop the mag. It's fully loaded. Twelve in the magazine and one in the hole.

I slam the mag back in, check the safety, and tuck the big automatic behind my back. Jen Smith's eyes never leave mine. Her bottom lip quivers and she whispers so only I can hear. "The slightest chance is better than no chance. Bring my baby home."

I nod, share a glance with Molly and Coop, and we leave the way we came.

CHAPTER 39

The rain and hail are gone, but the road is still wet and slick. Thunder and lightning play in the sky, and some unseen, unknown force twists and rolls with the clouds above, a power reflected somewhere in the deepest parts of me.

Something is wrong with the world. Something is wrong with me.

Molly rolls down her window, letting in air thick with moisture, and looks up. "I've never seen anything like this. It's . . . beautiful, like an impressionist painting of the sky, not the actual sky."

Coop has his window down too. "Only if Stephen King was an impressionist. I prefer sunsets. That sort of thing. Not end-of-the-world stuff."

"It's nature," Molly says. "Unique."

I look up. Molly and Coop are both right. It's creepy and unnatural, but beautiful all the same. Orange light leaks from somewhere in dark and gray swirls, like the light of the moon is fighting the night. But it's more for me. The power above pulses in my bones. It's both exciting and terrifying. Dad never said anything about *this*.

During the drive on County Road 8, at the same spot Hanna's phone last showed, all our phones lose signal.

"Ugh," Coop complains. "It's like we're in the nineties or something."

The road twists and turns, and I take the side road to the old barrel plant. It's way back in the woods in a larger defunct industrial park from even before the nineties. We pass by several buildings, all dilapidated and closed. One building has been kept up though. The grass was mowed sometime before the colder weather, too. I turn off my lights and drive slowly.

A chain-link fence surrounds the old building. The fence is topped with enough barbed wire to eviscerate a woolly mammoth, all of it at least a century newer than anything else.

The warehouse is dark, and no cars are visible in the parking lot. An old, dilapidated sign stands tall on a metal pole. The faded H&H logo is still visible despite years of wear.

"This is it," I say, trying to ignore the fact that I can feel the storm above us, gathering, waiting.

"Are you sure about this?" Coop asks.

I take a deep, steadying breath. "My plans are crap, all of them, but I'm going in that building. If Hanna's inside, she's coming out with me and that's it."

"Lucas too," Molly says.

"Uh, right. Of course. Lucas too."

I find a dirt road covered with pine needles and take it. The Beast's suspension squeaks on the uneven ground, and a few times, the tires lose traction on the pine straw cutting into the thin layer of mud below. It would not do well to get stuck, so I'm forced to back up and park on the side of the street.

"I'm going," I say.

Coop leans forward into the front seat. "I'm going too."

"No, you're not. I need both of you to stay here and be an extra set of eyes. Molly's driving. Keep the car running. If there is even a hint of danger, run. Get out of this dead zone and call . . . someone. Nobody from Rush Springs."

"Who?" Molly asks.

"I don't know. DM some reporters. Let everybody know. Drive straight to the FBI office in Little Rock and start talking. Post everything on social media. Tell the world. It may be the only way. Just give me twenty minutes first. If you can."

"I'm going," Coop says, defiant. "You need backup."

"And leave me alone out here?" Molly asks Coop. It's a low blow, and by the slight raise of her eyebrows Molly gives me, she knows it.

Coop sputters. "I—well. I— Okay, fine. Just don't go blaming me if Jude gets murdered."

"Twenty minutes," I say.

Molly hugs me fiercely. "Be safe, Jude. If you can't do anything, get out." She releases me. "You don't always have to be the hero."

I nod, hit the trunk release under the dash, and get out of the Beast. The thick, cool air assaults me as I make my way to the back of the car. I open the trunk all the way and pull up the carpet on the inside edge, where the spare tire sits, and take the duct tape and the small pocketknife I have stashed there.

Duct tape. Never leave home without it.

I turn to the warehouse and remember Mrs. Smith's gun. The big gun was uncomfortable tucked into my blue jeans. When I got in the Beast, I took it out and laid it under the seat. *Bring no weapon but yourself.* The rule echoes in my head, and I know the rightness of it. But this is not that. I am not answering the call of the Dream. This is a rescue mission, not a murder.

I go back to the driver's side and open my door. Molly's already behind the wheel.

"Ahh, excuse me." I reach down, my face close to Molly's and reach under her seat. As I pull the gun out, Molly leans forward and whispers in my ear. "Be safe."

The warmth of her breath sends a shiver down my spine. I stand, putting the Beretta behind my back again.

Molly's eyes are so round as she looks up at me. "And come back," she says.

"I will," I say, my voice calm and clear. I head toward the fence. The rain has completely stopped, even the lightning gone, but the storm still lingers. The jog up the hill doesn't take long. The warehouse is dark, the night is still. Would the Stroups take Hanna someplace Stan knew about? Maybe. Maybe not. Either way, I'm about to find out.

The ground is muddy near the fence. My clean white sneakers sink into the soft earth, the ground pulling back at me as I walk. I remove Dad's jacket and throw it over my shoulder. Making sure the Beretta is still secure in the small of my back, I place the duct tape on my wrist like an oversized bracelet. I approach the fence. It's a ten-footer.

I throw Dad's jacket over the barbed wire. "Sorry, Pop."

I climb the fence, moving over where Dad's jacket drapes the barbed wire. Even so, a spike punctures through the coat and bites deep into the heel of my palm, and another rips my pants as I hoist my leg over to the other side.

I land inside the fence as softly as I can. My hand is bleeding, so I make a fist and jog across the abandoned parking lot to the warehouse, leaving Dad's jacket behind.

I skirt the building looking for a way in, and immediately something catches my attention: a faint odor on the breeze. Up ahead, no more than ten feet away, I spot the back corner of the building. The scent gets stronger as I near the edge. The smell is distinct, reminding me of my childhood and trips with Mom in the car. Cigarette smoke. Someone is smoking nearby.

I put my shoulder to the edge of the building and peer around the corner, careful not to expose myself. A figure has his back to me. Smoke curls around a man I recognize. It's one of the BBs.

I take a slow breath. I'm in the right place.

A light dimly illuminates the right side of the big guy's body. A back door. An open back door.

I pull the gun from behind my back and slide around the corner, and I consider bashing the B with the butt of the automatic. In the movies, people are knocked unconscious with a swift blow to the head.

In real life, a blow strong enough to render a person unconscious is not that easy to deliver. Not with the butt of a pistol, anyway.

I should have brought the crowbar instead of the duct tape.

I can't let him scream. If he does, and anyone else is here, I'm toast.

I choose door number two.

I creep up to him, the wind concealing any noise I make. When I'm close enough, I place the cold barrel at the base of the B's neck as I cock the hammer.

With an auto, cocking the hammer isn't necessary, but the click of the trigger mechanism engaging is just so satisfying. And so very distinct. This B knows what's up, and he stiffens.

"Move an inch and you're dead," I whisper.

The cigarette falls from his fingers and hits the ground, sparking on the asphalt. "Who—" he starts, but I tap him hard on the skull with the barrel. "Not a word either," I hiss. "On your knees."

The big guy does as he's told. "Put your hands behind your back." Again, he complies, and with one hand I slide the duct tape off my wrist, using my hip to move it. I quickly pull off a strip with my teeth and bind the B's hands.

Next, I loop the tape around his legs. The sound of the tape coming free pierces the night, and I wince at all the noise I'm making, but it can't be helped. His legs and hands bound, I connect the two behind him and hunch him over like a trussed-up pig. He hits the asphalt with a satisfying flop. "Hey," he growls, "whoever you are, you're—"

I move so he can see me. So he can see the gun too. "I'm what? Dead? Is that what you were going to say?"

I see the B clearly now. It's Brian. I think, still not sure. If it is Brian, he's a very beat-up Brian. One eye is black, and his lip is busted and swollen. "You," he says.

I nod. "That's right, me. What happened to your face?"

He smiles. "I fell down some stairs."

"Those stairs wouldn't be named Lucas Munson, would they?"

He glares at me but says nothing. I tape his mouth shut, careful to make sure he can still breathe. He grunts and squirms when I stand. I kick him once in the ribs. He grunts and stops moving, glaring up at me with hate-filled eyes. "That's for pointing a gun at me. If I hear a peep out of you, I'll come back and kick you some more." I leave him, still glaring, but quiet.

I slide inside and find myself in a long hallway. Six doors line the hall. I curse under my breath. I don't have time for this, but I have no choice. I open each one. The first three are empty. The next three are full of boxes, but still no Hanna. I open the door at the end of the hall, and it exits into a larger room. A machine full of knobs and gears fills half the space, but still no Hanna. I take a minute to search behind the machine just in case, but all I find are cobwebs.

I take the only door left and enter a dark room. Above, small rectangular windows let in a minuscule amount of light. It takes a minute before my eyes adjust to the inky darkness. I'm in the main warehouse now, and it's as large as a basketball gym. A faint glow comes from way across the room in the shape of a door.

I don't want anyone to know I'm here, and I want to preserve my night vision, so I resist the urge to use my phone for light.

I make it to the door without breaking my neck, falling in a pit, or tripping on a hunk of forgotten machinery. I listen and hear nothing. My hand goes to the knob and I turn it, swinging the door open and pointing the gun in the room. Hanna sits behind a desk, a large metal bar bolted to the top and her right wrist handcuffed to it.

"Jude?" she asks, as I sweep the room with the gun. "It's you." Her speech is slurred, and I wonder if she's hurt.

The room is small, an old office with a drop-down ceiling. Besides the desk, there is no other furniture.

I hurry to Hanna, stuffing the gun in the back of my pants, and take a closer look. The cuffs are standard-issue police. The single iron bar welded to the steel desk is definitely DIY. I don't see any obvious signs that Hanna's hurt—no blood, no bruises, and, for what it's worth, she doesn't appear to be in pain. "You okay?" I ask. "Did they hurt you?"

"Nah," she says. "They, uh, didn't hurt me." There is a noticeable lack of emotion in her voice, and I wonder if she's being honest.

"You sure?"

"Of course, I'm sure," she says, her words sharp as a razor, the old Hanna back for the moment. "How did you find me?"

I don't have time to explain it, so I give her the short version. "Your mom and your—Stan—helped us."

Hanna lets out a deep breath. "I didn't know what they'd do, Jude. Thought they might leave me and run off to Tahaati—uh." She blinks, and keeps her eyes shut for a few seconds. When her eyelids open, her eyes don't want to focus. "Tahiti, I mean."

Something's up. The Hanna I know would be barking orders, making plans, and telling me what I'm doing wrong, but I don't have time to ponder her odd behavior. I have to get her out of here. "Where's the key?"

"Brian had it," Hanna says. "Josh and Billy left, I think. Brian stayed behind. He tried to smoke in here, and I told him to get lost. Like, boundaries, right?"

"Brian has the key?" I ask as soon as she's done rambling.

"Yeah," Hanna says. "That's what I said. Pay attention."

I slap my forehead.

"What?" Hanna asks.

"I left Brian taped up outside. I didn't search him. Give me a minute."

I head to the door, but Hanna stops me. "Wait," she says. "The key . . ." Her words trail off. She shakes her head. "The key *might* be in here. Yeah, the key is almost definitely here. Brian put it somewhere before he left."

"Great," I say and wait for her to tell me where. She stares at me but doesn't elaborate. "Hanna," I say gently. "Where's the key?"

She blinks at me. "There's, like, more than one. Josh said that, I think. *Josh.*" She makes a disgusted sound. "He has such a punchable face. I'd *really* like to punch his stupid face."

I'm now positive something is wrong. "Focus, Hanna. Where did Brian put his key?"

Hanna licks her lips, concentrating as she scans the room. She points at an antiquated plastic wall file next to the door. "There."

I go to it and reach inside. My fingers touch metal. I pull a ring of keys out. I groan. There's like a hundred keys on it. It takes a minute, but I find a cuff key.

"Got it," I say.

"Sweeeet," Hanna says.

I walk over to her with the keys, examining her closer. "You sure you're okay? No one hit you in the head? You sound—off."

"I'm fine," Hanna snaps, sitting straighter and regaining some vigor. "No one hit me. My head is fine. Are you going to unlock me or what?"

I already have the key in the cuff as she asks the question.

"Oh," she says as the cuff falls off her wrist. "Thanks."

I drop the keys on the table. "That's soooo much better," Hanna says rubbing where the cuff had been. "Did you see a bathroom on your way in?"

"You need a bathroom? Now?"

She groans. It's way over the top, like a second grader who didn't get her snack. "I've been chained for . . . I don't know, but literally no bathroom breaks. I really have to go." Her eyes won't or can't focus on me. She giggles. "Go . . . *go* . . . go."

I finally understand. "What did they give you?"

243

She frowns and stands on unsteady feet. "I don't know," she hisses, but her anger is ruined by a little giggle. She sighs dramatically. "They made me, okay? Something to make me calm. I don't do drugs, and they gave me waaay too much. Little pink pills. How do they pack so much in them?" She slides the chair back with her legs, almost falling, and takes a step toward me, but it's more of a stumble. I grab her arm to steady her, and she falls into me, our faces only inches apart. "Jude," she says.

"Yes?" I ask, trying to stand her up straighter. She's not big, but it's like she's a loose bag of bones. "Jude," she says more forcefully.

I delay my efforts to right her and look up into her face. She's all up in my grill. For a moment, our eyes lock.

She licks her lips and lets out a breath. Her eyes focus on me as if seeing me for the first time. She squints and frowns. "If you try to kiss me, I'm going to knock your teeth out."

"Kiss you? What? No. You're messed up. Just chill, okay? We've got to get out of here."

"Whatever," she says. "You're too . . . anyway . . ."

She can't finish her thought, and I think that's for the best.

Together, we stumble out the door into the dark warehouse. How long has it been? Molly and Coop are leaving in twenty. I fish in my pocket for my phone, pulling in out. I turn on the light. I have to give Hanna way more help than I at first thought. She's stumbling and dragging her feet. I snake one arm around her slim waist to keep her steady.

"Wait," she says. "What about Lucas?"

I stop, almost tripping. "Lucas," I say. I want to laugh and cry all at once. I keep forgetting about Munson. "Where is he?"

She points in the dark, and I swing my phone in the same direction. The light illuminates a row of doors on the wall to the right. "They took him in there when we got here. They beat him. They wouldn't stop hitting him."

"Which door," I say.

"There." Hanna points and giggles. "No, there." She points to the door next to it. "Wait, not that one." She straightens and scratches her cheek, obviously confused.

"This is taking too long," I say.

"Relax, I'm working on it. We came in, they split us up . . ." Hanna points. "Over there. Shine the light over there."

I shine the light.

"There, that door. Right there."

"You sure?"

"Yes!"

I help her as we backtrack. She trips, and I keep her from hitting the floor. Despite our situation, Hanna is chatty. "Why do you think Lucas and I are together, anyway?" She doesn't let me respond. "It's so *typical*. Can't two people just be friends? Why does there always have to be . . . expectations?"

"I don't think y'all are together," I say.

"Oh," Hanna says. "Why not?"

"Lucas told me. Is this important?"

"No. Not really. Just whatever."

I lean her against the wall and open the door to a pitch-black room.

The light of my phone cuts through the dark. Lucas lies in the floor in a black suit, zip ties on wrists behind his back. Zip ties on his feet. Zip ties interlocking the two, twisting him in a much crueler rendition of how I left the B out back. He's awake. His tie, used as a gag, is fastened around his head, sadistically pulling his lips back in a manic grin. A cut glistens red above his right eye and dried blood cakes his face. His left eye, red and puffy, is nearly swollen shut, and his white dress shirt is pink and red with blood.

"Mhmph . . . mhmph . . . mhmph," he mumbles, managing to make it sound like cursing. I pull Hanna into the room and help her down.

She moans and covers her eyes. "Is the room spinning? It feels like it's spinning."

I pull out my pocketknife and make quick work of Lucas's bonds. He pulls his tie from his mouth as soon as his hands are free. "Are they still here?" he says, standing stiffly, his figure imposing in the small space. He pulls his suit coat off and throws it on the floor.

Hanna giggles, eliciting a frown from Munson. "Is she okay?"

"Peachy. They gave her something. Can we talk about this later? I have one of the Bs tied up. Everyone else is gone. We gotta go."

Lucas walks over and picks Hanna up in one motion and places her on his shoulder, like a precious sack of potatoes.

Hanna moans but doesn't complain. She's coming down off whatever drugs they gave her, and it doesn't appear to be pleasant.

"Show-off," I mutter at his casual display of strength.

I lead the way out the door, heading across the warehouse floor, my phone lighting the way. Munson is all up on my six, breathing down my neck. "How did you find us?"

"That's a question for another time," I say. "Let's get Hanna out of here first."

Munson grunts. "Fine. Move faster, then."

He gives me a little shove from behind. I stumble forward, annoyance and adrenaline shooting through me but picking up my pace all the same. Despite the odds, we're almost clear. In ten minutes, we *will* be clear.

A door shuts somewhere in the building. The unmistakable clang of metal. I skid to a stop, trying to triangulate where the sound came from. Munson almost runs into my back. "What was that?" he pants.

Before I can answer, the door we're headed to bangs open, and the lights above flicker on.

Josh Stroup and Chief Jamison come into the room, their pistols leveled at us.

There is no cover. Nowhere to run. Nowhere to hide. My instincts tell me to draw my weapon and open fire. Two against one. Not great odds—on the verge of suicide, depending on how skilled the bad guys are, but I also know the odds of Josh Stroup letting any of us go.

Before I can even process that thought, more people enter. Coop followed by Molly. Molly's eyes are wide and apologetic. Coop looks like he might puke.

The next person to enter the room is none other than Big Hank Stroup himself, complete with white cowboy hat, a smile on his lips, and a salesman's twinkle in his eye. He, at least, doesn't have a gun.

Unfortunately for the good guys, both the BBs behind him do.

My hand moves to my side, away from the Beretta at the small of my back.

Two against one would have been bad. Four against one is suicide.

CHAPTER 40

"Well, well, well," Big Hank says, nailing the evil-cowboy drawl to a T. "Jude Erickson, we meet again. You seem to be turning up a lot lately in my business. I gotta say, I don't care for it much."

"He's got a gun," a very irritated Brian says, pointing his pistol at me.

Big Hank widens his eyes in mock alarm. "A gun? Well, that ain't very all-American football of you. Where you got it hid? Let me guess. Behind your back. Yep. The small of the back does make a good pocket for it, now don't it? Why don't you move real slow and lay that gun on the floor?"

Four guns point at me. If I so much as sneeze, I'm dead. Josh Stroup, fresh bruising covering most of the left side of his face, looks eager to do damage, especially to Munson, who he keeps glaring at.

Lucas sits Hanna gently on the floor and stands tall, stupid all over his bloody face.

"Don't," I say to him. He glances at me. I shake my head. He's got to see this situation for what it is. Molly and Coop are beside Josh, the BBs behind them. There is no way to protect them if bullets start to fly.

Munson grimaces but stays still, for now, and I want to scream. Deep inside, something stirs. The metal building shudders, and the wind howls outside.

Big Hank's eyes drift up. His gaze comes back, finding me. "That gun, now. Slow, too."

I pull the Beretta from its place, holding it with the barrel down and my finger away from the trigger. My chest burns, and my limbs tingle.

A *ting* on the metal roof strikes above, followed by more and more. Hank snorts. "This weather." His eyes narrow at me. "Waiting on you, hoss. Place it on the floor, gently now."

I place the gun on the concrete floor, careful to move as slow as I can. It would suck to get shot before they plan on shooting me.

"Now, kick that nasty thing over here," Hank says.

I do like I'm told. The gun slides on the concrete, right to Hank. He stops it with a snakeskin cowboy boot, bends, and picks it up. "Now, this is a nice weapon. You steal this, son? No, no, no. Don't tell me." He pauses, smiling big. "Anyone else know you're here? The accountant and his wife, I imagine. Who else? Law enforcement?" He hesitates. "Particularly, law enforcement of the federal kind?"

I blink.

Hank shakes his head, and the jovial, wise-cracking country boy is gone. His face, carved with laugh lines, hardens. "Don't you dare lie to me, boy." He scowls. "I see it. I see those wheels turning. That's not the play here. You're going to tell me how you found us. Then you're going to make me believe you." He sweeps the room with his hand holding the gun. "You need to understand your situation. You're in an oasis where technology has ceased to exist. Spent a lot of cash on the latest jammers and blockers. You might as well be on the moon. No one knows you're here. No one ever will. You get me? You understand your predicament? I will hurt you."

Jamison shifts on his feet. "Hank," he says. "I don't know about—"

Hank's face twists with barely suppressed rage. "Not now, *Fred*!" He rubs at his clean-shaven face with his free hand, the Beretta pointing at the floor in his other. His hand falls away from his face, and like a switch being flipped, Big Hank, the smiling billboard cowboy, is back. "Come on now. What y'all waitin' for? Round 'em up. Right here on the floor." He gives Jamison a reassuring smile. "We're just going to have a talk, Fred. Relax. Now move."

Billy pushes Coop, who comes flying our way. I catch him before he can fall. Josh grabs Molly by the arm, twisting it behind her with a malicious snarl. Molly yelps in pain as she's forced toward our group.

I take two steps toward Josh and Molly. Out of the corner of my eye, Munson tries the same, but Hanna is latched to his leg.

Every gun in the room points at my chest.

"Stop!" Big Hank roars. He points at Josh. "Let that girl go, you damn fool."

Josh eyes his father with the same malevolence he directed at Munson a few seconds ago. His face slackens and he shrugs, letting Molly's arm go and pushing her forward. The storm churns in my chest, and the whole building shudders.

"Sit," Big Hank says.

Molly staggers over to me, her face down in shame, and her thick red hair covering her face. She stumbles into me, and I help her down as we sit. Coop sits on the other side of her, moving close like he wants to protect her too.

Molly leans against me, and I place an arm around her.

Munson hasn't made any indication he might cooperate. He's glaring at our captors one by one, no doubt imagining which bits he'd like to tear off first. Hanna still clutches his leg, saving him from himself.

Hank gives Munson a respectful nod. "You are a big ole boy, ain't ya? Messed my boys up pretty good." He points Mrs. Smith's gun at Munson's head. "But bullets don't care much for muscle."

Munson doesn't flinch, the dumb in his posture growing.

"Sit down," I tell him.

He turns his glare on me for a second. Big Hank drops the gun, pointing it at Hanna. "Or maybe I'll just shoot *her*."

Lucas trembles with rage, but he sits down, unentangling Hanna from his leg and letting her slump against him.

Something hot burns behind my eyes and the whole warehouse shudders with the storm. Everyone looks up.

Hank glances at his son. "Is there supposed to be tornadoes tonight?"

Josh shrugs, not even looking at his father. "How should I know?"

Hank makes a disgusted sound and shakes his head. "Anyway. I need answers and quick. First: Anyone else know you're here? And I mean anyone at all. And second: Who's been talkin' about my affairs?" He glares right at Hanna. "There's a lot of people here. A lot of people poking around where they shouldn't."

When no one offers up any info, the real Hank peeks from behind the curtain again. "Somebody start talkin'!" he screams.

"Shoot one of them," Josh says with relish. "You won't be able to shut the rest up after that."

"Shut your damned mouth!" Hank screams again. "If you'd of handled your business, we wouldn't be in this situation. I wanted the daughter. Now we got *five* people to deal with."

Josh's face turns red. From anger or embarrassment, I can't tell.

"I'll tell you what you want to know," I say.

Munson makes a noise between a growl and a grunt. "Think if you do like he says, he'll let us leave, Jude? Don't be stupid."

"No," I say. "He offered me money once. You're a businessman, right, Hank?"

Hank's salesman grin is almost as wide as the brim of his hat. It's a smile that could never lie. "That's right, son. This is all one big misunderstanding. You got information on how I might run a better business, I'd be much obliged."

"And we can leave if I help? All of us?"

Hank grins and nods like he's about to seal the deal on a luxury manufactured home. "Well no. Not the girl. Not directly anyhow." He's smart enough not to make the lie too big. "You see, her parents owe me something, and she's gotta be my guest for a while. Now the rest of you? Sure. In fact, I bet my boy would be glad to see the back of that one." He nods at Munson.

The look that crosses Josh's face is one part hate and four parts rage. If by some miracle I'm wrong about Hank's intentions, Josh's intentions are crystal clear. Munson's never going home. None of us are.

Josh stops glaring at his father for a moment to give the BBs a slow nod. I'm not sure what is happening, but the BBs do. Hank and Jamison are oblivious to the silent conversation going on between the younger men.

"We won't keep Miss Smith long," Hank continues. "A day or two, tops. You other kids can go home." He raises a finger. "But you have to stay quiet about tonight. We can talk rewards for good behavior after that. Now spill."

"Don't be a dumbass, Jude," Munson says. "He's lying."

I ignore him. Hank just smiles.

I do my best to let terror echo in my words. It isn't that big of a stretch. "I-I can show you." I take a chance and try to stand.

"No," Molly whispers, holding me. "Just do what they say."

"It's okay," I say, pulling free of her, standing as slow as I can. Every gun in the room finds me. Josh takes a step forward, taking a bead on my head. "My phone," I screech like I might wet my pants. Again, not that big of a stretch. "I'm getting my phone."

"Go ahead," Big Hank says, smiling that smile of his. "It's a worthless hunk of junk here, but show me what you got. And go slow. Real slow." He bends his elbow up and rests the pistol on his shoulder.

Munson looks like he wants to murder me. Molly's head is bowed, her hair in her face, like she can't watch what's about to happen. Coop's jaw is slack with disbelief and puzzlement. Hanna, though . . . She doesn't look sick anymore. Her eyes are focused on me. Calm. Ready for whatever's about to happen. She trusts me. Totally.

Or maybe it's the drugs.

Either way, a surge of confidence pulses through me. Hanna Smith believes in me. We're probably still going to die, but Hanna believes. For some odd reason, at this moment, that means the world to me.

I hold out a placating hand and carefully remove my phone from my pocket. "It's an app," I say. "Something friends do. Gives us an idea where everyone's at, so we can hang out." It's not the truth, but close. Those are the best lies.

"None of that stuff works here," Hank says.

"You're right," I say, "but Hanna's phone showed up a few miles from here. Stan knew about this place, and we put two and two together."

Hank frowns at me and cuts his eyes to Josh.

"No," Josh says. "She doesn't have her phone. She never did."

"You sure about that?" I ask Josh, opening my weather app, and holding out my phone. The app is blank. It won't load, but that doesn't matter. I just need Hank to let me get closer.

Hail pecks at the roof above, gaining in intensity. The rain pours down, and the wind howls.

Behind me Hanna clears her throat. I glance back. She's holding her phone up for the world to see.

"My *son*," Hank says with scorn. "Got his daddy's looks and his momma's smarts."

"I told Billy to search her," Josh protests as he glares at his father.

Billy doesn't look very pleased being blamed, but, then again, neither of the BBs ever look pleased.

"Show me that damn phone, football stud," Hank says, stepping closer, the gun down, squinting at my screen.

I take a tentative step toward Hank. "Yeah, and if you look here, it shows where—"

Hank leans in even closer as I point to nothing at the top of the screen. He's overconfident. So many guns pointed at a bunch of unarmed teenagers. Josh should have warned him. Billy and Brian too. They know. They saw what I could do at the Banjo. A ton of people did. One video from that night is going viral, but I doubt Big Hank's into that sort of stuff.

I drop the phone and spring forward with a lifetime of training and all my God-given athleticism. Hank brings the gun up, but he's too late. I grab the gun while redirecting the barrel. The loudest clap of thunder I have ever heard crashes outside. Motion catches my attention in my periphery as people move, but Josh and the goon squad are going to be too late. My body moves like a machine as I control the weapon and pull an overbalanced Hank in close. He gasps as I rotate the gun one hundred and eighty degrees. His finger, in the guard, breaks with a satisfying crack of bone.

Even as Big Hank screams, I'm moving, twirling the thin man so he's between me and his boys. I don't place the gun to the side of his head like in the movies. Instead, I press it to the base of his skull, my left arm wrapping the smaller man tight and my head barely visible behind his.

"Stop," I yell.

Jamison's gun is the only one not pointed at me. His barrel is down and his posture screams uncertainty. He's the unknown. He's the only one hesitant about killing us all. I need to reinforce that. "You don't want to do this, Chief Jamison."

His lip twitches. "Let Hank go." He makes a decision and points his gun at me. Or at his boss. I'm making the target as small as possible. Billy slides closer to Jamison, his weapon on me.

I slide back until I bump into someone sitting on the floor. I think it's Coop, but I don't look back. "Everybody, get up," I say. "We're leaving."

Brian moves, trying to flank me. "Stop," I tell him in a voice as cold as Big Hank's heart. Brian doesn't even blink, just keeps moving. "You think I'm playing?"

Brian glances at Josh, who lifts his chin. Brian, like a good dog, stops at Josh's command.

It's Billy who does something odd. He tucks his gun into the front of his pants and moves behind Jamison. Billy grins wide as he rears back. I see what's going to happen an instant before Billy's huge fist slams into the back of Jamison's head.

Chief Jamison is rocked by the blow. He drops his gun and almost falls, but Billy grabs him, his right arm around the other man's neck, pulling Jamison close.

I feel frozen in place, unable to do anything but watch the madness unfold in front of me.

Jamison's eyes widen as Billy puts him in a rear naked choke. It's used in combat training and martial arts. I know it well. If done properly, you can render someone unconscious by restricting blood and oxygen from reaching the brain. It is a useful tool in subduing someone, but if it's done wrong, or for too long, you can cause serious injury or even kill the other person.

Jamison's eyes flutter even as he tries to hit Billy, throwing his fists up and over his shoulder, doing as much damage as butterfly kisses. It only takes seconds. Jamison's arms fall to his side, and his body goes limp. Billy drops him like a pile of dirty laundry.

The bad guys are turning on each other, but I doubt it's improving our situation. We should all run, but even as I think this, it's too late.

Big Hank sputters. "What in the name of all that's good are you doing?"

Billy ignores him as he takes a zip tie from his pocket and restrains Jamison, securing the police chief's hands behind his back.

"I asked you a question," Big Hank says, some of the authority coming back to his voice.

Josh Stroup sighs dramatically and points his gun at his father's chest. "You know, Pops, you should watch the way you speak to people."

"Don't—" Hank starts. "What are you doing, Josh?"

"It's a coup. You don't have the stomach for what needs doing anymore, old man. You're soft. You were actually thinking about letting them go? Letting that accountant walk too?"

"I wasn't going to let anyone go, you dammed fool," Hanks says.

Josh shrugs. "Whatever."

"Son," Hank says, for once lost for words.

"*Son*?" Josh asks. "You know you call everyone *son*. *Son* this and *son* that. You use that word so much it don't mean nothing." He nods at the BBs, and they spread out. Jamison moans on the floor. He's slowly coming to, trying to get free.

The BBs keep moving, flanking me.

"Stop," I yell, but they don't listen.

Josh laughs. "Or what?" he feigns concern. "You gonna shoot my daddy?" He moves the gun up so that he's pointing it at his father's head. "Please do. I think I'm ready for my inheritance."

Hank trembles as I hold him close. His voice is filled with anger and betrayal. "Why?" he asks.

"*Why?*" Josh mocks his father. "I have so many reasons, old man. We don't have enough hours in the day." Josh moves his gun a fraction, aiming at the thin sliver of my head poking up behind his father's back. He closes one eye and bites his lip in mock concentration, like he's drawing a bead on me. "Drop the gun, boy."

To drop the gun is death. I know that, but my human shield is worthless. I point the gun at Josh and push his father away. Hank trips and falls on the concrete with a curse.

In my head and in my chest, pressure builds like something inside wants out. Overhead, the building shakes with the wind and hail.

"Whoo-hoo!" Josh yelps with glee. He's hopping from one foot to the other, excited, actually excited. "You know what we got here, boys?" he screams over the storm. "We got a deadlock." Josh's eyes are alight with joy. "You shoot me, my boys shoot you. Man, kid. You want a job? You've got stones. I'll give you that. Big Hank's is under new management, and I'm hiring." He laughs. "Nah, on second thought, you'll be too dead to apply."

My head pounds with the storm. I am a cup overflowing.

Any second and Josh is going to take a shot. He'll kill me and all my friends and sleep like a baby tonight.

The odd calm I've experienced before fights the past few weeks settles in. The hail hammering the roof slackens and stops, matching my emotions, and the silence that follows is like the grave.

My decision is made. This is what I am. This is what my father made me.

I pull the trigger.

CHAPTER 41

lick. The Beretta misfires. Josh shows me his teeth. I pull the trigger again, again, and again in quick succession. *Click, click, click.* The weight of the gun is right. It's loaded.

I run the slide, attempting to eject the bad cartridge, but no cartridge ejects, and the gun jams with the slide open. "That's not . . . possible," I mumble.

But it is. Unlucky, but possible.

"Whoo!" Josh hoots. "That's what I'm talking about!" He cackles as he speaks, and I wonder if he's been dipping into his product. "Thought you had me for a second. Now drop the gun or we start shooting."

I could clear the jam and make it work, but Josh could kill me five times before I could do that. I can't believe it. It's tragic bordering on impossible. I drop the gun.

"Why, Son?" Big Hank wheezes from the floor. "Why?"

Josh walks toward me, his eyes on me, smiling his predatory smile. As he passes his father, he points his pistol at him and pulls the trigger. *Bang.* The gunshot is loud in the warehouse.

Big Hank screams, twitches, curls up in a ball, and screams some more. Josh shoots him again, and this time Big Hank goes still. Josh never once takes his eyes off me. He stops, closer, but out of my reach.

Behind me, Coop begins to cry. I understand. I've seen death in my dreams, but this is different. This is horrible.

Josh takes a deep breath and smiles. "Now . . . we're going to have some fun."

The BBs move toward us, and Munson rises like a bloodied and bruised mountain. The BBs raise their weapons.

"Stop!" Hanna, using Munson to pull herself up, stands on shaky legs. "Stop!" she screams again.

Munson pants like a rabid dog about to attack. The BBs point their pistols at him, ignoring the rest of us. Josh Stroup laughs. "My, what a forceful, commanding voice you have there."

Hanna glares at Josh. "You need me." Her words are slurred but not nearly as bad as earlier.

"Do I?"

"You . . . you need my father," she says.

Josh's smile widens. "Accountants, lawyers, they're a dime a dozen. And Stan's got liabilities. I mean, can you keep your mouth shut, Hanna? Are you trustworthy? I don't think you are."

Hanna takes a shaky step toward Josh, then another.

Josh motions Hanna toward him with the gun and his free hand. "Come on. You can do it."

Munson tries to hold her back, but Hanna swats at his hand. "Stop it, Lucas! Just . . . hold on."

"Whoo-hoo," Josh hoots, enjoying his newfound status as top dog. He sniffs and rubs his nose. "Feisty, this one."

The BBs laugh appropriately.

Hanna staggers next to me, and I consider stopping her, but she trusted me earlier. I think I'll trust *her* now. Things aren't always what they seem, and Hanna is smarter than me.

Out of the corner of my eye, Jamison gets to his knees. His hands are still zip-tied behind his back, but Billy really should have secured his legs. He's to the bad guys' backs and looks like he's about to do something stupid.

Good.

Hanna takes a few unsteady steps to Josh. Then a few more. "Stan is good at what he does. You of all people should know that."

"Really?" Josh says with a wolfish grin, enjoying this game. "Me of all people, huh? Is there something you'd like to confess?"

Hanna takes two more awkward steps, stumbles, and falls into Josh.

Josh looks over at Brian, smiling. "Damn, son. How much did you give her?"

Brian shrugs. "Enough."

Josh laughs, but the laugh is cut off as Hanna's knee comes up, right into Josh's downstairs business.

The guttural groan that escapes Josh's lips might be the most pitiful sound I've ever heard. He drops his gun to clatter on the floor.

Jamison makes his move, standing and running at Billy. He hits the big kid with a lowered shoulder, and they tumble to the ground. Munson sprints and leaps into the fray with all the suddenness and ferocity of a grizzly bear, wailing on poor Billy like an MMA fighter.

Without thinking, I turn to Brian. He'd been distracted by Jamison's attack on his other half, but now his attention—and the barrel of his pistol—swings back to Munson. I can't cover the distance in time to keep him from shooting.

The discarded Beretta is at my feet. I stoop as Brian lines up a shot. I grab the jammed gun and throw it with all my strength. Brian sees it too late, and it takes him in the forehead. His knees go slack and buckle. I sprint to him before he can recover, and kick him in the head. He falls hard, hitting his head again on concrete. He goes still, and I pick up his gun, scanning the surrounding scene.

Hanna points a gun at a kneeling Josh. Munson and Jamison have Billy unconscious and bleeding. It takes a second for it to sink in.

We did it. Hanna. It was Hanna. She did it. She saved us.

Josh Stroup screams. "No! No! No!" He jumps up. Hanna backs away, pointing the gun. "No!" he screams, turns, and runs away. Hanna points the gun at his back. For three heartbeats, I think she's going to shoot, but she lowers her weapon as Josh reaches a door with an old, dusty EXIT sign above it. He fumbles with his keys and unlocks the door. He's gone in seconds, leaving without looking back.

Hanna shudders and drops the gun to her side. I take one step toward her, when something metal and the size of a soda can bounces once, twice, three times on the concrete.

I look in the direction it came from. A black gloved hand throws another of the objects into the room. At the last second, I recognize what they are. The world is gone in explosions and flashes of light bright as the sun.

My chest is rocked with the concussion of the explosion. I'm blind, I'm deaf. My eyes, ears, and chest burn. I'm on the floor, rolling. Flash-bangs. Someone thew flash-bangs into the room.

I'm aware of someone, many someones, yelling, but I can't make out what they're saying. Something hard slams into me, and I'm flipped to my back.

Long seconds pass, and my vision clears in increments. A man in black, pointing an assault rifle at my head, stands over me, his boot in my chest. The placard across his chest reads FBI. Other men dressed the same are cuffing or otherwise subduing everyone in the room.

One of the black-clad men comes to stand over me. "Found him!" he yells, and three other men come over and pull me up by the arms. The men haul me from the room without explanation.

CHAPTER 42

The van they stuff me in is right outside the warehouse. "Wait," was the only explanation I was given. I still hear a faint ringing in my ears, but my vision is fine. More than anything, I want answers.

The van is sparse, no windows, just a lone light in the ceiling above casting dim illumination into a gunmetal interior. I sit on one of the two benches lining each side of the van. A steel wall with a small window separates the back from the driver's compartment. The back door is the only way in or out. The latch is locked. I tried it already.

The back door opens, and a man in a suit and tie hops into the van. He smiles at me, his ballistic vest tight over his suit jacket. A tablet is under one arm. He looks around, hunched over, his head almost scraping the low ceiling, as if waiting for me to invite him to sit. When I don't, he shrugs and plops down on the bench opposite me. Like all his buddies, an FBI placard is stuck to his vest. He opens the tablet and punches in his password, looking up at me with wide eyes, like he's about to perform a magic trick.

"Jude Erickson," he says, like greeting an old frat brother.

He's thirtyish, with slick black hair combed back and gelled to perfection. I hate him already.

"You are a very interesting young man," he says without giving his name. He taps at the tablet and turns it so I can see. I recognize it right away. It's the video from the Banjo that's currently going viral. "This you?"

I don't answer. He knows.

"That is some quick hands. You have any special training?"

He's asking questions, but he already knows the answers. I won't play his game. "Tell me about my friends," I say. "Are they okay?"

The man gives me a smile that I bet has got his butt kicked more than once. "Everyone but Big Hank Stroup is fine. Unfortunately, Josh Stroup evaded capture."

"Evaded capture?" I ask dryly. "He ran out the back door."

The man tilts his head in acknowledgement. "We came in all haste and didn't have numbers to cover all points of entry. Don't worry, we'll get him."

I huff at that. "Sure, whatever. How did you even know we were here?"

No-Name doesn't seem bothered or surprised by my question. In fact, he's pleasant, overfriendly, and not super professional. "Well. Stan Smith and his wife came to their senses and called us."

"Is that right? Because last I talked to them, they were terrified someone in the FBI was on Big Hank's payroll."

The man leans back, making himself comfortable. "They were right to be worried. Two weeks ago, an agent with an impeccable record failed a polygraph. It was close. She almost passed." He shrugs. "But she didn't. Big Hank wasn't known to us until then. It's remarkable really. He's been hiding in plain sight for decades." He holds out one hand as if asking if I have any more questions. When I don't respond, he continues. "Great, I need a statement now."

I tap my foot. "Fine. Where do I start?"

The man smirks. It's an odd gesture, given the situation. "Well, Jude. Why don't you start from the *beginning*?" The way he says *beginning* makes me do a double take. He waits for me to start, his face giving nothing away.

I'm annoyed, tired, and the flash-bang probably didn't do my brain any favors. I want to go home.

I tell him what happened, starting with the call from Hanna a few hours ago. No-Name records the interview with his tablet, asking appropriate questions here and there. It doesn't take long.

When I'm done, he places the tablet in his lap. "Thank you very much, Jude. We will be in touch to go over the details, but I think I have what I need. You are free to leave."

I get up from my seat, my back stiff as I still have to stoop. I half expect the door to be locked, but it pops open as I tug on the latch.

"Sweet dreams, Mr. Erickson," the man says airily.

I freeze and look at him. His face and demeanor have changed. He's not the bumbling FBI bro anymore. He's something else. Something I may have underestimated.

He grips my arm, hard. "Finish this. Time isn't on your side. They won't wait forever."

I pull my arm free. "You know. You're with *them*." I don't say who *them* is. I don't need to.

No-Name grunts. "We are all just actors on the stage the Old Blood built. They believe you may have a part to play in the coming conflict, but even they must follow the rules. Play your part. Do your duty. Kill the killer."

"I am so *sick* of all of this," I tell him, danger rising in my words. The man doesn't so much as blink.

Is he like me? Is he a Dreamer too?

I laugh joylessly. "Kill . . . the killer," I repeat back to him with all the disgust I feel. "So easy, huh? Tommy Davis," I say my friend's name, watching the man's face for any sign, any reaction that would tell me whether Tommy is truly the one.

The man's face is a mask, giving nothing away. "Thank you for your cooperation, Mr. Erickson. You should probably go now."

I consider him for a few heartbeats more. He's done talking.

I leave the van to find my friends. The night is cool and a wind blows, but the storm is completely gone. There are flashing lights but not a ton of people. For something like this, I would expect more.

Nothing about this is right, and I have no answers.

Old Blood, coming conflict? What was that?

The world, it seems, is a much, much bigger place than I ever imagined.

I don't like it. I don't like it at all.

CHAPTER 43

Almost twenty-four hours have passed and there has not been a single news story of what went down. The story should be all over the news, but it's not. Not a peep.

Hanna's parents did call the FBI, but Stan Smith is free. He hasn't been arrested or even questioned. Hanna says no one has even come to talk to them.

It's wrong. All wrong.

But I know what's happening. No-Name told me. He also told me what I had to do.

The house isn't as large as Hanna's. It's not a rich person's house. It's a high school football coach's house. The Beast's engine rumbles as it idles in Coach Davis's driveway.

I get out of my car and walk up to the front door and knock. Within seconds, a smiling Tommy opens the door. "What's up, Jude? Come on in."

Tommy turns his back on me and leads the way. I close the door behind me and follow him. We're alone. I know it from a few weeks ago in Coach D's office. Coach D said he and his wife were going on a fishing trip the day after homecoming. My phone call earlier today confirmed it. Coach D told me Tommy knew where the old fishing gear was. All I had to do was come by.

Hanna is safe, hanging with Molly at Molly's house. Wonder of wonders, the two seem to be becoming friends. I'm thankful they're together and safe.

I follow Tommy through the living room. The TV is playing a college football game. An aerial view shows a huge stadium packed with thousands of people, most wearing red. The sound on the television is muted. Tommy stops to watch the screen and grabs the remote off the TV stand. "You want to watch some of the game? That AJ kid's got an arm. I love watching him spin it."

"Thanks, I-I can't though. I actually have some people waiting on me."

Tommy looks disappointed as he places the remote back down. "Yeah, all right. What you got going on tonight? Date night?"

"Kind of."

"Cool," he says, but it's obvious he thought we'd hang out for a while. "So, I already brought some stuff down. It's out in the garage. Hope you have enough room for it all. Dad thinks making new fishermen is like a holy calling. Give a man a fish, feed him for a day. Give him a bunch of old fishing junk . . . you know."

"I don't think that's how it goes," I say, my voice flat.

Tommy side-eyes me. "Is everything okay, man? You seem a little uptight."

"I'm kinda in a hurry, is all."

He frowns, and I have an urge to apologize. Forget that. Tommy Davis is a murderer. I'm doing the right thing. The only thing.

Tommy's eyes narrow, and I realize I've been staring at him, unblinking for a few seconds past normal.

"You sure you're okay?" he asks, concern in his voice. It's not real. It can't be.

"I'm fine," I snap.

Tommy looks at me like I have three eyes. "Bro? You are definitely not all right."

I force myself to calm down. The living room isn't the place for what I've got to do. "Sorry," I say, forcing a self-deprecating smile onto my face as I search for a reason for my mood. "Girl problems," I say, not sure why I went there.

Tommy's expression softens. "Ouch," he says. "I get that." He looks like he's going to give me some sage, older dude advice, but he smiles instead. "I don't think I can help. I'm kind of a disaster when it comes to the ladies. Come on. Let's get you outfitted."

I follow him through the kitchen, making our way to the garage. The butcher block is strewn with snacks. Tommy was expecting me to stay. Our conversation in the cafeteria about all his friends ditching him when he got clean comes back to me. I don't let my mind go there. He's not worthy of my sympathy. His whole personality has been a disguise. I mean, I was only in school with him for a year. How well do I really know him?

I think of that night, being knocked down the stairs. The person had moved fast, decisively, just like an athlete. I replay the video from the mall in my head. I think of the pictures in Tommy's book, his manifesto of hate.

I let the anger build.

In the garage, a dark blue SUV is parked on one side. The other side is empty. The ladder to the attic is down, and four or five poles and two tackle boxes lie on the concrete floor. There's also a box of clothes and a pair of old waders. "It was a pain getting this stuff down," Tommy says with a laugh.

I bite my lip. Tommy Davis is about to have an accident. He's going to fall from the attic and hit his head. It will be quick. Fast. Merciful.

I step closer to him, making a show of studying the tackle, my heart pumping.

It's surreal. This can't be my life. I'm about to kill Tommy Davis.

"Just pick whatever you want," Tommy says. "Honestly, take it all. Dad tried to get me into fishing, but it's not my thing. It's like hurry up and wait, you know?"

I grab Tommy by the shirt, slide my leg behind him, and throw him onto the concrete. He lets out a startled yelp as I position myself on top of him. Tommy's not small. He's athletic and muscular, but I have him in a full mount. He fights me for a moment, and I slide up into a high mount with my knees in his armpits. He's lost now, doesn't know how to get free. "What are you doing, Jude? This isn't funny, man. You could have—"

I slap him open-handed across the face to get his attention. He thinks I'm goofing around. Time to set him straight. "I know what you did."

Pure bafflement crosses Tommy's face. It turns quickly to anger. "Get off me."

This wasn't the plan. I talked it over with Molly, worked it all out. I was supposed to smash his head against the concrete and make it look like he fell from the attic, but I changed my mind. I need to hear him confess.

And he *will* confess.

"You left a book at the mall," I say. "This summer, in the food court. It was pictures of Hanna Smith. Messed up pictures. A week later, you tried to kill her. I know she's your half sister. How could you, Tommy? How could you try and kill her? She didn't do anything to you."

Tommy's voice is high and shrill. "What are you talking about?"

I slap him again, harder this time. "Stop, Tommy. There's video from the mall. I saw you. Her dad is your father, only he didn't want to have anything to do with you, wouldn't even talk to you. Thought you'd teach him a lesson, take Hanna from him." I slap him again, but what I want to do is punch him. I want to punch him until he tells me the truth. I hesitate, my fist raised, ready for a strike.

Tommy's confused, angry. He tries to get free, bucking and straining against me, but Dad taught me well, and I have him good. Eventually, he stops fighting. His eyes drift up to me, and like a curtain being drawn back, all emotion fades from his face.

He smiles up at me without an ounce of warmth, blood on his teeth. "You want to beat me?" he asks calmly. More blood leaks into his mouth. "Nah," he says, his usually happy demeanor frigid now. "I see it. You want to kill me." He gives a hollow laugh. The person below me is almost unrecognizable. This is definitely not the Tommy I know. His face contorts. "Go ahead!" he screams. "I deserve it. I'm worthless, man! Everybody knows it. I did things, lied, cheated, stole! You don't even know!" His breaths are ragged, and his eyes are bulging. "Do the world a favor." His lips tremble and there is a manic gleam in his eyes. "Do it!" he screams.

My fist poised for the strike shakes. Tommy confessed to everything . . . everything but attempted murder. "Tell me you're not a murderer, Tommy." I grind my teeth. "Please."

Tommy swallows hard and finds a measure of composure. "I'm a lot of things," he says, his eyes defiant. "But I've never tried to kill anyone, much less Hanna Smith."

He doesn't offer any other explanation, and despite all the evidence pointing to Tommy, I believe him. God help me, I believe him. The anger I've been fostering vanishes in an instant, leaving me exhausted. I push myself up, disentangling my legs, and stand.

Tommy bounces up. He spits blood on the concrete, mad.

I make some space for him, but I'm not in the mood. If he wants to fight, I'll break his nose. "Tell me you didn't try to kill Hanna," I say.

"I already did," he says. "Do you even know me? Get serious, man."

"I am serious," I say. "Dead serious. And I need you to say it clearly. I saw the book you left at the mall. Tell me you didn't try to kill her."

Tommy shakes his head belligerently. "What book? I don't know what you're talking about."

"In the food court," I say. "This summer you forgot your bag in the food court and there was a book in it."

A small portion of the fire dies in Tommy's eyes. He hesitates. "The bag. This summer? Nah, man. It was drugs, Jude. Not a book. Drugs, all right? It was a drop. It's what we junkies do."

"It wasn't drugs," I tell him. "It was a book full of stuff, bad stuff. Psycho stuff about killing Hanna."

"No," he says, like maybe he's not sure now. "I owed Josh Stroup from back before I got clean. He told me one drop and my debt would be paid. He gave me the bag, told me where to go."

An overwhelming sense of relief runs through me as Tommy speaks and the pieces finally fall into place. "Josh," I say. "Josh Stroup gave you the bag?"

"Yeah, man," Tommy says. "That's what I just said."

I pump my fist up in the air, all my energy back. "I knew it," I say. I look at Tommy. "I *knew* it."

"What'd you know?" Tommy asks.

I laugh, letting out days of frustration. I collect my thoughts. Tommy deserves an explanation. "Josh was setting you up," I say. "He tried to kill Hanna about a week after you dropped the bag off at the mall. There was evidence in the bag pointing to you as the murderer."

It all makes perfect sense. Josh Stroup is the killer. I knew it. I've known it all along.

Tommy's anger is gone, replaced by disgust. He slaps his forehead. "Perfect," Tommy says. "I knew I should have looked. Told me to keep the bag closed. Said I couldn't resist seeing all that dope and not having a taste. Said if I opened the bag, he'd know, the deal was off, and my debt would come due right then. I didn't have the money. I did what he told me."

Tommy spits blood on the concrete again, this time more to clear his mouth than in anger. I slapped him harder than I thought. He wipes his mouth with the back of his hand. "But why would Josh Stroup want to hurt Hanna?"

I lean back against a workbench, my whole body screaming to sit. The up and down of emotions is wrecking me. "Stan's messed up with the Stroups," I say. "Hanna found out something she shouldn't— It doesn't matter." I take one of the deepest, best breaths of my life. Killing Tommy would have been hard. Killing Josh, not so much. I just have to find him now.

Tommy's face pales. "I would've had an overdose, I bet. The Stroups would have made sure of it. So, Hanna's okay, right?"

I nod. "Yeah, she's fine. She's hanging with Molly. She's not a big fan of going home right now."

"Molly? Who's Molly?"

"You know who she is. Molly Goldman. In my class. Red hair."

Tommy looks down. "Yeah, I know her, kind of." He clears his throat. "That's not good, man. Yeah, that's bad." There is deep concern in his voice, but I'm not sure why.

"Are we cool?" I ask him. "I'm sorry I hit you. Seriously. I messed up. I'll make this up to you."

"No, man," Tommy says, and the alarm in his voice is undeniable. "I don't care about that." Tommy scratches his neck. "You need to call Hanna, man. Tell her to get away from that girl."

An uncomfortable laugh escapes me. "What are you talking about?"

"Yeah, so I went to Josh's early to get the package—the bag—but there was a car in the drive. I circled around a few times. They didn't see me, but I saw her. I saw them. Together. Josh and that girl Molly. They were, like, making out in the driveway."

"No," I say, drawing the word out. "Not Molly Goldman." I take my phone from my pocket and find a picture of me and Molly together, acting goofy. "Not this girl, right?"

"Sorry, man," Tommy says. "But that's definitely her."

"No," I say again. "Molly wouldn't be at Josh's. They wouldn't be—" I swallow unable to say the words. "They wouldn't be doing that."

"It was her. I swear it. I saw her real good. Drives a little blue Chevy."

"No," I sputter. "That's not . . ."

Ice. My body goes cold. Ice.

Molly?

Molly.

My Molly.

Hanna can stay with me, Molly said. *Just until she wants to go home.*

I was grateful. Molly wanted to help.

Molly. There has to be another explanation. Josh is manipulating her, using her in some way. It has to be. Josh is the killer. Molly . . .

I close my eyes. It can't be real. It can't be. I open my eyes. Tommy is staring at me, worried.

Outside, thunder booms, and I can hear the rain begin to fall hard against the garage door.

CHAPTER 44

Lightning dances in the sky and the rain falls in sheets. The Beast's engine rumbles like a dinosaur. The headlights cut through the driving rain as an ungodly wind nearly blows the Beast off the road. One hand is on the wheel. I press the phone to my ear with my free hand. Hanna's phone rings and rings and rings, finally going to voice mail.

Hey, this is Hanna. You know what to do.

I curse as a gust of wind makes me swerve into the other lane. I drop the phone and regain control of my car. Tears want to form in my eyes. The release of emotions would be more than welcome, but the truth hurts so bad that if I gave in and let myself feel anything, I would lose myself in grief. That can't happen. Later I will mourn. Later, I will try to understand what happened. *Ice.* That is what I am. That is what I have to be.

Lightning flashes bright, striking a tree on the side of the road. A limb falls and I swerve, the limb crashing inches from my passenger-side door. In the distance, a tornado siren begins to wail. Tornadoes in September. It's not the norm.

But normal is a distant memory.

The wind rocks the Beast again as I grab the phone from my lap and hit Hanna's number again. Someone answers on the first ring.

"Jude?"

"Hann—" I stop. "Molly," I say instead.

Molly's voice is full of concern and compassion. "Is it done?"

My mind spins. "Where's Hanna?" I ask, barely able to hear as rain thrashes down. The whipping wind makes it almost impossible to keep the Beast on the road with just one hand.

"She's here," Molly says. "Don't worry."

I swallow. "Are you driving?" I ask. "It sounds like you're in a car."

She answers my question with a question. "Did you do it quick like you decided?"

I want to scream. I didn't decide anything. It was Molly. She steered me, maneuvered me, made me think it was my decision, but it wasn't. I need time to understand. What else? Her black eye that night. She said it was Marcus and Marcus backed up her story. But what if the accident was staged? An excuse for future injuries. Molly stopped me from shooting Josh at the Banjo. Mrs. Smith's gun that jammed. She was alone with it while I got the duct tape out of the trunk. It was her—all of it. Molly.

"It's done," I say. "Yeah, I did it quick, so he wouldn't suffer. Can I speak with Hanna? I need to, ah, I need to ask her something." Molly is silent. I'm less than a quarter mile from her house. I need to stall her.

Molly's voice is cold, accusatory. The opposite of the Molly I know. "You didn't do it, did you?" Not since the first day I met her in third grade have I heard this person, this Molly. Brake lights ahead make me slow.

"I did," I lie. "I did it. Tommy's dead. I'm really messed up." I slow as the traffic in front of me backs up. It's only a car or two, but some grandmother must be coming home from Sunday night church. The three cars ahead of me are doing ten miles an hour. I punch the gas and pass all three cars on a double yellow. In the side-view mirror, illuminated in crackling lightning, way off behind me, a funnel cloud descends, a black swirling vortex of night.

"You're a terrible liar, Jude," this cold Molly tells me. "I knew you wouldn't do it."

I want to vomit. I want to scream. I want to cry. Not Molly. Please, God, not her. "Molly," I say, as level and as calm as I can manage. "Why?"

Molly pauses for a long moment, as if that one question stopped time. Finally, she answers. "Hanna should have minded her own business, Jude. She got in the way of things. That's it."

Despite her words. Despite her simple admission of guilt. Despite knowing in my core Molly is not who I thought she was, can now never be what I wanted her to be . . . still, I have a small ounce of hope that this is all some mistake, a catastrophic misunderstanding. "Don't do it," I say. "You don't have to do this. Don't hurt Hanna. You haven't done anything wrong. Not yet."

Molly's voice is a whisper, and I'm positive she's in a car. "Haven't I though? We'll be at the Bluehole, Jude."

"The Bluehole?" I ask, unable to keep the confusion from my words.

Her voice cracks as she speaks. It's a voice full of pain and regret, such a contrast from a few seconds ago. "I can't help myself, Jude. It's like you said. I'll do it again. I'll hurt her, even—even though I don't want to anymore. I made mistakes." Her words sear me to the bone. "But then you came along, Jude. *You.* But it's so hard." She pauses, whimpers. It's such a low, scared, miserable sound. "The Bluehole, Jude. Come save me from myself." Lightning, the largest bolt I have ever seen, lights up the night like day. "Hurry, Jude," Molly says, and the line goes dead.

I let the phone fall from my limp fingers and almost miss my turn. I recover fast enough to swerve off the main road onto the old country road leading to the Bluehole. It's not close and traveling through the storm will take time.

The Bluehole. This is so bad. The pit of water, bottomless some say, would be the perfect place to dump a body.

Once you go in, you never come out.

I don't have a choice. I can make this right. It's not too late.

Outside, over the roar of a storm, every tornado siren in Rush Springs blares. My car stereo comes to life, glowing in my car's interior with a ghostly blue light. White noise crackles on the speakers and someone—no, *something*, ancient and terrible—calls my name. *Juuude. Juuude, Juuude.* My name rumbles amid the snaps and crackles coming from my speakers.

I slam the gas pedal to the floor, and the Beast lurches forward. *Juuuuuuuuuude.* Something hungry calls my name. *Juuuuuuude.*

I shiver but drive on anyway, trying to ignore the sounds coming from my radio. I don't have time for this. Not now.

Juuuuuuude.

I drive on, trying to ignore the monster in my radio.

CHAPTER 45

Less than thirty yards from the turnoff, the old dirt road leading to the Bluehole turns slick as ice. The Beast's wheels start to spin in the mud. Ahead, deep furrows the four-by-fours have left over the years are already melting into a thick black soup under the constant rain.

The Beast fishtails, the wheels humming as they spin. In the next second, I come to a complete halt. For another few seconds, I try to move forward, the accelerator to the floor, but it's no use. The Beast was never meant for mudding.

I leave the car running and step out into the night. The rain has let up a fraction, and the lightning has stopped altogether, but the rain's still falling and it's cold. The tornado siren roars from town, rising and falling, as I sprint down the muddy road to the Bluehole.

Just audible over the siren is a faint roaring, a distant sound behind me and to the left. It sounds like a train, kind of, but it's not a train. I've heard this sound before. Once you've heard one, there is no mistaking the sound of a tornado.

Mud and water splash under my feet, grabbing at me, trying to hold me in place, trying to stop me. A lone bolt of lightning cracks a short distance away, and for an instant, the woods are lit with a white light. A hundred yards ahead, the forest on either side of the trail opens up. Hanna's Jeep is parked in the rocky clearing with its headlights on; they cut through the empty dark to the edge of the cliff, failing to illuminate the vast chasm beyond.

The mud sucks at my sneakers, so I swerve to the edge of the woods, trying to get out of the worst of it. Three deer, bedded down in the short scrub pine, jump up. A doe and two yearlings. They dash off, up the trail, and cut back into the woods. Behind me, the roaring intensifies.

I sprint to Hanna's Jeep. It's parked close to the open expanse of the Bluehole, the cliff's edge less than twenty yards away. The driver's side window is dark with an expensive tint job, so I have to plant my face to the wet glass to see inside. Something is in the back. Something moving. I cry out, words without meaning, as I open the door and climb up onto the driver's seat. Hanna, bound and gagged, looks up. Her eyes are bright with emotion. As soon as I remove her gag, she's screaming. "It was her! I told you it was her!"

Some type of cord or nylon rope binds her. The thin binding has cut into Hanna's wrists, causing them to bleed. I take out my pocketknife, insert the blade under the cords encircling her wrists, and pull up. The sharp knife makes quick work of the cord, and I move to her feet.

Hanna rubs at her wrists. Tears are in her voice, but she's more angry than sad. "That—that girl. I should have listened to my gut. She was on my list from the start."

I cut the cords binding her legs. "Where is she?"

"Close. I don't know. They drove me here and got out."

My heart lurches. "Did she . . ." I can't say it. "Did she jump?"

"Jump? Are you an idiot? She has a gun, Jude. Josh is here too. They're in this together. We have to get out of here."

She pushes past me, and I follow her out of the Jeep and back into the weather. The wind rips at me. Around the rim of the barren rock that makes the old bauxite mine, pines and scrub oak bend beneath the storm. Lightning flashes and thunder cracks.

In the light of the storm, the entire expanse of the Bluehole is illuminated, a hole in the earth a quarter mile wide and half as deep. Lightning flashes again, once, twice, three times. The rock face of the far wall glistens wet in the night, narrow streams of water cascading over the edge in miniature waterfalls. The only visible sliver of the water far below churns angry, swirling like a witch's cauldron.

Hanna searches the front seat for a second or two, then turns on me. "The keys aren't here," she says over the storm.

The storm. I need it to stop. I need there to be stillness so I can think.

The storm calms in seconds, the swirling, howling wind gone, and the sudden lack of noise and motion fills me with dread. *Did I do that?* Mist falls, light and insistent, and the clouds above part.

Hanna looks up. "This is so insane. You have a lot of explaining to do, Jude."

I say nothing as the moon, large and bright, is revealed. For an instant, I think I see something silhouetted in the moon's glow. Something hungry, on leathery wings, but then it's gone, and Hanna is staring at me.

Bang! My right arm burns as if a thousand hornets attacked the meat of my right shoulder. I spin, pushing Hanna behind me on instinct. Molly stands in the rain, her clothes as wet as mine, her hair plastered to her face, and the gun pointed at my chest. Josh Stroup, wet to the bone and smiling like a demon, stands to the right of her, his arms wrapped around her waist.

"Did I hurt you, Jude?" Molly asks. Her eyes laugh at me, and it is so hard to look at her.

Warmth spreads down my arm and the entire limb pulses with my heart, but for all that, the pain is gone. Maybe it's a graze, or maybe it hit a major vessel and I'm bleeding out, in shock and dying as I stand here. I can't tell.

I force myself to meet Molly's gaze. My voice is raw when I speak. "Is he making you do this?"

"Make her?" Josh asks. "You think you know her? You can't *make* this girl do anything." He looks at Molly with a certain kind of crazy.

"We're taking over my family business," he says. "Me and Molly. Tell him, baby."

Molly trembles, a smile sliding cross her face. She turns to him. They kiss, hard and passionate, Molly always keeping her eyes on me. Josh's hands move over her body, making my spine crawl and my heart ache. Molly breaks the kiss, and Josh lets her go as she steps closer.

"Careful," Josh warns Molly. "He's fast."

"I know," Molly snaps.

The mist and a small breeze are all that's left of the storm. The moon is streetlight bright, surrounded by still angry swirling clouds. The tornado sirens sound distantly from town.

"Why?" I ask Molly. "The truth this time."

Molly's eyes hold so much energy, so much anticipation, so much joy. She wants to tell me. She needs to tell me. Her focus turns to Hanna, but she keeps the gun on me. "No one messes with my plans," Molly says. "Especially not rich, stuck-up bitches."

Hanna comes around me, and it's all I can do to hold her back. "Why did you try to kill me? Lucas? Tell me this wasn't about Lucas Munson!"

"Lucas?" Molly's laugh is quick and shrill. "Of course not. Pay attention!" She pauses, enjoying the moment. "You didn't even recognize her. So far beneath you, you don't even notice." Her words are scornful and full of reproach.

"Who?" Hanna asks, exasperated. "Who didn't I recognize?"

"I had to take all her pictures down before you came over. Make sure they'd be gone this weekend. But we have our own business website. All you had to do was look, but you are so caught up in your own problems, you don't notice people like me. Like my mother. My mother!" Molly screams. "She gave you the tissue in the FBI parking lot. You were going to rat your own father out and ruin all of Josh and my plans. But you got caught. Mom was there with a remodel job, and she sees Hanna Smith crying in the parking lot. She knew you! She told me everything, and I told Josh."

I swallow. Love or money.

It hurts so bad.

Love or money.

It was both.

Hanna tries to get around me again. "You're crazy!"

Josh whoops. "Crazy hot."

"Shut up, Josh," Molly says, her voice venom.

Josh gazes at Molly with a fire and hunger way past sanity. "You've never been hotter than right now, Molly Goldman." He steps up next to her. "Shoot 'em, baby."

Hanna makes a choking, sobbing sound that turns to a sad chuckle. "You're not going to get away with this. The FBI is involved. Josh is going to jail."

Molly's grin goes thin. "An unfortunate complication, but we have plans. Do you know how much money we have? Not the pennies your dad helped steal. Big Hank had offshore accounts. We have access to that. Almost a hundred million dollars." She licks her lips. "Did you hear me? A *hundred* million. We're leaving and never coming back."

"Hold on now," Josh says. "That wasn't the FBI. I bet it was Haskell over in Tennessee, making a play. Lawyers say there is nothing. Nada. Nobody's looking for me." His face darkens. "Haskell is going to learn what it means to come at *me*."

"*Haskell doesn't matter,*" Molly says through clenched teeth. "We've talked about this."

"Yeah. I know," Josh says like a petulant child. "And we'll talk about it some more."

"We're leaving," Molly says, brooking no argument.

"Sure, we're leaving. Aruba awaits. We might be coming back is all I'm saying."

Molly grits her teeth but doesn't argue.

I shake my head, unable to comprehend what's happening.

Molly sees my head shake. "Don't be mad, Jude," she says. "I told you this summer. I'm not Elizabeth Proctor. I'm Abigail Williams. I'm the Big Bad."

Her words cut deep. She thinks this is a joke. "This is real," I say, pain coursing through every syllable, "not some stupid play."

"Isn't it though?" she says, a sad smile on her lips, and for an instant, she's the real Molly, the one I've known since third grade. The Molly I want to hold and be with. "I have feelings for you, Jude. Strong, deep, true feelings." Her eyebrows lift, and her eyes become wide and bright. "But you kidnapped Hanna, a girl you're obsessed with. You *kidnapped* her. What were you thinking? You're sick, Jude."

I blink at the rain running in my eyes. And it is rain. It's not tears. It's not tears.

"I saw you on the bench in the mall," Molly says, all the sweetness gone. "You were so bad at hiding what you were doing. I saw you watching Hanna Smith. I knew then it was fate. Hanna had to die, and I needed someone to take the blame. We already had Tommy and the book, but I thought *two* prime suspects would be so much better than one. The hammer, Jude. Did you ever wonder why a hammer? It was a roofing hammer. Billy stole one from your dad's job site. It had someone's name on it. Perfect. I leave it at the scene. The police trace it back to your dad. Back to you. More chaos. More confusion."

"No," I say, unable to take what I'm hearing. She's rationalizing her actions. Making her seem like this cool, calculating criminal. Love or money. But I forgot that I know better.

The Dream. I was in Molly's head. I experienced the murder with her emotions. I take a deep breath. "It excited you," I say. "The sense of power. The joy in getting the final, last word. You say it was about keeping Hanna quiet, but you wanted to do it. You liked it. You got off on it. That's it. You tried to kill Hanna," my voice catches, "because you wanted to."

Molly shrugs. "Josh wanted to go. I told him no. I wanted to do it."

"I could have loved you," I say, my voice cracking.

Molly laughs at my pain. "Love? You're pathetic. You know that? Pathetic.

"They're going to blame *you*, Jude. You are going to kill Hanna, and then kill yourself. I've been playing you from day one, Jude. How does that feel?"

The utter maliciousness in her voice is hard to understand. I can't speak.

Her face softens and the corner of her lips turns down, and there is such sadness in her voice. "I was trying to help. I knew Jude was delusional, but I never thought he was dangerous." Her face loses all remorse, a grin replacing it. "How's that? Am I a good actor, Jude? The cops will hear that, then that little geek Coop will start talking about dreams and murder and everyone will know how crazy you are. You know he will. I'll talk too. *He was sick*," she says, her voice quavering. "I knew, but I-I was falling for him. I wanted to help."

"Damn, you're hot, Molly Goldman," Josh says, stepping close again and putting his arms around her. Molly lets him.

Something hard and brittle snaps in my chest, and I am filled with warmth. The wind picks up, growing louder with each beat of my heart. Above, the clouds swirl and grow in seconds, covering the moon. Everyone, including Molly, looks up. The wind begins to howl louder, faster, swirling around us.

And I hear it, the sound I've been waiting for.

Molly hears it too. She licks her lips, her head turning to the road. Blue lights faintly reflect off her and a police siren squawks. "You called the police?" Molly asks, a pouting frown curling her lips down.

Josh pulls at her arm as the wind doubles. "Shoot 'em now. We still have time."

Molly pulls free of Josh, anger distorting her features. The rain begins to fall harder, and the wind picks up dust as the approaching police sirens grow louder. "No help," she spits at me. "Isn't that one of your rules?"

"A life for a life. Kill the killer?" I ask. "Do you think I could do that? Kill you?"

Josh keeps glancing at the lights. "Come on, shoot 'em. We gotta go. We can get out the back. I know the way."

Molly's hand tightens on the gun. She's going to shoot. She's going to kill me, then Hanna.

No.

The roaring above triples in intensity as the wind swirls around us. The gun in Molly's hand trembles, and I want it to move. I need it to move. The wind explodes, and the gun is nearly ripped from Molly's grasp, her arm going wide as the wind pushes, moving the barrel away just as the gun goes off. I flinch at the discharge and the flash of the muzzle.

Anger fills me.

At Molly, at myself, at my stupid life. The anger and storm course through me like life's blood. The connection to the wind, rain, and storm solidifies in my mind as Molly brings the gun back down, but Molly doesn't have a chance.

For I am the storm.

I push at the gun with my will, focusing all my mental strength. All that is me and is the storm. The wind is part of me, an extension of my body. It does as I command. The gun goes flying out of Molly's hand, spinning away into the night. Molly is spun too, hard. She cries out as she goes down, landing on the rocky ground.

Josh rushes toward me, but I unleash my anger on him. The wind picks him up, and he's thrown like a pebble, up high into the air, moving toward the Bluehole. His arms flail, and he screams, but I don't care. I need him to go, to be gone, out of the equation.

Up over the cliff, out over the drop, he is hurled like a leaf in the wind. Some part of me lost in the destruction, the raw power of the storm and my fury, breaks free. "No," I whisper against the howling wind, trying to stop what is happening. To take it back. I want him gone, but not this.

For an instant, Josh is suspended in time, no longer going up, not yet falling. I hold him in place, but it's hard, so hard, and I have no idea how any of this works. The wind fights itself, fights me, pushing and pulling. "No!" I scream this time as I lose control completely.

Josh Stroup drops like a stone. Gone into the abyss, spitting curses and pleas for help, barely audible over the wind. Above the Bluehole, a vortex of black turns and twists, a tornado forming, the eye swirls down, growing larger, reaching toward the earth. Debris flies around me. Hanna grabs hold of me as her Jeep's suspension squeaks. I lean against the wind as rocks slide on the ground and the tornado descends.

Molly screams and rushes at me and Hanna. A limb, blown by the storm, strikes her in the head, and she stumbles past us, staggering toward the cliff's edge, clutching where the limb hit her. In the light of Hanna's Jeep and the closing red and blue police lights, she looks back at me, disorientation and hurt in her eyes. She runs toward the Bluehole.

"Molly!" I say, the anger and raw emotion vanishing.

In that second, the wind lessens, the swirling vortex recedes back up into the sky as if it never was. I pull away from Hanna and run after Molly.

Molly slides to a stop, inches from the cliff. The Bluehole is in front of her. She has nowhere to run. She turns. A gash on her forehead leaks blood. She backs up, her heels on the lip of the cliff, her eyes wide and wild.

"Don't move!"

Her heel slips. "Jude," she wails. She tumbles backward.

I dive, grasping her ankle. My body slides with her weight, pulling me a quarter over the lip of the chasm. Molly's leg is slick with rain, the black water so far below.

Once you go in, you never come out.

Molly looks up at me, her long hair falling down, terror in her eyes. "Help me, Jude! Pull me up!"

A life for a life. The words echo in my mind. And I know they are true. I know they are true to the core of my being. Something primordial and desperate demands I drop her into the dark hungry water. And it would be so easy. All I have to do is let go.

Molly's life for Hanna's life. One second is all it would take.

Dad would come home. All of this—this nightmare—would be over. Done. Open my hand. Molly *is* the killer. She earned her fate.

The wind stirs, the tornado begging to be unleashed, to destroy, rip, and punish. A sharp pain shoots through my skull, almost making me release Molly. The wind picks up, harder and harder, swirling, and in that gale something speaks. A voice as big as time, as small as a breath of air. *Choose,* it whispers.

Molly screams my name—begging, pleading—and I scream back, a guttural wail as the pain in my head throbs, demanding I open my hand. That I pass judgment. That I fulfill my duty. But the voice. The voice . . .

I am a Dreamer, meant to bring justice to the wicked. It is what Dad taught me. It would make my life right to end Molly. My very nature demands it. I have a duty. A duty that the Society would tell me is sacred and ancient.

To hell with that.

I scream. A bellow coming from deep within me, sounding not at all like myself, not at all human. Something tethered finally breaking free.

I clasp my other hand over Molly's ankle, and I pull, straining to get her over the edge without us both falling. I struggle, wiggling back, inch by inch, hauling Molly up as the police sirens and flashing lights fill the clearing.

The pain in my head and the wind are gone. I feel nothing of the storm. The air, still full of ozone, is as still as my soul. Something inside me has shifted, altered, changed, but I don't have time to ponder what it all means.

I get a knee under me, then it's all leverage. I pull a crying, sobbing Molly all the way up, my arms aching with the effort. After a moment, I manage to get her to her feet. She's rubbery and weak but latches on to me with surprising strength. "Thank you, thank you, thank you," she says over and over as I help her move away from the edge.

I hold her as sirens wail and blue and red lights strobe across the rocky ground. "We'll get you help," I tell her. "There's something wrong with you, but we can—"

Molly screams, high and shrill, backs up and punches me in the face. She catches me right on the nose, bringing instant tears to my eyes. I take a step back as Molly turns and runs.

A shadow moves in the police lights. Hanna steps out of nowhere and trips Molly. Molly gains her feet in seconds, but Hanna's ready, delivering an uppercut that even Dad would be proud of. The first thing to hit the ground is the back of Molly's head.

Hanna looms over her, a vengeful goddess in light and shadow. "That's for trying to kill me."

Molly groans but doesn't try to get up.

By Hanna's Jeep, state police officers are getting out of their four-by-fours. Tommy Davis stands with an officer, pointing, talking. Turns out Coach D's brother is a state police officer. I never knew. Good old Tommy brought his uncle. He brought the cavalry.

I look up into the night sky. The clouds part and dissolve into nothing, and the storm is gone like it had never been.

The moon, bright and cold, all-seeing and uncaring, shines down on us all.

CHAPTER 46

It takes all night to sort out the mess.

The paramedics wrapping my arm told me I was lucky. The bullet grazed me.

Lucky. It makes me want to laugh.

The police took Molly into custody. She didn't say a word. Her face was impassive, devoid of emotion, but something in her eyes looked broken. I wonder on that, my heart wrecked. Even now. Even knowing who and what Molly is, I want her. I want her to be who I thought she was. I want that Molly, the one I've known all my life. That Molly is *real*. Not the other one. But the logical part of my brain knows the awful truth. Molly was never the person I thought she was.

At the police station, Molly's parents sit in the waiting room. Her mother leans against her father. Her father watches me as I walk by, giving me the slightest of apologetic nods, his dark eyes sad and haunted.

The police ask questions, and I answer most of them truthfully. They don't push me, satisfied with my answers. Once the questions are over, I find out why. They show me video taken from Molly's parents' house: Josh and Molly carrying a tied up and kicking Hanna out the front door.

The Beast, mud caked thick on the wheels, is parked right outside the front exit. I get in and leave the state police headquarters, driving home, my radio silent and my windows rolled down. The morning air is crisp, promising a mild September day in Rush Springs. Not a single cloud in the fall sky.

Dad is waiting for me when I get home. He sits in his chair, the lights off with the morning light filtering through the blinds. We watch each other for a long time, Dad's expression unreadable. He stands and walks over, embracing me in a fierce hug. It's as if all the stress, all the heartache, all the pain I've been through over the past weeks, hits me at once, and I cry like a child.

In that moment, I am not a six-foot-one, two-hundred-pound seventeen-year-old. I am not a Dreamer, a trained killer. I am my father's son. I am just a boy who needs his father. The feelings I've pushed down, the emotions I've tried to control, now run free. I let it all go.

My father holds me, and I let him. Later we will talk, later there will be questions, later I will get some answers.

Right now, I need to be held.

EPILOGUE

I open my dorm window and let the morning air in. It is an unseasonably crisp August morning, the first day of class at Harris College.

Two in-state colleges offered me football scholarships after my high school football career ended, UCA and Arkansas Tech. I was all set to pick one of the two, when Harris offered.

It was too good of an opportunity to pass up. Harris is a private school, way too expensive for me, and one of the top schools not just in Arkansas but in the South. It was a no-brainer.

Life is funny sometimes. After years of hating on private school kids, now I'm one of them.

I've been here for months, training and practicing. Our first football game is in a week, and it looks like I will redshirt, not play this year, but practice, watch, and learn. It's cool with me. Football pays for everything. Room and board, books, tuition. They even pay me a stipend for work study. I'm playing the sport I love and going to class. College is all right by me.

The week after my night at the Bluehole, the other shoe dropped and the story about Big Hank came out. It was national news.

Hillbilly drug lord gunned down by his own son and two accomplices. Officer Fred Jamison turned state's evidence. He pled guilty to several charges of conspiracy and drug trafficking in exchange for a light sentence and witness protection after time served. Drug cartels, it seems, don't like it when their biggest distributor in the Southeast gets dismantled piece by piece.

Brian and Billy became famous. Local and nationwide news had the same stock footage of them being paraded around in ill-fitting suits and handcuffs. They never smiled for the camera, not once.

The official story is that Josh Stroup is on the lam, probably in Mexico somewhere, loose, armed and dangerous, but I know better. I dream about him sometimes, his body arching out over the great expanse of the Bluehole. Josh Stroup will never bother anyone again. Of that, I am sure.

We won the rest of our games, going 9–1 in the regular season. The best record since 1991, and our first appearance in the playoffs in four years. Two more wins and one devastating loss in the state championship game ended our season. But Dad was there for every snap, cheering me on from the stands. Mom was there too. After all that went down, we decided the Society could go to hell. Mom and Dad even sat together during the state final.

The town was proud of us. We were proud of ourselves. No other team in Bedford High School history had ever gone further. Even so, a shadow lay over the whole town. Evil had hidden in our midst, an evil that had roots in every part of Rush Springs. Worse still, was when those roots were pulled from the earth, many wondered if keeping them in place would have been the better choice. Big Hank had almost as many legit businesses as he did illegal ones, and many honest, hardworking people lost their jobs.

Stan Smith's name was never mentioned once in all the news stories on TV or on the net. His involvement in the drug empire was swept under the rug for reasons I'm not completely sure of. Hanna doesn't know why either. Mrs. Smith left her husband and Hanna went with her, moving far away from Rush Springs.

Molly is in a mental health facility being evaluated for her ability to stand trial. She's been there for a while. No one knows why a decision hasn't been made yet, but Dad thinks it may have something to do with the Society. She's tried to contact me twice since that night at the Bluehole, once by an email I trashed without reading, and once by a phone call whose voice mail I deleted without listening to.

Despite what I might want, I will never be fully free of her. The gunshot wound to my right deltoid is a thin pale scar now. Molly, in a sad way, will always be with me.

"Ready for our first day of class, big guy?" my roommate asks.

I scan Coop from head to toe. He looks like a walking billboard. Everything he has on, from his sweatshirt to his hat, has a Harris College logo on it. His shirt is a roaring lion, our mascot, with Harris Football printed below it. His hat is embossed with the stylized marble pillars of the Honors College. "Hmmm," I grunt. "You look . . . commercialized."

Coop snorts. "It's called school spirit. I don't go halfway. I'm all in, bro."

"There's still a tag on your shirt," I say, pointing to his left shoulder.

"Oh, thanks," he says. He cranes his neck, finds the tag, pops it free, and stuffs it in a pocket.

I can only smile. I got into Harris because I'm good at football. Coop got in because he's smart. "I'm glad you're here, buddy," I tell him.

He grins. "This isn't high school. You can't cheat off me anymore."

"I never did."

Coop shrugs. "Yeah, well, just saying." He rubs his hands together. "You ready? Let's do this. Chancellor's list, baby."

"I'd settle for dean's list. Heck, I'll settle for above a three point."

"Nah, Jude. You're riding with me now. You ain't alone, my dude."

"Ain't?" I ask. "Maybe I'll do comp without your help."

"Whatever. You just want Hanna to be your study buddy."

I grimace. "No, I don't."

"Why not?" Coop goes to his desk and gets his backpack. "Hanna's awesome, Jude. And for some reason I think she's into you. Embrace it."

I shake my head. Truth is, I'm not in a great place.

Molly is always on my mind. The girl who shot me and tried to kill Hanna twice. The girl locked up, who I now know is incapable of healthy human emotion. I have baggage, loads of baggage, and it's unfair to Hanna to push things. And despite Coop's opinion, I'm not sure Hanna wants me to.

"I'm bad at girls," I say. "Really. Super. Bad."

"Who you talking to?" Coop says with a grin. "Like I don't know."

Unconsciously, I rub at the scar on my arm. Coop eyes me but doesn't say anything. "Let's go," I say, grabbing my backpack. "I don't want to be late to my first college class ever."

"All right," Coop says. "Let's get this party started."

As I head for the door, my phone buzzes in my pocket. I pull it free but don't recognize the number. It's probably a reporter, wanting an exclusive. I've had a few of those. I consider ignoring it, but it might be the police again. I answer the call. "Hello?"

"Jude Erickson," a man asks.

"Go on, Coop," I say. "I'll catch up."

Coop makes a hurry-up motion and leaves our dorm room.

"Look," I say. "If this is about an interview—"

"I'm not a reporter," the man says, cutting me off. "My name is Mark Stilts, and I'm with the Society."

My blood goes cold, my voice colder. "The same Society that kidnapped my dad?"

Mark Stilts seems unperturbed by my words. "The same," he says, but goes no further, forcing me to ask the next question.

"What do you want?"

"I imagine your father explained things?"

"He told me y'all kidnapped him and locked him up, yeah."

"Not that," the man says, his voice sharp as a razor. "About *you*. About your obligations going forward."

If the man were here in front of me, I'm not sure I could resist breaking his nose. These people nearly ruined my life.

But Dad had explained things. The Society would overlook me drawing national attention to myself not once, but twice. They would forgive me the transgression of not murdering my girlfriend and would even allow me to live. *If* I got in line and followed Society rules from now on. Dad was surprised by the offer. Problem was, I wasn't going to do what they wanted.

"I won't be your executioner. Not anymore."

The man clucks his tongue like an English butler might, not that I've ever heard an English butler cluck his tongue. "Yet Josh Stroup is gone . . . forever."

"That—" I stammer, "was an accident."

"What happened to Josh Stroup isn't inconsequential," Mark says. "One could argue he was the instigating factor in the attempted murder of Hanna Smith, and, by default, the killer. People have, in fact, made that argument. It's one of the reasons you're still alive."

I don't say anything. The fact some in the Society want me dead isn't really news.

"I am not your enemy, Jude," Mark says. "You are of great interest to me and a significant faction within the Society. We are the Old Blood, those who can trace our line back to antiquity." I straighten at the name. Old Blood wasn't a word I'd heard until the FBI guy in the van.

"I myself," Mark says with an arrogance I have rarely heard, "am a direct descendant of Constantine the Great."

I guess he thinks dropping some ancient dude's name will impress me. I'm not impressed. Mark might be the least impressive person I've talked to all week.

When I don't respond to his flex, he grunts and continues. "We are the Old Blood, and we have been watching you your entire life."

"Wow," I say deadpan. "That's the creepiest thing anyone has ever said to me."

Mark gives an amused chuckle. "You have no idea what any of this means, do you? You are one of us. There is no other possibility. Only one of the Old Blood would be capable of what you have done. The weather patterns that follow your exploits are not without precedent, but they are exceedingly rare. The girl you spared has been talking to her doctors. Extraordinary events happened that night. Extraordinary, indeed. Can you still feel the storms within you?"

I swallow, remembering the raw power of the storm that night. The truth is, I can't. Since that night at the Bluehole, storms are just storms. I don't have any connection to the weather anymore. Part of me wants to ask Mark more, to grill him on what it all means, but I won't. These people are evil. They tried to kill my father, and they drove my mother away. I don't want their help. I'll figure it out on my own.

I've been silent for several seconds and Mark moves on. "Will you allow me to help you, Jude? We want to bring you in, share our knowledge, show you our ways."

My throat is tight when I speak. "No thanks, *Mark*. Not interested."

Mark lets out a long breath. "Very well. We are prepared to give you time. Will you do me a favor?"

"I think we've covered that."

"Go to your bed and look under your pillow."

I hesitate but don't argue as I walk to my bunk, glancing at the picture of me and Mom. We took it at the lake this summer. Three years is a long time, but we're making up for it.

I bend over and slide my hand under my pillow. My fingers brush something cold. I grasp it and pull it out. I stare at the coin in my hand. Three scythes crossed, making a wheel with their long blades. I've never seen it before.

"Someone was here. In my room," I say as much to myself as to Mark.

"The coin is yours now. Whether you like it or not, you are one of us. That symbol," Mark says, "is ancient. This is a war, Jude. And you are a soldier. This is bigger than one girl's life. One person's life. Have you seen them, Jude? Have you heard them?"

"I don't know what you're talking about," I say, but I know.

"The Hungry Ones," he whispers. "In your dreams. The veil is thin. It grows thinner with each passing year. You have heard them, seen them. Have you not? You must tell me if you have."

Mark definitely has my attention now. I talked with Dad about the waking nightmare where I stood in a field of wheat, but when I was certain Dad didn't have a clue, I changed the subject, and never told him about the monster that cried my name. Or the voice in my radio. Or the wind talking to me. But the voice in the wind was real, and it gave me a choice. And I made my choice.

Mark takes my silence for acknowledgement. "So, you have. Extraordinary." A hint of televangelist seeps into his voice. "Each time we Dream, Jude, each time we save an innocent and destroy evil, we make the barrier between our world and theirs stronger. This is our true purpose. We are so much more than your father knows, more than most Dreamers know. From the night of your birth, we have been watching you. The tornado that wrecked the hospital. Your father had no clue what it meant."

I clear my throat. "I'm not buying what you're selling, *Mark*. Not anymore. No," I say, more certain. "Don't call me again."

I end the call and put my phone away. The cold coin is still in my hand. I don't want it. It creeps me out.

I toss it on my bed and step out into the hall. Coop is there looking guilty. "It was them, wasn't it? Just like your dad said."

"You heard?"

Coop nods.

"It was," I admit.

"So, what are we going to do?"

Coop. My friend. My unlikely best friend. He didn't blink, asking what *we* would do. Once in my life, I thought I was a killer, destined to be like my father, alone and dangerous to those who would murder and destroy lives.

I love Dad, but I don't want to be like him anymore. For his part, he doesn't want me to be like him either. When the time comes again—and it will come—I'll do what must be done, but only with what I can live with. One thing I know for sure, I won't be an executioner.

I am my own man now, and I will make my own way.

"*We*," I say to Coop, "are going to class."

Coop smiles, and his face lights up. "Now you're talking."

ACKNOWLEDGMENTS

Many years ago, I told my wife I wanted to write. After a brief pause, she told me I should. Thanks for that, Martha. Love you.

To Mom and Dad, who rarely said no to a new book. To my brother Greg, who let me read his dog-eared copy of *The Fellowship of the Ring* in 1980-something.

To Josie, Alec, and Evelyn for letting me practice with bedtime stories.

To Maria Dong and J. Elle, who read early versions of *Kill Call* and encouraged me in countless ways.

To Jenna Lincoln for her mentorship and friendship.

To Michael Mammay for his words of encouragement at just the right time.

To my writing group whom I lean on all the time, Emily Thiede, Brook Kuhn, Ryan Van Loan, Eliza Langhans, J.A. Crawford, Lyla Lawless, Melody Steiner, Brighton Rose, Lisa Schunemann, Margie Fuston, and Erin.

To all the people at CamCat, Sue Arroyo, Helga Schier, Olivia Hammerman, Meredith Lyons, Abigail Miles, Laura Wooffitt, Penni Askew, Christie Stratos, and especially to my editor Elana Gibson, who helped me mold this book into something more than it would have been.

To Bill and Cade for keeping my feet firmly on the ground.

To Ken, Francis, and Carol for keeping my days fun and full of laughs.

And to the readers who have taken the time to read this far. Thank you all.

ABOUT THE AUTHOR

Jeff Wooten lives in Arkansas with his wife, three kids, and one dog. He is a full-time physical therapist who works with kids and adults with orthopedic issues.

If you liked Jeff Wooten's *Kill Call*, you'll also enjoy Nicole M. Wolverton's *A Misfortune of Lake Monsters*.

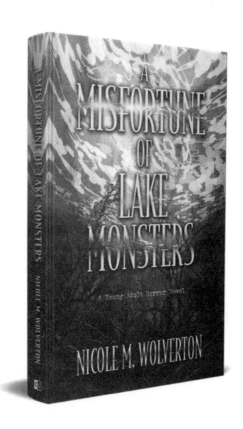

CHAPTER ONE

LEMON

If it weren't for the dry suit strangling me from toes to tonsils, hypothermia would have set in thirty minutes ago—and graduating from high school with all my digits intact is a record I want to hold on to. Inside the Old Lucy costume, my toes and fingers scrunch. The good news is that I can feel them. Being the gooey human center of a neoprene and latex lake monster burrito isn't my favorite way to spend a Sunday night, but here's more good news: things are about to wrap up because a cluster of shadowy figures is suddenly flitting like moths around the hazy lights on the dock about a hundred meters away.

That *this* is what's passing for good news is full-on crap, but whatever—it's go time. A sudden flash of heat in my veins chases away the March-cold Lake Lokakoma water, and I clear my throat. It's sandpapered near raw from the oxygen I've been sucking from the tank strapped to my back. "Now, Lemon, it hain't no different than takin' a breath on land," is what Pappap's told me on more than one occasion. He keeps saying I'll get used to it—like the longer I'm the supersecret Old Lucy impersonator, it'll all magically feel normal one day.

Nothing about this is normal and never will be. Not swimming around the lake in a monster costume on a dreary night. Not hiding behind the boulders at Peter's Island to keep watch for people on the dock. And definitely not being trapped in Devil's Elbow for the rest of my natural life.

The crisp air fills my lungs, even though it feels like it has to claw over what feels like broken glass to do so. Best get used to it now

instead of wallowing in my misery. Hey, I *want* to wallow, but now
isn't the time. I can wallow when I'm dead . . . or at least after this
impersonation is done. I check the silver dive watch strapped over
the iridescent scales on my wrist and calculate how much time is left
on my oxygen tank. Every thought in my head pares down until all
I can do is visualize the Old Lucy impersonation routine, exactly as
Pappap taught me. Nothing too showy. Just give them a taste, just a
glimpse. And let them hear Old Lucy roar.

Light drizzle pings off the surface of the water and smacks my
chin. I duck back behind the boulder, clear my throat again, and rip
out a high-pitched ululation of the Old Lucy cry, complete with a long,
eerie note that hangs over the lake as heavy as mist.

No wonder the oxygen doesn't hurt Pappap's throat—he probably
doesn't have any pain receptors in there anymore after a lifetime of
ululating. *Damn.* Also, I hate the word ululating with a fiery burning
passion—it makes me think too much about the little punching bag
in the back of my throat.

A girl's voice is the first thing that comes sliding across the water.
"Did you hear that?"

And then a guy's whoop. "Old Lucy's out there! Can you see her?"

"I can't see anything—it's dark as shit tonight."

I fit the regulator back into my mouth, swallow around the stale
air from the tank, and adjust my goggles before clicking the face mask
back into place. The new moon makes for a sky that might as well be
a black hole, sucking the whole of Devil's Elbow and all the towns
around it into nothingness. Low clouds obscure the stars, and there's a
thick gloom hanging just above the water—all the better for that extra
bit of mystery. It's the perfect night to stage an Old Lucy appearance,
whether I like it or not.

The urge to think *and I don't* is hard to resist. It's like the words
swim through my brain in big flaming black letters. Even the sweet

almond perfume of the early blooming forsythias from the island temporarily masking the stink of sweat-embedded monster suit latex isn't enough to cheer me out of this funk. The cold water closes over me as I sink into the lake. I've practiced the sighting route so many times that even my seemingly perma-depressed mood isn't a distraction. I've dreamed this route, woken up swimming through my blankets like a water bug. Ten yards clear of the island, five yards toward the dock for the tail flick. My body corkscrews up through the water like a drill, and I jackknife to thrust my legs and hips and the latex tail upward, and for a brief moment the absence of water resistance is glorious, and I'm something close to triumphant. Then the realization of what I'm doing thwacks me, and it's tempered to mere grim satisfaction—the tail flick was probably loud enough to attract notice from the dock, and that's the whole key to a super-secret monster impersonation.

Then it's off to the bottom of the lake, to the submerged wreck of a car that's been there for as long as I can remember. The rough texture of the old rope that Pappap installed as a guide is evident even through my monster mitts. Hand over hand, I pull myself along the line and shoot up to the surface again, just out of sight of the dock. There are a few spots like that between here and our boat house—I splash around, make some noise, and hope the people on the dock can hear it. Even the satisfied feeling is fading now, though I've successfully just pulled off my first solo Old Lucy impersonation. Whoop-di-doo.

The neoprene strangles tighter. Being trapped inside a genera-tions-old fake monster costume is just the perfect metaphor for this dumpster fire.

The bridge of my nose prickles. I dive toward the bed of the lake and practice fake smiling around the regulator for the benefit of my grandparents while swimming for home. *I am a grateful granddaughter. I am a grateful granddaughter. I am a grateful—*

More spine-tingling reads from CamCat Books . . .

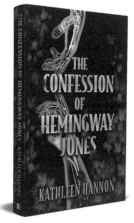

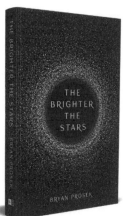

Available now, wherever books are sold.

CamCat
Books

VISIT US ONLINE FOR MORE BOOKS TO LIVE IN:
CAMCATBOOKS.COM

SIGN UP FOR CAMCAT'S FICTION NEWSLETTER FOR
COVER REVEALS, EBOOK DEALS, AND MORE EXCLUSIVE CONTENT.

CamCatBooks   @CamCatBooks   @CamCat_Books   @CamCatBooks